DARKVALE
DRAGONS

DARKVALE DRAGONS

BOOKS 1-3

CONNOR CROWE

FATED FIRE FOUNDRY

When the kids are away, the mates will play...

Sign up here for your FREE copy of ONE KNOTTY NIGHT, a special story that's too hot for Amazon!
https://dl.bookfunnel.com/c1d8qcu6h8

Join my Facebook group Connor's Coven for live streams, giveaways, and sneak peeks. It's the most fun you can have without being arrested ;)

https://www.facebook.com/groups/connorscoven/

THE DRAGON'S RUNAWAY OMEGA

DARKVALE BOOK 1

They had chosen me to die.

I stood stock still, reading the name on the parchment for the thousandth time. My shaking hands nearly dropped the paper.

Alec Cipher.

Me.

I couldn't think for the blood rushing in my ears. I couldn't breathe for the mass of people crowding around me.

I had been Chosen.

———

MY FAMILY AREN'T EXACTLY what you could call progressive. I grew up and lived in the small village of

Steamshire. The people, while kind, had a mountain of superstitions.

Don't bathe after dark.

Never stand directly behind someone.

And absolutely do not stare at a fire. Ever.

They said looking directly at a fire was basically inviting a dragon into your home.

And that's how this whole mess got started.

A tribe of dragons lived not far to the east. Despite their bloody history, I'd never even seen one. But history and superstition had a way of influencing the villagers more than cold hard facts ever could. The Elders of the village decided to make an annual offering to the dragon tribe in exchange for their continued safety.

A human offering.

Lucky me.

No one knew what happened to the Chosen. They assured us that it wasn't some kind of grisly human sacrifice, but what evidence did I have to go on? Each season, they pulled a name from all of the omegas of adult age. They exalted the Chosen as some sort of hero, but I knew better than that. They left with the shamans, and never returned.

Why they chose only omegas was beyond me. I'd cursed my bloodline more than once, wishing I had the alpha blood of some of my peers. They got the better treatment of everything. I'd say it wasn't fair, but I was old enough to know that real life is hardly ever fair.

I was an omega, just like my mother and brother. And that meant I was on the chopping block for their little ritual.

I started when Elder Marin tapped me on the shoulder. He had a long, bushy white beard and eyebrows that nearly covered his vision. "Congratulations, Alec. This is such a great honor."

His greasy smile made me want to barf.

I shook his hand weakly. "Thank you," I mumbled, not daring to meet his gaze.

"You have tonight to pack your things and say your goodbyes. You must meet with the shamans at dawn."

A stone of dread dropped into my stomach, weighing me down into the earth. At dawn. The sun was already setting. I didn't have much time. I swallowed the thick lump of fear that stuck in my throat.

"Please," I croaked. "You don't need to do this."

His eyes grew hard. "We must protect our village from the dragon threat. Why do you think we've had so many years of peace?" A vein bulged in his forehead.

I should have known better than to challenge him. But I was a dead man. What did it matter?

"The Choosing is final. I'll see you at dawn." With a whisk of his robes, he turned and walked away, leaving my heart thudding in my chest.

A heart that, if I didn't do something, would soon stop forever.

I knew that the Elders were only doing what they thought was right. They were only doing what they'd always done.

But it was time for a new order. I wasn't going to be part of their game.

———

I RUSHED to my family's tent, sniffing away the tears that threatened to overflow.

They'd already heard the news, of course. But they needed to hear it from me. My mother, my little brother...without me, they'd be alone.

My mother Cilla's health had deteriorated year by year, and as it was, I brought in most of the food and money to keep our little family alive. What were they going to do without me?

My little brother Samson was too young to work in the village. He helped me with cooking and gathering at home, and when he came of age he could find some paying work for the Council.

Until then, though, it was up to me.

But now I was leaving them.

I pushed open the tent flap to my family's home. Cilla and Samson were already there, waiting for me. Mother looked tired, but no other emotion crossed her face. Perhaps she had already felt so much she couldn't summon the tears anymore. Her eyes drooped low with dark circles from too many nights of missed sleep. Her mouth froze in a thin line, and tangles of hair that had once been blonde hung limply from her forehead.

She didn't look at me. She never did. Always at the floor. At her feet. At anything but her own son.

Samson, on the other hand, was a mess.

He flew forward and attached himself to my leg as soon as I entered, sobbing great ugly sobs and drooling on my pant leg.

"Aleeeeec…" Samson wailed, burying his face in my leg. He made a snorting sound with his nose. I rubbed my hand through his curly hair and crouched down until we were at eye level with one another.

"Hey," I said softly, giving his hand a squeeze. Samson sniffed and swiped at his face with the other hand. "It's going to be all right."

His eyes flickered and another tear spilled over, running down his streaked face. Samson's lip quivered. "How do you know?" he asked.

"I'm going to make it all right," I responded. I looked him straight in the eye. "Take good care of Mom for me, okay? Can you do that?"

He sniffed again and nodded.

"Are you coming back?" Samson asked, still clinging to me like a lifeline.

I winced. What could I even say to that? "I don't know," I said finally. That would have to be good enough.

After a time, he spoke again. "I love you."

I smiled and leaned my forehead against his own. He didn't deserve this. None of us did. "I love you too, Sam." It took all my willpower to keep my voice steady. I had to be strong. For him.

Straightening, I gave him one last hug and stepped over to where my mother sat in her rocking chair. Her eyes barely registered my movement, simply staring off into space. They were coated with a milky pallor that heralded the loss of her vision. She was getting worse, then. I swallowed hard and took her hand.

"Mom."

"Alec."

We sat in silence like that for who knows how long, just holding hands and comforting one another. There was nothing I could say that the Elders hadn't already said.

"I'm sorry," I let out finally, holding her close to me. "I'm sorry."

"Oh, Alec. Such is the way of our people. It's fine. Really."

I grimaced. It was very much not fine, but Mother had never been one to show emotion openly.

"I don't want to leave you."

Her skin had taken on an almost translucent quality in her age, showing spots, freckles, and veins underneath. She felt so cold, so frail. But so strong at the same time.

She blinked up at me with those glassy eyes and I thought I could see the beginnings of tears.

"Go on, dear. Do your duty."

She gave me a weak smile and kept on rocking, pulling a blanket around her lap.

I had so many things I wanted to say. So many memories, feelings, dreams. They crystallized on my tongue like maple candies and stuck there, refusing to move further.

"I love you, Mom." That was the last sentence I could muster.

I TOSSED and turned that night in my small cot,

listening to the steady snoring of Sam and my mother. Tonight was my last night with them. And in the morning, I'd be shipped off to the shamans, to go who-knows-where and do who-knows-what. One thing was for certain, though.

I probably wasn't going to come back. And I probably wasn't going to survive.

My teeth chattered together as I wrapped the thin blanket closer around myself. Who was I kidding? I wasn't going to get any sleep tonight.

The sound of hoof beats and the sharp snap of something hitting the ground roused me from my sleepless haze.

Who was traveling this late at night? Steamshire was so far out of the way we barely ever had any traffic. The occasional passing caravan was a major event for our sleepy little village. But a small wagon passing in the dead of night? Strange, indeed.

Curious, I peeked out of the tent and saw a small carriage with a wagon attached. Must be some kind of merchant. The silhouette of a man stepped out of the carriage, backlit by the pale light of the full moon. He made small soothing sounds at the horses, then crouched down next to the wagon. He straightened almost instantly, hands on his hips.

He wasn't going anywhere fast.

As the man dug into his wagon and pulled out a box of tools, a wild idea struck me.

This carriage could be the ticket to my freedom.

The stars twinkled and shone above with the moon, casting a desperate light on the last hours of darkness.

It would be dawn soon.

And my time was running out.

I glanced back at my mother and brother, still sleeping. Still oblivious.

The wagon looked spacious enough to hold plenty of goods, and had a canvas cover to protect it from the elements. If only I could get inside...

Fear and apprehension seized me.

I had no idea who this man was, where he was going, or what he might do if he found me.

But was the uncertain future as a stowaway better than my certain demise?

The seconds ticked by as I thought, weighing the pros and cons. I'd never even been outside of Steamshire. I'd lived in this village my entire life, sheltered by their rules and traditions. I had no idea what was out there.

For all I knew, the carriage man could be an enemy. He could kill me, or worse.

The Elders had wasted no time warning us what happened to stray omegas.

Still, a spark of possibility fluttered in my heart. I could take this chance. I could escape, right here, right now.

And I'd keep my promise to Samson. I'd come back. I'd rescue him and all the other omegas too. But first, I had to get out of here.

I set my jaw, balled my fists, and made up my mind.

Tonight, I was leaving Steamshire.

————

IT DIDN'T TAKE long to gather my paltry belongings. I'd already packed a bag for my meeting with the shamans. It wasn't much.

A set of extra clothes. A water skin. And my most prized, most secret possession.

A small, fossilized fang.

I turned it over in my hands, feeling the smooth ivory texture. I'd found it when digging in the dirt as a child, and my mother had thrown it out as soon as she saw I had it.

Little did she know, I'd snuck out to retrieve it again, digging through our trash to find my prize. Even covered in dirt and stink, the fang fascinated me.

Like a relic from a bygone past, it represented all the things I didn't know. All the things we were told were dangerous, foul, evil. The dragons.

Mother told us a dragon killed our father shortly after I was born. I was too young; I didn't remember any of it. But dragon hysteria ran high in the village every year since, whisperings and rumors of a new onslaught. That's when they started the Offering.

The fang was the last thing I had left of my father.

I squeezed my eyes shut, clasping it tight.

I'll avenge you.

With a last look at my family, I hefted my bag over my shoulder and stole away into the night.

LUCIEN

S nap! The splintering of the wood and the tilting of the carriage caught me by surprise.

Cursing, I threw my legs off the carriage and around to the left side where I'd heard the noise. It was well past midnight, but I didn't mind.

I'd gotten used to doing late night shipments.

Kneeling in the dust, I peered at the wheels of the carriage. The axle had hit a rock and splintered, leaving the wheel unstable. I let out a breath and ran a hand through my hair.

"Just my luck," I mumbled. My most important shipment of the year and the carriage decided to fall apart on me. Typical.

I stood and circled around to the wagon I was pulling, looking at my haul. These goods weren't gonna transport themselves, and if they weren't delivered by tomorrow...

I grit my teeth. I'd just have to fix the damn thing.

A few fires flickered not far away, throwing long shadows on me and the carriage as I worked. Some small village, probably. I didn't come this way often. Didn't know anyone lived all the way out here.

I patted the horses, trying to soothe them. "We'll be on our way soon," I whispered, running a hand down their long, tangled manes. "Don't worry."

Crouching in the dust, I got a better look at the splintered axle. I grimaced. Worse than I thought. Best thing I could do for now was brace it and make the delivery. Alarfort, by my calculation, wasn't far now. I'd get it fixed up there. Just had to get there in one piece.

I thanked the Goddess for my night vision. She only knew where I'd be without it—fumbling around in the dark trying to fix a broken axle, probably crushing my hand in the process.

My bloodline had its perks.

I let out a breath as the old memories came back, lapping at the shores of my mind like the incoming tide. A stirring of fire flickered in my heart, a long dormant ember.

That life was over.

I grabbed the toolkit I kept for emergencies and went to work.

———

WELL, it wasn't the neatest job I'd ever done, but it would hold until Alarfort.

At least, I hoped it would.

I wiped my hands on my pants and sighed. My lips and throat dried and cracked in the desert-like air. I reached into the carriage for my water flask. Empty.

Tilting my head back, I tapped the last few drops of water into my mouth, my tongue lapping them up all too easily. They did little to quench the parched feeling, and my tongue still felt like sandpaper.

My ears pricked up, listening to the world around me. A cool, rushing sound. Water. And not far, either. Hidden behind a mound of brush and tapering down a steep slope, a small creek puttered along. Too steep to bring the horses, though. I'd have to go it alone.

The trickling sound grew louder now that I knew what to listen for. My mouth and stomach ached at the thought. What I wouldn't give for a good drink, or wash off the dust and grime of the day...

I had to keep moving, didn't I?

But the temptation grew stronger. Even my eyes felt

dry. No amount of blinking could get rid of that gritty feeling.

I looked around warily. I knew better than to leave my shipment unattended. I really did. But the lack of food, water, and sleep had short-circuited something in my brain, and all I could think about was the delicious cool water down there in the creek.

"Be right back," I whispered to the horses, and took off at a sprint.

———

WATER. Glorious, refreshing water.

I drank greedily, desperately. The cool drops from the creek rejuvenated my parched throat, my skin, the thin layer of dust that seemed to cover everything. Wonderful.

But I could not linger.

Topping off my canteen, I clambered back up the bank and to my carriage.

Good. The horses hadn't run off.

I chanced a quick peek into the wagon. Didn't look like anything was missing or had been moved. Good, then.

Time to go.

I double-checked the brace I'd put on the broken axle and crawled back into the driver's seat.

"Well, that was a nice intermission," I mumbled to myself. With a flick of the reins, we were bumping along the barren road once more.

I must admit, there were more than a few harrowing moments when we hit a rut or the wood beneath me squeaked dangerously. The brace held, though, and the sun was just starting to peek over the horizon when I pulled into Crowley's Inn.

A stable boy came out to help with the horses and I ensured they were fed and watered for the night. My body cried out for sleep, but there was something I needed to do first.

Couldn't leave all this precious cargo out in the open, now could I?

"Whatcha got there, mister?" the stable boy asked as he led the horses away. He couldn't have been more than twelve or thirteen years old, but already had the beginnings of muscle tone one gets from manual labor.

"None of your business," I said, not really paying attention. The boy said nothing. Trained not to press further, I'd guess. Good lad.

My thoughts, and gaze, moved elsewhere.

Something was moving in my wagon.

My heart skipped a beat as I mumbled a thank you to the boy and slipped him a coin.

The sound came again.

Something was definitely moving in there.

And last I checked, I didn't have any live cargo.

The taste of fire crackled through my chest onto my tongue and my eyes narrowed into slits. What had I picked up along the way?

Silently cursing myself for leaving my cargo, I crept toward the wagon. A strange memory tickled at the back of my mind. In a moment of delirious thought, I imagined opening the wagon and seeing my mate again.

Sparks crackled on my tongue, but I knew they would go no further than that.

I was no longer a dragon.

————

CALDO FAIWIND HAD BEEN everything to me. My hope, my light, my soul.

I still remembered the night I met him, so many years ago. The Goddess had smiled upon us that day, he used to tell me.

We were an unstoppable pair. Even as I rose through

the ranks to become Clan Alpha of the Firefangs, he stayed by my side.

But the peace we enjoyed those too-few years soon vanished into the machinations of war.

Rival clans encroached on our territory, soon stealing more than just our resources. One bloody raid after another left our forces weakened and our clan only a shadow of its former glory.

Then they struck the damning blow—a mutiny from within I'd been too blind to prevent.

Caldo fell before my eyes, and there was nothing I could do to stop it.

My heart broke that day, and you know what they say about the heart of a dragon. Once broken, the shifter is trapped as mortal—as human—forever.

The wagon bumped and clattered down the dusty road as I hid under the scratchy blanket. Creaking crates were my travel companions, surrounding me with their musty smell. I wondered what might be inside them, and who would be transporting such cargo in the dead of night.

A tendril of fear wound its way through my gut. What if he was one of the black market dealers the villagers told stories about?

I closed my eyes and brought in a deep breath through my nose. It was dark, cold, and I couldn't see where I was going.

But all that had mattered in the moment was that I was going away from Steamshire.

I had plenty of time to consider my predicament as the carriage wound its way down the dirt roads. I'd never been so far from home before, and if circumstances were different I would have liked to see the landscape rolling by.

But I was just a stowaway. A risky one, at that. I had to stay low, stay out of sight, and at the next stop, get away as soon as possible. With any luck, the merchant would stop at a town for the night and I could make my way from there.

A hand shot to my side where my small coin pouch jingled. It wasn't much, but hopefully it would be enough to put me up for the night. Then I could figure out what to do next.

Anything was better than being a dragon sacrifice.

————

THE WAGON CAME to a stop as the first rays of sun started to peek into the holding area. I blinked and jolted awake, yawning.

Hadn't realized I'd fallen asleep. I rubbed my eyes and took a moment to get my bearings.

This wasn't my bed...

But then it all came rushing back to me.

I wasn't safe in my tent in Steamshire anymore.

I wasn't safe at all.

I was a stowaway on a carriage heading out of town, and I had to get out of here. Fast.

Stretching my limbs, I listened for footsteps. There were two voices. A young boy, by the sound of it, and someone else. Much deeper. A warm, rumbly timbre washed over me like hot molasses and a whisper of electricity shot through my chest.

Where there should have been fear bloomed a curiosity, a fascination I couldn't name. He sounded familiar in some way, like a far-off memory shrouded in mist. I shook my head and tried to clear the thoughts.

As soon as I heard footsteps heading away, I needed to make my escape.

My unwitting travel partner be damned.

The sounds of travel quieted and the footsteps grew fainter. It was time.

Ever so slowly, I peeked my head out from under the blanket.

That's when I came face to face with Mr. Mysterious himself.

———

"THE HELL ARE YOU DOING HERE?" the man growled, grabbing me by my collar and yanking. I tumbled out of the wagon and into the dirt, gagging. "You're a damn Cog spy, aren't you?"

I tried to protest, but managed only a few squeaking sounds as he crushed my windpipe.

He released me, his lip curling in disgust. I hit the ground with a bone-jarring thud, coughing and wheezing as oxygen rushed back into my lungs.

"Talk," he commanded, and I felt the same rush of electric energy again.

What was going on?

"What? I'm—" I coughed, "—not a spy! I'm sorry, I just...needed to get away and—" A fit of coughs seized me again.

Our eyes met for the first time. Only, his eyes weren't like any human's eyes I'd ever seen. Bright orange with black slits for pupils, his gaze felt like fire itself. In that moment, all the old stories came back to me.

Dragon.

I stared, open-mouthed, at the man before me. He cut an imposing figure, all hard muscle and unyielding power. A tremble of apprehension rolled through me, but a pleasant shiver as well. A dragon. My very first dragon.

Wait till Sam hears about this!

"You're a dragon," I breathed.

"And you're a fool," he spat. "I'd roast you right here, but you're too stupid to be a spy. Go on, and don't let me catch you again. My mercy will not be extended twice."

He waved me away and I stumbled to my feet. The energy I felt pouring off of him still echoed through me, body and soul. His voice had a hard edge to it, sure, but there was something...off about it. I couldn't put my finger on what it was.

I turned to leave when he called out to me again.

"What's your name?"

I froze. What did it matter?

"My name for yours," I said, not turning around.

"Hah," he huffed. "Fine. My name is Lucien."

Lucien. I tasted the name on my tongue, feeling the sparks of excitement still dancing there.

"Alec," I said finally.

A heavy pause hung between us. "Be careful out there, Alec."

With a few footsteps and the yawn of the heavy inn door, he was gone.

———

ONE SILVER and four coppers later, I had a small

dinner and a cramped room at one of the more unsavory inns. Excuse me, I should say "budget-friendly." The air hung heavy with the stench of alcohol and body odor. Moths fluttered around the lamp hanging precariously from the ceiling. It swayed ever so slightly as some kind of thumping noise came from above.

Well, it was better than nothing.

I lay awake on the scratchy pallet bed, staring at the cracked paint on the ceiling. The last day and a half felt like a blur, a misremembered dream. Yet here I was.

I pulled out the rucksack I'd brought along and changed into a fresh pair of clothes, grateful at least for the clean garments. Food, clothing, safety.

Not to mention my mission.

I thought again about my family. About Steamshire.

What had they thought when they woke and found I had disappeared? Were they upset? Was Sam sobbing into my mother's dress, even now?

I swallowed back tears.

I did what I had to do.

And I wasn't going to leave and let them suffer in silence. My escape was a gift, and I didn't intend to waste it. With this new opportunity, I'd be able to meet allies, get stronger, and eventually, return to Steamshire to free the omegas once and for all.

But first—I needed a good night's sleep.

"You can save the world in the morning," I mumbled to myself, and burrowed into the pillows.

———

I WOKE to the sound of splintering wood.

The door flew off its hinges and clattered across the floor, jolting me immediately from sleep. Even through my sleep-haze, I could see the shining red uniform of an Enforcer.

Here.

He called over his shoulder, "We found the runaway!" I heard footsteps echoing down the hallway, and knew he wasn't alone.

With a yelp, I threw myself out of bed and into action. Grabbing my bag, my eyes surveyed the room with a glance.

One hulking Enforcer blocked the doorway, dangling a pair of handcuffs and a bloodthirsty grin. Shouts and commotion grew closer as the men closed in. Wouldn't be getting out that way. Right above the bed, an ancient window blackened with dust and age peered out into the alleyway.

My one chance at escape.

"Oh, no you don't!" the Enforcer yelled, lumbering toward me. He lunged forward, grabbing at my ankles, but I dodged out of the way just in time. Throwing my weight against the window latch, it groaned as the rust of ages fell away and swung open, the cool air blustering in at once.

The Enforcer's lunge threw him off balance and I used the momentary distraction to my advantage. I leapt upward and grabbed the window sill, kicking my legs against the wall to boost myself higher.

The hard ground stared up at me from a dizzying height. I could stay and let them take me, or I could make the leap of faith.

I closed my eyes, gripped the fang in my fist, and jumped.

My feet hit the ground and crumpled beneath me, pain shooting up my legs all the way to my head. My hands hit the ground next, scraping against the frozen ground. It was better than landing on gravel, but not much better.

The pain pumped through me with a healthy dose of adrenaline, keeping me focused on my prize. Escape. Escape. Escape.

I stumbled to my feet and ran.

Shouts and footsteps sounded behind me. I pushed my

legs harder, my bag bumping against my legs as I ran. Breath came hard and heavy, spilling out into warm puffs of air.

All reason had fled, and I ran like a trapped animal, fighting only to survive. Villagers and animals alike stared at me as I ran, but I paid them no mind. If I put enough distance between me and my pursuers maybe, just maybe, I'd be safe.

You should have known better than to run, a dark voice mocked in my head. *You should have known they would find you. Who do you think you are, anyway?*

My foot caught on an exposed tree root and I fell forward as if in slow motion. I put out my already raw hands to catch my fall, knowing that this time, there would be no escape.

I tumbled into the dirt with a cry. My body didn't listen to the signals I was screaming at it. I couldn't move, I couldn't see, I could only hear the roaring of my pulse in my ears and the taste of iron in my mouth and...

"Back off." The deep, commanding voice sent a slice of hope through my aching body.

"What was that?" A voice came from behind me. Incredulous. I heard the scraping of metal as a blade was drawn.

"I said. Back off."

"You lousy draconian scum!"

I rolled out of the way as the men charged. My savior drew his own blade and joined in, moving in a blur of silver and orange. He danced across the field as if it were a game, deflecting their blades at each turn.

They had him on the defensive, though. Lucien backed up step by step as the guards advanced on him, and the ground didn't last forever. No, a steep ravine cut through the village, cutting it in two. I'd learned that much when looking for a place to sleep. It separated the well-to-do from the impoverished, in some kind of perverse segregation. There were bridges, sure. But there was no bridge here.

Lucien continued to backtrack and my eyes widened as he neared the abyss.

"Watch out!" I cried before I could stop myself, and his eyes snapped to me for only a second.

That second was long enough for him to let down his guard.

Sensing the opening, the Enforcer charged, knocking him into the dirt. Blades flew from their hands as they hit the ground together, locked in hand-to-hand combat.

I held my breath and considered running. With the guards' focus distracted away from me, I could escape.

So why wasn't I?

I couldn't tear my eyes away as Lucien and the guard

grappled with one another. Lucien rolled to the side, taking the Enforcer with him. That brought him within range of a fallen blade and he grabbed it, slamming it into the man's ribcage without hesitation.

He yelled a broken yell, blood flecking his lips and oozing out from the wound in his chest.

With a roar, Lucien pushed the man away and off his blade, leaving him in the dust to die.

But two more men came running.

"What are you waiting for?" he screamed at me as he resumed his fighting stance. "Go!"

I clambered to my feet and took off, his words knocking me out of my trance. The clash of steel rang out behind me and I was afraid to look back, all too sure of what I'd see.

I ducked behind the tall rock wall that surrounded the town, resting my back against the stones and taking a moment's breath. The sounds of battle still rang out behind me, but my stamina stores were gone. I panted and heaved outside against the wall, bile forcing its way up onto the dirt. I spat and wiped my mouth, sinking into the dirt as darkness wrapped itself around me.

————

"OUR PATHS CROSS AGAIN." The voice brought

me back to reality. I opened my eyes. Lucien stood there, offering me his hand.

He was alive.

Covered in blood and ripped clothing, but alive.

I sat there gaping at him.

"Are you going to sit there like an idiot or are we going to get out of here? Come on!"

He grabbed my hand and pulled me to my feet. I stumbled and fell against him, trying to regain my balance. His chest was a hard wall of muscle, and the strangest smell assaulted my nostrils. It poured off of him in waves when we touched, the smell of pine and fire and honey. I'd never smelled anything so delicious in my life, and the curl of desire in my belly reminded me of one thing: I was an omega.

This alpha in front of me, dragon or not, had triggered something in my most primal nature. Something I hadn't known existed.

But it was ridiculous, right?

When he righted me and I chanced another look in his glowing eyes, I wasn't sure of anything anymore.

4

LUCIEN

T he Goddess was really having a laugh at me this time.

My shipment was late, the town was crawling with Enforcers, and I kept running into that insufferable human. Whenever I tried to leave and wash my hands of the situation, there he was again. And when I saw him being chased by the Enforcers?

Well, I did what I had to do.

They had no love for my kind. It bordered on genocide. Being in this town at all was against the law, depending on who you talked to. My network, my stealth, and my powers of persuasion had allowed me to get this far.

I dispatched them to save my own skin. Nothing else. The fact that I'd also rescued Alec was secondary.

As much as I tried to hide my nature, people could still

tell if they looked closely. At first glance, we could pass as human, but there were always little discrepancies between our human shifts and their own. Not least of which our fiery irises that belied our heritage.

Never mind the fact that I couldn't even shift. I was hardly a threat to anyone like this. Humans didn't care. The second the word dragon crested someone's tongue, it was all "grab the torch and pitchforks!" Give me a break.

Now, for whatever reason, this little human's fate had been tied up with my own.

I couldn't deny he was handsome. That much was obvious. A cool, sort of youthful energy flowed off of him. He cut a nice figure, almost as tall as I was. He was built, for an omega, and his shaggy curls fell across his forehead in a riot of inky black that made me want to run my fingers through them.

I shook my head, appalled at the thought.

The fact that he was an omega and I was an alpha meant nothing. I ran across omegas every day, but none of them affected me like this. He was a human, and I still didn't trust him. He'd been trespassing on me, after all! The thought of him feeding information to my enemies still froze my blood cold, but there was something...hopeful about him. I couldn't put my finger on what it was. By all accounts, I should have left him there to be devoured by the Enforcers. I should have left town immediately and continued on my way.

But my dormant dragon had other ideas.

———

I SHIFTED my gaze to the side. Alec sat next to me in the carriage, gazing at the landscape with a far-off expression. It was like he'd never seen grass before or something.

Questions bubbled up through my mind, but I tamped them back down. Even bringing him along with me was a terrible idea. If he really was a spy, I was playing right into his hands. But I'd yet to figure out what irked me about him. And my dragon wasn't going to let him go until I did.

"We're nearing Briarwood," I said as we came to a fork in the road. I nudged the reins to the left and we trotted on. The barren desert lands had all but faded away, giving way to lush meadows and the promise of water. A great forest rose up against the horizon, the tall pines stretching toward the sky. Briarwood Forest. My final destination.

I wiped sweat from my brow as the midday sun beat down upon us. The road hadn't been traveled in some time, by the look of it. Shrubs and weeds obscured the path and forgotten ruts dug deep into the soil. I'd be glad to finally get rid of this cargo. If I was a superstitious man, I'd say it was cursed. With all the strange occurrences that had happened since I picked it up, almost certainly.

"Now when I give the word, you will hide in the wagon, you hear me? I've some business to attend to and I won't have it interrupted."

Alec smirked. "You mean you're actually giving me permission this time?"

I rolled my eyes. "Watch it. I could throw you out on the road right here, you know." I tried to keep a fierce edge to my voice, but a hint of mirth showed through.

"As you command, O Scaly One," he joked, throwing up an arm in a mock salute.

I grumbled, but said nothing.

———

"WHOA." I pulled the horses to a halt as we came to the edge of the forest. It looked even more intimidating up close, the evergreen trees dwarfing any I'd seen previous. The scent of pine and sap exuded from the forest in waves, but there was something else, a subtler smell on the undercurrent.

Blood.

My dragon knew that scent all too well. I just didn't expect to smell it here. Now.

I took a deep breath and steeled myself. Nothing to get bent out of shape about. Probably a dead animal or something.

"It's time for you to hide. Now remember, stay out of sight and let me do the talking."

"Right." Alec climbed down from the carriage and the wagon swayed to the side as he crawled inside.

"You good?" I called back to him.

"Yeah," came the muffled reply, and I shook the reins to make our way into the woods.

The thick canopy provided some blessed shade from the sun but blanketed the forest floor in a cool, dreary darkness. The kind of darkness that if you weren't careful, could come up and bite you when you least expected it. I focused my vision, my dragon eyes taking over.

The path veered from difficult to basically nonexistent. Moss and vines crawled across the ground and the foliage was so dense it spilled out onto the road. Or what had once been the road. The horses resisted and let out a whinny. They weren't going to make it over this kind of terrain.

I cursed myself again for picking up this damned delivery. It better be really important, to make me come all the way out here. But the nature of my work was always unpredictable. I knew that. I'd seen my share of dangerous situations and had always made it out on top. This time would be no different. I just had to remind myself of that.

I slid off my seat and walked around to the wagon, peering inside. If I didn't know any better I wouldn't have known a young man hid inside. He had a knack for hiding, I had to give him that. I lifted up the canvas cover and he jumped, eyes snapping to mine.

"What?" he hissed.

"Road's too rough. Gonna have to go on foot. Here, hand me those cases." I pointed at the wooden crates sitting beside him. He pushed them forward, the muscles in his forearms bulging. I tried not to stare...much.

Damn this human, and damn the way my dragon stirred in my chest. It wasn't going to happen. Not now, not ever.

"What's in these? It's heavy as bricks!"

"What did I tell you about asking questions?" I hefted the crates out of the wagon and onto the forest floor.

"Not to." His shoulders slumped.

"Come on now, cheer up. It's not far, and I'll be right back. Just stay low and watch the carriage. You'll likely be fine, but if anything happens there's a spare blade in the side compartment there." I pointed. "You know how to use a blade, right?"

"Oh. Yeah." The uneasy waver of his voice didn't inspire a lot of confidence.

I lifted the crates and turned to leave when I heard his voice again.

"Lucien?"

"Yeah?"

"Be careful."

I stepped carefully over the vines and twigs, glad my back was to him. He couldn't see the smile blooming across my face.

5

ALEC

Why the stranger had left me alone with his vehicle was unclear. But it showed some measure of trust, even if he didn't want to admit it. And for that, I had to be grateful.

I kept still in the wagon and listened. The chirp of crickets. The shuffling of the horses. The wind as it rustled the leaves all around us.

I'd never seen so much green in one place before. We'd had small gardens of hardy plants back in Steamshire, sure, but nothing like this. I watched in amazement as we traveled down the winding road, grass as far as the eye could see. It was beautiful.

And the trees! Giants of wood and greenery rose all around me, thrusting their powerful arms to the heavens. The air hung heavy with mist and the sparkling reflections of dew.

The faint sound of voices echoed through the trees and I froze. It must be Lucien, finally delivering whatever it was he was carrying. I frowned, thinking about how antsy he got when I asked questions. What could have been so bad?

I had tried to peek into the crates when hiding the first time. Black, sticky tar lined the seams, sealing the crates tight.

So much for that plan.

The voices echoed closer, and I could make out a few words if I strained to listen.

Medicine. Children. Dragons.

An explosion rang out through the trees, the birds scattering all at once. My blood ran cold and I reached for the secret blade, my heart pounding. What was going on?

I'd used farm tools to gather crops and chop wood, sure. But using a blade to defend myself? Never.

"No time like the present," I muttered, gripping the worn leather handle. It was about the length of my forearm, tapering to a razor-sharp point. The kind meant for stabbing, not slicing. A worn engraving caught my eye near the hilt and I squinted in the dim light.

Caldo Faiwind.

Who the heck was that?

Another blast shook the cabin, jolting the thoughts away. With the knife in one hand, I ever so slowly peeked outside.

Smoke rose from the treetops not far away. Flames devoured the dry brush, roaring with orange fury and spreading by the second. My heart caught in my throat. Did Lucien do that? And more importantly, was he okay?

At the thought of Lucien, I felt a tug at my subconscious, the same feeling of a long-forgotten memory. A rash of emotions flooded through me at once. Fear. Anger. Power. Loss. Need. I blinked my eyes and saw flames. Flames everywhere.

My limbs moved despite themselves and I threw myself out of the wagon, advancing toward the inferno. Rationally, my mind screamed at me to run. But something deeper pulled me forward, a primal instinct that smothered all other feeling.

I'd only heard stories of it happening to others. I might have thought I was crazy, otherwise.

Maybe I still did.

They said omegas only got like this in the presence of a mate.

But that couldn't be right at all.

The heat poured toward me in waves as sweat flecked my brow. I saw the shattered remains of a wooden crate, then another. Fear, then a terrible anger took hold and refused to let go. Who had done this to him?

"Lucien!" I called, gagging on the smoke. "Lucien!"

A long pause, then, "Alec?" The voice was weak, but close by.

I rushed toward the sound, the same ethereal force pulling me along.

Lucien lay on his back, clothes singed and blade missing. His eyes lit up when he saw me, and the force inside me grew stronger.

The fire was gaining, and fast. Smoke filled my lungs and obscured my vision. I blinked away ashes as I crouched down next to him, offering my hand.

"Alec, I told you—"

"Shut up and listen to me. We've got to get you out of here."

He stared, his mouth hanging open a little. Without a word, he grabbed my hand. His normally warm weight was cool and clammy. Not good.

"Can you stand?"

Lucien grunted in response. With a wince, he heaved himself upright. His eyes still held a glassy stare, and his skin carried so much dirt I couldn't tell just how badly he'd been hurt.

"Bastards turned on me," he muttered, swaying to the side. I hooked an arm around my neck and put one of my own around his waist. Pinpricks of desire shot off like fireworks, but that was the least of my concern. The fire was getting closer.

"Come on," I urged. We hobbled through the rubble, the carriage in sight. Not too much further...

Lucien's breathing grew labored. I hadn't realized how much work it was to carry the weight of a full-grown man across an overgrown jungle. I'd helped my brother learn to walk when he was little, sure, but that was different. My energy was rapidly waning.

"Lean here," I suggested as we came to the wagon. With a long breath, he propped himself against the wagon's beams and I dove into the back, folding the blanket into a makeshift cot. "Lay down."

He eyed me, the mischievous glint in his dragon irises still there. "Not used to omegas bossing me around." His lips turned up at the corners.

"Lay down," I repeated, pointing at the cot.

"You don't know the area." Lucien crossed his arms.

"And you can't drive in your condition."

"I heal faster than humans, I'll be fine."

Gods, he was stubborn.

"Be that as it may, you need rest to heal. Not even dragons can avoid that."

I held his gaze, challenging him. His eyes flashed, lip curled. Finally, his shoulders slumped.

"Fine," he spat. "But only till I'm feeling better."

"Of course. Wouldn't dream of stealing your carriage."

Lucien raised an eyebrow.

"I said I wouldn't!"

He rumbled deep in his chest, then crawled into the back of the wagon and positioned himself on top of the blankets. Propping himself up on an elbow, he looked at me. "Go north, and don't stop."

With that settled, I circled around to the carriage side. The fire still roared and crackled, the ground underfoot starting to hiss and smoke as the heat grew closer.

"Let's go," I urged the horses, and we set off away from the flames.

6

LUCIEN

Thank the Goddess for my accelerated healing. The bruises and burns melted away as I lay on top of the scratchy blanket. The ground bumped and rolled beneath us as the forest fell away.

It was just enough time to reflect on how ridiculous this situation was.

An omega, a human omega at that, had put his life on the line to save me. What did he have to do that for?

You know why, a little voice in my chest warned. The same reason you can't let him go.

I ground my teeth. I'd already had a mate. Caldo. I didn't want another one, and even if I did, I never expected it to be like this.

I'd heard dragons could mate with humans, but it was

only a rumor, a whispered story around the clan gossips.

Was it really possible?

I shook my head. Even if it was, it didn't matter. My dragon powers were already gone, I'd been exiled from my clan, and I had to run dangerous smuggling jobs to survive. It was no place for a human.

And yet he'd come back for me.

The thought sat in the back of my throat like heartburn, leaving me twisting and turning on the cot. With a frustrated huff, I sat up.

"Stop," I called, and Alec pulled on the reins.

"You say something?"

"Yeah, I said stop. I'm feeling better now. Want to come back up front."

It wasn't a total lie, but I couldn't lay back here with my thoughts any longer, either.

The carriage shifted as he got down from his seat and then he appeared at the back of the wagon. Another surge of energy flared through my chest at the sight of him. His eyes drooped slightly with exhaustion, but he still carried that indomitable spirit I'd seen in him the first day.

"Looks like you're the one that needs some rest," I teased.

Alec scoffed. "I'm fine."

"All the same, I think I should take over for a while."

"You sure you're okay? That was awfully fast."

"What part about dragon do you not understand?" I grinned at him, enjoying the banter. I pushed myself off the ledge. I stumbled a bit as I stood, but I corrected myself quickly enough. I hoped he hadn't seen.

Outside of the wagon, I could get a better sense of my bearings. Good. He'd listened.

We were about an hour north of the forest now, which meant we were coming up on Timberthorn.

Home sweet home.

I climbed into the driver's seat and Alec scooted over to sit beside me. We started off in silence, until the words on my tongue wouldn't stay there any longer.

"Thank you."

"For what?" Alec asked, snapping his gaze to mine. He'd been lost in the scenery again, a wrinkle of confusion creasing his forehead.

"For coming back for me, back there. I...I should have been more prepared." The bitter taste of defeat burned on my tongue as I remembered the battle that had bested me. The battle that had taken my mate and my unborn son along with it.

"I couldn't leave you there to die."

The words rang in my ears. He'd never know how much that simple admission meant to me.

"Well, thanks."

We rode in companionable silence, Alec blissfully unaware of the growing knot of dread in my stomach.

———

WE'D TRAVELED down a sloped path into a tunnel that led underground. A locked iron grate stood in our way. No key could open this gate, though. I waved my hand over the bars and spoke a secret word. With a click, the grate scraped open, leaving a long, winding tunnel ahead.

"How did you do that?" Alec asked as we entered and closed the gate behind us.

"Magitech," I said, my mind elsewhere. "There's a current of magical energy flowing through all of us, though many aren't able to harness it directly. Our Engineers have honed this skill to create all kinds of contraptions, though. We wouldn't be here without them."

The tunnel wound on, lit only by flickering torches. Alec stood closer now, as if afraid I'd disappear into the blackness. Finally, the tunnel opened up and we arrived in Timberthorn Compound: my home away from home.

"What is this place?" Alec asked, whipping his head around to take in the sights. His gaze was everywhere at once, staring with a slack jawed wonder.

"My home."

"No way," he breathed. "It's incredible."

"You should have seen the clan at its height." I sighed wistfully. "But some other time." I couldn't get occupied with that right now.

The dirt road turned to gravel, then cobblestone. Huts spotted the landscape and smoke billowed from one in the center, the smell of roasted meat intoxicating.

"That smells delicious," Alec said.

"It tastes even better."

I pulled up beside my hut, a small thatched-roof place with stone walls. It wasn't much, especially after what I was used to back in Darkvale, but it was home. I unhitched the horses and led them to water, securing the wagon and carriage in the meantime. Alec followed me, watching every move with a sort of hushed reverence.

"This is a clan of *dragons*," he said in wonder.

"Not quite," I said, busying myself with the water pump. "It's more like our little outsider's club."

Alec tilted his head.

"We..." I started, not wanting to meet his gaze. My cheeks flushed with shame. "I'll tell you later. Let's eat, shall we? I'm starving."

He lit up at that. "Me too!"

"Then let's get going." I stood and brushed myself off. The horses slurped at the trough noisily, the wagon was lashed to a post nearby, and the smell of roasted meat got stronger with every breath. It had been a long day.

We walked toward the center of the compound together. Smoke rose from an earthen chimney and vented out into the night sky. Ansel, the local engineer, had put together a screening mechanism that dissipated the smoke through several vents. This way, any curious pursuers wouldn't be tipped off by our cook fires.

I pushed aside the hide door and stepped into the common area, my senses assaulted with the smells of dinner. Myrony had really outdone herself tonight.

A line began to form in front of Myrony's great cook pot. She stirred it with a giant wooden spoon and doled out a portion to each visitor. They smiled and greeted one another, bumped shoulders, and settled into their meals. The den turned boisterous with the snacking sounds of hungry dragons.

Alec stayed close by my side, watching the display with a mixture of fascination and horror.

"Dragons are a bit...messy," I laughed, and got in line.

I'd notice that mohawk anywhere. I tapped the guy in front of me on the shoulder.

"Bryn! Long time no see, man!"

He spun around and returned the greeting. "Lucien! When did you get back in?"

"Just today. I was out on business, you know how it is." The side of my face quirked upward in a subtle wink. Bryn nodded.

"Do I ever," he said, stretching his arms out behind his back. "I'm starving." His eyes flicked to the human next to me. "Who's the human?"

I bristled, drawing Alec closer. "He's my guest."

"Guest, huh?" Bryn said, grabbing a plate and moving down the line. "That's what all your business amounted to this time?" He snorted. "You're really branching out, Luc. It's like I don't know you anymore."

The rumbling of fire vibrated through my chest again. I punched him in the shoulder on instinct.

"What was that for?" He rubbed the bruise.

"The human was an unexpected addition to the journey. Now you are to treat him as you would any of our brothers and sisters. Understood?" I leveled my gaze at him. Even in our little refugee camp, I held some measure of power. There were those who defected when The Paradox threw me out. They sought me here, and we started anew.

Bryn shook his head and sighed. "Was just messing with you man, no need to get bent out of shape."

I grumbled and my face grew hot with guilt. Of course he was. He was my best friend. Why had I acted so irrationally?

I scrubbed a hand across my face and plastered on a smile. "No harm done," I told him.

Alec held out his right hand toward Bryn. "It's a pleasure to meet you."

Bryn eyed the hand, then Alec, then me.

"You're supposed to shake it," I whispered. "It's what the humans do in greeting."

"Oh! Right." Bryn gave a nervous laugh and shook Alec's hand. Way to get off to a good start, the inner voice chided me.

Shut it. I clenched my teeth.

The line had moved considerably, and Bryn was up next. He took his turn and pivoted toward the long tables. "I'll grab a seat?" he asked, pointing.

"Go ahead."

We were next. I stepped forward and Myrony noticed

me immediately. "Lucien! How good it is to see you again!"

I leaned forward and gave her a small hug from over the steaming pot. "And you too, of course, My."

"And who's this you have with you?" She smiled at Alec, dimples creasing her rosy cheeks. Myrony was the closest thing we had to a mother figure here. She went out of her way to make everyone feel welcome, even if they were a little odd or different. After all, that was what this retreat in Timberthorn was all about.

The Outcast Club.

"I've brought a friend," I said evenly, nodding to Alec. He stuck his hand out and My pulled him into a hug instead, a cute little squeak escaping from him at the sudden contact. I laughed, nearly dropping my bowl of food. "She's just affectionate, is all."

"So happy to have you here, dear. I hope you like beef stew." Her eyes danced as she filled Alec's bowl to the brim. "Enjoy!"

"She's...enthusiastic." Alec chuckled, balancing his bowl with steady, slow steps.

"She's like that with everyone," I offered.

"She's lovely."

I grinned, the same sparkling heat traveling up my spine all the way down to my fingertips. "Yeah. She is."

7

ALEC

I couldn't eat another bite. The stew was warm, delicious, and so filling my stomach felt fit to burst. I yawned and looked over to Lucien, who wore the same kind of food-coma expression. "What now?"

"There's the matter of sleeping arrangements," he started.

My heart skipped a beat.

Surely, he didn't mean...

"You're free to sleep in my quarters."

He saw my eyes widen.

"I won't be there, don't worry. I'll take first watch." He amended his offer quickly, his face growing red.

Yeah, cause why would I want that?

"Are you sure?" I asked. "I couldn't take your bed from you."

"I'm sure," Lucien said in that commanding tone. He rested a hand on my shoulder and the chemistry flowed between us like a live wire once more. "It's no problem at all. Shall I show you the way?" He stood and offered me his hand.

"Thank you."

It was a good thing I had Lucien leading the way. I would have gotten lost in a heartbeat. The tunnels twisted and turned back on themselves, raising and lowering and intersecting. I tried to paint a visual map in my mind, but with every new corner we turned what I thought I knew turned on its head.

"Your head spinning yet?" Lucien teased, taking a hard right.

I scoffed. "Hardly."

"Hmm." He grabbed a ladder against the wall, starting to ascend. I watched him rise.

"Don't sit there all day, come on!"

I snapped my mouth shut and followed. The ladder creaked as I climbed, but seemed stable enough. Steel bolts attached it to the walls, although how sturdy walls of packed mud were, I wasn't certain.

After clambering onto the landing, Lucien stood in

front of an iron-plated door. "Your sleep awaits." He made an exaggerated bowing gesture and turned the knob.

Lucien's bedroom.

I stepped inside, feeling the plush carpet between my toes. The warm, flickering glow of candlelight dimly lit the room and a large spherical bulb hung from the center of the room, glowing with the same orange light.

I stepped closer and peered into the orb. There was no wood, but fire danced just as merrily as it would in a full hearth. How was such a thing possible?

"Dragon fire," Lucien said, as if sensing my thoughts. "Another bit of magitech. Our fire can be bottled, harnessed, modified." His voice faltered.

"It's incredible," I breathed, looking around. "You sure you'll be all right out there?"

"I will," he said. I wasn't sure I believed him.

"Go on now." He shooed at me with his hands. "Get some rest. I'll be keeping watch outside if you need me."

"Lucien?" The name tumbled from my lips like the tide, unstoppable now that the words had started flowing.

"Mmm?" He turned.

"What happened to your clan?" I snapped my lips shut

as soon as I'd said it. Far too personal. Far too nosy. But there it was.

Lucien froze, his hand on the doorknob. Neither of us moved.

"It's a long story." He pursed his lips, as if considering his next words. "I could ask you the same question, though. Who are you? Why did I find you hiding in my wagon? Bet there's someone worried about you out there."

My heart ached with the truth of his words. Mother. Samson. I had to make it up to them.

I furrowed my brow and squeezed my eyes shut. "My secret for yours."

Lucien chuckled at that. "You drive a hard bargain, I'll give you that. But you've got a deal. Remind me in the morning. We will talk then."

My heart lifted a bit. I hadn't expected him to actually tell me. "Promise?"

His eyes met mine, all molten lava and warm honey. "Promise," he said with a smile.

The door clicked closed, and I lay back on the fluffy pillows, watching the wavering light of the dragon fire.

8

ALEC

The smell of burning wood floated through the air. I sniffed, half-asleep.

It reminded me of the campfires we used to build in Steamshire. It reminded me of home.

I blinked open my eyes.

Only this time, I wasn't home. Far from it.

I was in a dragon's den. The one place my people feared most.

And yet, I hadn't been eaten yet. I hadn't even been mistreated. A lifetime of stories and rumors and warnings to the contrary, I wasn't quite sure who to believe anymore. Perhaps the dragons were just being nice to me to lure me into a false sense of security. Perhaps they would roast me in my sleep.

Or perhaps, just perhaps, the Elders were wrong.

It was a heretical statement. I knew that. A pang of guilt rose in my chest even at the thought. But I was far from them now. They couldn't get me here.

I sat up and stretched, yawning. Despite the stress of the last few days, I'd enjoyed one of the best nights of sleep I'd had in a while. For a temporary settlement, Lucien's bedroom was ridiculously comfortable.

Lucien.

My thoughts flickered back to the alpha dragon who'd taken me in. He had no reason to be nice to me. I was the one trespassing, after all. So why did he keep coming back? Why did it feel like we were connected by some cosmic force I couldn't explain, and didn't want to?

Mate. The thought lingered in my mind, reaching to the very depths of my being. I shivered. There had to be some mistake. I'd never even had a heat like the other boys. All the hype around mating and babies seemed a little overblown, to be honest. I thought I was happy doing my own thing, providing for my family, eking out my simple little existence in Steamshire, all the while dreaming of more.

How wrong I was.

The door opened and startled me from my thoughts.

Lucien backed into the room, holding a tray piled high with fresh fruit. My mouth watered at the sight.

"Rise and shine, sleeping beauty. Thought you might be hungry."

"You thought right." I tried to ignore it, but I couldn't help but notice the way my heart skipped a beat when he called me a beauty. "Thank you. This is wonderful."

And it was.

Lucien scratched a spot behind his ear and stared at the floor with a pleased look on his face. "I don't know about that," he mumbled.

"That's ok. I do."

I dove into the plate of fruit he'd brought, juices dribbling down my chin. "Thank you, really," I said through berry-stained lips.

He laughed. "I didn't know feeding our guest was considered such luxury treatment."

I threw a grape at him. It bounced off his broad chest and rolled away. "You know what I mean."

Lucien smirked with a raised eyebrow. We continued to eat in silence.

"Did you get some sleep?" I asked.

"Did you?"

"That's not the question I asked."

"I managed."

I gave a disapproving groan.

"So Alec, you ever gonna tell me your last name?" The question came out of nowhere.

"Oh, uh." I scrambled, my mind momentarily blank. "Cipher. Alec Cipher." Somehow, it felt almost too intimate sharing my full name like that. Like I was exposing myself to him.

"Hmm." Lucien smiled. "Cipher. Like a puzzle."

I snorted. "Something like that."

"It fits you," Lucien said after taking a long swig of water from the jug he'd brought.

"How's that?"

"You are quite the puzzle to me, Alec." His voice took on that warm, melty tenor again, vibrating all the way to my bones. The fiery orbs trapped me in their gaze, locked in time like an insect in amber.

This time, I couldn't stop the blush from raging through my cheeks.

"That reminds me," I pointed out. "We were going to share secrets."

His eyes flashed as he leaned back, picking at the rinds of the melon he'd devoured. "You remembered."

"Of course, I did," I said, bristling. How would I forget something like that?

"You first," he offered.

"Oh no, you don't. I asked you first. It's only fair."

Lucien gave a dramatic sigh, putting a hand to his chest. "Fiiine." He rolled his eyes at me, but a good-natured smirk still creased his face. "Get comfortable. It's a long one."

———

"...AND THAT'S WHAT HAPPENED," he finished, his voice shaking with emotion.

I'd been listening silently, but inside my heart was crying out in a million ways. The connection I felt to the alpha dragon grew stronger with each word, each trial, each defeat. When he was finally done, I felt empty. Raw. Like it had just happened to me. I could only imagine what it was like for him.

I reached out and put a tentative hand on his shoulder to comfort him. He didn't flinch away. To my surprise, he covered my hand with his own, leaning his head to the side. Lucien's stubble brushed my hand with a tickle. And still the fire raged through me.

Guilt, too. New and raw in its intensity, it cut a rough slash through my heart. Lucien had a mate. Caldo. The man whose name had been engraved on his blade.

I couldn't imagine losing a mate. To have someone so deeply intertwined with your soul, and to have them ripped away...it was no wonder dragons lost their powers because of it.

Who was I to think we could have had anything together? I was just a nosy human, and I knew enough about dragons to know they mated for life. There was no way he'd give that up for someone like me. In fact, the very idea was an insult to Caldo's memory.

"I'm so sorry," I said finally, when words came. "That's terrible. All of it."

He squeezed my hand, warmth spreading up my fingertips. Did he know what he was doing to me?

"I was the Clan Alpha, you know. Before it all happened." Lucien continued speaking, his voice far away. It was almost as if he were just recounting it to himself as an afterthought. Not speaking for an audience.

"I had everything. Or I thought I did."

"And now?"

"Taking it a day at a time." Lucien drained the flask and stretched. "Now it's your turn." He gave me a teasing grin.

I grumbled and rolled my eyes, turning to face him. I put my hands in his own before I thought better of it. I was searching for a little physical comfort, but it did much more than that. Lucien linked our fingers, and the warmth of his touch nearly took my breath away. What was I talking about again?

"You know relations have been...strained between humans and shifters," I started.

Lucien barked out a laugh. "That's one way to put it."

"My village...they're really scared of you guys. I grew up hearing nothing but how awful dragons were, how they wiped out whole villages without blinking an eye. They treated dragons like some kind of gods. I doubt any of them have ever even seen one, now that I think about it."

"That's ridiculous," Lucien sputtered. "I've heard a lot of crazy theories, but gods? Come on." His face darkened with a hidden sadness I couldn't name. "What do they do about it?"

The hole in my heart grew as I thought about the night of the Choosing Ceremony. I remembered my name being called. I remembered the parchment and the cries of my mother and brother.

"They make a sacrifice." I whispered the words, barely able to continue.

Lucien flared into action at that, gripping my shoulders and yanking me out of my memories. His eyes bored into mine and his voice came out as a roar. "They tried to kill you." It wasn't a question. His nails sharpened into claws, digging into my shoulders. I sucked in a breath as fear pulsed through my veins.

I closed my eyes as they welled with tears, my head slumping. The words wouldn't come.

Lucien did something I didn't expect. He pulled me close, holding me against his chest. A warm, hard plane of muscle met me there. It was surprisingly comfortable. He ran a hand through my curls and one over my back. A strange combination of fear, adrenaline, and something else entirely tingled through every pore.

"You will be safe here." He said at length, his jaw tight. The conviction in his voice left no room for doubt.

In the moment, that was all I needed to hear.

We sat there, our chests rising and falling as the glowing embers silhouetted us below.

———

"CAN I ASK YOU SOMETHING?" Lucien spoke up after a time.

"Yeah?" I turned to face him.

"Do you ever feel...weird when I'm around?"

I raised my eyebrow, laughing. "Weird? What do you mean?"

Lucien wrung his hands, searching for the words. "Like...I dunno. A current. A feeling."

I realized with a shock he was talking about the same cosmic pull I'd felt toward him. The same one that screamed *mate.* My heart sped up a few beats. He felt it too?

"That's how I found you, in the forest. How I knew you were in trouble." The words were out before I had a chance to censor them. Truth time.

His presence enveloped me, my body temperature rising. Suddenly the room was too small. Too warm. Beads of sweat broke out on my forehead and my mouth grew dry. All I could feel was the heat, waves of heat, washing over my body like a hurricane. That, and the rush of blood and desire to my groin.

Heat.

Oh no.

"I gotta know if this is normal," Lucien growled breathlessly, his eyes just as wild as mine. If he sensed my predicament, he didn't show it.

"Try me," I whispered. Even the feel of his breath on my skin was too much. Too sensitive.

I wanted him.

May I be damned, but I wanted him.

We stared at each other for a moment, points of light

zapping between us, then he leaned forward and kissed me.

An explosion of delight rippled through me, opening the floodgates to a new, surging river of need.

This couldn't be happening.

But it was.

I kissed him back, moaning into his mouth as the warm lips teased mine. He tasted like he smelled—cinnamon and honey, surprisingly sweet. There was a bit of an herbal taste there too, just barely. He was delicious.

I shot out my tongue and Lucien rumbled in response as I probed his lips. He fisted a hand in my hair and pulled me closer, the kiss turning desperate.

A low, feral rumble vibrated from his chest outward and he tore himself away as a roar broke free.

I scooted back a few steps, heart hammering. Every hair stood on end, every nerve alight. Lucien's face contorted, his irises dilated to fill the entire eye with flaming orange light. He shuddered and shook as if a cold wind had seized him.

"Lucien!" I screamed, concern taking over.

Those mighty eyes met mine in recognition. The flames simmered, cooled, stabilized. He righted his body, and now only gazed at me with a tired expression.

"What happened?" I dared to ask.

Lucien stared at me in awe, examining his hands and feeling his face as if he'd never seen them before.

"I...I can't believe it. My dragon..."

I held my breath. Everyone said a broken-hearted dragon could never heal. Could never shift again.

"He was dormant for so long. They told me it was final. But ever since I met you, this...energy, this current, has been stirring deep within me. The dragon noticed, like waking from a long sleep. And when we kissed just then, it was like everything made sense, for the shortest of moments. It's like I was alive once more."

I sucked in a breath. "That must have been some kiss," I teased. "Are you okay?"

"More than okay," he growled, advancing on me. "Fucking fantastic."

We clashed together again, more physical this time. Sparks flew in my vision and waves of heat rolled off of me in a way I knew the alpha could sense.

I was having my first heat in the presence of a smoking-hot dragon.

There was only one way this could go.

"Sounds like we better experiment some more," I gasped. My lips tore away to nuzzle at the side of his neck where his pheromones were strongest. They washed over me and fueled the fire, blocking out any rational thought.

Mine. Mate. Mine.

"I like the way you think," Lucien growled and lifted me into his arms in one smooth motion, carrying me to the bed.

My body burned for him, but not even my heart could cover up the niggling wave of doubt and grief.

"But Caldo," I started, looking into Lucien's eyes. They were both gentle and fierce at the same time, crystallized into a golden gem.

His face softened and he laid me on the bed gently, the blankets and pillows welcoming me. "He watches over us all from the Great Beyond. And I've realized something. If he were here, he'd laugh at how complacent we've become. He'd want me to fight. He'd want me to crush those sons of bitches that took him from me. And I finally know how we can do just that. You're the key, Alec. The Goddess threw you in my path for a reason. And now I know why."

"Tradition be damned, I want you. My dragon wants you. And my dragon will not be refused."

9

LUCIEN

I didn't know what had come over me.

Or rather, I did, but didn't want to believe it.

I hadn't felt so alive in years. And to think, all it took was a stray human omega crossing my path.

I hadn't felt my dragon respond this way to anyone, ever. Even with Caldo. And that scared me.

But in that moment, lust was greater than fear.

The rush of power as I held him close was intoxicating, making my head spin. I couldn't even imagine what it would feel like to be inside of him.

Alec looked up at me with eyes hooded with pleasure. His skin burned and sweated, his eyes wild.

So, he was feeling this too.

I lay down on top of him and nuzzled his neck, nipping

at the sensitive skin there. That produced a delightful yelp from my omega, so I did it again on the other side. He writhed in my touch, hips raising up desperately to meet mine.

We were much too clothed for this.

I tore off my own shirt in a smooth motion, noticing the sharp intake of breath from Alec.

"God, you're gorgeous," Alec mumbled, his hands exploring the broad muscled planes of my chest down to my abs and finally teasing along the waistline. It was my turn to hiss in surprise.

"Needy omega, aren't you?" I grinned, brushing a lock of hair from his face.

He didn't say anything, only nodded. I grabbed his wrists and pushed them away, holding them together with one strong hand. He was so much smaller and lighter than me. It was kinda adorable, actually.

I pinned his wrists above his head with one hand and set the other to the buttons on his shirt. I leaned in close, my lips inches from his. My dragon rumbled in my chest again, pushing outwards. The sparks that flew between us were maddening, but I wanted to prolong this.

For both our sakes.

"Please," Alec mouthed, arching toward me.

"Shh," I smiled, putting a finger to his lips. They were warm and swollen from kissing, formed into a perfect rosy pout that stirred my cock even more.

I released my hold on his wrists long enough to remove his shirt, throwing it to the side.

"You're not so bad yourself," I rumbled, burying my face in the curls of chest hair.

Alec moaned and clutched at me, fingers digging into my flesh. I could feel the hard evidence of his arousal poking through his trousers, desperate to break free.

"You sure you want to do this?" I hesitated at his waistband. Once this night was over, there would be no going back. For either of us. But I'd finally understood the way Alec's presence pulled at me. The way Caldo would have smiled and given us his blessing, if he were alive. I needed to be strong. I needed to avenge him.

I needed to learn to love again.

Alec locked eyes with mine and I felt another roar bubbling up through my throat. My vision blurred.

"I'm sure."

With a growl, I grabbed the waistband of his pants and pulled downward, exposing his ass. It glistened already with wet, hot slick that took my breath away. And his cock...my Goddess.

He was big for an omega, his length jutting proudly

upward and pulsing with each beat of his heart. Heat and pheromones overwhelmed my senses and before I knew what I was doing I dove downward, burying my face in his crotch.

I took in a deep scent, letting the musky smell of him surround me. I'd never smelled anything so good in my life! My dragon agreed as the flames inside stoked higher.

Alec gasped under my ministrations, his fingers winding through my hair. I didn't mind, it felt good. Good to be wanted.

I nuzzled my way down to his cock and licked the tip of it, watching as Alec shivered beneath me.

"Oh...that's nice," he groaned, arching his back.

"You haven't seen anything yet," I teased, then dipped my head lower, taking him all the way in. My tongue lapped at his shaft as it tickled the back of my throat. My nose was planted firmly in the tuft of hair above his shaft and the whiff of pheromones that hit me nearly made me come right then and there.

"God—" Alec breathed. His breaths came faster now, his skin at a fever pitch. It was time.

"Not God. My name is Lucien." I grinned evilly at him, winding a hand down to stroke his opening. He was so slick, so ready. I coated my fingers in his juices and sniffed them again. I could never get enough of that smell if I had it next to me twenty-four hours a day.

"Lucien!" he cried out as I inserted a finger, probing the tight muscle there. His hips lifted of their own volition, providing me easier access. Grabbing a pillow, I stuffed it under him.

There we go.

And what an view it was. My hands roamed the perfect globes, squeezing and kneading the muscle there. It was the perfect combination of taut and squeezable. Not to mention—

Smack!

Very smackable.

Alec yelped at the sudden impact, his eyes wide. "You like that?" I asked, readying my hand to strike again.

He nodded and made a soft keening sound, wiggling his hips at me. My cock stiffened even further, painful against my briefs. I groaned at the sensation. This omega was going to be the end of me.

I spanked him again, relishing the soft mewling sounds of pain and pleasure. Alec panted for breath as I paused for a moment. Rubbing my fingers against his hole, I inserted one, then two.

"Goddess you're tight," I groaned, drawing away to drop my own briefs. I couldn't stand it anymore. My cock sprang free, bouncing up against my stomach. A drip of precum had already formed at the head, desperate for release.

I took my shaft and pressed it up against Alec's slick opening, rubbing it back and forth, teasing him. Alec writhed his hips toward me. It was adorable, not to mention really fucking hot.

"Give me that cock," Alec gasped through gritted teeth, still trying to angle himself against me.

He didn't have to tell me twice.

I pressed the head of my cock against him and slowly, ever so slowly, it slipped past the ring of muscle and in. We groaned in unison as the mating of our bodies set off fireworks before my eyes. I took a moment to get used to the sensation, and for Alec to get used to the stretch. I leaned forward and cupped his face. He grinned with me in a heat-induced haze.

"You're beautiful," I whispered, stroking his chin.

"Shut up and fuck me."

I had to laugh. One-track mind, this one.

"You asked for it," I growled, my dragon rumbling low in my chest. He was waking up from his protracted slumber, and he was hungry.

With a clean thrust of my hips I pressed into him, all the way to the hilt. The sensation was dizzying; I could only imagine what it must have felt like for Alec. He sighed and relaxed, his body loosening as a lazy sort of delight washed over his face. "That's nice," he said, wiggling his hips against me.

The friction set me off even more, and suddenly I was beside myself, consumed with lust and greed and desire. The dragon had taken over, plundering his hole hard and fast and hot. I panted with each thrust, pulling him closer, pushing myself deeper. The keening sounds he made only spurred me forward, desperate for more.

Mate. *Mine*. Mate.

The dragon roared within me as I picked up the pace, sweat now forming in dew drops across my body. A rush of power and energy flowed into me, this time not just from the endorphin high of sex. My vision blurred and changed, taking on the dragon's enhanced qualities. A tickle between my shoulder blades prodded at my consciousness. Wings.

The world fell away, the only sounds those of our labored breathing and the slick, heavy thrusts into Alec's perfect channel. I knew people would say this was wrong.

But Goddess, it felt so right.

My knot began to swell within him, even as the rational voice in the back of my head warned what this meant. My dragon was having none of it.

Alec's gaze never left my own, watching me wide-eyed as his hands roamed anywhere they could touch. He threw his head back and moaned as my knot grew and stretched him even further.

My balls tightened, my vision narrowed. For all that was good in this world. For my clan. For Caldo. I would carry on. I would fight.

The primal roar could be contained no longer and it ripped itself free, echoing through the cave walls as I dumped my seed into Alec's waiting channel. My knot swelled to full, locking us together as alpha and omega. As Alec and Lucien. As two souls united in a moment of passion.

Thoughts and emotions flooded through my mind as we joined, melding into one.

I'd show Alec's Elders. I'd show The Paradox. I'd show them all.

I was back.

I woke up naked and nestled in Lucien's arms. My heat had passed; in its place lay a cool, calm assurance. I lay there for a few moments more, feeling Lucien's heart beat against my own.

I couldn't believe I'd just done that.

Visions of the passionate night we'd shared flickered back to me in full detail, stirring my cock.

I'd not only met a dragon. I'd mated with one.

If only the Elders could see me now.

I glanced down my naked body, noting the prickles of energy that still raced along my skin.

I felt different. Stronger, somehow. *More.*

My gaze moved to Lucien's sleeping form. For a dragon, he sure slept like an innocent baby. Hair spread out around him in a halo and his mouth hung slightly open, his chest rising and falling with each whispered breath.

He was beautiful. He was mine.

The reality of the situation was just starting to dawn on me when a knock came at the door, fast and hard.

Lucien woke with a start, flailing through the covers as he blinked his eyes open. "What?" he mumbled blearily.

"Lucien? You in there?" a small voice came from the other side of the door.

A pause. "Who's asking? I'm a little busy at the moment." He yawned and fell back on to the pillows, rubbing his forehead.

"I hate to disturb you, but it's urgent, so get unbusy."

Lucien closed his eyes and let out a long slow breath through his flared nostrils. "Be right there," he called and threw himself out of bed.

"What's going on?" I asked, rubbing my eyes. I'd been looking forward to some morning cuddles, to be honest, but it didn't look like that was going to happen now.

Lucien grumbled as he threw on some clothes. "I don't know, but apparently it can't wait." He leaned over and planted a kiss on my forehead. "I'll be right back. I promise. Stay here."

As if I was going to leave the warm, cozy sanctuary anytime soon. "Be careful out there," I said before I thought better of it.

He turned to me and smiled. "You know I always am, irralo."

Before I could ask what that word meant, he left the room and the door closed with a gentle thud.

I lay there, staring at the ceiling. Irralo. I repeated the syllables. What did it mean? I assumed it was some kind of pet name. Perhaps from some ancestral language.

The seconds ticked by. I grew restless. My thoughts ping-ponged off one another, filling my head with chaos. Where was he? What was going on? Did I *really* just mate with a dragon?

I swung my legs over the side of the bed and padded over to the bathroom. A nice shower should clear things up.

The steam of the bathroom soothed my frayed nerves and the hot water washed away all evidence of our little tryst the night before. As I ran the bar of soap over my stomach, I felt the tiniest twinge of movement there. Like a bubble popping, or a feather-light touch. I thought I'd imagined it the first time, but then it came again.

I nearly dropped the soap, my mind suddenly racing.

I was an omega. He was an alpha. And I'd been in heat.

I shook my head, letting out a nervous laugh. We were two whole different species. I'd never heard of dragons and humans breeding together. I didn't even know if it was biologically possible.

But I probably should have considered that *before* I got down and dirty.

I held my breath as the twinge came again. It was probably nothing. I was just hungry, was all. I finished washing up and wrapped myself in one of the plush robes Lucien left hanging in the bathroom. It almost pushed away any worry still burrowing into my mind.

Almost.

I was flipping through a book on dragon history I found on Lucien's nightstand when he returned. I looked up.

Lucien's face no longer held the easy confidence or the joy I'd seen last night. His forehead creased, his eyebrows scrunched together, the corners of his lips tugged downward.

Something was wrong, and he wasn't doing a very good job of hiding it.

I flipped the book closed and patted the bed next to me.

"What's the matter?"

Lucien walked over to the bed and sat as if in a daze, his eyes still locked into some far-off glance.

"Lucien?" I prodded him. I rested a hand on his shoulder, trying to decipher his expression. He didn't react.

"You okay? What happened?" I was really starting to get worried now.

Lucien let out a breath and his shoulders sagged. "They've found us," he said at length.

Fear lanced through me like lightning, along with something else. A fierce protectiveness, an indignation that someone would hurt my mate this way. "Who's they?" I dared to ask.

"The group that got me into this whole mess in the first place. When they stole my mate, my own clan turned against me. I was blind. I didn't see, or chose not to see, how many of their followers had infiltrated our ranks. They kicked me out, stripped me of my command, my power, my everything. The Iron Paradox." He spat the last words with such malice even I shivered where I sat.

I knew I should probably know what he was talking about, but I didn't. "The Iron Paradox?" I asked gently.

"They're a sect of shifters with some...shall we say... extreme beliefs. But they're charismatic as hell, and persuasive, especially to the young ones. Their followers are called Cogs. Disgusting, isn't it? They know they're all cogs in a greater war machine, and they like it. Revel in it, even."

"And they're the ones that found us?" My heart quickened at the thought. Suddenly, our little cave compound didn't feel so safe anymore.

"When we moved out here, I took only my most trusted and valued clan members. They stood with me, even through the midst of the mutiny. I have no reason to doubt their loyalty. But one of the magitech wards malfunctioned last night and alerted them to our presence. The Iron Paradox has taken control of Darkvale, and their troops are on their way now. To wipe us out once and for all."

The words settled onto me with a violent finality.

"What do we do?" I winced. I already knew the answer.

"Grab your things, and stay close to me. We're evacuating."

———

I GUESS I should be no stranger to being on the run by now. What I wouldn't give for a decent night's rest again, though. My eyes burned and my muscles ached, not to mention the strange fluttering sensation deep in my stomach. But none of that mattered right now.

I threw the few things I'd taken out back into my bag and slung it over my shoulder. Lucien was ready in record time, his own bag prepped and ready to go. Almost as if he'd been expecting this day to come.

My heart ached for him. To be thrown out of his own home, to have his people turn against him in that way... it must have been horrible. And then to lose his mate on top of all that?

I'd never measure up.

There it was, the niggling guilt again. The worry that I was only a means to an end, a way for Lucien to regain his powers and take back his throne. I didn't mind helping, sure, but were we really going to play up this whole mate thing if he didn't really mean it?

But I was getting ahead of myself. I didn't know if he meant it or not. I didn't know what was going to happen to me, or us, after this. And if the fluttering in my stomach was any indication, things were about to get a lot more complicated.

I cradled my belly and followed Lucien through the compound back to the center hub, where everyone gathered. They carried their packs, their children, and hushed, frightened faces. Only a few of them had weapons. I grimaced. If we were ambushed, we were toast.

But perhaps the dragon shifters had some tricks up their sleeve yet. They couldn't have all lost their powers like Lucien, right? That meant...

I sucked in a breath.

I was going to see a real live dragon.

Ever since finding that fang in the dirt outside Steamshire, I'd wondered what the dragons were really like. There were the stories they told us around the campfire at night, filled with evil spirits, blood, and fire. But what were they really like? I remembered asking over and over if anyone had ever actually seen one. They seemed to think that was an inappropriate question, and eventually I stopped asking.

Take that, stuffy old Steamshire.

"Your attention, everyone." Lucien stepped up onto a dais at the center of the room, looking out at the crowds that had gathered. "I've called you here today for some dire news. The Iron Paradox has learned of our location, and they are sending troops here as we speak." The crowd rumbled with alarm. A child cried out, burying his head in his mother's shoulder.

"When we first came to this place, you remember what I told you all back then. I will say it again to you now. You are my most trusted, most loyal brothers and sisters. We have become more than just members of the same clan. We have become family. And that is why I ask you now, will you fight with me? Will you fight for our rightful land and drive back the invaders?" He raised his hand high, Caldo's dagger pointing to the heavens.

A cheer rippled through the crowd, taking on a form all its own. Those who had weapons brandished them, and those who didn't roared so loudly I felt the entire cavern shake. I covered my ears from the sound, and they were still ringing even as the cheers died away.

Right. Den full of dragons.

I gazed at Lucien up on the stand, beating his chest and thrusting his sword to the sky. I thought he struck a commanding presence before, but this was something else altogether. He exuded power, presence, energy, and something else I hadn't noticed before. Hope.

These people had left their clan to come with Lucien and build a new clan together. I had to respect that. And even in the face of almost-certain defeat, they were ready and stand and fight for their people, their land, their clan.

And their Alpha.

A sense of pride rushed through me. That was *my* Alpha.

"And there's something else I would like you all to know, as well." Lucien's voice boomed from the platform and I snapped my gaze to him. He met my eyes for a fraction of a second and winked.

"I believe there's a way to reverse the Curse of the Dragonheart."

A surprised mumble went through the crowd. I heard whispers all around me.

"Didn't think it was possible…"

"A broken heart…"

"Poor Caldo…"

"When we lost Caldo to the Cogs and their Paradox, it was a dark time for all of us. You've all heard the stories. A broken-hearted dragon, they said, will never shift again. His powers lay dormant for the rest of his days, his dragon suppressed under the weight of grief in his heart. Until now, I, like all of you, thought there was nothing we could do about it. I was determined to live and make the most of what I had left, just like all of you when you chose to follow me. But then something happened I didn't expect. I met a human on the road. "

More rumbles of confusion. Many shifters were wary of humans, and with good reason. After all the things my people had said and done to them, I couldn't blame them. But perhaps there was some core misunderstanding between cultures that they didn't quite get. Maybe all this fighting was over something as simple as a failed translation.

"And it was this human, my brothers and sisters," Lucien continued, his voice raising with pride, "that taught me the true meaning of bravery. He may not be like us, he may be from a different background, a different race, a different village. But he has become more than that. He has become my mate."

Shouts of surprise. Dragons mated for life. Not often was it that a dragon would take two mates in his lifetime, much less an Alpha of his position.

"I know what you may be thinking. Do not see this as a slight against Caldo. I have made my peace with his passing. He remains here, among all of us, in our hearts. And with my new mate, I have discovered something. The Paradox won't know what hit them."

With a triumphant roar, he leaned back and flames spewed from his throat, rising toward the sky in a column of flame. The crowd stepped back, everyone talking and shouting at once.

"His dragon..."

"It's back..."

"The curse..."

A chill ran through me at the sight of his fire-breathing, all the way to my toes. Even though the air hung crisp and hot with the acrid scent of fire, a different sort of heat wove its way through my bones. That was my alpha. My dragon. My mate.

To see him breathe fire like that was to fully realize his potential as a dragon. His powers were coming back. I'd done that. The pride of it all filled me up like a warm honey, radiating out toward the crowd as they turned their heads to look at me.

"My mate, Alec Cipher!" Lucien boomed, pointing at me. Everyone who wasn't staring already turned their heads and suddenly dozens of eyes were on me.

Oh crap, was I supposed to make a speech or something?

I cleared my throat and straightened my back under their expectant gaze.

"Hello, everyone." I tried to project my voice so they all could hear but my voice cracked. "I have met some of you already, but I hope to meet you all in the coming days. Lucien and I are a team. I know many of you are wary of my kind, and for good reason. But I assure you, I harbor no ill will toward your people. I simply want to learn more about your clan and your culture, if I can. I hope, in time, we will come to understand one another, and work together for our common causes, instead of fighting these petty battles."

Rumblings of assent. "Hear, hear!" a voice shouted from the back.

"And there you have it. The time has come. Let us take to the air, and take back what is ours!" called Lucien.

Roars shook the cave walls once more, and this time I was prepared. I probably should have been scared, a horde of dragons roaring all around me. But if I listened closely enough, I could hear something else in their roars than just blind bloodlust. I heard loyalty. I heard bravery. I heard hope.

It was with that fever pitch that the crowd moved and shuffled, pouring out of the cave mouth with Lucien at the helm and me scrambling to catch up. The sun rose over the horizon, large and sleepy, and it was a new day.

I'd never seen a dragon shift before.

As the men and women poured out onto the plains, they let out guttural growls as their primal nature took over. I couldn't tear my eyes away.

Their skin bulged, ripped, re-mended with scales and claws and teeth. Wings sprouted from their back, unfurling against the sky. Each of them was a slightly different color, but they all had the pupils of molten flame I'd seen in Lucien.

Speaking of, where was he?

I ducked through the crowd. Being a human in a group of shifting dragons is a precarious position, let me tell you. Dragons are *big*, and it's not like we had a ton of room out here. I scooted off, the image of one of their massive tails crushing me still fresh in my mind.

"Lucien!" I called through the chaos.

Then I saw him.

I craned my neck upward, taking in his full form. And what a form it was. Towering over me, Lucien struck an even more imposing figure in dragon form. Onyx black scales rippled across his skin like polished jewels or the purest ink. His four feet were tipped with long ivory talons, not unlike the one I'd found all those years ago. His eyes were what gave him away, though.

Filled with light and fire, the irises latched onto mine and enveloped me in a sea of flame. Warm breath puffed out from his nostrils. My heart raced as I reached out a shaking hand. Lucien lowered his snout to eye level. He was so big. His head was easily the size of my entire body. How did something this ferocious fit inside the man? I could only stare on in awe.

My hand inched closer and I held my breath. The scales were smooth, hard, with almost a velvety feel to them. Lucien rumbled next to me, nuzzling against my hand. He emanated warmth and power and prowess. He was the Clan Alpha dragon, after all.

A voice echoed through my mind.

I am sorry, irralo, as I am not strong enough to carry a rider just yet. My powers are still returning, and you need to be safe.

I let out a breath. *What, you're leaving me?* I thought

back. The pain of it spiked through me all the way down to my belly, where the fluttering still continued.

Not leaving. Never leaving, my blessed one. I must join my people in battle, but Lessa will take you to safety. She's a friend and ally, one of my most trusted comrades. Listen to her, she will lead the children and omegas to a safe house. We must protect our bloodline at all costs.

I clung to him, hugging his warm snout. *I want to come with you.*

I wish that you could, irralo. We will meet again soon, and when the dust clears, I will never leave you again. That is my promise, on the bones of my people I swear it.

He projected an image of a crackling hearth, good music, and a hearty stew bubbling in a pot. *We will have all of that and more, precious one.*

The images and sensations filled me like warm honey, soothing away my worries for a second.

You are my mate, and you are everything to me now. Stay safe, little one. I must go to join my brothers.

The word mate lingered in my mind, echoing through my bones. Mate. Whatever this bond was, it went deeper than just friends or lovers. It was more than that. Primal. As if the gods of nature themselves ordained it.

Come back to me soon, I thought with a final caress.

I will, he promised. His wings expanded to their full length and he rose off the ground, dust and grass blowing around me as he flapped those giant wings.

Thundering footsteps shook the ground behind me. I felt the warm breath of a dragon.

I turned.

So, this must be Lessa. She would lead us to safety.

"Lessa Sarvonis, at your service." She dipped her head in what could have been a bow.

Whoa, a talking dragon! Whereas Lucien had only communicated with me telepathically in dragon form, Lessa spoke aloud. It was not a rumbly, dragony sound. Just a normal human voice, which was kind of amusing coming from such a huge dragon. I smiled.

She was smaller than Lucien, but no less elegant. Her scales shimmered an iridescent green, the light bouncing off of them in prisms of color. Her eyes were softer, a paler yellow than the others I'd seen. Even though her mouth held dozens of razor sharp fangs, it almost seemed as if she was smiling.

"Thank you." I dipped my head, still awed by her beauty.

And to think, I had been scared of dragons with the rest of them only weeks ago!

A gathering of children, a few parents, and a few elders

congregated behind her. They looked on, some with hopeful faces, some mottled with fear. I caught the eye of a rosy-cheeked boy with black curls and gave him a smile. He shyly turned and buried his head in his mother's skirt.

"We must get moving," Lessa announced to the group. "Each of you has been assigned a role as flyer or rider. We will be heading in the opposite direction of the immediate threat, but you must keep on your guard. Do not leave the formation for any reason whatsoever, you hear me? If we stay together, we live together. The safe house isn't far, and it's protected by magitech wards. All the same, we must be vigilant. Do you understand?"

A rumbling of nods and assent.

A thought struck me. Wait a second... Flyers and riders?

"You're with me, hun."

"What?" I gasped. "Oh no, no no no. I'm not riding you, I can't, I—"

"Lucien will have my hide if I leave you here, so be a good boy and climb on."

I backed away, sweat prickling on my forehead. No way! This was crazy! I couldn't ride a dragon. I'd fall off and die! I'd been exposed to a lot of new things as of late, but riding a dragon was solidly on the nope list.

"I'm scared of heights!" I blurted out, my breaths coming faster as my heart raced in double time.

She groaned and rolled her giant yellow eyes. "Oh, you humans and your heights! Let me put it this way: do you want to live or not? Your choice, darling."

I grit my teeth and sucked in a breath through my nose. She was right. Didn't mean I liked it, but she was right.

I had to do this.

Not only for my sake, but for Lucien. For the clan. And for whatever was growing inside of me.

I took a deep breath and grabbed onto her scales right above the front leg joint. She leaned down slowly, her stomach touching the ground so I could climb up easier.

"That's it, there you go. Right over the wings, that's the best spot."

I clambered up onto the dragon's back, my heart still going a million miles a minute. This was crazy. This was crazy. This was crazy.

But I had to live. I didn't escape and claim my freedom just to die a coward.

There are two pockets on my back there, do you see them?"

"Just a moment!"" I grunted, still trying to right myself on the slippery scales. I felt the strong, hard muscle beneath and the subtle rising and falling of breath. I ran my hands over the spinal area until I found what she was talking about—two small pockets on the dragon's back, right between the wings. Almost like handles.

"Grab on and don't let go!" she yelled, and with a thrust of those mighty muscles she launched into the air.

I screamed and squeezed my eyes shut, hanging on for dear life. Air whooshed around me and roared in my ears as I felt us ascend. I white-knuckled the pockets of flesh and squeezed with my legs as hard as I could.

"It's just like riding a horse, it's just like riding a horse, it's just like riding a horse..." I mumbled to myself as a mantra.

Yeah, a big, scaly, flying horse. That could breathe fire.

"Who you calling a horse?" Lessa teased. Her powerful wings beat back and forth to drive us even higher into the clouds. Soon we'd gained a sort of rhythm, a rising and falling as smooth as the breath through her lungs.

"You can open your eyes now, you know. Most humans never get to see the world from the air. I hear it's quite the experience."

I'll pass, I thought silently, but as time passed and the air whipped against my face, I grew curious.

I opened my left eye just a peek.

First, a blinding, brilliant light. The sun. When I'd adjusted to the glare, I saw so much more.

Skies blue as a perfect gem surrounded us, white puffy clouds floating by like wads of cotton. I'd never seen them so close. Up here, they were white wisps without any real form or shape, just drifting along as we cut through the air. I gulped, steeled myself, and looked down.

What I saw there took my breath away.

The land rose up around us, all green and brown and tan. I could see clearly now the shapes of farmland, the little cubes of houses, the flickering pinpricks of fires. Large bodies of water stared up at me, still and serene. My initial fear and vertigo was soon replaced by a wondrous fascination as I stared at the world below. It was like looking at a map, but in real life. If I stared closely enough I could see tiny specks moving about their day. People.

"It's incredible," I yelled, but my voice was lost in the wind.

"We're approaching the mountains," Lessa called back to me. "You're in for a treat."

I looked to the horizon and my eyes widened.

Tall, milky-white spires jutted against the sky, their proud beauty standing against the backdrop of stone and brush.

My mouth hung open as I took them in. I'd heard about mountains before, sure, but I'd never seen them. Seeing them from above was another matter altogether. I felt so small and so large at the same time, viewing the earth from this angle. Was this what the dragons saw all the time?

It certainly gave one a sense of perspective.

"Hang on, we're almost there."

I renewed my grip on Lessa's hide as she dipped into an air current, her wings straightening and gliding downward.

The mountains came into focus, stone and snow and grass. They looked so ethereal up here, like props in a diorama. And yet this was our world. A shiver passed through me as we flew through what could have been a cloud, though I didn't see anything. It was like floating through a layer of soap bubbles in a bathtub. The feeling only lasted a fraction of a second before it was gone.

"What was that?" I yelled to Lessa.

"That's the wards that Pakka set up. He's been scouting this place out for just this contingency for some time. And he's damn good with magitech."

"Magitech?" I asked before she took a hard right and I had to grab on for dear life again.

"Magic plus technology. Now look. We're here."

I gazed down at the rapidly rising ground. Where before there had been only bare stone now lay a little settlement. It hadn't been there a minute ago! I blinked and rubbed my eyes.

"An extra layer of protection from prying eyes," she said. The ground rose faster and faster, making me a bit nauseous. The old fear kicked in again and I slammed my eyes shut, panting through my nose. There were a few more seconds of gliding, then with a thump, she alighted on the ground.

Warm, solid ground. Thank Goddess.

"We're here," Lessa said, craning her head around to look at me. I was still locked up in a frightened ball, clasping onto her scales as tightly as I could. "We're safe now, hun. Come on. Let's get you inside."

Dragons landed all around us, shaking the ground. Ever so slowly, I lessened my grip, fingers and legs aching from being held in the same position for so long. I stretched my fingers, making a fist, then letting it go. I was going to be sore for sure. I swung my leg over the dragon's side. Intending to make a smooth dismount, the slickness of the scales disarmed me and I rolled off Lessa's back, landing with a thump in the dirt.

"Puh." I spat dirt out of my mouth and wobbled to my feet, rubbing my bruised tailbone. "You could have warned me." I grumbled at Lessa, and I thought I could see a smirk for sure. If dragons could smirk, that is.

The settlement we approached was not unlike the one I'd left behind in Steamshire. Why they didn't use the mountains to carve out a new cave I wasn't certain, but I supposed time was of the essence. I brushed myself off and followed the line of people heading into the village.

The dragons began to shift back into their human forms, a mist surrounding them as they became flesh and blood once more. Finally, I could see Lessa's human form. She was just as elegant as a human as she was in dragon form. Long blond tresses hung around her neck and she wore a coil of gold around her neck. Her skin was pale, spotted with a few freckles from the sun. It was cute.

She noticed me staring and made a shooing gesture. "Don't just stand there, go on in. I'll be right there."

I blushed and jogged to catch up with the line of parents and children.

Children.

The word floated in my throat again, like the faintest touch of a feather or a ladybug alighting on my skin. It triggered something in me I couldn't name, couldn't explain.

Children. Family. Mate. Mine.

I had an idea what was going on, but I didn't want to believe it. Not yet.

A dragon and a human?

Preposterous.

A voice roused me from my stupor.

"Name? Sir, your name?"

I blinked and looked up. A short man stood there with a book, taking a headcount, no doubt.

"Cipher. Alec Cipher."

"Very well, in you go."

He ushered me past and I stepped into the settlement, my mind still racing. Was I going to have a child? With Lucien, of all people? We'd had sex, and I was in heat...

I was an idiot.

Lessa tapped me on the shoulder and I spun around. "We've prepped a tent for you over here, come on."

I grinned and followed her, a warm sort of gratitude lighting me up not for the first time. I was nothing like them, but they treated me as one of their own. They took care of me, looked out for me. More than Steamshire ever had, anyway.

"Lessa?" I called, jogging to catch up with her.

"Yeah?" Her wavy blond hair tossed over her shoulder as she turned.

"Thanks," I mumbled, staring at the ground. "Really. For everything."

"You're the Clan Alpha's mate," she said matter-of-factly. "Human or not, we're sworn to you just as much as we are to him."

Another wave of sickness came over me just then. I doubled over and heaved, nothing coming out. Lessa rushed forward and brushed hair out of my face.

"I knew it."

"Knew what?" I asked, though my throat was raw. Nausea came back in waves, leaving me wheezing and coughing in the middle of camp. She grabbed my shoulder and muscled me inside a tent, sitting me down on a cot.

"Sit. Drink." She pushed a glass of water at me.

I eyed her but gulped it down, the cool contents soothing on my battered throat.

After a moment, the wave of nausea passed. The world stopped spinning. Lessa sat in a chair next to the cot, fidgeting with her hands. "What was it that you knew?" I asked when I found my voice again.

"Your sickness."

I tried to play it off with a casual wave of my hand. "Motion sickness. Riding a dragon, especially for the first time, is messy business."

Her eyes narrowed. "I know better than that, hun. The smell's coming off you in waves. The whole camp is gonna know before long."

It took me a few seconds to click the pieces together in my mind. I had known it, but the outside confirmation made it that much more real.

"You're pregnant, hun. With our Alpha's baby."

I gagged and heaved as anther crash of sickness took me. My mind raced with the knowledge. I was going to be a parent.

Oh, Goddess. I was going to be a parent. I didn't know anything about parenting!

"Are you sure?" I asked.

Lessa gave me an embarrassed smile. "You did...mate with him, did you not?"

Now it was my turn to blush. Did everyone have to know about that?

"Yes," I sputtered, "But—"

"You didn't know dragons and humans could breed, did you?" She gave a tiny musical laugh. "Well, I can't say its common, but it does happen from time to time. I've only ever seen it once before, myself."

"Am I going to be okay?" The words tumbled out, the foremost thought on my mind. A half dragon baby... inside me? It filled me with a fear, to be sure, but there was also something else. A pure, unfettered joy. I was going to have a baby.

His baby.

Our baby.

"Where's Lucien?" I asked her. I needed him now more than ever, and if he didn't come back...

"He'll come back," Lessa assured me. "He always does."

I wasn't so sure, but lay back on the cot Lessa had prepared for me. My stomach and chest ached from the wheezing and heaving. My mouth had a dry, cottony feel to it.

And I was pregnant.

I'd never quite seen the point of omegas fawning over babies and pregnancy. Omegas rarely got pregnant in Steamshire, and when they did it was a huge production. Parties, lavish gifts, ceremonies, the whole shebang. No wonder I was so turned off by the idea.

But this was different.

I was carrying a baby inside me. A half dragon baby, at that. I wondered if the little one would be able to shift like his father. The thought spiked such a glow of pride through me I almost understood why other omegas got so excited about the prospect.

My own little family.

Lessa called out to me as she ducked through the tent flap. "Stay here and don't move. I'm going to get you something for that nausea and check on the others. I'll be right back."

With a fluttering of canvas, she stepped outside and I was alone for the first time in quite a while.

I lay there with my thoughts, turning the idea over and over in my mind. Pregnant. Me.

I almost wanted to scoff at the ridiculousness of it all. If someone had told me last year, or even last month, that I was going to be pregnant with a dragon's baby, I would have laughed and knocked them into next week. That kind of thing didn't happen.

But it happened to me.

I thought about Lucien again, wondering where he was., if he was all right. Especially with this new development, I needed him to be here with me. But I knew that he had an important mission to complete. I knew that, but it didn't stop the selfish thoughts from forcing their way in.

I missed him.

Lucien, are you there? I tried to reach out through our psychic link, but hit a wall. I heard nothing, just static. Fear gripped me for a second or two until Lessa ducked back into the tent, carrying a bowl of steaming-hot broth.

She must have noticed my face screwed up in concentration.

"Trying to reach him on the Link? He's too far, hun."

"What?"

"He may be your mate, but even the Link has its limits. Try not to worry. I know it's difficult, but he will return. I promise you that. Come now, have some of this broth. It's got herbs for the sickness."

I scowled at her and sighed. Letting go of my worry about Lucien wasn't going to be easy. Barely even possible. But I grimaced and took a spoonful of broth, determined to stay strong until he returned.

12

LUCIEN

My long-dormant wings flapped through the air as the ground fell away.

Goddess, how I'd missed this.

The joints were achy, rusty almost. I hadn't used them in so long. But the further I flew, the higher I ascended, that weariness fell away and a sense of clarity I hadn't experienced in years fell over me.

I was flying.

I thought I'd never shift again. I thought it was all over for me, that I would live the rest of my life in exile, scraping by a meager existence with odd jobs.

But now I was a dragon once more, and I was leading my people into battle.

A feeling struck me just then, hot and instantaneous like a bolt of lightning.

It was Alec.

He needed me.

I tried to reach out to him, to tell him it would be all right.

Only static. The Link was out of range.

Cursing inwardly, I thought about my little mate I'd left in Lessa's care. Flashbacks to our night of passion ripped through my mind.

Then all the pieces came together at once.

The way he smelled when we left. The way he'd clung to me, afraid to see me go. The way he'd looked that night, naked and stunning in the throes in his passion.

Alec was pregnant.

And I was a fool.

The thought nearly toppled me out of the sky. Oh, Goddess. He's pregnant.

It took every ounce of willpower I had not to turn tail and head back to him right this instant. I needed to be there for him. For both of them.

I remembered with great pain Caldo's pregnancy. The way he grew, the glow it gave him when he laughed. Caldo, my mate, my heart, my everything. He was snatched away too soon, my son never able to meet the world.

I couldn't let that happen again. Not this time.

I beat my wings harder, ascending above the pack and pulling ahead. I needed space. I needed air.

An unfamiliar emotion washed over me. Fear. Cold, unadulterated fear.

I didn't know how to bring up a child in this tumultuous world. With Caldo, things were different. Things were simpler then, more peaceful then. But how could I be a good father when my clan was at war? How could I be a good commander, a good mate, and a good father all at the same time?

"Cogs incoming!" The warning cry took me away from my worries and back into the moment.

All of that could wait.

Right now, I had a job to do.

Fire built in my chest as I prepared to let it fly. For my child, I would fight. I would fight until my dying breath if that meant my mate and child could live. I wouldn't make the same mistake as last time.

I couldn't.

———

THE SKY GLOWED RED with flame. Teeth and blood and wings and claws. Dragons clashed together with earth-rending roars all around me. A golden drake flew toward me, its eyes alight with bloodlust.

The thought of Alec strengthened me and I roared, letting out a jet of flame across the sky. The golden drake rolled and tumbled out of the way of the flame, regaining his altitude gracefully. I'd never seen a dragon so smooth in the air before. It was like he (or she) was a ballerina dancer, gliding through the air currents with ease.

I pushed myself forward, eyes narrowing on my target.

The soft, fleshy underbelly.

The drake was too quick, once again. Momentum carried me past them and I lost my balance, clawing at the air. Fire flashed behind me and I dodged on instinct, but not before my tail got singed.

The scales us dragons wore were like plate armor, rough and impervious to most weapons. Piercing or slashing damage didn't do much good. But the scales were like metal, adaptable to the temperatures around us. We were cold-blooded, after all. The fire on my scales heated them up and burned me, as I let out a screech, rounding on the golden one.

They hissed, brandishing their wings. A taunt!

I wasn't going to fall for that this time.

I peered through the chaos of blood and bone and fire.

There, in the distance. A speck of light growing closer by the second.

The reinforcements were here—the second wave of dragons.

I feinted and my attacker fell for it, swaying to the left just as I lunged forward. My head collided with their underbelly, knocking the air and fire out in a great blast of flame. My claws scrabbled to find purchase, digging deep against flesh and scales.

The drake didn't go down without a fight. They flailed against me, claws tearing at my back, my wings, my face. I tried to unleash another bout of flame right into their gut but no spark came. No matter. I had teeth.

I burrowed my fangs deep into the soft flesh, adrenaline dulling the pain of scratches and claws all around me. A leg swiped forward and across my eye, tearing me away from my prize.

I screeched as the world blurred and darkened in a blood-red haze. Pain blustered through me, white-hot.

Where was that bastard?

A mass pummeled into me from behind and I was falling, the ground rushing toward me with dizzying speed.

Snippets of thought and sensation flooded through my mind as I fell. Caldo. Alec. The baby.

Oh, Goddess... the baby.

Fire and blood raged in the skies above, and I crashed into the forest below.

13

ALEC

Days passed and turned into weeks.

Still no sign of Lucien.

I tried not to let it get to me. Too much, anyway. I wasn't the only one with a missing mate, and it seemed there was a silent understanding: just take it one day a time and help out where you can.

So that was what I did. Better than sitting in my tent worrying.

Lessa kept me busy in the camp, helping with the cooking and taking care of the children. The morning sickness had finally passed after countless bowls of herbal broth and I felt stronger again.

The children of the camp were adorable, I soon found out. I'd always had a way with kids in Steamshire, but never thought I'd be rearing my own someday. Oh, how wrong I was.

"Alec!" a small boy cried out as he ran toward me. I picked him up and he squealed with delight. He was about six years old and already full of energy. His blond curls fell all across his face and highlighted the perfect toothy smile he always wore.

"Hey there, Finley. What are you getting into today? Not too much trouble, I hope?"

"Don't listen to him, he's all lies." A deep laugh came from behind me and I turned.

Adrian, Finley's omega father, stood there with a bright smile on his lips. He held a towel in his hand and his clothes were speckled with water droplets.

"Looks like someone needs a bath," I chided Finley, bouncing him up and down.

Adrian looked on with a weary smile. "Thank you, Alec. You know how he is about water." He rolled his eyes and laughed. "I keep telling him it won't put his fire out, but he doesn't believe me."

"Of course not," I agreed. "You're the big, mean grown-up."

We both had a laugh at that, remembering our own childhoods.

Even though Adrian was a dragon shifter, we'd bonded

over shared experiences in the time I'd spent at camp. Adrian's mate was off at battle as well, and it helped having a friend who I could confide in. It also didn't hurt that his little munchkin Finley was the cutest thing I'd ever laid eyes on.

"What was it like?" I asked suddenly, the question rising within me. I'd refrained from asking anyone else about pregnancy or birth, but the truth of it was I had no idea what to expect.

"What? The birth?" Adrian asked as I transferred the squawking child back into his arms. He shook his head, a wisp of nostalgia clouding his eyes. "I couldn't describe it if I tried. It's at once the most amazing and most painful thing I've ever done. And I wouldn't trade it for the world."

"That sounds nice."

"It is. Can't wait to meet your little one."

"Neither can I," I said with a smile.

Another thought still gripped me, and since I was asking uncomfortable questions...

"Why do they hide us here? Why won't they let us help? Let us fight?"

Adrian pursed his lips, thinking for a moment. "Omegas are tough. But you already knew that. Hell, we can have babies! What's more hardcore than that?"

I snorted.

"We do help, in our own way. Alphas might act like they're all high and mighty sometimes, but really, it's the omegas who run things. They would be nothing without us after all."

I thought back to the Curse of the Dragonheart, Caldo, the connection I'd felt lace us together as we mated that night.

"I just hope they come back soon," I said, my voice small.

Adrian freed a hand and put it on my shoulder. "You and me both, Alec. Now if you'll excuse me, this little monster needs a bath."

He continued on his quest to give the little dragon boy a bath, but I had one more question.

"Hey, Adrian?"

He turned.

"What does irralo mean?" The word had stuck in my mind ever since Lucien had said it to me the first time. It had to be some word from their native language but I still didn't know what it meant.

Adrian's face changed, a calm, knowing joy lighting up his features. "It means he truly cares about you." With a smile, he turned and walked on, leaving me with my thoughts.

———

AS I CHOPPED veggies for the night's dinner, thoughts and worries of the life I'd left behind came back to me. As much as I'd tried to pretend the clan was my new home now, it wasn't. I still had a family out there. A brother who needed me. A mother whose health weakened with each passing day. I had never meant to leave them. I simply wanted to get free so that I could return stronger, more powerful.

The mission burned itself on the inside of my mind like a brand. I had to go back, and save the omegas from the same fate I had. Especially given what I knew now, I couldn't let the harmful ideas of Steamshire affect them any longer. I saw now what happened when hate reigned. The Iron Paradox.

I nicked my finger and gasped, sucking at the cut. "Go on and clean up," Myrony prodded me. "I'll finish here."

"You sure?"

"I'm sure," she waved me away. "I don't want blood in my food."

Fair enough.

After cleaning and bandaging my finger, I still had about half an hour before dinner would be ready. My mind was still occupied with thoughts of Steamshire, so I turned to my tent and pulled out a piece of paper.

Dear Samson and Cilla,

I am writing this letter to let you know I am alive and I am safe. I have found refuge with the Firefang clan of dragons. Before you panic, I have learned many new things about them. Dragons are not harmful by nature. In fact, they have their own families and dreams and desires just as we do. Along the way, I've fallen in love with one of them, and I am now carrying his child. I plan to return in the near future, and I don't want you to be afraid. Steamshire is no place for children, I know that now. Especially omega children. I want you to know that...

I frowned at the parchment. I couldn't send this, no matter how much I wanted to. It would give away our location, and that would put both of our peoples in danger.

I crumpled the parchment and tossed it aside, burying my head in my hands. If only there was some way I could talk to them...

But for now, I had to keep my head low. Lucien made a promise. And dragons never broke a promise.

I'll come back for you, I whispered to myself in a silent litany. *I will. I promise.*

The dinner bell rang, and I stepped past a mountain of unfinished letters. So many things left unsaid.

I hadn't expected to be out in the field this long. Especially since I had a mate with a baby on the way.

That fall into the forest was a nasty one. Served me right for getting caught off my guard. And I still wasn't up to full strength yet. My own bravado had cost me on that one.

I wasn't out of commission, but my eye was still healing from the golden drake's attack. My vision wasn't completely gone in that eye, but it probably would never be the same, either. It had taken me some time to get used to the new depth perception, but it could be worse, I reminded myself.

Bless my people, though. Bless the chosen family I'd put together. They had come to my aid immediately, before things could get much worse. We ended up winning the battle that day, but the war was just beginning.

I needed to be home. With Alec. With the baby.

But war has a way of getting to you. Getting under your skin. Becoming part of your blood.

We were camped in a small outpost near Starstone, about ten miles south of Darkvale, my people's ancestral home. The home we hoped to take back from the pretenders.

Our numbers had thinned, but then again so had theirs. The days blurred together as we ate, slept, kept watch, marched, fought, ate, slept, and did it all over again.

My men were starting to tire, as was I. Their weary faces and slumped postures told me all I needed to know. It was only when a scout burst into my tent with a new report did my spirits start to lift.

"Alpha Commander," he said with a bow as he entered.

I bristled. "You know I don't care for all that formality, Lazarus. Just tell me what's on that scroll of yours."

He straightened, looking crestfallen. Unrolling the parchment, he read it to me.

"We have discovered the opening to a small tunnel about two miles west that leads into the city walls. Perhaps built for transporting resources, this could be a potential avenue for ambush."

I rubbed my chin. I didn't remember any tunnel in Darkvale. But things had changed under the new leadership, that much was certain.

"Tell me more about this tunnel," I said, my mind already whirring with strategy.

"It's about seven feet tall and three feet wide. Should be enough for our men to get through—in human form, of course."

"Hmm. And where does it let out?"

"We expect it leads to a granary or storehouse, as we found spilled grain and discarded twine in the tunnels."

"Is this the only tunnel you found?"

"Yes, sir. We've scoured the area and have not discovered any others."

I drew in a breath. "Thank you, Lazarus. You may go."

He turned.

"Leave the report here."

"Of course, sir." He placed it on the table and left.

I had tried not to let my excitement show in the scout's presence, but this could be the big break we were looking for. Throughout our siege, it seemed like the Cogs had inexhaustible resources. Now I knew how they were smuggling goods in and out.

I peered at the scrawled maps and reports closer, considering the pros and cons. If we could sneak in there with a small battalion and take them by surprise...

This could finally break the stalemate.

I gathered up the papers and swooped out of the tent. Time to run this by my officers.

———

THE TUNNELS WERE dark and rough-hewn, the only smooth part about them the packed-earth floor. At least we didn't have to worry about tripping. It had been well-traveled enough—ruts from some sort of wheeled container laced the path here and there. What were they transporting...and why?

"Keep on your guard," I'd warned them before entering. We crept slowly, relying on our night vision instead of a Dragonfire lamp. One false move and we'd all be toast. Literally.

Six of my best fighters had followed me into the tunnel. They'd volunteered, of course. I couldn't force any of them to go on such an uncertain mission. But if the reports were correct, this could be our key to turning the tides of battle.

We'd left at midnight, when most of the Cogs would be sleeping. Sure, they'd have night guards, but those were much easier to dispatch than a whole horde.

Why they had left the entrance to the tunnel unlocked was beyond me. It could have been simple carelessness. It could have been a trap.

I crossed my talons and hoped it was the former. All the same, we needed to be prepared to fight.

Jaxon, one of the team's engineers and a fierce fighter in his own right, had brought with him two dragon-crafted explosive devices. They could be remotely triggered if necessary, and packed enough firepower to blow the whole granary sky-high if it came to that.

Get rid of their resources, get rid of their morale. It was that easy. The siege would soon break, and we'd overwhelm their weakened forces.

At least now we knew how they were sustaining themselves during the siege.

"Goddess-damned tunnels," Marlowe spat. "Should have known."

"Shh," I hushed him. "I hear something."

We stopped in our tracks, every man's ears pricked up, listening.

Footsteps.

But not hurried, urgent footsteps. No. Slow, plodding footsteps, rhythmic against the dirt. Step, step, step. Pause. Step, step, step. Pause.

They had a guard down here. Of course, they did.

But why hadn't he heard us and sounded the alarm yet?

We crept on, each step measured and silent. None of us dared to breathe. I peered around a corner, flattening myself against the wall. That was when I saw the truth of it.

There was no guard at all. It was simply some sort of recording, looping over and over. Step, step, step. Pause. Step, step, step. Pause.

I let out a breath, but more questions than ever crowded my brain. Why even bother?

"I don't like the look of this," Marlowe muttered to me.

"Nor do I." I furrowed my brow, trying to think what their game was. Were they really that understaffed?

"Not like we can go back now." Jaxon shrugged, and I had to agree. We'd come this far. We needed to see this through, mysteries and all.

"Come on," I whispered, and we turned the corner.

We slunk past the recording without any apparent recognition, though the thought of it still froze my blood cold.

As if on cue, my next step was onto an unstable patch of dirt. When I put my weight on it, a pressure plate sunk down into the floor with an audible click. I froze.

Oh, crap.

The klaxon of sirens rang out above us and the ground shook as footsteps, real footsteps, echoed ahead.

I closed my eyes.

I'd doomed us all.

"Incoming!" I yelled, drawing my weapon. The others did the same, poised to fight.

The tunnel wasn't really wide enough for more than one man to stand across, but when we saw the Cogs pouring into the tunnel, flames at the ready and weapons drawn, all hell broke loose.

I rushed forward, slashing through their front lines, my eyes glazed over with blood and adrenaline. My brothers followed me, squeezing through the tight spaces where they could. A blade swiped out at me and I ducked, narrowly missing the sharpened edge. In fact, I think I may have gotten a little bit of a haircut. I swung around and drove my sword deep into the man's belly, using his momentary loss of balance to my advantage. He gasped and gurgled, then fell to the floor.

"Lucien!" a voice called, and I turned from the onslaught to see Jaxon lying motionless, the remote for the explosives still gripped in his hand. Blood dribbled from his mouth and his eyes stared at nothing.

Another man dead. Another man I'd failed.

But a small red light on the remote flashed, echoing a

last hope through the dim light of the tunnel. He'd armed the explosives.

"Retreat!" I yelled, turning from the tide of Cogs streaming into the tunnel. I leapt over fallen soldiers and ducked down to grab the remote as I passed Jaxon's fallen form. I said a silent prayer for him as I ran, beseeching the Goddess to have mercy on his soul. It was all I could do now.

Marlowe caught up with me, panting. "We had them! What are you doing?"

I showed him the remote and his eyes widened. "I have an idea. Keep running and don't stop."

He pushed on with the rest of my men as I slowed and took one last look down the tunnel. The Cogs were gaining on us, and I saw the flash of fire bellow out from one's throat as I grit my teeth and pressed the button.

———

IT HAPPENED ALL AT ONCE. Flames flew toward me as the ground shook like the fiercest earthquake. I clung to the wall, still running, my vision clouded over with soot and smoke and dirt. A rage of heat seared my backside but I didn't stop to see what it was. Rocks and dirt tumbled from the ceiling as the tunnel caved in on itself. I dodged a falling stone and kept my focus on the point of light up ahead. The surface. Safety.

The ground crumbled beneath me and I lost my footing, grabbing onto a tree root anchored nearby as I fell. The root held firm and yanked me to a stop, my joints screaming. With a groan and the last of my energy I hoisted myself up and crawled out and away, not daring to look behind me. A hand stuck out from the opening and I saw Marlowe peering down at me. "Come on!" he yelled.

I put on another burst of speed and grabbed his arm with both hands. My feet clawed at the wall, trying to lift myself up. That, combined with Marlowe's help, lifted me out of the tunnel and face down on the grass, broken, bloody, and beaten.

But alive.

The tunnel rumbled one last time and the entrance fell in with a rain of dust and rubble. Jaxon's death would not have been in vain. We'd sealed off their supply tunnel and buried the Cogs.

The momentary advantage wouldn't last forever, though. Now that they were cut off, we had to move quickly. We had to go in for the kill.

ALEC

I'd fallen asleep in my tent, the days mundane and ritual now. I'd said a silent prayer before bed, wishing for Lucien's safe return. A lot of good it did.

Although the morning sickness had passed, my stomach had started to inflate like a balloon. It seemed like an awfully accelerated process at first until I'd asked Adrian more about dragon gestation periods.

Instead of the human timespan of nine months, dragon babies were born in only three.

Great. So that meant I'd already had all the fun of the first trimester in just a few short weeks. No wonder I felt like I'd been run over by a truck. I tossed and turned, trying to get comfortable with my newly pregnant body.

It was harder than it looked.

———

IT WAS a night like any other when I was captured.

I woke to the sound of steel and shouting. Close.

Throwing myself out of bed, I chanced a peek outside my tent flap. Rookie mistake.

A pair of cold, beady eyes locked onto mine. "Found 'im!" His grubby hand pointed at my tent and even more men came running.

I shrank back inside, heart hammering. Whoever these men were, they were no friends of mine. Mercenaries, by the look of their dress. But why would someone send mercenaries here?

My blood ran cold. There were only two options.

Either Steamshire had caught up to me and sent out their cronies to make an example of me, or The Paradox thought they could use me as strategic leverage.

I wasn't sure which one was worse.

Where were all the dragons? I thought frantically as I searched the tent for something to defend myself with. These men were no dragons. They should have been burnt to a crisp the moment they set foot on our land. Then again, they shouldn't have been able to find it in the first place.

A blue flash of light blinded me and the flimsy walls of

my tent disintegrated. I stared on at the glowing ice-blue eyes of the men encroaching on me.

Sorcerers.

Feared by human and shifter alike, the Sorcerers were an ancient race gifted with magical affinities. Most of their kind had died out over the years, but few still remained in secrecy.

And apparently, they were mercenaries now for the highest bidder.

My stomach roiled as I looked around for any escape. Sorcerers converged on me from all sides and magical energy bound me to the spot, paralyzing my limbs. I couldn't move, I couldn't escape, I couldn't get free...

My breaths came fast and heavy, and the last thing I remember thinking before they lowered me out of consciousness was *please, don't hurt the baby...*

————

A BUCKET of cold water splashed over my head and my eyes flew open with a gasp.

"Now listen here, Alec."

One of the Sorcerers stood before me, pacing back and forth all judiciously while he eyed me like a piece of meat. Magical bonds lashed my hands and feet together, rendering me motionless.

The baby.

I still felt a presence there, deep inside. If anything had happened to them...

"Your little hellspawn is fine," the Sorcerer said, noticing my panic. "That was part of the terms."

"Who hired you?" I growled, yanking at my restraints. They held fast.

"That's confidential."

"You little—"

"I'd watch your mouth if I were you. We are only tasked with keeping you and the babe alive, after all. We can have a lot of fun within those boundaries." He folded his hands and stepped toward me with an evil gleam in his eye.

I instinctively shrank away.

"You're quite the wanted man, Alec. You should have seen the bidding war."

I clenched my fists and unclenched them, breathing heavy through my nose.

"Let me go." My voice shook.

"And lose my client's bargaining chip? Not likely."

A wave of sickness crashed over me and I fought to hold back the bile. I was a man! Not something to be tossed around for political gain!

"Where's Lucien?" I asked. The question burned its way through my throat. I didn't have any confidence that they would tell the truth, but I had to know.

"Your mate has been causing quite the grievance for my client."

I let out a breath. So, he was still alive.

"They decided that the only way to get him to see reason was to turn the tables on him, emotionally. You are his mate, are you not?"

I closed my eyes, refusing to look at him.

The seconds ticked by. My muscles ached. My stomach fluttered. The baby was hungry.

Footsteps. A door opened and closed. The room grew silent.

I opened my eyes again, taking in my surroundings.

A cold stone cell surrounded me. Windowless save for a small slit of light over on the right-hand wall. A torch flickered nearby. The spartan room held no luxury. A simple chair, cot, small table, and chamber pot. That was it.

I tried to reach out to Lucien again across the Link. Static, but weaker this time. Like a badly tuned radio station. I pushed further, almost able to hear the sound of his voice.

Lucien, I projected, not knowing if he could hear me.

It's Alec. Please. I've been captured by Sorcerers. I don't know where I am.

I'm scared.

The connection grew fainter again and I slumped against the wall, exhausted.

No one was coming to save me.

There'd likely be some kind of ransom on my head. Something to lure Lucien away from Darkvale. I knew if it had been me dealing with Lucien's capture, I would stop at nothing to get him back.

And they knew that, too. That was just what they wanted.

With the distraction of the Commander's mate held hostage, The Paradox could crush Lucien's forces once and for all.

Please, I thought again, reaching through the spider webs of our minds. *Do the right thing.*

I stared at the ceiling, let out a breath, and waited.

We were on the brink of victory when I felt the message come through.

We'd broken the siege and breached their walls. The tides were turning in our favor. All that was left was to seek out The Paradox's leader, the Master Cog, and eliminate him.

But then I felt the nauseous shiver of something gone horribly wrong.

The message was garbled and I could barely make out the words. But it was Alec. And he was in danger.

One of the only words I could understand was "Sorcerer." And that was enough to stop me in my tracks.

My blood ran cold with the words. Sorcerer. How in

the five hells had he gotten mixed up with those awful mages?

My stomach clenched. I knew exactly how. The few remaining Sorcerers pawned off their power to the highest bidder. I didn't think The Paradox would stoop that low, or that they had the funds in the first place. Clearly, I'd underestimated them. And now they had Alec. I'd failed my mate. Again.

The gut-wrenching guilt would have to wait. If anything happened to him, or the baby…

I held my breath.

"Marlowe!" I shouted through the din.

"Sir!"

"I'm putting you in charge, all right? Wipe out those Iron bastards once and for all. Take back our home. I've got to go."

His voice betrayed his surprise and fear. "What? You're leaving us? Now?" He lunged and drove a sword through an oncoming Cog. "Little busy, aren't we?" He grunted and pushed the man away from him, blood spattering his clothes.

"It's Alec. The Sorcerers got him."

Marlowe's face blanched. Then he set his lips in a firm line and nodded silently. "Go to your mate. But be careful. We'll hold down the fort."

"Behind you!" I yelled. A Cog sniper aimed right at him and fired a poisoned arrow.

He rolled away just in time and the arrow buried itself in the ground. He glanced back up at me with a small smile. "Thanks, man."

"Don't mention it." I clapped him on the back. "Tell the men of my choice."

"I will."

"Goddess-speed. Glendaria smiles on you."

"Goddess-speed," he agreed, then ran off into the fray once more.

I realized right then and there that I'd made a choice, and an important one. The sounds of battle raged on behind me as I ran, taking advantage of the momentary distraction to escape undetected.

When faced with my ancestral home pitted against my pregnant mate, it was no contest. I'd made the decision before. The wrong one. The reason I fought so hard was for our future together, and without him, what future did I have?

I rushed away from the walls as the sounds grew fainter behind me. I had confidence that Marlowe could lead the men to victory in my stead. I just hoped that this time, I wouldn't be too late to save my mate.

———

THE SORCERERS KNEW how to disrupt the energies around them, making it hard for shifters to access their powers temporarily. To a normal dragon, this could come as quite a shock and the moment of panic was usually enough for them to lose the advantage. But I was no normal dragon.

I'd been cursed when I lost Caldo, and had to learn how to get by without my dragon powers. I'd learned to be deadly and effective in both the human and dragon realms. And that was my ace in the hole. Their magic may have been powerful, but I still had a few tricks up my sleeve.

Not to mention the burning fury that billowed through me like an inferno. My mate! My chosen! My child. Strength and energy poured into my veins as my dragon, fully awake now, fed on the emotion. The anger spurred me on and the stirring inside me reached a fever pitch.

I gave over to the sensation and leapt into the air, the shift tearing my body apart and putting it back together in a new form.

With a flap of my new, stronger wings, I took to the air, my mind focused on only one thing.

They would pay for taking him. They would pay in blood.

I lost track of the days, and with it, the hope I'd held grew thinner and thinner.

He wasn't coming.

Perhaps he never got my message. Perhaps he decided saving his hometown and his people was more important than saving one human.

Perhaps he'd already forgotten about me.

My captors weren't actively malicious, but I certainly wasn't living in the lap of luxury either. Magical barriers kept me from leaving the one room I'd found myself in, and my bonds were released only twice a day for me to eat the slop they called food.

I was starting to look—and feel—very pregnant. I supposed that was why they'd held off on harming me. I didn't have to ask to know who had done this.

The Iron Paradox.

They wanted me alive, as a pawn in their game.

Then why hadn't Lucien come?

I started from a haze of half-sleep when the door creaked open. For a split second, a wisp of hope wove through me, thinking he had finally arrived.

That hope dashed on the rocks in an instant as a man entered I'd never seen before. He didn't wear the mercenary reds of the Sorcerers. Much the opposite, in fact.

He wore a long black robe, the ends of it trailing the floor. I could see his boots sticking out, caked with mud and something even darker. I shuddered. A hood obscured most of the man's face, but I could see his lips and chin, a scar dragging itself down toward his neck.

He motioned to the Sorcerer guarding the door. The guard left and closed the door behind him with a bow.

Was this the mysterious client?

The man stepped closer and lowered his hood, giving me a full view of his ghastly face.

The eyes said dragon, but he held himself differently than any dragon I'd seen. His posture was hunched as if a great weight bore him down. His face sported years, no, decades of wrinkles, but his eyes still gleamed with vicious fire.

"There you are." He appraised me, those horrible eyes looking me up and down.

I breathed through my nose and clamped my lips shut, avoiding his gaze.

"Alec Cipher. The human." Disdain dripped from his lips. He folded his hands and tilted his head. "I'm not sure what he sees in you."

A growl ripped itself free despite myself. I railed against my restraints, vision clouded with red. All of the anger, the heartbreak, the pain spilled out at this man. How could he act so casual?

"Is that any way to treat your host?" he chided. Footsteps glided over to the one window and covered it, blanketing the room in darkness.

My heart rate picked up and I sent out a last panicked message over the Link. Glowing orange eyes bore through the darkness and settled on me. "Do you know who I am?" He was close now, that much I could tell. I felt the warm, rancid breath on my face and strained to turn away.

The floating eyes backed up and considered me. Whew. A chance to breathe.

"My name is Arion Knox. Still not ringing a bell? My, he didn't tell you anything, did he?"

My hands clenched into fists behind me and I ground

my teeth. Lucien wouldn't hide things from me...would he?

"Lucien and I used to be friends, you know. It's really too bad he chose a different path."

"You mean choosing not to be a dick?" I spat, seething. "You're from The Paradox, aren't you?"

He advanced on me and I felt something sharp scrape at my throat. "Foolish boy. I *am* The Paradox."

I didn't dare breathe. The cold steel of Knox's blade lay against my throat, defying me to move.

That's when I heard him, faint and distant, but I heard him.

Hang in there. Coming.

My world shifted as I clung to the words.

Lucien.

A spike of adrenaline splintered through my veins. Resolve solidified. I needed to buy time.

"You're right," I said finally. "He hasn't told me anything. Why don't you?" As long as I could keep him talking, I was safe.

The floating eyes hung there for a moment, blinking. The knife fell away.

"Very well."

Footsteps. Pacing.

"I know you're trying to buy time. It won't do you any good. It was my intention to lure your alpha here, you know. The Sorcerers are well prepared to dispatch him."

A desperate moan escaped as all the air rushed out of me. It was all a trap. Of course, it was. And Lucien was heading right for it.

"I suppose, however, I can indulge you until he arrives. Least I can do." I couldn't see his face through the dark, but I could just feel the greasy grin that plastered across his face.

"You may be wondering, why Iron Paradox? Why such a name? It all started with something that flows in all of us...blood. There was a time when dragons ruled these lands, free and unfettered. It wasn't until the rise of the human villages that things began to get complicated.

"A dragon's bloodline is sacred. We carry the ancient prowess of our ancestors inside of us. We were the dominant species. But the humans, powerless and scared, didn't like that. They spread across our lands, paying no mind to the destruction they caused. They hunted us. Loathed us. Drove us back.

"Why, then, should we give any care to the human savages?"

I almost felt for him, in a way. He never asked for his

home to be destroyed, to be ruined and regulated by the follies of man. But he had to understand that we weren't all like that. And if his beef was with the humans, why was he out to destroy Lucien and his family?

"Some of our number thought it wise to cooperate with the humans. They said that working together and putting aside our differences was the only way to peace. They were fools."

"You're the fool!" I cried, heart pumping. "You don't have to keep fighting like this!"

"Oh, but I do. You see, as long as our kind are divided, we can never be truly free. Glendaria spoke to me. That's right, the Goddess chose me. She tasked me with purifying our bloodline and claiming ownership of our world once more. Soft-hearted shifters like your pathetic mate have no place here. The more people like him dilute our blood by fraternizing with the enemy, the weaker we become."

"And yet you've allied with the Sorcerers?" I continued through gritted teeth. *Hurry, Lucien. Hurry.*

Arion laughed. "Allied is a strong word. We've merely contracted with them to further our own needs. They pose no threat to us, and as long as the coin keeps flowing it matters not who they're fighting for. Besides, their numbers are small. Human tribes took care of that. They're quite good at wiping out anyone unlike their own, you know."

My heart burned as I thought of Steamshire and the fervor with which they hated dragons. Perhaps Arion was right.

"Lucien, and all those who support his claim, must die. It's simple as that. Only then can our race rise again."

Any sympathy I had for him went out the window. No. That was the way of hate. The way of Steamshire. The way of The Paradox.

"You'll never win," I bit off the words. "The world is changing. Adapt or die."

"Funny you should say that." Arion advanced on me once more, his face only inches from mine. "When you're the one that will die."

A thump at the door.

"Come in, come in, Lucien! I know you're out there."

My heart leapt into my chest as I peered through the darkness.

The door creaked, cracked, then exploded open, flying off its hinges. Light spilled into the room and I squinted my eyes against the sudden brightness.

Standing there, muscles bulging and caked with blood, was Lucien.

"I see you've bested my guards," Arion said casually, though I could hear the faintest hint of fear.

"I see you've taken my mate," Lucien replied, charging.

He pummeled headlong into Arion's gut, the air whooshing out of him as they flew forward and crashed onto the floor.

Arion roared and coughed, his eyes widening.

"The Sorcerers, remember? Nullifies our dragon powers."

"Guards!" Arion screeched, flailing under Lucien's grip. "Guards!"

"They won't be coming," Lucien said.

"How did you manage to—"

"Practice. Years and years of practice. I should thank you, really. For teaching me to stand on my own. For teaching me not to rely on my heritage. That's what you're all about, right?"

"You ungrateful—"

"The world isn't just for dragonkind anymore. It's for all of us. And you're on the wrong side of history. The Paradox is over, Arion. Give it up. We've taken Darkvale. And here you are, hiding like a coward."

"Lucien...my old friend..." He gasped out the words as Lucien's strong arm pressed against his windpipe.

"You are no friend of mine." The words echoed through the cavern with utter conviction, and with a sure stroke he slashed the man's throat. The air fell silent, rank with the smell of blood.

Adrenaline still buzzed through me, setting each nerve alight. The shackles around my wrists and feet fell away, no longer beholden to their master.

My arms hung limply, the muscles crying out from lack of use. Lucien pushed Knox away and came to my side, rubbing my sore wrists.

His forehead rested against my own, damp with sweat and blood.

"Alec," he breathed. "Are you okay? Is the baby okay?"

"Yeah," I managed. "I think so."

"Goddess, I thought I'd lost you." He threw his arms around me and held me tight, warm finally spreading through my bones once more.

"I thought you weren't coming," I said sheepishly, burying my face in his shoulder.

He grabbed my shoulders and drew back, searching my eyes. "You are my mate. I will never leave you again."

"The others..." I started.

"Shhh," he soothed, brushing a hand through my hair. After all I'd been through my body and mind were both wiped. I needed a nap. Preferably a week-long one. "Let's get you out of here."

"Is it safe?" I asked, clinging to him as he helped me to my feet. My ankles had swollen horribly, both from the pregnancy and the restraints. I wobbled but leaned on Lucien for support. He held steady. Lucien. My rock.

"If we hurry," he said with a grin, taking my hand. "Let's go."

ALEC

Riding on Lessa's back had been a slightly nauseating experience, my pregnancy and fear of heights notwithstanding.

Riding with my mate was a different experience altogether.

His sleek black scales glittered in the light, sending prisms of color across my vision. I grasped his warm body, feeling the muscles move and flex beneath me. Wind rushed through my hair, but it was a good feeling. Not a scary one.

I even looked down once or twice.

I knew the moment I clambered onto his back that this would be different. I heard him speaking to me in my mind. But what's more, I felt him there too. It was as if he and I were one, two parts of a whole fused together in some primal dance. I blinked and saw the world in brilliant color, aware of each blade of grass, each movement on the horizon.

"Is this what the world looks like to you all the time?" I asked in awe.

"Only in dragon form," he rumbled, pushing us higher.

My hands still shook a little. The fear of heights didn't go away instantly, but with Lucien by my side it was much more bearable.

We flew for what seemed like ages, toward the setting sun. I'd never seen a sunset from the sky before, and I couldn't tear my eyes away. Reds and golds mixed with a deep, deep purple in a gradient that cast the whole world in a dusky light. The beginnings of stars began to peek through, and the pale sliver of moon.

The air cooled and I leaned forward, laying myself against Lucien's strong neck as we flew. My pregnant belly got in the way and I ended up in an awkward half-crouch position. I scooted and scrambled, but couldn't quite get comfortable. That was okay, though. The view was too spectacular to miss.

Get some rest, he soothed me through the Link. *I won't let you fall.*

The stars came out, a million twinkling points of light. They seemed so close now, as if I could reach out and touch one. Or that if I raised my hand I might come away with a smattering of stardust. It was a perfect night, cool and clear, and I had my dragon mate and my baby resting inside me. I'd lost track of time, but with the way I felt and my belly bulged, it must be getting close. I felt a kick in response and placed a hand there, smiling.

"I can't wait to meet you," I whispered, and lay my head against my dragon's smooth scales.

———

WE'RE HERE. Lucien's voice through the Link roused me into full wakefulness. At first, I saw only darkness. The world had descended into the full shadow of night and only specks of campfires dotted the landscape. As I waited for my eyes to adjust, Lucien sent me a glimpse of his vision.

The world came into view once more, unhindered by the darkness. I saw the outline of trees and valleys and rivers. I saw a town encircled with stone walls and a blood-red banner emblazoned in gold.

"You have night vision?" I gasped.

"How else would I make all those midnight deliveries?" He chuckled.

"Like a normal person."

That earned me a raucous, roaring laugh. "Dunno if you've noticed, sweet one, but I am not quite normal."

I grinned. "You sure aren't."

"Hold fast, we're descending."

He didn't have to tell me twice. I gripped the fleshy pockets as tight as I could without squashing my belly and clamped my legs against his undulating muscles. The ice-chill of fear still prickled through my scalp, but it was easily overtaken by another feeling.

Wonder.

"That is the mark of my clan," Lucien pointed out as we neared the banners. "Marlowe and his men have done it, then."

"Done what?"

"Routed The Paradox. Re-occupied the city. At last. Welcome home."

Pride flowed through Lucien in waves and so too through me as I watched the rising walls reach toward us. Home. Now that was a word I hadn't considered in a while.

On the one hand, it made me think of Steamshire. My brother. All the omegas I'd left behind. My mother, sick and getting sicker.

But a new definition sprung up in my mind as well. I felt the fluttering in my stomach, the warmth of my mate beneath me, and the soul bound connection that flowed through both of us, sharing more than I'd ever shared in my life.

Maybe this could be my home, as well.

Lucien alighted on the ground, his talons touching down gently in the dirt. Dust scattered around us and I shifted a little in my seat but hung on tight. Then we were still.

I let out a breath.

Solid ground.

Solid, safe ground.

My legs protested as I crawled from Lucien's back, my posture still stuck in a bowlegged position. I stumbled as I slid from his back but caught myself, leaning on him for support.

"Stand back," Lucien warned. "I must shift back."

I regained my balance and took a few steps away, my legs still wobbly. In a rush of light and color, the dragon faded away and in its place kneeled a man.

My man. Lucien.

I ran forward and threw my arms around him, catching him off guard. He nearly toppled with a laugh and gripped me tight, nuzzling his face into my neck.

I sucked in a breath as his breath tickled my skin all the way down to my cock.

He tilted his head and nipped at my ear, eliciting a quiet squeak on my part. Need coursed through me in an instant, and I found myself not caring where we were or who could see us. I wanted him. I wanted him bad.

A clearing of a throat cut my lust short and I extricated myself, the blush already burning my face.

Lessa stood there, hands on her hips and a knowing smile on her face. "Thank the Goddess you're both all right. We were starting to worry."

"Lessa!" I cried, the air rushing out of me. She was alive. After my capture, I shuddered to think what had happened to the compound. How had the Sorcerers subdued so many dragons at once? "I'm so sorry." The words blurted out as I faced the bubbling guilt.

"Not your fault, hun. None of us could have predicted the Sorcerers getting involved. They've been lost for decades now, but it seems they're regaining strength. Concerning indeed, but all the more reason we must stick together as a family."

Family. There was that word again.

Thrown from a world where oppression and sickness were commonplace into this new and fantastical realm, I still found it too good to be true sometimes. These people—these dragons—had done so much for me already. I just wished I had a way to repay them.

"Thank you. Again."

"You're family now," she said simply. "Firefangs never give up on family."

Lucien grabbed my hand and squeezed it. Maybe I would get my happy ending after all. But there was something I needed to do first.

"Lucien, remember what I told you about my village?"

He furrowed his brow, then nodded in recognition. "Ah yes, Steamshire. From what I've gathered, it sounds like they've got their own little Paradox forming. We must be wary."

"What if we could do something to help? To support both our peoples?" It wasn't enough for me to escape the Elders, The Paradox, and my untimely fate. The others needed the same chance that I did.

Lucien rumbled deep in his chest, considering. "I'll bring it up with the clan and see what we can do. There are some things we must attend to first, though. I'm to go see Marlowe for a debriefing on the battle and—"

At that moment, a spike of pain lanced through my abdomen like someone had just punched me in the gut. It came again, my muscles squeezing and contracting. I doubled over and looked to my alpha in fear and shock.

Adrian muscled his way through the growing crowd,

and I'd never been so glad to see my friend. His eyes widened in recognition.

"What's happening?" Lucien rushed to me, laying a hand on my back. His touch did little to soothe the spasms of pain still racking through me.

"The baby's coming," I gasped, sweat starting to build on my forehead.

"But it's not time yet, it's—"

"Listen, you stupid Alpha, the baby is coming! NOW!" I doubled over again, trying to focus on my breathing.

Could my body even handle birthing a half-dragon baby?

I didn't want to think about that right now.

The world faded away, lost in a sea of people and hands and voices and pain. Adrian's voice pierced through the fog. "Let's get him inside! Someone call Dr. Parley!"

Lucien was there, holding my hand. I blinked. He tried to hide it, but his face was riddled with concern. I squeezed his hand weakly and smiled. Lucien brushed a hand through my hair. "You're going to be fine."

I hope so, I thought darkly. *I sure hope so.*

"**I** fucking hate you! Don't ever come near my ass again!"

My mate screamed, his face pinched and sweaty.

I had to suppress a laugh. Alec got quite...colorful in the throes of labor.

Hell, I could never do it. The strength I saw shining there in his eyes inspired me.

Doctor Parley and his assistant Anna came rushing, carting him off to the medical tent. I followed on foot, rushing past the mass of people welcoming me home or hoping for a word.

"Outta my way! Mate's having a baby!"

Thoughts and fears crashed in on my mind like waves at high tide.

Would he be all right? Would the baby be all right? What if he needs me? What can I do? Can I even be a father?

The thoughts looped and started again, over and over.

I paced back and forth outside the medical tent. As the Alpha of the clan, and Alec's mate, I should have been the strong one.

But something came over me when I saw Alec first go into labor. I saw the future spill out around me. I saw the past. They aligned and linked up, connecting and scattering into the unknown, the unknowable. Things would never be the same, on multiple fronts.

Oh, Goddess, a baby.

A deranged scream came from inside the tent and I couldn't wait any longer. I barged in, heart hammering.

"Lucien!" Alec cried when he saw me, his face taut and eyes glassy with exertion. "Lucien, the baby..." He panted and his eyes rolled back in his head as he let out another yell.

"Push!" Doctor Parley ordered, working swiftly beneath the sheet that covered Alec's lower half.

"He's coming!" the doctor announced.

He. My heart skipped a beat. A baby boy.

A high-pitched cry rung out and Alec's body relaxed, slumping into the cot.

Silence.

And the sounds of our baby's first cry.

Parley handed off the baby to his assistant to clean off after snipping the umbilical cord. Seconds later, she returned, a pale-blanketed bundle screaming bloody murder.

I couldn't tear my eyes off him, even when the assistant handed the baby to Alec's waiting arms.

My chest swelled with delight, pride, wonder. My baby. Our baby.

Our son.

Alec held the bundle close, the cries quieting as he settled into Alec's embrace. Alec couldn't stop smiling. You couldn't wipe the smile off of his face with a baseball bat. Despite the ordeal he'd just endured, I'd never seen such unfettered joy.

A tuft of black hair lined the baby's head, a stark contrast to the pale pink skin. Tiny hands reached out and grasped at nothing. I stepped forward and offered a finger. The baby grabbed it, warm fingers wrapping around the digit.

"Hey there, little guy," I cooed. "Welcome to Darkvale."

Big, shining golden eyes turned to me and I sucked in a

breath. Vertical pupils, burning with a latent fire. Dragon.

We'd done it.

"What will we name him, Lucien?" Alec asked, tearing his gaze away for a second to look up at me. "Any ideas?"

"You choose," I offered. "He's your son as much as mine."

Alec thought for a moment. He planted a soft kiss on the boy's forehead, eyes still shining with delight.

"What do you think about Corin?" he said, more to the baby than to me.

"Corin," I repeated, tasting the word. It suited him. Corin. Once again, the trail of possibilities unfolded in front of me. Corin Cipher. Or was it Corin Black? My son. My heir.

"It's perfect."

"He's perfect," Alec agreed. No truer words had been said.

———

EXHAUSTION FINALLY TOOK its toll on me a few hours after the birth. Everyone was doing swimmingly, Alec and the baby napping off and on. The alpha part of me wanted to be there for everything, to protect him if anything went wrong. But sleep kept tugging at me, and I finally gave into it in a chair next to Alec's bed.

The quiet solitude didn't last long. Word traveled like wildfire and soon the tent was packed with friends and well-wishers. A new baby was a rare and magical event for the Firefangs, especially in the last years we'd spent in exile. The fact that this baby would one day inherit the title of Clan Alpha made them all the more excited to meet him.

But as we greeted family after family, I could sense the interaction wearing on Alec. He smiled and shook hands with everyone, cordial as ever. But when I peeked outside the tent and saw a line starting to form, I had to put a stop to it.

"I know you all wish to share in the celebration of our new son. Rest assured, we appreciate each and every one of you. It is because of your efforts that we are here today. Make no mistake, we will hold a baby shower in the near future when both Alec and the baby are well rested. For now, however, I ask that you leave us to bond with our son."

There were a few disappointed murmurs, but no one wanted to go against the Clan Alpha's word. Slowly, they shuffled off, leaving us with blessed silence.

I stepped back into the tent where Alec was feeding Corin. A weak smile broke out over his face. "Thank you for that," he sighed.

"You need your rest. Everyone else can wait."

———

ABOUT A WEEK AFTER THE BIRTH, Alec hit me with a question I didn't expect.

We'd fallen into something of a routine, though everything was different now. My clansmen worked tirelessly to repair the damaged buildings and reboot the cycle of industry. Farmland was tended, the granary raided, new living quarters and kitchens and watch towers set up. They did all this with minimal direction from me, and for that I was thankful.

Alec and I had our hands full.

No one ever told me how much *work* having a baby was. As adorable as his cute little button nose and flashing eyes were, it seemed like he was always hungry, sleepy, or just needed to be held and cuddled. Sleep became a faint memory as Alec and I tended Corin at all hours of the night. It was exhausting, sure, but I wouldn't have traded it for the world. When I looked into those golden eyes and saw my son smile, it was all worth it.

Finally, I had a family. Our family.

The well-wishers and rubbernecks soon tapered off, leaving us to care for the baby in peace. As Alec recovered, I did everything I could to make him comfortable. What was a good alpha if he didn't look after his mate?

So, when Alec asked me that question, I was caught a little off guard.

"So, are we safe now? Is it over?" Alec held Corin on his hip and bounced him up and down as the baby cooed and gurgled.

I blinked, filtering his words. My mind had been so occupied with the birth of our son that I'd pushed all memory of the war and The Paradox far, far away.

A gnawing guilt and fear bubbled in my gut. When would the other shoe drop?

"I think so," I said wearily. "We've wiped out their main faction and eliminated their leader. But there could still be splinter groups out there. I've posted men on watch each night and we're working on rebuilding the fortifications. For now, we rest, recover, and stay on our guard."

Darkvale had fallen far since the time I'd ruled. The Paradox's neglect had left many of the structures in shambles and it was taking the clansmen longer than expected just to clean everything up. I still saw flickers of the home I'd once known, but they were faint, fleeting. No matter. We'd build a new Darkvale. A better one.

Alec pursed his lips and nodded. "I guess you can never

wipe out hate completely." His voice had a sad tinge to it, but an accepting one.

"Isn't that the truth," I agreed, putting an arm around his shoulder.

"Oh, and Lucien?" He spoke up as if suddenly remembering something.

"Yeah?"

"Remember when I told you about Steamshire? Did you ever get a chance to talk to your clansmen?"

Ah yes, his save-the-omegas project. What had I done to deserve such a full-hearted and noble omega? He escaped from oppression only to turn it around and bring that hope to others. I saw the light of determination in his eyes, the set of his jaw, the way his whole body came alive when he spoke of his homeland.

I supposed it wasn't too different from my nostalgia for Darkvale and my longing to return.

"You have helped me reclaim my home. And now I will help you reclaim yours. I've spoken with the clan, and they've given their blessing. We can leave as soon as you're ready."

Alec's eyes widened. "So soon? You're not needed here?"

I shrugged. "Sure, but my mate comes first."

Alec laid his head on my shoulder and smiled, letting

out a breath. Corin reached out his stubby hand toward me again and I offered a finger, letting him squeeze at it.

"I love you," Alec said, voice distant. For a moment, I wasn't sure if he was speaking to Corin or me.

"Both of you," he added, and my heart flooded with joy.

I planted a kiss on his forehead, my dragon rumbling with delight. "I love you too, irralo."

He turned his head to me. "You never told me what that means."

Ah. He was right. It came so easily, so naturally to me that I forgot he was not in tune with the Dragon Tongue.

I tipped his chin toward mine, pecking a kiss on his nose, then those sumptuous lips.

"It's from the Dragon Tongue of my people. We don't often use it anymore, even among ourselves. The Dragon Tongue is reserved for religious ceremonies and bursts of extreme emotion, these days. It is the most sacred form of endearment we have. Translated into English? It means little storm. You are my little storm, Alec. You and our son. And I've never been so grateful for a trespasser in my life."

Alec laughed and held me close. Whatever happened in the future, it didn't matter right now. I had my mate, my perfect little storm, and my son.

20

ALEC

I busied myself for the next few days taking care of Corin and preparing for our trip.

If I kept busy, kept moving, I wouldn't have time to second-guess myself. I wouldn't have time to chicken out.

The gravity of my mission still hung over me, heavy and cloying like a thick mist. When I thought of Samson and my mother, and all the other omegas I'd befriended back in Steamshire, I knew there was no choice.

I had to do this.

I was loading extra food supplies into the saddlebags Lucien had provided when he came into the room. He held a huge bundle of clothes in his arms and could barely see over it, so when he tripped over a pile of dishes I'd organized, it made a horrific noise.

Needless to say, Corin was now wide awake. His shrieks pierced the room and echoed through my ears. Lucien gave a sheepish grin and picked himself off, moving over to the crib.

"Shhh," he soothed Corin, picking him up and holding him to his chest. "It's all right. Daddy's here." He made soft humming noises at a pitch so low it rumbled the walls.

The crying subsided slowly, to be replaced by the gentle breathing of sleep.

"See, you can just call me the baby whisperer." Lucien smirked at me as I sealed the packs and picked up the dishes.

"What was that?" I whispered, raising an eyebrow.

Lucien shrugged. "Something I remember my mom used to do for me. The dragon blood in him must have reacted to it. Our own little form of lullaby."

I turned to him. "I'm glad I have you." And I was. More than I could ever say.

He pulled me close, sparks of desire still racing through my skin whenever we touched. Would this ever get old?

"You have me is right. Body and soul."

"I'm thinking more about the body right now though..."

"Oh yeah?" Lucien challenged with a wicked grin. "Tell me more." He came closer, his hips meeting mine in a clash of skin and fire. My cock swelled, reaching toward him.

"The baby..." I said breathlessly.

"What of it?" Lucien rumbled, nuzzling at my neck. I threw my head back and sighed. He knew that was my favorite spot. Want to win any argument, be forgiven for any crime? Just kiss me right there. It was a weakness, for sure.

But it felt too good to be ashamed of.

"You got everything packed?" Lucien's voice tickled my ear and sent chills down my spine.

"Yeah," I gasped as he ground his hips against mine. "We need to get going—"

"Not yet," Lucien said, his eyes flashing with fire. "There's something I need to do first."

I felt so small, so vulnerable beneath him. But paradoxically, it was also these times when I felt most powerful, most at peace. Lucien knew me inside and out. Loved me. Cared for me. And I trusted him wholeheartedly.

Putting myself in his capable hands was just another extension of that intimate connection we shared. A chance for all the world to melt away, for us and us alone.

"The baby..." I protested again, but even I didn't believe

my own words. I wanted him. Needed him. Here. Now.

"We'll just have to be quiet." Lucien grinned, taking my hand. "Think you can do that?"

I let out a shaky breath, my cock throbbing against my pants. "Yeah."

This time, I wasn't gripped by omega heat. I could feel every touch, every kiss, every sensation as it coiled through me like delicious smoke. My mind floated in a haze of lust, but it was my lust. My choice. Not some omega's imperative. And that only excited me more.

I wanted this man. This dragon. Mine. Mine.

Irralo.

I shuddered as I thought of the words, clinging to Lucien's body as we lay down together on the pile of blankets he'd brought in from the wash. They were a bit lumpy, but soft and luxurious on my skin, enveloping us in a warm cocoon of wool and cotton. I looked into his eyes, flashing ever stronger with desire, and kissed him.

———

"GODDESS, YOU SMELL GOOD." Lucien worked his way down my face, chin, neck, and was delving under my shirt to nip at the collarbones there.

"Thought we were being quiet," I hissed with a grin.

"Guess you'll just have to shut me up, then."

A wild idea crossed my mind. "With pleasure."

I shimmied out of my pants, my cock springing free. Lucien sucked in a breath, looking wide-eyed at me, then at my cock.

I didn't say anything, just gave him a meaningful nod downward.

A low rumble shuddered through Lucien's chest and he delved downward, licking and kissing as he went.

I lay back on the mass of blankets, breathing steady as he kissed my stomach, my hips, the inside of my thighs. His mouth orbited around that center of essential need and I grit my teeth to keep from crying out. I shot out a hand and grabbed his hair, fisting it in my passion. Another rumbling chuckle.

Then he took me into his mouth.

I cursed under my breath, the sensation of his hot mouth around my cock all-consuming. Lucien's gaze flickered upward, catching my own, and I craned my neck to watch him. He slowly moved down the shaft, his lips and tongue caressing every plane and ridge and vein. I'd never felt so electrified in all my life. Hell, this was better than heat.

Lucien worked himself into a rhythm, slurping and

tasting my cock all the way to the hilt then back up to the head and down again. I lay back, my mind blank of everything but the overwhelming sensations. I clenched my jaw and breathed through my nose, fast and hard. Quiet. Gotta be quiet.

My mate picked up speed and a little whimper escaped, teasing all the areas that were already on fire and alight with sensitivity.

This man, this dragon, was going to drive me crazy.

He worked his way into a fever pitch, my cock swelling impossibly against him and my slick dampening the blankets beneath us. My balls tightened and a wave of pure energy floated through my body, short-circuiting every sense from head to toe.

"I'm gonna—" I breathed, unable to hold back any longer.

With a groan, I released into his mouth, my vision starry as I pumped into him again and again. I pulsed and shuddered in his grasp as he held me firm, slurping up every last drop of my cum. At length, he rose and grinned at me with a slobbery smile, his own eyes still hooded with desire.

"I love you," I breathed. My body relaxed, finally coming down from the high.

"It's not over yet," he teased and grabbed my hips. I flipped over in an instant. The head of his cock, fat and hard, pressed against my dripping opening. Oh, Goddess. Yes, *please*.

"Be a good boy and stay quiet for me, okay? If you make too much noise I'll have to stop." Lucien's voice was right next to my ear. I nodded, biting my lip.

He speared into me with a single smooth motion, my hole stretching to accommodate him all at once. I bit down on my lip hard, the pleasure and pain racking through me. Dragon dicks were no joke, okay?

I felt each ridge of his shaft press into me, lighting up the tight warm walls of muscle there. His cock twitched and I shivered in response. My head swam. Lucien anchored me, holding my arms to my side as he pressed himself deeper. I breathed into the blankets as sparks flew, igniting passageways of nerve endings I hadn't known existed.

"God," I groaned into the makeshift bed.

He pulled out, deliriously slow, inch by inch. I felt each ridge and nub of his draconian member, teasing me the way no human cock could. He slid back in, faster this time, all the way to the hilt. I collapsed into the blankets with a breath. Stars shone before my eyes.

The world narrowed around us, all other worries or cares falling away. In the moment, I didn't have to worry about returning to Steamshire, or what the Elders might think, or even how my family had fared. Right now, I was full of love and light and I was flying, adrift on the clouds of our most intimate connection.

The onslaught continued without mercy, the long hard length of him pressing into me again and again, hitting that delicious sweet spot at just the right angle, just the right place, and suddenly I was hardening again, that shouldn't even be possible, and—

I groaned into the blankets, thankful they were there to muffle the sounds of my passion.

Lucien reached a crescendo and fell on top of me, his sweaty body covering mine, hips pumping frantically as if pulled by some power higher than us both. Cum pumped into my wanting hole in hot, thick spurts.

He pulled out before his knot had time to inflate to full, my head still spinning. Cum leaked out of me and onto the blankets.

"We're gonna need to wash these again," Lucien teased, brushing a lock of hair from my face as his breathing slowed.

"Yeah, we are," I agreed, and nuzzled into his chest as sleep took me.

The big day had arrived. We checked and double checked our packs and supplies to make sure we hadn't left anything. Lucien especially. He became obsessive in the last minutes, worrying over every little thing.

"Are you sure Corin will be okay to fly?" I hefted him from his crib and he woke groggily, nuzzling against me with a yawn. I didn't want him in the middle of all this, to be honest. But the thought of leaving him behind was too painful to consider. He was coming with me, or not coming at all.

"Dragon babes are tough, you know," Lucien had assured me a million times. "Even half-dragons. We would often go flying with the little ones when I was Clan Alpha of Darkvale. It gives them a taste for the air."

"If you say so." I stepped over to the custom saddle Lucien had commissioned for our journey. Not only was there a spot for me, there was a carefully reinforced "dragonseat" for the baby. I fingered the leather straps and smooth buckles. Had to be better than bouncing around bareback.

A wicked grin split my face as I flashed back to our tryst the day before. Heh. Bareback.

"If that's everything?" I asked, turning toward Lucien. He checked things off a list and rubbed his chin.

"I feel sure we've forgotten something, but I can't think of what..."

I put a hand around his waist and gave him a peck on the cheek. "Whatever it is, we'll be okay. Let's get going while there's still light out. Come on."

Lucien hefted the supplies in his strong arms and brought them outside to a wide grassy field. "Bring the saddle!" he called.

It was a little awkward holding the saddle and the baby. Okay, more than a little awkward. The leather straps dangled to the ground as I clasped it with one hand while balancing Corin with the other. But I made it outside with both the saddle and the baby intact.

I placed the saddle down on the ground next to the rest of the supplies and Lucien stepped forward.

He took my hands and looked into my eyes. "I know

this is going to be dangerous for you. But I want you to know that I am with you. Now and always. I am with you."

I leaned my head onto Lucien's chest, listening for a moment the soft spell of his breathing and the beating of his heart. We may have come from different cultures, different peoples, but the love we shared overcame all of that.

I just hoped that love could overcome hate in Steamshire as well.

"Stand back. I'm going to shift."

Corin and I gave him a wide berth, watching open mouthed as the transformation began. No matter how many times I saw him shift, it was still just as fascinating, just as awe-inducing as the first time.

A large onyx dragon stood before us, claws thundering to the ground as the process completed.

He was magnificent.

He was mine.

To my surprise, Corin stayed silent through the process, only watching with a wide-eyed sense of wonder. Any human baby would have been screaming bloody murder. I planted a kiss on the top of his head. "Daddy's a dragon now, Corin. Did you know that? He's special. Just like you."

Corin chirped and made a grabbing motion with his hands.

"You wanna go see him?"

We walked toward the towering dragon and I could already feel the heat pouring off of his scales. His brilliant golden eyes were no less powerful than the day I'd met him, but they held a softness now as he looked upon us.

Can he hear us? I sent over the Link.

Not yet. It takes time to develop. Soon, though.

"This is your daddy, Corin. Say hi."

Corin gurgled with delight and pressed a hand to Lucien's shining scales.

A different sound came from him then, a not entirely human sound. A small reptilian squawk and a flash of those haunting amber eyes.

Irralo, was all I could hear through the Link. *My little storm.*

When the connection broke, Corin turned back to me and lay his head on my chest, the momentary lapse into dragonhood all but forgotten. He yawned and drooled a bit on my shirt. I didn't mind. He looked too adorable.

What was that? I asked through the Link.

He knows who I am. And he knows who he is, too. He'll be a powerful one. I can feel it.

My heart swelled with pride as I held my son close. We'd done a good job. Ten fingers, ten toes, and a smile that could light up any room.

Grab the supplies and secure the saddle. Daylight won't last forever.

The thought snapped me back to our mission. Adrian arrived to take over baby duty and I set to work once more, the glowing pride of parenthood still pulsing through my veins.

————

WE SAILED through the sky on black wings, the ride even smoother than I could have imagined. Corin faced me in his secured "dragonseat", looking with awe at the sky around him. He cried a bit as we ascended, but wonder soon replaced his fear and he grew silent, simply staring.

"This saddle is incredible!" I yelled through the rush of wind around us. "Who made it?"

"Ah, you have Teria Willowfern to thank for that. She's one of the best craftswomen I've ever met, and I accept only the best for my mate and son. You can meet her when we return. I'm sure she'd be thrilled to hear your praise."

"I'd like that."

I glanced at a map Lucien had packed. A big blackened X lay over the village of Steamshire, nearly too small to warrant a mention. My breath caught in my throat. I was really doing this.

I could see my family again. See everyone again.

The emotion swept over me like the wind. I'd been so focused on rescuing the omegas and taking care of Corin that I'd completely neglected to think about the real reason I was returning. My family. My friends. My people.

What would they think when they saw me? Would they be happy? Scared? Sad?

Would they try to kill me on the spot, just like they did with the legendary dragons of old? I shivered, though the warmth from Lucien's scales was more than enough.

Come what may, we were heading right into the belly of the beast.

But if I could save my brother, save my friends, save my mother, even...maybe it would all be worthwhile.

I glanced at the map again and pushed the other thoughts out of my mind. "Bear west past that mountain range. There's a forest nearby, you can shift there and we'll head into town. Won't be far from there."

My heart rate picked up. Not far from there.

"Will do," Lucien acknowledged, and I prepared for the coming confrontation.

———

MY STOMACH still clenched in knots as we descended. I didn't think I would ever get over my fear of heights completely, but riding with my mate was about as close as I was gonna get. I held Corin's hands as he wailed, unused to the pressure change. We landed about a mile outside of town, under cover of dense foliage. We'd come from behind the mountains, which meant that scouts wouldn't have seen our approach.

Not unless they'd seriously ramped up their forces, anyway.

I placed Corin in a carrier against my chest as Lucien shifted back into human form.

"You ready for this?" he asked, placing a hand on my shoulder.

"As I'll ever be."

We walked, hand in hand, toward the clearing. Toward my home.

As planned, Lucien emerged from the woods first. It wasn't long before I heard shouts of confusion from the scouts keeping watch. I wanted to leap out right then and there, to defend him and tell everyone it was all right. But that would spoil the plan we'd so painstakingly put together.

So, I took a deep breath, held Corin close, and waited.

"I mean you no harm," Lucien said, stepping calmly toward the walls of the village. He wore a hood to conceal the glowing of his eyes, but that wouldn't last long once they got a good look at him.

"Who goes there?" a guard at the gate demanded, leveling his lance. I couldn't help but imagine the sickening vision of that sharpened metal tip piercing Lucien's gut, ending his life.

Please be careful, I whispered over the Link, hoping he would hear me.

"I mean you no harm," Lucien said again, hands outstretched in a gesture of innocence. "I am unarmed, but a weary traveler seeking only the safety of your village. Please, show me mercy."

Any minute now...they would notice. They would see. Then all hell would break loose.

The guards looked to one another and lowered their lances slowly. With a creak, the gate opened.

I held my breath. I couldn't believe they were actually letting him in.

I crept forward, soothing Corin with an absent hand rubbing his back. He was being good so far, but if he decided to speak up, our cover would be blown.

Lucien entered the gates and they clattered shut behind him. I strained my ears to hear what was going on, but the walls successfully blocked any sound.

I clenched my jaw. What was going on in there? And where was the sign? Lucien was supposed to signal for me to come out of hiding, but the seconds dragged on into minutes. It felt more like hours.

Fear and determination got the best of me. I was done hiding in the shadows. That life was over.

I burst out of the forest and strode toward the gate, the guards shocked in recognition.

"It is Alec Cipher, son of Cilla Cipher, and the Season's Chosen. I have returned and you will let me in. Now."

The guards visibly gulped and opened the gate without a word. My heart roared in my chest, my ears, my stomach.

For family, I lodged the intention in my heart, and passed through.

"It's him!"

"He's back!"

"The Chosen!"

The voices gathered around me as I stepped into the village. Faces I'd once known looked down at me with a mixture of surprise and horror. More so than me, they stared at the babe I carried.

At the sound of the commotion the five Elders pushed through the crowds, their inky blue robes billowing and blocking out the light. Elder Marin was first to converge upon me, his eyes bulging.

"Mr. Cipher! Come to turn yourself in, have you?"

"No, Elder Marin, I haven't."

"Then what brings you here to defile our peaceful

village? And what of this stranger? Do you lead traitors into our midst?"

I opened my mouth to speak but Lucien lowered his hood and gave the crowd an eyeful.

The shouts of terror and confusion grew louder, and the Elders' faces blanched as they caught sight of his draconian pupils.

Marin turned on me, sputtering. "You see! This is what happens when we do not complete the Chosen Ceremony. This traitor, this defiler, has brought dragons to Steamshire! He seeks to destroy us all!"

The fervor in his voice roused the nearby villagers and they crowded around us, angry hands grasping and clawing. I backed up, hitting the wall. Corin cried out in terror and Lucien was at my side, shielding me.

"Let me explain," Lucien bellowed, his voice steely and laced with power.

Just then, the crowd parted to let through the two people I missed most: Samson and my mother.

Her unseeing eyes searched the place and Samson screamed.

"Alec! Watch out!"

Lucien growled deep in his chest but I steadied him. *No*, I whispered through our Link. *That's him. That's my brother.*

Lucien stood down and let me pass. Samson threw himself at me, his eyes watery. "Alec..." he sobbed. "I thought you were..."

"I did too," I soothed, hugging him. "I'm sorry I had to leave. But I came back. I'm going to get you and Mom out of here."

He looked up at me with alarm.

"Don't tell me you've fornicated with one of these beasts!" Elder Thrain gasped, the disdain dripping from his voice. He eyed the baby and then Lucien in turn. His lip curled with hatred and disgust.

"Why doesn't Alec tell us what's going on here," Elder Marin hissed with steely venom. "Tell us why you've betrayed your own kind."

I took a deep breath. *Here goes nothing.*

"Yes," I said loudly enough for all the crowd to hear. "Yes, I ran. I didn't know what would happen to me. I didn't know where I would go. But I met a dragon along the way, and with it a whole clan. They took me in, even though I was human. They didn't have to. But they have showed me such kindness. Such generosity. One dragon especially. Lucien?"

Lucien's shift overtook him and he exploded into a mass of shimmering scales and claws and teeth. He looked down at the cowering crowd and let out a mighty roar.

"This is my mate!" I yelled, placing a hand on his scales. "And this is our son!"

The crowd devolved into full-on chaos.

"Traitor!"

"Blasphemy!"

"Whore!"

The insults flew at me left and right like bricks to my heart. Each one chipped away a little more of my resolve, a little more of my attempted calm. For Lucien, and for Corin.

I scanned the crowd again, looking in vain for my mother and brother. They'd been swallowed up by the masses, nowhere to be seen.

"Samson!" I cried, receiving no answer.

"Kill him!"

"Kill the beast!"

I needed a better vantage point. I needed to find him.

Clambering up the slick scales on Lucien's side, I ascended and took my place on his back. Lucien straightened to his full height and I could look over the town from above. More people than I had ever seen gathered at once crowded the village square, pushing and screaming and fighting one another for a look at the dragon and his bastard baby.

Lucien let out another roar, echoing through the village and shaking the walls. The people froze in fear, stunned. One of the many powers of dragonkind. This was my chance.

"I challenge you!" I yelled at top volume. "All of you here! Alphas and omegas alike. Think about your lifestyle here. Think about how these beliefs have shaped your actions and thoughts. Hate and fear will only beget more of the same."

"There is a way out." I flung the words with conviction, adrenaline rushing through me like the tide. "Lucien and I, and his clan, are building a new community. We believe that only by combining our forces, by living together as human and shifter, can we truly be free. We welcome you to join us, to start over with a blank slate. If you are tired of your future being thrown away by an ancient edict you had no part in, if you are tired of the Elders convincing you it is an honor and a privilege to be selected, then I challenge you this day. Come with us. Let's build it! We will provide safety, food, care, learning. There is a life outside these walls. I have seen it. All you have to do is reach out and take it. We will take you there. But it is up to each of you, each mother and child, each alpha and omega. Look inside yourself. Choose hope over fear. I am not here to tell you it will be easy. I tell you it will be worth it. What does your soul hunger for, deep down inside? Hate and injustice? Or freedom and choice? That is the challenge I pose to you here today. Will you join me?"

The crowd murmured, everyone looking to one another as the dragon-stun wore off.

I could see the gears turning. I could see the beginnings of fresh new thought blooming in their minds.

Of course, then the Elders cut in once more.

"This is absolute blasphemy! Look at him, tainted with sin. He's fornicated with the enemy, brought his demon spawn upon us! He's no friend of ours. Get him!"

People crushed in around us and I fell from Lucien's back.

Oh no, the baby.

I landed on my feet by some miracle of acrobatics but my knees buckled, scraping into the dirt as Corin began to cry.

Lucien lunged forward, trying to hold off the crowds.

Then I felt a greasy hand around my throat.

"Lucien!" I screamed, gagging. Corin squealed in terror and Lucien whirled around, his eyes an inferno.

"Alec is ours, you hear, ours!" Elder Marin held me fast, paying no mind to the baby. He was crazy! Insane! I struggled against his grip, trying to get free.

Lucien thundered toward us, but there was nothing he could do with me and Corin as a meat shield.

"You've defiled him, and for that we will never forgive

you. Leave now, before we wipe you from the face of the Earth. This is your one chance."

I threw my leg backward, connecting with Marin's groin. He groaned and loosed his grip as I ducked to the side, holding Corin against me.

"You filthy omega, no good for anything but—"

Heat blew past me as fire spewed from Lucien's maw, roasting Marin where he stood. A long, tortured scream echoed through the square. I shielded my vision and covered Corin's eyes, waiting for it to be over.

Then everything was silent.

"Anyone else have questions?" Lucien turned on the crowd, many of them already fleeing. I scanned the throng of people. The Elders were gone.

Cowards.

Samson stepped forward, his mother's hand in his own.

"I will go with you, Alec."

My heart soared. I even saw the slightest hint of a smile on my mother's face.

He ran to me and took my hand. Corin's crying quieted. He didn't seem hurt, thank the Goddess.

"Samson," I breathed. Before I had a chance to say anything else, more omegas stepped forward.

"And I." Jerran, a childhood friend and fellow omega.

"And I." Lonya, my brother's classmate.

"And I." Walter, the alpha schoolmaster, came forward. He held his two omega children by the hand and they smiled at me and Lucien. There was a hint of fear, sure. But there was something there I hadn't ever seen in Steamshire before.

Hope.

Steamshire shook with the sound of young omegas standing for their rights, their future, and their freedom.

It was working. It was actually working. I stayed by Lucien's side as the families came forward.

"Thank you. All of you," I said, tears threatening to spill over. Emotion washed over me at the sight of my people choosing hope over fear. They had made the decision to try something new, even though it was scary and uncertain. They wanted to change. And that was enough.

"Come along," I offered, climbing onto Lucien's back. We thundered toward the gates. With one look at the dragon and the mass of people following him, the guards scattered.

The children in tow gazed in awe as they saw the world around them. For many, this would be the first time they'd ever been outside the village walls.

We headed east toward the waypoint, where Firefangs would be waiting to transport the new recruits.

Samson ran up beside me, craning his neck to catch my eye. "I'm glad you came back," he said as we moved off toward the setting sun.

"I'm glad I did too."

A new life lay ahead for dragons and humans alike. With my mate, my son, and my family, I didn't need anything else.

THE DRAGON'S SECOND-CHANCE OMEGA

DARKVALE BOOK 2

"You want a date? Fine. I'll give you a date. I'll go with you to the Flower Festival—on one condition."

"And what's that?" I threw back, waiting for the answer. The fact that he was playing along at all stunned me.

"Best me in a duel." Marlowe said it so casually, with a quirk of his lips into a wicked smile. He knew he was pushing my buttons, and he loved it.

I sputtered as I looked him up and down. Even though we'd been friends throughout our childhood, Marlowe had always been the strong one. Especially after he presented as Alpha.

"Those are the terms. Better get to practicing, Nik." Marlowe turned and went back to chopping wood. The conversation was over. I watched for a few seconds longer, eyeing the rippling muscles and the way they moved as he swung the axe through blocks of wood. A fine sheen of sweat made his skin shine in the sunlight, and made my own mouth dry.

I'd finally done it. I'd finally asked him out.

He didn't say no, but...

Another log split in half with the force of his mighty axe. I swallowed and snapped my gaping mouth shut. I knew Marlowe was strong, but seeing it like this was getting my dragon fifty shades of flustered. How would I ever beat someone like him in a duel?

I shoved my hands in my pockets and turned on my heel, away from my friend and the other alphas working nearby. It was a nice enough day, sunny with just a hint of breeze. The blood-red banners of the Firefang Clan rippled against the stone walls just like they always had. I headed off toward the Clan Alpha's quarters with a thought. He'd know what to do.

I chewed my lip as I made my way across town. I couldn't stop replaying the scene in my mind. Marlowe hadn't said no. I had to remind myself of that. And that thought alone both thrilled and terrified me. I'd only been crushing on him since forever, but nothing I did seemed to get his attention. When he joined the army, I saw him less and less. I thought my chance was gone.

But he'd returned to station in Darkvale at the request of Clan Alpha Lucien, and I saw my chance. Normally it would be unusual for an omega to make the first move, but no one had ever called me usual. And for a man like Marlowe, it was easier to kill a man than reveal his true feelings. I had to give him something to work with.

Even when we were kids, Marlowe had always been like this. Teasing, play fighting, always competitive, always looking for a win.

Would he win here as well?

My steps soon led to the Clan Alpha's chambers deep within the fortress of Darkvale.

Though Clan Alpha Lucien was an alpha, he was friendly with everyone. He ruled the Firefangs with his mate Caldo, always looking out for the elderly, the children, the omegas. It was through these overlooked peoples, Lucien was known to say, that we make true progress.

I raised my hand to the solid wooden door to knock when I heard a breathy sigh from within. I drew back my hand, embarrassed.

Guess I can just come back later...

Still frozen, still blushing, I heard Lucien's voice ring out just as I was about to make a run for it.

"Come on in, Nikolas."

"It's not urgent. I can come back if I'm interrupting..."

My voice stuck in my throat like honey. Lucien wasn't at his usual haunt and the door to his private chamber was closed. What did I think was gonna happen?

Footsteps echoed on the other side of the door and the latch opened with a creak. Lucien opened the door a crack and smiled. "Not at all, come on in."

Both he and Caldo were clothed and other than the slight twinkle of a shared secret in their eyes all seemed normal.

"Thanks," I mumbled as I sunk into one of the huge cushions Lucien kept around as chairs.

"What's on your mind?" Lucien asked. He faced away from me, digging into a cabinet and making quite the racket. A small cacophony later, he fished out a few cups and filled them with spirits from a decanter nearby. "Sit, drink. Let's talk."

That's what I liked about Lucien. Despite being busy with his duties as both Clan Alpha and Caldo's mate, he always had time to speak to one of his clansmen. In the Firefangs, we were family.

"I did it," I said after taking a sip of the bracing liquor. "I asked Marlowe on a date."

"Did you now?" Lucien's eyes lit up and he gave me a toothy grin. He pulled up a chair and sat on it backward, his chin resting on the back as he straddled the seat. "Took you long enough. How did it go?"

I rolled my eyes and pursed my lips. "I'm not quite sure, actually. It was kinda awkward."

"But he didn't say no?"

"He didn't."

"What did he say, then?"

I buried my face in my hands, skin burning. "He wants to fight me. He said he'd go with me to the Flower Festival if I could beat him in a duel. Does he not see how impossible that is?"

Caldo burst out laughing from across the room.

"What?" I asked, a little annoyed. I didn't come here to get laughed at!

Caldo sniffed and caught his breath. "Typical Marlowe," he said, shaking his head. "Type A alpha if I ever did meet one. What he means, Nik, is that he likes you. He wouldn't offer that to just anyone."

I blinked, considering the prospect. "Really? Why couldn't he just say so?"

"He's a stubborn one, that's for sure. But you knew that already. I'm willing to bet that under that rough and tough exterior he sees something in you. He just doesn't know how to say it."

My heart thudded in my chest as a thrill surged through me. It seemed too good to be true. My best friend. Could we really be more?

"I'll never be able to beat him," I whined. "He knows that, too. He's so strong!"

Lucien grinned, showing all his teeth. He had a plan. "Who said strength was the only way to win? What do you say to a little training with Caldo and I?"

I swallowed the lump of anxiety in my throat and in its stead rose a swell of gratitude. What would I do without them? "You think it will work?" I asked, raising an eyebrow. My whole friendship with Marlowe was on the line, and by asking him out I'd opened Pandora's Box of Feels. No going back.

"Let's get you your man," Caldo said, and took my hand.

———

"ALPHAS LIKE MARLOWE are all lumbering muscle. But you have something he doesn't." Lucien circled around me, locked into a fighting stance. "I don't know if you've noticed, but that guy is a solid brick of a man. Let's just say I'm glad he's on our side."

"So how do I beat him?"

"You wear him down, just like you're gonna do here. You dodge and weave. He won't be able to keep up and when he tires, you'll have him right where you want him."

"Grab 'im by the balls!" Caldo suggested from the sidelines, eyebrows waggling. "Works every time!"

Lucien rolled his eyes. "Or you can be like Caldo and play dirty."

I had to laugh at that. "I just don't understand this whole duel thing. Why can't he just say what he means?" All this seemed awfully over the top for something as simple as a date.

"This is just how he processes things. He's never been so good with emotion, you know that."

"I wish he could say that." My shoulders slumped.

"I bet he wishes he could too."

A smile crept over my face. He had a point.

"Now come on, we've got a lot of work to do if you're gonna beat his alpha ass tomorrow!"

My heart thudded faster and fire surged through my veins. My dragon thundered within my chest, relishing the idea of being so physical with Marlowe after all these years. Grappling with my friend, falling down into the dirt together, tumbling over and over as Marlowe grabbed me and held me close...it was enough to rouse my cock right then and there.

"Save that for the battle," Lucien teased, noticing my faraway glance.

I blushed and swiped away the thoughts, but my

dragon was persistent. I couldn't believe I was going through with this.

"Now come at me," Lucien taunted. "And focus!"

———

I'D NEVER BEEN SO SORE in my life. Every muscle ached, pushed to their limits. The training Lucien and Caldo put me through was merciless, but they assured me it would turn the tides in my favor. I lay in bed like an invalid, staring at the ceiling as my limbs throbbed. If I was too sore to fight, it wouldn't matter anyway.

I stared out the small window into the clear night sky. The moon was full tonight—that boded well. I whispered a prayer to Glendaria and tugged the covers around me.

Best me in a duel. The smile and glint of his eyes still rang through my mind. Tomorrow would change everything.

———

THINGS not to do on the day your crush wants to fight you for a date: oversleep and show up late.

Things I did: just that.

I woke up in a panic, throwing the covers off and

stumbling out of bed as soon as I saw the sun in the sky. Much higher than expected. I was late.

Way to impress your crush, Nik.

I threw on some clothes and rushed out the door, sprinting to Marlowe's place. I knew the path by heart but this time it carried with it a tension that hadn't been there before. I wasn't going to Marlowe's to hang out with my buddy like we always did. I was going to fight him. To prove to him I could be his mate.

Could I?

And if it didn't work out...what then?

I shivered. Best not to think of that.

Marlowe was there waiting for me when I arrived, a knowing grin on his face. He looked me up and down as I panted. We hadn't even gotten started and I was already out of breath. His lips quirked up at the corners and he pushed away from the wall he leaned on. "Good to see you could make it. Thought you'd changed your mind."

"Never."

His eyes flashed. "You still wanna do this, then?"

I took a deep breath, appraising my friend. If all went well here today, we would be more than just friends. Maybe even mates.

"I do. And when I win, you're gonna take me to the

Flower Festival." The cockiness in my voice belied the nervousness that shook me to my core. I hoped he wouldn't notice. Beneath the fear and jitters there was something else, too—a feral, consuming heat that threatened to destroy me. My dragon knew what he wanted, and he wanted Marlowe. Bad.

Marlowe raised an eyebrow. "Watch your words, omega. You better be able to back those up." He threw me a cocky grin and led me inside.

A large open space spread out before us. Nothing to get in our way. Nothing to hide behind, either.

We'd always been like this, I mused as I followed him. Always teasing, always taunting one another. But this time, the stakes were higher. Much higher.

"Rules?" I asked as I joined him in the center of the room.

"Human form only. No shifts, no weapons. Winner is first to make the other yield. Other than that?" He grinned wickedly. "Anything goes."

Anything. I swallowed the words as the idea shot straight down my spine to my cock. The deep timbre of Marlowe's taunting voice worked its way into my heart like honeyed wine, stoking the flames of passion there. The time to act was now. No more stealing glances. No more teasing one another like children. If this was what it took to prove myself, then this was what I'd do.

I drew in a deep breath through my nose and blew it out, stretching my still-sore limbs. If my hormones got the best of me now, I'd lose for sure.

"Fair enough," I replied, balling my hands into fists.

Marlowe rolled his neck and cracked his knuckles. "Let's do this. You and me, Nik. Come on!"

I said a quick prayer to the goddess Glendaria and adopted a fighting stance, trying to remember what Lucien and Caldo had taught me. Trying to access thoughts felt like wading through mud. Adrenaline, lust, and terror had shut down all rational thought and clouded my mind, leaving me alone. I had to act.

Marlowe growled and ripped his shirt off. The fabric fell away, showing the firm abs and the bulging muscles in the dim light. My mouth went dry at the sight and my dragon cried, desperate for release. I gulped.

"See something you like, Nik?" Marlowe held out his arms. "Come and get it then."

Didn't have to tell me twice. My dragon pulled me forward, ready for a fight.

Marlowe lunged toward me and swiped the air with his huge hands. I dodged at the last second, ducking beneath his grip like I'd learned. It became a sort of dance, weaving and dodging my way out of each advance. This worked my attacker into an even more feral frenzy. I was no longer his best friend Nik. I was prey.

"Come back here and fight!" He roared, lumbering toward me. "Stop moving around!"

I ducked into a roll and regained my feet behind him. Then I had an idea. I barreled into him, throwing all my weight into the lunge. This caught him off balance and we both went down, crashing into the ground on top of one another. His heated skin, slick with sweat, slipped out of my grip and Marlowe took advantage, grabbing me and flipping me over.

The wind rushed out of my lungs and I wheezed, staring up at him with wide eyes. He was huge. Marlowe hovered over me and blocked out the light, his eyes alight with the adrenaline of battle.

In that moment, I did the only thing I could think to do. I wriggled my hands free, grabbed his head, and kissed him.

To my surprise, Marlowe didn't flinch away in disgust. Instead he took control and forced his lips over mine, biting and sucking at the swollen skin there. He delved his tongue into my mouth and around my own. A deep, shuddering moan rumbled free.

"What are you doing?" I breathed.

"Pressing my advantage," Marlowe rumbled. "Anything goes, remember?"

I growled and swung my legs to the side of his torso, pulling him away from me. We tumbled together and then I was on top again, grabbing his wrists and pinning him down. It took all my weight and strength, but I straddled his chest and held him immobile for a few precious seconds.

My cock pressed through my trousers and into his chest, looking for that delicious friction.

"Someone's a little excited," Marlowe noted.

"And you're not?" I quipped. I ground my hips against him, reveling in the hot and heavy groans coming from my alpha.

I sunk down and kissed the area between his neck and shoulder, scraping my teeth against the flesh there. Goddess, he smelled like heaven. Iron and fire and musk. Wings itched at my shoulder blades, aching to come out. I bit my lip and suckled at him harder.

He could have easily thrown me off of him. But he didn't.

"Don't tell me you knew this would happen?" I asked between my little love bites.

"Fuck you," Marlowe spat and turned the tables, twisting his arms out of my grip at last.

"Fuck me?" I shot back. "That wasn't part of the rules."

"It is now," he roared. Marlowe grabbed hold of my

shirt and ripped it away, fabric tearing. "Yeah, like that."

The cool air brushed past my bare skin and pebbled my already-sensitive nipples. I flailed my arms and legs against him but couldn't find purchase. Finally they found their way around Mar's neck and I pulled, forcing his face down to crotch level.

"Suck it," I growled, heat burning through every pore. I couldn't think straight anymore, or maybe I never had. I needed him. Burned for him. The fight didn't matter. Quenching this raging desire did. "Suck my fucking cock." My hips thrust upward of their own volition.

"No!" Marlowe twisted his head out of the way, shuddering in my grip.

"Yes," I growled and fisted a hand through his hair. I pulled him closer, grinding against his face.

What I didn't notice was Marlowe slipping his hand down my pants. He squeezed my ass and I hissed, suddenly aware of the position we were in.

This was supposed to be a duel, a hand to hand fight. How did we end up here?

No more questions. No more reason.

Need him. Need him now.

"Take those fucking pants off, boy." Marlowe's voice took on the same steely command as it did when he trained the troops. It sent a thrill of electricity from head to foot.

"Make me," I sneered.

"I will."

He grabbed the waistband and yanked, my pants flying upward and off. My cock bounced free, already throbbing.

Marlowe pushed my legs away and leaned over me, one arm holding me down and the other ever so softly stroking my cock. Sparks flashed before my eyes as the waves of desire grew only stronger. He was winning.

Maybe I wanted that.

I struggled beneath him, but Marlowe held firm. I was no match for his raw power.

He kept up the torturous motion on my cock as it twitched beneath him. I tried to thrust my hips upward, get more, but he held me down. "What's the matter, pretty boy? Say it."

"No," I hissed through my teeth. He fisted my cock and I groaned, throwing my head backward. My back arched, my breath came in gasps. After all the nights fantasizing about something like this, nothing held a candle to what was happening right now.

"What's going on down here, I wonder?" Marlowe snaked a finger lower to my dripping hole.

"Ah, fuck!" I moaned as he probed the ring of muscle there. Goddess, it felt so good. I couldn't even imagine how he would feel within me—

"Now fight me, omega! Fight me!" Marlowe jerked away in an instant. Whiplash seized me, every pore and nerve tense and ready to spring. Mar's voice was nothing more than a feral roar, but my dragon understood every word.

Fire threatened to consume my body as we tangled together. Our bare chests and sweaty skin pressed so close made my head spin and worked my dragon into a frenzy. Fire and iron and blood and magic, he was mine, he was mine...

Mate! The dragon screeched from the depths of my soul. Mate! Mate!

I gathered my strength and pawed at Marlowe's pants, unfastening them at the waist. He didn't resist, even helped me a bit. He kicked them aside and we were right back at it, rolling around on the ground naked, grunting and straining to subdue the other. I was tiring, but so was he. The animalistic grunts, the hot pants of breath, the slick and sweaty skin kept me going.

Our hard cocks pressed into one another and our eyes were like fire. There was nothing better than this, the thought wove through my hazy mind.

I couldn't take my eyes off of Marlowe's straining cock. Sure, I'd fantasized about it more than a few times. But seeing it in person was another matter completely. I reached down and wrapped a hand around it, marveling at the girth of it. My fingers barely fit around his rod and I sucked in a breath thinking how it might feel inside of me.

Could I even take the whole thing?

"Mmmm," Marlowe let out in a low sigh as I worked my hand up and down his length. "That's nice."

Without warning he grabbed my arms and spun me around, slamming me onto my back. I coughed and looked up at him, his hulking frame hovering above me. Heat poured off of his sweaty body in waves, and more than that, the alpha pheromones he gave off were simply too good to resist. I took a long drag through my nose, letting his personal musk fill my senses.

Yes. Goddess, yes.

"Do you yield yet?" Marlowe's voice brought me back to the moment. His jaw clenched, his voice strained. He was holding himself back.

"Never," I hissed through my teeth. I wanted to egg him on. I wanted to see where this would go.

"You asked for it," my alpha growled and brought his hand to my slick, dripping opening. He coated his fingers in my juices and brought them to his nose, sniffing deeply before sucking them into his mouth.

He rumbled deep in his chest, closing his eyes as he

tasted me. Goddess, that was so fucking hot. My cock twitched and strained against Marlowe's body and my breath came out in frenzied pants.

"You're so wet," Marlowe groaned. "Would be a shame not to put that to use."

I narrowed my eyes, all thought blanked out by the feeling of him on top of me, the fire raging within my soul, our dragons so close to one another, straining to meet, to play, to mate.

"Do it!" I groaned through gritted teeth. We'd reached a crescendo. A point of no return. If I was gonna tumble over this cliff, I was taking him with me.

Marlowe let out a booming draconic roar and the head of his cock speared through my channel. I gasped as it filled me, stretching beyond anything I'd felt before. Amidst the haze of momentary pain there was something else—heat. Raging, unrelenting heat.

I bucked my hips toward him, drawing his hard throbbing cock deeper into my channel. Marlowe's eyes widened and he grinned incredulously.

I sighed and threw my head back, stars dancing before my eyes. Electric currents zapped and sparkled between us, weaving an ancient connection that only true mates could experience.

"After all this time?" Mar said, his voice awed. "Why didn't you ever say anything?"

The old fears came rushing back. The old memories. "Thought you had your sights set on another," I said sheepishly, my voice deepening into a moan as he slid all the way in, balls deep in my tight channel. "Never thought you'd see me like that."

And now here they were, close as two men could be. Their sweaty bodies writhed together as one, Marlowe seating himself deep within.

"Shut up," Marlowe mumbled. He put a finger over my lips and I clicked my teeth, threatening to bite it.

Goddess, this was so fucking good. Better than flying. Better than Myrony's best stew. Better than maple candies.

"Always you, Nik. Always you. I'm just sorry it took this long." My alpha's voice carried a hint of sadness now as he remembered some long-forgotten pain. "I was too blinded by my fears to do anything about it. Thought I could block it all out. But then you asked me, and my walls came tumbling down. I've wanted you for so fucking long."

He thrust into me again, probing the sensitive spot deep inside. I moaned and lifted my hips, straining for more.

"That makes two of us," I breathed. "Now show me that you mean it!"

We turned into a single mass of growling, sweating

flesh. Marlowe drove his cock home again and again, building the tension and fire to unquenchable levels.

"Goddess, you're tight," Mar groaned, kissing my lips, my neck, my chest. He picked up the rhythm, a frantic flicker in his eyes.

"Last chance," he bit off the words as our gaze locked together. I held him there, pumping my hips and matching his thrusts. The circuit was nearly complete. "Do you yield, Nikolas Lastir?"

"Never," I said with conviction, and held him to me as he tumbled over the edge, jerking and thrusting as he came. His knot swelled against me, locking us together as mates. The stretch made me dizzy, made me see stars. I couldn't take it any longer and groaned, thrusting beneath him. Hot gobs of cum shot over my chest, smearing onto sweaty skin.

But more than that, the sense of something greater overcame me. A celestial connection that had been forged here today, binding together our bodies, our minds, our spirits. Marlowe and Nikolas. Alpha and omega. Mates. Family.

We lay there for some time, still knotted together, still holding one another close. It took a few minutes for my breathing to return to normal. For all the sweat to dry. I fluttered open my eyelids and saw Marlowe there, gazing at me with a sleepy grin. "So how about that date?"

Marlowe laughed, tousling my hair and kissing my forehead. "Wait, who won the duel?" He furrowed his eyebrows, thinking.

"Does it matter?" I chuckled.

"You are my mate. My best friend. My confidante. There is no greater win than that."

I nuzzled into him, still sniffing at the primal musk that coated his skin. Mate. This dragon is my mate. Mine. Forever.

I snapped my eyes open, propping up on an elbow. "You knew this was going to happen."

"I did not." Marlowe held up his hands in an innocent gesture. "I had my hopes, though." He winked.

I groaned. "You're ridiculous." Try as I might, I couldn't stop the grin from spreading over my face.

"You mean ridiculously sexy?" Marlowe quipped, nudging me.

We laughed, holding one another close, knotted together both in body and soul.

"And yes, I will take you to the Flower Festival. It's a date." Marlowe rested his forehead against mine, his breath slowing as he slipped away to slumber.

Right here, in this moment, was all I ever wanted. We weren't just friends anymore. We were mates. And nothing could stop us now.

MARLOWE

W e had 'em by the balls.

Supply lines cut short. The fortress surrounded. It was only a matter of time.

Darkvale would be ours.

My heart raced with adrenaline and the endorphins of battle. Finally, after five years of hiding and preparing, we were fighting back. Finally, we could return home.

"Firefangs!" I roared in a lusty battle cry, fire building in my chest. The walls of Darkvale stood tall, reinforced with stone and mortar. The magical dome over the city made simply flying over the walls impossible, but we could still knock them down. And if we couldn't get in, they couldn't get out. Siege 101.

I flapped my wings harder, gaining speed, then tucked them to my side as I slammed into the wall like a torpedo. I braced myself against the impact and it shuddered me to the bone. But the walls shuddered too, cracks of plaster and stone coming free.

"To the walls!" I cried, and my battalion followed suit around me. The sky thundered with the sound of dragons pummeling the stone walls like battering rams, over and over again.

Thank the Goddess for my armored scales, but I was starting to feel a little dizzy. In human form I'd have broken just about every bone in my body by now. But we couldn't stop just yet.

The wall was weakening.

I projected my voice, booming through the walls into the city I'd once called home. "Your time is up, Paradox! We've cut off your supply lines. We've caved in your tunnels. There is no way out. You can surrender peacefully, or we shall burn this castle to the ground!"

A few beats of blessed silence, then a shuffling sound echoed behind the walls. A sniveling voice responded.

"You wouldn't dare. Cut off your nose to spite your face? Not likely."

The high-pitched whine stirred the rage inside me even more. I caught sight of a glowing orange eye through a chink in the wall and grinned, showing off my rows of razor-sharp teeth. "Try me."

A great explosion of crumbling stone sounded to my left and I swerved, narrowly missing the falling debris. As the dust cleared, I could see that Tork our demolitions expert had breached the wall, light spilling into the human-sized hole he'd left behind.

I wasted no time. "For Darkvale!" I called, and forced my shift down deep into my chest. It wasn't easy—my dragon was in full-on bloodlust mode—but as my hands and feet returned to normal I clawed through the breach and into my old home.

Not all of the Paradox fighters were in their shifts. The enclosed space made sure of that. I roared and lunged forward, ducking to the side as a column of fire erupted from a nearby dragon.

I heard shouts and war cries behind me, and I didn't dare chance a glance but I knew my team had followed. They poured into the city like water through a broken dam, eyes blazing with determination and fire.

"For Darkvale!" The shouts rung out, and I was filled with an arresting sort of pride.

We'd done it.

But the fight wasn't over yet.

I dodged and weaved through the morass of men and dragons, grabbing a broken wooden staff off the ground to use as a weapon. The dragon inside roared in triumph, begging to be released once more.

I tamped the feeling down, focusing only on the makeshift spear in my hand and the flood of my enemies around me.

"Watch it, Mar!" Tork's voice carried over the storm and I swiveled around, my staff meeting the blade meant for my back. The wood vibrated with the impact and I almost dropped it. But my attacker would have liked that too much.

The rust-colored face of a Paradox fighter grinned deliriously down at me, pressing his advantage. His eyes shone a rare green instead of the standard yellow or orange. An Elemental dragon.

I dug my heels into the earth and held on. Our muscles bulged, our teeth bared in bloody grins as we fought for dominance. "Give it up, lowblood," the attacker growled.

"Never," I promised, and threw all my weight and strength into a forward lunge, throwing my attacker off balance. I took the opportunity and drove the sharpened edge of the stake deep into his stomach. He gasped and gurgled, eyes wide. In a final act of defiance the ground shook and changed, the particles vibrating under my feet. Goddess-damned Elementals!

The dirt beneath me became muddy and thin like a slop of quicksand and soon I felt myself sinking, slurping into the Earth. The Elemental was sinking, too, but he had the look of a man who knew he got in the last word. His life force drained away through his abdomen in a bloody haze, but he kept his gaze fixed on me, watching as I tried to clamber my way out of the pit.

Try as I might, I sunk only deeper, in up to my knees now. I watched with wide eyes as the battle raged around me, swords and fire and claws filling the air with the thunder of dragons. My arms scrabbled around on the dirt, looking for something, anything I could anchor myself on. Nothing came.

"Grab on!" Tork yelled and offered me a hand. It was coated in sweat and slipped through my fingers as I sank further. He desperately wiped it and leaned down.

"Pull!"

This time he held firm and I used his body as an anchor to climb free, my boots popping free of the suction-like substance with a final pop. I sprawled on the ground, staring at the sky for only a second before I was back on my feet.

"Close one there," Tork said, handing me a blade. "Fuckin' Elementals."

"He's dead," I assured him, and we rejoined the fray.

I grabbed a running officer by the collar and gave him my most intimidating roar. "Where is Arion? Where is your leader?"

The man cowed beneath my gaze but held a sickly grin that told me he knew something I didn't. I hated it.

"He's not here," the man chuckled. "You're too late."

My dragon would stay silent no longer. A feral roar ripped itself from my throat and sparked a fire, roasting the man where he stood. I dropped the charred corpse to the ground and looked around, my eyes clouded with bloodlust.

Find the leaders. Kill them. Kill them all!

Behind the red haze of battle, another ache began to take hold. A deep, heart-rending ache of nostalgia, guilt, grief.

I was home. I hadn't set foot in these walls in five years, and oh, how things had changed….how *I* had changed…

"Marlowe, we've got them!" The voice roused me from my thoughts and two of my officers approached. Two enemy Cogs in shackles sank to their knees in front of me, their tired, dusty faces full of pure hatred.

"We've got two commanding officers here. They seem to be in charge. Knox's nowhere to be found."

"Coward," I muttered and appraised the two men in front of me. They wore the silver uniforms of Paradox officials and their faces were hard, mean. They didn't meet my gaze. Didn't want to admit defeat, no doubt.

"Where is your leader?" I asked them just as I had the other soldier.

They didn't say anything for a moment, then the man on the left narrowed his eyes and peered straight at me, voice full of malice. "You think we're gonna tell you, lowblood scum?"

There was that phrase again. Lowblood.

I fought to keep my voice even. "Tell me and I might let you live."

The man spat in response, a lump of phlegm landing near my feet. I turned and left them to my officers.

"Roast them," I said casually, and walked away as the sounds of their screams echoed behind me.

My mind buzzed with a million questions, ached with a million little paper cuts. I was home, and yet...it didn't feel like I thought it would. I should have been happy.

Instead, I felt nothing.

The city grew silent save for the moaning of the fallen. The fight was over. We'd won. The stink of blood was heavy in the air, on my skin, under my scales. I rounded a corner and slumped against a stone column. My hands and face reveled in the cool, smooth surface as if I was feeling it for the first time. This courtyard was where I used to play hide and seek as a kid. I was home. Finally, I was home.

"There's no sign of Nikolas, sir." Arthur, my scout, stepped toward me. He shrugged and winced and at the same time.

I closed my eyes and let out a breath as grief washed over me anew. Of course not. How foolish could I have been to think he'd still be here? Still be alive?

The sick, gnawing agony in my gut twisted like a knife. I was home...but without Nik, did it even matter?

That part of my life was over. Had been over, for years now. So why couldn't I get him out of my head?

"If I may, sir," Arthur started. He pulled out a handkerchief and offered it to me.

"You may not." I bit off the words and straightened, assuming the role of the cold military commander once more. Feelings had no place on a battlefield, and there was much work to be done.

"Gather the troops. I wish to speak with them."

"Right away, sir." Arthur hurried off. I stared at the dome above us, enjoying a few more seconds of peace.

———

"IT IS through each and every one of your efforts that we are standing here today, in the city of our forefathers. No longer shall we run and hide in fear.

No longer shall we be relegated to the shadows. We've routed the Paradox. Darkvale is ours once more."

Cheers thundered through the crowd in a way that only dragons could.

"I know that if Clan Alpha Lucien were here, he would say the same. He's had to leave on some urgent business, but has left command with me in his stead. He shall return soon, but in the meantime, let's get this place cleaned up. We want a new Darkvale to show him when he returns, you hear me?"

I looked out at the crowd of men and women I'd fought, lived, and dreamed with for the last five years. Through forests, caves, tunnels, shanties, they'd been there for me. We'd been there for each other. And we'd finally done it. At long last, we'd done it.

Darkvale was ours once more. But at what cost?

"Tonight, we will honor our fallen. Tonight, we will spend time with our families. We will hug our children. We will prepare for our new life. Tomorrow, we build."

A voice from the back spoke up. Kari, one of our strongest soldiers. "What of the survivors?" She asked. "We've dispatched the Cog officers, but there are still many villagers left within these walls. What of them?"

My heart jumped in my chest. Maybe, just maybe...Nik would be there.

"We'll give them a choice." I said finally. "They can bend the knee, or they can die."

Kari nodded in acknowledgment. I continued. "Come daybreak, Arthur will go around to each home and take note of the remaining individuals. They will need to swear fealty to Clan Alpha Lucien officially when he returns, of course, but we need to let them know the terms now so that they can make their choice. Are there any more questions?"

The crowd was quiet, shuffling back and forth on tired feet.

"Very well. You're dismissed."

The crowd dispersed, and as it did I felt the same weight of longing drape back over me like a blanket. I couldn't escape it. Sooner or later, I would have to face the facts.

The man I'd loved—the man I'd left behind—was gone.

2

NIKOLAS

The acrid scent of smoke filled the air and wove its way into my lungs. You'd think a dragon would be used to a little smoke smell, right?

But this was more than just a little smoke. It smelled like the whole city was burning. And here I was, trapped in a very-flammable house with no way out.

Those damn Paradox bastards.

A sliver of hope rose in my chest as I went around, clattering the shutters against the pollution. The sounds of steel and shouting echoed off the walls. Battle. Someone was fighting. But who? And who was winning?

The thought of finally getting out of here was tempting, but I'd learned five years ago that things rarely work out the way you expect.

The night Darkvale fell was both the best and the worst day of my life.

He was handsome. He was alpha. And he wanted me. In the midst of our passion, fire and terror rained from the sky. I didn't know it then, but it was the final mutiny that would oust Clan Alpha Lucien and bring the city under Paradox control.

I remembered him running outside to see what was going on, dressed in only a robe. He never came back. The chaos and violence tore us away from one another and I screamed myself hoarse trying to find him. No response came.

When the Paradox soldiers—they called themselves Cogs—knocked down my door, I knew it was over.

For the first few days or even weeks in captivity, I remained convinced that my mate would come back to rescue me. Even if he didn't, surely Clan Alpha Lucien would...right? I prayed to the Goddess Glendaria night and day, begging, beseeching, pleading, bargaining. Nothing worked.

Weeks stretched into months stretched into years. They never came. None of them.

Now I was trapped here in this Goddess-damned house that might as well be a prison cell. I had food, clothes, supplies, sure. But the walls were coated with a magical tar-like substance that suppressed my shift and made sure I couldn't escape.

They never physically hurt me, at least not directly. For that I was thankful. But I was no better than an animal to them, a permanent hostage, a plaything.

"Dad?" The small voice caught my ear and I turned from the window.

A four-year-old girl with pigtails looked up at me.

Oh yeah, and there was that. He'd also left me with an unplanned parting gift: a baby.

He never even knew.

I looked at her as if seeing her for the first time, all rosy cheeks and mussed hair and an innocent smile that could light up any day. She wasn't much of a baby anymore, I mused. Far from it. Lyria was four years old, nearly five, and just as spirited as her alpha father. It was a shame she never got a chance to meet him.

"Dad, what's going on?"

I stepped forward and held her close. "Nothing, sweetie. Go to your room and don't make a sound. Can you do that for me?"

She nodded, wide-eyed.

The door shook as a clattering knock echoed through the house. Someone was outside. My heart leapt into my chest.

"Go now," I whispered and she ran off without a word.

I grabbed a kitchen knife from the counter and crept toward the door, holding my breath. Not like a puny kitchen knife would do much against a dragon, but I had to try.

An image flashed through my mind as I clasped the doorknob. It was ridiculous, but I almost expected to see my lost mate on the other side, smiling wide as ever.

But it wasn't.

Of course it wasn't.

I opened the door to a man in uniform, bearing the red and gold sigil of the Firefangs. My blood ran cold at the sight. My Goddess, they'd finally done it.

"Arthur Linn here to take a census. The Firefangs have occupied Darkvale and routed the Paradox traitors. Pledge your fealty to Clan Alpha Lucien and no harm shall come to you. Refuse, and meet the dragon's justice." The officer read off of a scroll then snapped his gaze to mine. There was a flicker of recognition, or perhaps confusion. Only a moment, though.

A wave of emotion flowed through me like a storm. It was Lucien and his late mate Caldo that had helped me gain Marlowe's favor in the first place. And now Lucien was back. That could only mean...

I swallowed, flashing back to the man I'd seen from the peephole in the wall not long ago. Fire and steel and dragons raged outside, and one man in particular led them all. He stormed through the breach like nothing could stop him, bellowing as he cut down Cogs left and right. When I saw it, I thought it was a hallucination. Just my brain wanting to see my long lost mate one more time before I died.

But it was no hallucination.

Peter Marlowe had returned. After all this time, he'd returned.

Who was I to think he'd want anything to do with me? He betrayed me. He left me to raise a child alone in Paradox territory. I couldn't forgive him for that.

And yet, I couldn't ignore the stirring of hope in my heart. A part of myself still longed for him, and I hated myself for it.

"Get lost," I growled at the servant, my lip curling in disgust. The pain of Marlowe's betrayal still coursed through me, clouding my thoughts. "I'll speak to Lucien myself."

Arthur clenched his jaw and made a damning mark on his scroll. "Very well, then. I do hope you will reconsider."

With that he was gone, off to the next house. He launched into the same spiel about fealty, Lucien, and the Firefangs. I sunk down onto a chair and clapped my hands over my ears.

We were free at long last. But I never thought it would feel like this.

3

MARLOWE

I woke with the sun. Strange, feeling the sunlight on my skin once more. After so long hiding underground, everything felt so bright. So colorful.

I threw myself out of the hammock, wobbling a bit as I got to my feet. My muscles screamed with exertion and soreness.

Yesterday, we'd attacked Darkvale.

Yesterday, we'd won.

I rubbed the sleep from my eyes and hastily dressed, eager to get on with the business of the day. A lump of guilt still lodged itself deep in my heart, but I had more than enough other tasks to focus on. Rebuilding a town was no easy feat, and if what Lucien had told me was correct, we were going to have quite the population influx soon.

There was no time for grief. In Lucien's stead, people looked to me as a leader. It was my job to act the part.

I brushed my dark hair back behind my ears and threw on my officer's uniform. When I exited my quarters my servant Arthur was already there, waiting for me.

Ever vigilant, that one.

"The census, sir." He followed me to the granary, not missing a beat. He waited by my side as I shouldered a bag of rice and carried it to Myrony, who'd already begun assessing the food stores. They'd gathered a few low-hanging fruits from nearby trees and the rice along with a couple choice herbs would make a filling lunch.

I finally turned to my unwanted shadow. "I just woke, Arthur, and my dragon's starving. Can't it wait?"

Arthur's shoulders slumped. "I'm afraid it cannot. I made my rounds with the census, sir. There are a few families on the west end of town who chose not to bend the knee. At least, not yet. Whether they're Paradox sympathizers or simply stubborn mules I cannot say. But we cannot have traitors in our midst. You know what happened last time."

My stomach tightened into a knot. I tasted bile in the back of my throat. Of course I knew what happened last time. Last time, we'd lost our home. And I'd lost Nik.

"What would you have me do, Arthur?" I sighed,

popping a few grapes into my mouth. The juices spread across my tongue, tangy and sweet at once. So much better than the stale rations we'd grown used to.

"I thought you might want to see to them personally."

There it was again. That tiny sliver of hope, flickering like a candle in the depths of my heart. Was Nik still out there?

"Very well," I said. "Give me the register and I'll drop by. But I'm finishing breakfast first."

Arthur nodded in response and handed over the scroll, taking his leave.

I sunk onto a bench. My joints creaked. Goddess, I hadn't had a good fight in so long. Yesterday's battle was exhilarating, to be sure, but I always seemed to forget how sore and tired I was afterward.

I propped up my head with a hand and looked to Myrony, hard at work sorting through the food and leaning over a small fire she'd started for the cooking pot.

"What do you think, My?" I asked by way of conversation.

"About what?" She asked, not taking her eyes off her work.

"All of this." I waved my hand around at the fortress. "We're finally home."

She gave me a small smile. "We are. Feels different, though, doesn't it?"

I frowned. "It does."

"Things aren't going to go back to normal, are they?" She didn't meet my gaze, staring into the cooking fire that flickered before us.

I grimaced, thinking of all the things we'd both lost. "No, they're not."

She straightened, wiping her ashy hands on her apron. "Well, eat up. You'll need your strength."

In more ways than one, I mused, and took a bite.

———

NOW THAT I had a full stomach, I could see to the rest of the day's business. I had to meet with the builders, post guards on the walls, and follow up with Myrony on inventory. Lucien would be returning any day now, and we needed to have things well in motion before that happened. He had a mate to look after. A mate with child. It was up to us to keep things running in his stead.

And apparently, now I had to go scout out some rogue villagers as well.

This day was getting crowded already. I wiped my brow and got to work.

The meeting with the builders went swiftly—I had Tork on hand to provide a little much needed muscle. The damage done to the structure was more than we'd hoped, but the builders assured me they could have it patched up in no time. And with someone like Tork at the helm helping clear the rubble, I didn't doubt it for a second.

The walls stood firm around us, in all but the place where we'd breached them coming in. The dome above held tight, filtering air through but remaining resilient to any fire or magical attacks. Our magitech engineers, in a feat of brilliance since unmatched, built a giant dome to protect Darkvale. At least the Paradox hadn't let that go to waste, I thought grimly.

The hole in the stone wall left us exposed, though. I gathered a few of my soldiers and posted them there on watch while the builders scurried around. First priority was getting the wall patched, then they could set to restoring the buildings. Sleeping quarters, a kitchen, an armory. Our numbers were smaller than they'd ever been, but not for long. The Firefangs would rise anew.

Guards paced the walls in each cardinal direction: north, south, east, and west. If anything, man or dragon, was coming, we'd see it.

I dawdled by speaking with a few of the villagers that had emerged from their homes. Subconsciously, I was still avoiding the rogue settlement Arthur had tasked me with investigating.

But it wasn't just that, a tiny voice reminded me. *You're afraid.*

I winced, swatting the thoughts away.

Alphas don't get afraid.

This one does.

I frowned and balled my hands into fists. I wanted to punch something, anything.

No matter how much I tried to distract my mind, I couldn't avoid the inevitable. Either Nik would be there, or he would not. Somehow, delaying the task made it feel a little more possible in my mind.

Once I visited the rogues, I'd know for sure one way or another. And that was perhaps more terrifying than not knowing at all.

———

FINALLY, I could delay no longer. I grabbed Arthur's register and set out on foot to the west. The houses there surprised me. I hadn't remembered any villagers living here last time I was in Darkvale, but that was five years ago now. The buildings were crude but sturdy, reinforced with black tar that resisted dragon fire. I clenched my jaw.

These weren't just humble huts. They were meant to keep someone in. Or someone out.

A voice clawed through my mind, reaching through ages of forgotten cobwebs and long-lost memories.

I knew that voice. Nik's voice.

The night Darkvale fell, I failed more than just my Clan Alpha. I failed my mate. Screams and fire ripped through the air and I stepped outside for only a moment. But that moment lasted for the next five years.

I left him, alone and naked. I was forced out of the city, forced into hiding. I thought he was right behind me. I thought maybe someone else had helped him escape and we just got separated in the chaos.

When the flames died down, he was nowhere to be found. And that's when I shut myself off completely.

It wasn't quite the same as Lucien's curse. My heart didn't break that day, no. I simply built a brick wall around it, blocking out any feeling. My days and nights turned to only one thing: war. It was the only thing I knew, only thing I was good at. And somehow, I had this delirious hope that if I could just stay moving, I'd finally forget about him. I'd finally find absolution.

But that was a fool's errand. Now I was back in Darkvale. And Nik was here. I could feel it.

The whispering voice grew stronger as I approached the western settlement. They were more like prisoner cells than houses, I realized with a shiver. Is that what they'd done with him? Trapped him in a sealed house to rot, or worse?

My dragon rose within me, all fury and fire. *I'm sorry,* I sent out into the void. *I'm sorry, I'm so sorry.*

No response came.

The tall stone door of the safe house loomed before me. There were only a few small windows to let light in, but they were shuttered. *Please let this be him,* I whispered in a silent litany to Glendaria as I raised my hand to knock. *Please let him be okay.*

I pounded on the door sharply, three times. I cleared my throat, waiting for a response. None came.

I knocked again. My breath caught in my throat this time and my mouth suddenly went dry. What if he had moved on? What if—Goddess forbid—he had mated another?

"This is Peter Marlowe of Firefang command. Open up at once." I tried to keep my voice firm, commanding. It only cracked once.

A long moment passed. I was about to turn and leave when the door creaked open, and there he was.

Nikolas Lastir, my best friend. My mate. The man I'd left behind.

It was still him, all right. But the years hadn't been kind. His face showed lines of weary grief and toil, eyes deep in their sockets. His blond hair hung down past his eyebrows and he had a sort of haunted expression about him, like he'd been possessed by a ghost. Or maybe he was one.

Nik was here all right. But one look at him solidified my fears. Everything had changed.

4
———

NIKOLAS

I couldn't tell you how many times I'd played out this situation in my mind, hoping that it would come true.

None of those wistful daydreams prepared me for the reality.

I swallowed against the lump in my throat and gritted my teeth against the roaring of blood in my ears. There he was, flesh and blood. My alpha. My mate.

Marlowe.

He looked older, sure, and sported more than a few new battle scars. It was the look on his face that really did me in, though.

His eyes searched mine, looking for a spark of recognition, for some assurance that I was still his.

After five years of silence, did it even matter?

"What do you want?" I said finally, voice low. "What are you doing here?"

Marlowe's face fell. "I came back, Nik." His voice broke. "I told you I would. We defeated the Paradox. We're free."

My dragon roared inside me, ready to pounce. I scowled and cursed before I could censor myself. "Fuck off with that. It's been five years. I haven't heard from you once. Too little, too late."

Marlowe sagged. "I don't know what you want me to do. I didn't mean to leave you. Everything happened so quickly. I did what I had to do."

"And what about us, Mar? What about that?" The words flung like daggers, slicing through the cold silence. "You even closed off your Link." My lip curled and I watched with some perverse enjoyment the look of shock on his face. "Coward."

Marlowe bared his teeth, a growl rumbling from low in his chest. We stood there, facing off, neither of us willing to make a move.

Finally, he shoved a piece of paper at me.

"Just...sign this paper. I'll leave you alone."

In a burst of hot anger, I dropped the paper and slammed the door in his face, shoulders heaving. A burst of fire rushed through every vein, every pore, and I roared in pain.

Lyria chose this moment to emerge from her room, eyes wide and watery at her omega father's predicament.

"Daddy!" She screeched, cowering in the corner.

The sound of my little girl was enough to return me to sanity. I shook from head to toe with anger, resentment, grief, fear.

How *dare* he come back like this? How *dare* he waltz right in and think things would go back to normal? Five years, five long years I spent toiling away by myself, raising a child, living like a trapped animal under the Paradox regime. And he did nothing. Nothing!

That's when the sobs began.

Lyria ran forward and threw her arms around me, anchoring me back into reality. "Daddy, what's wrong?"

I held her close, breathing in the scent of her hair, feeling the warmth of her skin. How could I even begin to explain?

"I'm sorry, sweetheart," I whispered and rubbed her back. "I'm sorry. Everything's all right."

"Who was that man?" She asked and felt me tense beneath her. I let out a breath. My eyes stared off into space.

I didn't respond. Couldn't. She didn't press, thank

Glendaria for that. We sat there together, holding one another and crying for all the things we'd lost.

It wasn't fair, my mind screeched at me. She didn't deserve this. She needed a happy, normal childhood. But after five years in captivity, what did normal even mean anymore?

And Marlowe...Goddess, Marlowe. He didn't even know he had a daughter. I wasn't even sure I wanted him to know now. My mind fought in all directions, the mate connection clashing with the hurt and betrayal in my heart.

Did he forget about me? Did he never even care?

Whatever the reason, I had this little one to take care of. I sniffed away my tears and held Lyria tight. She was my beacon of hope in this war-torn world, and no one, not even Marlowe, would take that away from me.

5

MARLOWE

I needed to fly.

Wings sprouted from my back and I leapt into the air, my strong back legs kicking off the ground. I couldn't go too high while the dome was in place, but I needed that space. Needed some air to breathe.

Raw emotion still flooded through me, searing at my hardened heart.

Coward.

The word burned itself into my chest like a brand, and I couldn't fly fast enough to escape it.

After five long years, I found him. I found my mate. He was alive, but his face had long lost the innocent gleam it once had. They had trapped him here like some kind of animal.

And I did nothing.

Just like the first time he confessed his feelings for me. I didn't know how to handle it then, and I sure didn't know how to handle it now. Last time, I ended up challenging him to a duel as a way to sort things out.

A very *sexy* duel, as it turned out.

A small grin broke out over my face as I remembered that moment. We went into it facing off like warriors, but our dragons wanted more than just a good fight. We fucked right then and there, sweat and muscle and panting breaths as we struggled for control, for dominance. It was the hottest sex I'd ever had.

Today I'd made the same mistake. By shoving away my feelings I'd hurt the person that meant most to me. He made me smile on my bad days, he brought light to my otherwise mundane life. At least, he did.

Now? I wasn't sure of anything anymore.

If today was any indication, he didn't want anything to do with me. That was fair. I was the one that left him trapped and alone. I could have tried to reach out to him. I could have done something to help. But could I have done it without compromising the clan's security?

Too late now.

I flapped my wings harder, ascending up to the level of the dome. Looking down on Darkvale made me feel a little better. Pride and patriotism covered the hurt for the briefest moment. The same walls and buildings I grew up in still stood. Men and women moved about the keep with purpose, each with a task to do. The builders gathered stone and mortar to repair the wall, Myrony and a group of helpers gathered food and supplies, and guardsmen paced the walls with sharp eyes, looking for any sign of movement.

This was my family. This was my home. All those years of hiding, of war, of fighting. This was what we fought for. We were home once more.

I settled on the ground next to the officer's quarters, shifting back into human form before entering. The men startled as I stepped in, looking up from a map spread out over a table.

"Commander Marlowe," Bryn stood and saluted. The other men did the same. All pesky formality, really.

"We've received reports of Sorcerers nearby, and I don't like the look of it."

I froze, panic twisting in my gut. Sorcerers. The very same that had captured Lucien's mate?

"What are they doing so close to our territory?" I asked, peering at the map they had laid out.

A small red x marked the spot, a valley not three miles from here shielded on all sides by cliffs. Also a perfect place to ambush them, should we wish to.

"Send out a few scouts for reconnaissance. I want to

know why they're there and what they're planning. Do not engage, unless in self defense. We need to keep on our guard."

"Very well." Bryn nodded.

"Any other news from the field?" I asked, pacing around to my seat at the head of the table. I clasped my hands together and rested my chin on them. I had no taste for war-room meetings right now. Not after being snubbed by Nik. But I tried to keep my voice interested, or at least formal. They depended on me.

"None," my officer Rayn added. "With your permission, we'd like to send an engineer over to the west end and remove the enchantments trapping the villagers there. You have confirmed their loyalty?" He looked at me with a question in his eyes.

My stomach seized into a knot again and I squeezed my eyes shut for a moment. Loyalty? Not quite, but treason? I didn't think Nik was capable of that either. If he didn't want to deal with me, fine. But he still owed himself to Lucien and the clan. "Yes," I said after a long breath. "Release them, thank you."

Rayn gestured to3 our chief engineer. "It will be done, sir." He stood and left.

"If that's everything?" I asked hopefully, rising from the chair. I needed to be alone right now.

"It is."

"You're dismissed." I waved a hand and they dispersed, muttering among themselves. I tried not to think about the looks of concern on their faces.

After the officer's meeting I wandered around Darkvale for a bit longer, checking in on the status of the builders, the gatherers, the hunters. When I could find no further diversions, I returned to my quarters and sunk into my hammock, staring up at the afternoon sky.

Clouds floated by in wisps of white, casting long shadows on the walls and people within them. The dome covering Darkvale refracted the light and shone rays of color down onto the ground, shimmering in the daytime sun.

All was going swimmingly. All except the matter of Nikolas, that was.

My stomach gurgled loudly. Myrony would start in on dinner soon, and perhaps if I went to help I could sneak a few bites before the bell. I knew that once dinner came, however, I'd have to face the villagers once again. I'd have to face him.

Of course they'd bring all the clansmen together for food. Why wouldn't they? We were family, after all. Firefangs were family. Not by blood, no, but by choice.

And our family was about to get bigger. Over two dozen villagers had stayed behind after we took Darkvale from the Cogs and pledged themselves to Clan Alpha Lucien. We'd have a proper ceremony once he returned, of course, but tonight we'd break bread with them for the first time.

I thought again about the engineers on their way to release the enchanted holding houses. Nik was in one of them, and that meant he would be at dinner too.

How long had they kept him in there? I furrowed my brow. I didn't want to know. The more I thought about him, the guiltier I felt. But I wasn't going anywhere, and nor was he. We'd have to get used to it, somehow.

I could move on. I'd have to. Nik sure had.

With that intention firmly in mind, I headed toward Myrony's kitchen. There were a few choice morsels with my name on them.

———

TIME PASSED QUICKER than I would have liked. Myrony kept me busy chopping veggies, lugging bags of grain, stirring the large pot while she tittered about the kitchen.

All too soon, I heard the reverberating clang of the dinner bell.

It was time.

I wiped my hands and emerged from the kitchen, surprised to find the square had been set up with rows of makeshift tables and benches. Flickering Dragonfire lanterns on staffs lined the eating area, and there was already a line forming at Myrony's cook pot.

My gaze swept over the crowd, looking for Nik. He was nowhere to be found. All the better, I grumbled in the back of my mind. Probably good to give him some space, anyway.

I nearly lost my footing when a small girl brushed past me, pigtails flying out behind her. My eyes widened when I caught a familiar scent. Nik's scent. Another scan of the crowd. He wasn't here.

Then a sick and horrible feeling dawned on me. That little girl...she couldn't be *his*, could she?

My feet stayed rooted to the spot, torn between running to Nik's or running back home. Don't worry about it, I tried to reassure myself. Get your dinner and turn in early. It's been a long day.

That it had, but I couldn't keep my eyes off of her. She had a wild, feral light to her eyes and the way she held herself reminded me of Nik. Then again, everything reminded me of Nik.

It wasn't until one of the villagers in the queue stopped her that my heart burst into double time.

"Hey there, sweetheart. Where's your daddy?"

She looked up at the woman with wide eyes. Kari wore soldier's garb and a sword strapped to her side, but she gazed upon the child kindly, like a mother might.

"He's not coming," the girl mumbled, staring at her feet.

"Why not?" Kari asked. "Is he sick?"

"No," she responded.

Kari put her hands on her hips and looked around the crowd. Finally she took the girls hand and led her toward the food. "Here, let's get you some food. Then we'll find your parents. Okay?"

She nodded silently.

"What's your name, dear?" Kari asked, handing her a plate and spoon.

"Lyria."

I couldn't help but watch. Couldn't help but hear. And then she said those damning words.

"And what's your daddy's name? Does he know you're here?"

"Nik said he wasn't hungry."

The words froze my blood cold. Nik. Oh Goddess, she *was* his! A flare of emotion surged through me and I nearly shifted on the spot, fire flashing through my pores in hot, raging anger.

Good job, Nik! Nice of you to tell me!

I ground my teeth, drawing in a shaky breath through my nose. Sparks burned on my tongue and I tasted ash.

Nik had made no mention of her when I came calling. I hadn't seen her, hadn't known she existed. I didn't even know if she was mine.

The thought made my head spin even more, and I sunk down onto one of the nearby benches. Nikolas had a child. And he didn't even tell me. I thought he was dead, for Goddess's sake! And now this?

One thing was for certain as the bustle of people crushed around me. I wasn't hungry anymore.

When the engineers came to remove the enchantments on the house, I thought it would feel different than it did. Like I would feel some sense of freedom, some sense of relief.

None came.

Even as the door opened freely in my hand and the world stretched out beyond, I couldn't bring myself to cross the threshold. Call it whatever you like, but I couldn't shake the feeling that the people out there weren't my friends.

They were my betrayers.

And I wasn't sure I'd survive another confrontation with my mate.

Lyria tugged at my sleeve, begging to go to the square.

She was hungry and tired of the rations the Paradox gave us. That much I knew.

So when the dinner bell rang, she took off like a bolt. Out of my grasp and out of the house.

I watched with terror as she fled, pigtails flying out behind her in the wind.

She looked so happy.

She could finally live freely.

The thought shook me out of my stupor and I flew out the door after her. Lyria was only four years old, soon to be five, and war-torn Darkvale was no place for an unattended child.

She had quite the head start though, and disappeared behind the buildings before I knew what had hit me.

Alarm bells screeched in my mind; how could I have let her get so far away from me? Who knew what would happen to her out there? Sure, it wasn't as if she'd gotten lost outside the city walls, but rubble was everywhere and construction was in full swing. No telling what she'd get into.

I fled up the hill toward the square, all fear and guilt forgotten. She was my daughter. My charge. And if I couldn't put my feelings aside and put her first, then what kind of parent was I?

I crested the hill, panting. Quite the crowd had

gathered in the square for the first Firefang dinner since the reclamation of Darkvale. I'd been invited, of course, but was too wrapped up in my own misery to care. I'd been so blind my own child wandered away from me.

My eyes scanned the crowd for blond pigtails. No sign of them. Then again, the Firefangs were known for their height and Lyria was just a child. She'd be swallowed up by any throng.

Silently cursing myself, I took a breath and ran down the hill toward the square. Surely someone had seen her. They could point me in the right direction.

Please, I whispered to Glendaria. *Let her be okay*.

The Firefangs were feasting, laughing, and drinking when I staggered onto the scene, sweaty hair stuck to my face. Someone had taken up a lute and begun to play, and a circle of men watched with enraptured glances. They clapped, stomped their feet, raised their mugs to the sky.

Still no sign of her.

"Lyria!" I called, my voice hoarse.

The sound mixed with the laughter and singing of the clansmen, lost to the breeze. I stumbled through the crowd, jostling plates of food and drink as I went.

"Lyria!" I called again, looking around frantically.

"Daddy?" I heard the little voice call and whipped my head around.

There she was, running toward me with outstretched arms. "Daddy!"

I took her into my arms, holding her close at eye level. "Thank the Goddess you're all right. Don't you ever do that again!" My voice shook as relief and the pent up fear spilled out of me.

Her lip quivered.

I sighed. "I'm so sorry, sweetheart." I held her to my chest and she wrapped her arms around me, smearing a snotty nose on my sleeve as she went.

Footsteps kicked up dust on the path. Well-worn combat boots walked toward me. I didn't have to look up to see who they belonged to.

"So this little munchkin's yours." It wasn't a question.

I straightened, still holding Lyria close.

"Yes, she is. Don't you remember what happened that night?"

Marlowe's face blanched. "She's..."

"Yours, yeah. But I'll be damned if you think you're gonna bring all your war and battle with you. She's just a kid. She needs a safe environment to grow up in."

"She needs her other father," Marlowe demanded, taking a step closer.

Lyria blinked up at me, concerned. I soothed her and petted her hair, still holding her to me as if I was afraid she'd fly away.

"This isn't the time or place." I said through gritted teeth. My eyes flitted to the still-largely-oblivious crowd, but if this kept up we'd be the center of attention in no time.

Marlowe crossed his arms and stood straighter, puffing out his chest. The full weight of his alpha pheromones wafted over me, heightening my senses and rousing the dragon within. Ever since he'd presented as alpha when we were children, it was his favorite dirty trick. He knew I couldn't resist him on a primal level. "Let's make it the time and place, then. I'll grab a plate of food for us, we'll go back to my quarters. Talk things out. Deal?"

I swallowed, looking from Lyria to Marlowe and back. Grief and apprehension still gripped me with equal measure, but I wanted to believe that things could be different. For Lyria's sake.

Marlowe was right about one thing, at least: the girl deserved to know her alpha father.

"Okay," I let out a breath. "Fine. Lead the way."

———

THE QUARTERS that Marlowe had taken up after returning to Darkvale were much nicer than mine. I guess that came as no surprise—he was alpha, and a commander. What was I but a puny omega left behind?

Well, nicer wasn't quite the word. More central, maybe. Oh, and not magically reinforced to suppress my shift or prevent my escape. There was that.

The red and gold banners of the Firefangs hung from the walls and a small hammock hung precariously in a corner.

"You sleep in a hammock?" I asked with a grin. Always seemed uncomfortable to me.

Marlowe shrugged as he placed the food down on the small table. "It's what I got used to out in the field. Can't really sleep in a proper bed anymore."

I huffed in amusement. He was still stubborn as ever.

"Now sit, eat. Let's talk."

Lyria gave me a wary glance and I squeezed her hand, nodding. We sat across the table from my former mate. The father of my child.

In the moment, though, my stomach growled painfully. I'd been so busy hurting that I hadn't noticed my hunger. Now that I saw the food in front of us, my mouth watered at the sight.

A big bowl of broth, two small loaves of bread, three

apples, a bunch of grapes, and a skinned fish lay on the platter, along with a few cherry tomatoes.

My daughter gazed at the food, then at me, as if looking for permission. "Go on, dig in," I urged her. "You're the hungry one."

She picked at a few of the grapes, eyes alight as they exploded on her tongue. She grabbed more, and then moved onto the bread, shoving it into her mouth as fast as she could.

"Careful now," Marlowe chuckled, watching her. "Don't make yourself sick."

"She's not had real food for quite some time," I glared across the table, my eyes hard. "Let her enjoy herself this once."

"All the more reason to be careful."

I held my gaze.

Marlowe clamped his lips shut and focused on his broth.

We ate in near total silence. Only the call of a bird overhead and the rumbling of the crowd carried over in the wind. That, and the sounds of silverware, plates, and food.

When the platter was empty and my glass drained I leveled my gaze at Marlowe again. Now that the initial shock had passed, I could see him a bit more clearly. He looked different, yes, but not terribly so. He was still handsome. There was no denying that.

His face had grown hard over the years. Harder even than before, and I hadn't known that was possible. I supposed that was one of the reasons I fell for him, though. I'd known him since we were kids, and I was one of the only people that knew him well enough to see beyond that brash exterior.

Underneath it all had been a caring, passionate, and dedicated mate. I wondered if that man was still in there.

Marlowe caught me looking and his face quirked up in a smile.

"Lyria," I said, placing my hand over hers. Her face showed nothing but confusion for a few moments before the pieces fit together. Lyria's mouth hung open, a bread crumb still dangling there.

"This is Marlowe. He and I go way back, don't we?" I eyed him meaningfully.

"Hey there," Marlowe grinned at Lyria. "I knew your dad way back when. I'm sorry I never got to meet you when..."

"What he means to say," I interrupted, squeezing Lyria's hand. "Is that he was gone for a very long time, but he's back now. He wants to be part of our family again."

Lyria sipped at her drink silently, eyes flitting from Marlowe to me. I wondered how much of this she understood. It was a complex topic for anyone to wrap their head around, much less a four-year-old.

My chest tightened as I waited for her reaction.

"Can I have more grapes?" she asked, ignoring the topic entirely.

Marlowe and I looked at one another and snorted with laughter. A grin broke across his face just as it did across mine. In that moment, I almost remembered the way things used to be. Why I'd fallen in love with him in the first place.

"What?" Lyria whined, looking up at me.

I took her hand. "Let's go get you your grapes, sweetheart."

She brightened at that, and I led her back out into the gathering.

———

A PILE OF FRUIT LATER, Lyria was looking sated and rather sleepy. She yawned and tugged on my shirt, pointing toward the west. Toward home.

"Looks like it's just about bedtime," Marlowe noted. "I'd be happy to walk you back home, or she can take a nap in the hammock if she wants..." he trailed off, as if thinking better of it.

"Thank you, but we really should get going. Come on, Lyria."

I looked over to her. She slumped over the table with her mouth open slightly, breaths coming in a slow, easy rhythm.

Marlowe grabbed my hand suddenly. The electric sparkles of chemistry I'd long since forgotten crackled across my skin just as powerfully as they had our first night together. I snapped my gaze up to his, where his dragon irises burned bright.

"Stay," he urged me. "A little longer. Please."

I froze, considering the options. I had no intention of going down this path with him again. At least, my rational mind didn't. It knew how badly I'd been hurt last time, and wanted to keep me from feeling that ever again.

My heart and my dragon, however, had other ideas.

I opened my mouth, then shut it, grasping for the words.

"We've got a lot of catching up to do." Marlowe ran a hand through his hair and stared at the ground. "I'm..." he gulped visibly. "I'm sorry, Nik. I am. I spent the last five years wishing I could change the past, but I can't, and it's killing me."

"You had no idea what it was like," I started, my voice a broken whisper. "Raising a daughter alone...being treated like a slave..."

He squeezed my hand. "Then tell me. I have all night. Here, let's help Lyria into bed."

As gently as possible, we helped Lyria to the hammock, who cradled herself into it easily. She woke and mumbled a bit, but I gave her a soothing smile and brushed the hair from her face. Poor thing was exhausted. Lyria yawned and fell back into an easy, peaceful sleep.

"She's beautiful," Marlowe said, not looking away from the hammock. "If I had only known..."

I gave him a grim smile, placing a hand on his shoulder. "There are things that both of us could have done better."

Marlowe covered my hand with his own, squeezing and rubbing the stubble of his cheek against me. "We were at war. Every day, hardly sleeping, never knowing if the next day would be my last..." His eyes widened and he grimaced. "Never knowing what happened to you."

"I'm glad you came back to me," I whispered before I could stop myself. I leaned my head against his chest and listened to the steady thump thump thump of his heart there. This was the Marlowe I remembered.

Marlowe ran a hand through my long blond hair and

kissed the top of my head, holding me close. "I told you I would. I'll always come back for you, Nikolas. And I'm just sorry it took me so long."

We stayed like that for what seemed like ages, and the cobwebs of time fell away piece by piece. The road back to being mates wasn't an easy one, and I didn't pretend that it would be. But we'd taken the first step, and that meant everything to me.

7

MARLOWE

We spent the night talking, sipping the wine I'd found in the cellar, talking and reminiscing about times past. It was a weird sort of duality.

One the one hand, here was this man, this mate that I had known my whole life. Who meant everything to me and who knew me better than anyone. Or at least, had at one time.

But there was a novelty to it all. The way my skin tingled when we touched, the way my heart leapt when he smiled at me, it was like first date jitters all over again.

Things were different now. That much was for sure. But now I had something worth fighting for.

Our little girl snored in the hammock and rolled over sleepily, mouth hanging open. The surge of pride and longing that washed over me was startling. My child. My daughter. My baby.

Ours.

I couldn't imagine what it must have been like for Nikolas to raise her alone, not knowing if I'd ever return. Not to mention the living conditions they'd forced him into. Living essentially behind bars for years on end, never able to shift or join the outside world? My dragon rumbled with rage at the unfairness of it all. I wanted someone's head for this. I wanted blood.

But we'd already defeated the main Paradox forces. We were safe now. We were home.

That didn't stop the righteous anger from burning me inside out. I didn't know how yet, but I was going to make this up to him. I had to make up for all those years I couldn't be around. I needed to be the mate, the alpha, and the father my family needed. Now more than ever.

The moon had reached its zenith when a knock came at the door. I glanced at Nik over the wine glasses and put the goblet down carefully, listening.

The knock came again.

A cold shiver passed through me from head to foot as I stood and stared at the door.

Someone was out there, and I wasn't expecting any visitors.

"Who goes there?" I called, trying to keep my voice low. I didn't want to scare Lyria.

"Urgent message from the scouts, sir. You're needed at the council hall immediately."

I blew out a breath through my nose and pale tendrils of smoke rose toward the ceiling.

I looked back to Nik, who wore an expression of weary resignation. "Go on," he waved me off. "Do your thing."

I stepped forward and placed a hand on his shoulder. "I'll come back. I will. That's a promise." I bent down and pecked a kiss on his forehead, then grabbed my cloak and rushed out the door.

This time, I wouldn't leave him stranded.

I followed the runner to the council hall where all the officers had already gathered. Guess I had a habit of running late.

"What's all this about?" I said, yawning and stretching. "Have you any idea what time it is?"

"We do," Rayn said. "That's why we called you here."

Two men marched into the clan hall, dragging a tall gangly man by the shoulders. His arms were in shackles, a black mask obscuring his mouth.

"We found the Sorcerer," Eron said, pushing the man to his knees. "We caught him skulking about outside. He knows something, I'm sure of it."

I smelled the ashy crackle of dragon fire and held out a hand to stop it. "He's more use to us alive." I paced around the man, noting his long tattered robes, his gaunt face, the way his eyes darted to and fro. Sorcerers were known to nullify the powers of dragon shifters, but with the proper precautions their talents could be subdued.

The mask covered his mouth so he could not form incantations, and the shackles were laced with a subtle poison that disrupted their magical auras. How they'd gotten hold of such a poison was beyond me; they must have found it when ransacking the Paradox's stores.

There was a reason that the Sorcerers were so dangerous. The poison and the ritual to imbue it was a dark, forbidden magic.

Just what had the Cogs been into here?

"Let him speak, but keep the shackles on 'im." I commanded, and Eron ripped the mask away. The Sorcerer gasped in a clean breath, still struggling against his restraints. He bared his ugly teeth at me, railing against his captors. They held firm. He wasn't going anywhere.

"Tell me your name, Sorcerer." I folded my hands, staring over them at the man in front of me. A tiny disruption vibrated through the air, but it wasn't enough to dull my powers. I could roast him right here if I had to.

The man stared at the ground, refusing to meet my gaze.

"You'll make it easier on yourself if you cooperate," I said evenly.

Seconds passed. The only sounds were the Sorcerer's labored breathing.

"Elias," he said finally.

"And is that your real name?" I cocked an eyebrow.

"Yes." He still didn't look at me.

I paced around to his side, admiring the handiwork of the shackles that kept him subdued. They shimmered with a sickly green light. Better him than me.

"Now tell me, Elias. What were you doing in my clan's territory? Were you hired by someone, or did you happen upon our land by coincidence?"

"Why would I tell you?" Long tendrils of shaggy hair hung down over his forehead. The strained years of seclusion had not done the ailing Sorcerer race any favors.

"We can help each other, I believe. You tell me what you've seen on your travels, and in return, I offer you the comfort of my home. You shall share our hearth in return for your loyalty. But be assured, Elias, betray that trust and you will burn in fires the like of which you've never imagined."

Elias raised his chin at long last, meeting my eyes. His gaze was a startling blue, clear and almost crystalline.

"We can work out a relationship that benefits the both of us. I am sure of it." I clipped off the last several words and sunk into a chair, staring at him at eye level.

He held my gaze, unflinching. Here was a man who knew how to hold his own. "You'd never believe me if I told you," Elias growled.

"Oh really? Try me, boy. I've seen rather a lot of unbelievable things recently." My lips turned up in an intimidating grin.

Elias snarled and a momentary disruption floated through the air again. He yanked at his bonds, teeth flashing in the light.

"Replace the mask," I said, waving him away. "Hold him until he's ready to talk."

The two officers wrestled the mask back over his face, the Sorcerer's eyes wide with alarm.

"I've got all the time in the world, Elias. But you don't." I gave him a last cold-hearted glare and turned my back to him. "Take him away."

Screams. Shouts. Then a thump, and the sound of a body dragging across the floor.

The door closed behind me and I sighed, rubbing my temples. I had no time for this. I needed to be with Nik.

But I needed to be here for my clan as well. Last time I'd made the wrong choice. Would I make it again?

I looked to the other clan members gathered in the hall. "I want double the guard presence, and if we so much as smell a Sorcerer nearby, you come to me first, understand?"

The men nodded.

"And what of Elias?"

"He will talk soon enough. Their kind are a selfish people. All we need to do is show him we're better than the other option. Do keep an eye on him, though. I don't want any...mishaps." I shivered to think what havoc a rogue Sorcerer could wreak on our recovering clan.

"As you wish, Commander."

"Any news on the Paradox? I'm not naive enough to think we've wiped them out for good."

"No sign of them as of yet, but perhaps the Sorcerer knows something. We'll keep an eye on him."

My mouth twisted into a scowl. The Sorcerers had a bloody reputation. Kidnapping the Clan Alpha's mate, pulling him away from battle at the eleventh hour...even if we could get Elias on our side, a Sorcerer was never to be trusted.

8

NIKOLAS

Reintegrating into clan life was going to be a challenge. Thank the Goddess I had my little Lyria to keep me on my toes.

In the past few days, the Firefangs had returned to claim Darkvale, Lucien had arrived with half a human village in tow, and the remaining residences were way, way too crowded.

No doubt about it—things were gonna be different around here.

I waited in Marlowe's hideout, sipping at his wine and thinking about the future. The moon rose and fell in the sky. The wine disappeared. Lyria sniffed and shifted in the hammock, but never woke completely. Poor thing, she was exhausted.

Sleep began to tug at my eyelids as well. I blinked and

shook my head, willing myself awake. I didn't want to leave. Not yet. Marlowe said he'd come back.

And I desperately wanted to believe him.

I knew he had duties as commander. I knew that our peace was still fragile. But it hurt, seeing him go like that. Would this one night of connection be all I got this time?

I stewed in my thoughts as my stomach clenched and unclenched. I never should have let my guard down. Not even for her.

My eyelids drooped again, and darkness fell over me like a blanket.

Movement behind me jolted me awake. My heart squeezed in fear, jumping into double-time. I whirled around.

Oh. It was him.

He was back.

"Marlowe," I mumbled, my voice hoarse from sleep. "What time is it?"

"Late," he answered. "Didn't know you'd still be here. How's Lyria?" Marlowe stepped over to the hammock and eyed the sleeping girl. His face softened, the lines of stress fading away. "She's a gem, isn't she?" His voice was soft, almost a whisper.

Pride lit up my face. "She is." He couldn't change the

subject completely, though. "What was all that about?" My heart still thrummed in my rib cage, the familiar tendrils of panic clawing their way through my gut. After five years in captivity, I wasn't sure I knew what safety felt like anymore.

"You sure she won't wake?" Marlowe asked, tilting a head at the hammock.

I moved to stand beside my mate. He smelled delicious, even with the undercurrent of fear vibrating through the air. I looked up at him and placed a hand on his shoulder. "She sleeps like a rock. Come on, sit down. You can talk to me."

We faced off, Marlowe's stoic expression waging war against my concerned one. Eventually, I won out. He let out a breath and stepped around me, sinking onto the bench at the table. "Wine's gone," he noted, looking at the bottle. "Someone's been busy." Marlowe let out a little laugh, raising an eyebrow at me.

"I was thirsty," I retorted with my hands on my hips. That, and I didn't know how else to deal with the sudden emotion flooding my body and soul.

After all these years, Marlowe was back. And he wanted to be there for our daughter.

But could it be that easy?

My head still swum with the alcohol, but I was clear-headed enough to take a seat and level my gaze at him.

"We're still at war, aren't we." It wasn't a question. The words rang out with all the finality of a death knell. For people like Marlowe, the fight was never over.

Marlowe chewed his lip for a moment in thought, then gave a curt nod. He leaned forward to wrap his arms around me. His breath was warm on my neck, tickling the skin there into gooseflesh. His scent drove my dragon wild, pushing against my skin, desperate to be one with him as we had in the past.

He was so close.

"Perhaps there are things more important than war," Marlowe rumbled into my ear. A shiver vibrated down my spine all the way to my cock, which grew with each passing second. "Like family."

The word echoed through the small room, filling me with a hope I hadn't had in five long years. *Family*.

"You mean it?" I asked, turning my head to match his gaze. His fiery pupils dilated and held me rapt.

"You know I do," he replied. "Your dragon knows, deep down. But will you believe it?"

I shivered again, even though there was no draft. The feeling went all the way down to my soul, to the depths of my dragon I'd kept at bay for so long. In its place roared a fire I'd all but forgotten. A fire for him.

"Let me prove myself to you." Marlowe's lips caressed the tender skin at my ear, moving down to my neck right where the omega pheromones were strongest. He took in a large whiff, groaning almost in pain. "I've missed that so much."

Before I could stop myself, I said, "I missed you."

"Let us fly again as we once did." Marlowe squeezed my hands in his own, taunting my dragon further. "Let us take to the skies, just the two of us."

Visions of cool, fresh air, stars, and clouds flashed through my mind. The feeling of pushing off the ground, of gliding on the air currents, of flapping my wings and finally getting to stretch—

"I can't." I drew away, shaking my head. "I've got a kid to look after now."

"And I bet you've never taken her to the skies either." Marlowe's voice took on a note of concern. "Our kind aren't meant to stay here on the ground. Suppressing your true nature like that...it's not healthy."

I recoiled. Now he was trying to tell me how to raise my kid? The thought stung.

"So you're the parenting expert now?" The bitterness of my words poisoned the lust I'd felt only moments before. "They *poisoned* me, Mar! They cursed that damn house so I couldn't shift! I couldn't get out, I couldn't use my powers, I couldn't escape..."

Marlowe's face crumpled. "Let me help you," he said at last, reaching out a hand.

"I don't need your help," I snapped with more venom in my voice than I intended. "We survived without your help for five years, Mar. Five long, hard years under Paradox control. Do you have any idea what that was like for me? For her?"

Marlowe's face crumpled. "No, but—"

"Daddy?" Lyria's tired voice snapped me out of my rage instantly. We both glanced over at the far side of the room where she'd woke and sat up, staring at both of us.

Shit, I cursed under my breath. *How much of that did she see?*

I swallowed the anger and hurt down deep, the same way I did every day that Marlowe was gone. I plastered on my father face and gave Lyria a smile that didn't quite reach my eyes.

"Hey there, darling. Have a good sleep?"

She blinked and yawned. "Yeah." She paused a moment, her lip wobbling. Then, "Why were you shouting?"

Her eyes were so full, so innocent. Guilt and shame hit me like a one-two punch straight to the heart.

"Lyria," I soothed. "Let's go home, hmm? I'll grab an extra tray of snacks for us. My treat."

She frowned at me with disbelieving eyes. I let out a sigh as the weight sunk deeper in my chest.

I took her small hand and helped her out of the hammock. She was still wobbly from sleep and clung to my pant leg. "Bye," she waved at Marlowe as I led her away.

Some timing, sweetheart, I thought wearily as we stepped out into the rising sun.

9

NIKOLAS

Days passed and I saw no hide nor hair of Marlowe. It was just as well. I could take care of my girl by myself. Always had.

He barely even knew her, or what we'd been through together. A strain of worry squeezed itself through my veins. Did he even know *me* anymore?

I left the house more and more often, venturing out with Lyria to the kitchens or simply to reacquaint myself with the streets that had once been home.

Things hadn't changed so much, in some ways. In others, they were irrevocably different. The stone structures were the same. The buildings and the roads led to the same places. Many of the people I'd known from back in the day. But they were different now.

So we all were.

Marlowe used to tell me that war changed a person. I never really knew what that meant until I saw it on their faces.

People moved with the determined, purposeful gait of one on a mission. They didn't hang back to talk with the neighbors or smile at passing children. Life in exile had forced them into strict regiment and routine. They were all like *him* now.

I grimaced at the bitter taste in my mouth. He'd come back, hadn't he? And they *did* manage to rout the Paradox from our walls.

It didn't matter. The machinations of politics meant nothing to me. The Iron Paradox was gone and the Firefangs ruled once more. That was enough.

It had to be.

I'd begun taking Lyria to interact with the other kids in the village. Thomas was starting a school for both human and dragons alike to learn and grow. It was quite the progressive concept, given that many human villages still loathed and feared dragonkind.

But that was another way that the Clan Alpha's new mate had surprised us all. When Lucien returned with a human mate in tow, I had to admit I was confused. Lucien had loved Caldo fiercely. Anyone could have seen that. But in that night of fire and death, Caldo had met a fate even worse than I had. He lay there, begging for his life, as he bled out onto the sands and they dragged me away.

Death was part of life, but to see it so cruelly taken? It turned my stomach sour. The oncoming morning sickness probably had something to do with it, too, in retrospect.

Lyria was spending the day with another of the shifter girls in the village when I decided to go see my old friend Lucien. He'd helped me once before. He was the one that helped me win Marlowe's heart in the first place. Surely, he'd know what to do.

The Clan Alpha's quarters looked much as I'd remembered them, only there were quite a few more people living there now. Lucien's human mate, Alec, had brought along his family from their village of Steamshire, and until new residences could be completed they were staying in the Alpha's quarters.

I opened the door to see a boy run past, tailed quickly by another boy chasing him. An aging woman sat by the fireplace, the clack-clack-clack of knitting needles a steady rhythm.

Ducking out of the way of their game with a smile, I crossed the threshold. Lucien looked up to see the visitor and grinned widely as he recognized me.

"Nikolas Lastir!" He boomed, clapping me on the back in an aggressive hug/chest-bump combo. "Goddess, it's good to see you. We'd thought you were dead."

I offered him a half-smile. I didn't come here to talk about my captivity. But everyone kept bringing it up.

"Listen, I just want to personally apologize, Nik. Had I known..." Lucien's voice trailed off and his forehead creased in concern.

"I'm fine," I brushed it off, though in my mind I was anything but. "I wanted to talk to you about something."

A spark of mischief glinted in his eye. "Just like old times?"

I had to give him a little smile at that. It seemed like so long ago now that I'd come to seek his counsel. Marlowe and I were nothing but childhood friends back then.

"Something like that," I said and took a seat.

"How's Marlowe, anyway? Is he..." Lucien cleared his throat. "Taking it okay? I haven't spoken to him much since the debriefing."

I gave a rueful chuckle. "That's what I wanted to talk to you about."

Lucien slid a platter of biscuits across the table. Their fluffy golden tops still steamed. "Go on, they're delicious."

I tried to politely decline, but Lucien pushed the plate

closer. "I demand it. You've got to try one. Tell him, Alec. Aren't they heavenly?"

We'd caught him in the middle of a bite and he nodded with a mouth full of food. After a moment he swallowed and added, "It's like a party in your mouth!"

We had a good laugh at that. The children ran and played, the woman clack-clack-clacked, and things were almost normal again.

Almost.

"Fine," I rolled my eyes and reached for the plate. "I'll try one of these magical biscuits. But I won't promise I'll like it." I stuck out my lip in a pout then took a tentative bite.

Flavors exploded on my tongue in an instant. Warm, flaky bread combined with a rich, buttery flavor and something else I couldn't name. I nearly moaned as I popped another bite into my mouth before noticing the snickering faces in front of me.

I cleared my throat and placed it down on the plate, swiping a few crumbs away from my lips. "They are..." I said with a blush, "Quite good. Never had anything like it."

The men erupted into laughter and I couldn't hold mine in any longer.

Lucien threw an arm around Alec's shoulder and gave it a squeeze. "You have Alec's clan to thank for that."

He pointed at the biscuit. "That's a human recipe. Incredible what they can do with food, isn't it?"

"Yeah," I agreed before scarfing down the rest of the biscuit. "I hope there's more where that came from." I grinned at Alec. "Are all your people such good cooks?"

Alec shook his head with an amused grin. "Only some of them."

"Now what's this about, Nik?" Lucien returned his gaze to me, propping his chin on his hands. "Trouble in paradise?"

I groaned and rolled my eyes. It was true, though. "You could say that. I just...I'm not sure what to do now that he's back. We were so close, and that night I thought I lost him forever."

Lucien closed his eyes and nodded. "I remember it well." Alec squeezed his hand. I hadn't been the only one to lose someone they loved that night.

"I thought we were gonna be together forever. Through anything. But he never came back. I couldn't find him, couldn't reach him on the Link. And as Darkvale burned they dragged me away."

Lucien's eyes opened again and he gave me a tired smile. "I offer you only my sincerest condolences. In all our time in the field, I never knew they would stoop that low. We'd been told that the city was cleared of

Firefangs. That there were no survivors. I can admit now that we were wrong."

No survivors. The thought sizzled on my skin like water on a hot pan. Is that why he never returned?

"You were able to overcome the Curse of the Dragonheart, clearly." I shifted in my seat and gestured to Alec. "But it doesn't appear Marlowe was ever afflicted. Why is that?"

The deepest fears in my heart told me that it was because he'd never loved me to begin with, that he could not break a heart he had not given to another. I feared it, with every fiber of my being. But what other reason could there be?

"Marlowe...well, you know how he is. I can assure you that he was quite affected by your disappearance, even though he may not show it."

"He was?" My voice was quiet to my ears.

"Marlowe is a man of action. Of black and white. Of problems and solutions. The problem came up that his mate, his lover, was missing. Instead of wallowing in the pain, he simply forced it away, bottled it up. You wouldn't think it at first glance, but I've been living and fighting with him in close proximity for half a decade. You learn things about one another no one knows. And let me tell you, Nik. It's eating him from the inside out."

I blinked at him, digesting the words.

From the inside out...

"I have a daughter, too." I blurted the words out.

Lucien's eyes widened for only a moment. "A secret baby...that does make things difficult."

"She's his!" My voice rose.

"Let me handle this one." Alec nudged Lucien and considered me. "Alphas can be like bricks sometimes," He offered with a grin. "Marlowe especially. But it sounds like he wants to make things right. He won't come 'round if you're all laggy about it though. Remember, you need to let him think it was all his idea in the first place. Even if it totally wasn't." Alec gave me a wink and Lucien sputtered.

"Hey!"

They cut off into flirtatious teasing as I turned over Alec's words in my mind. He had a point. Perhaps I was letting my grief cloud my judgement.

And after smelling him again for the first time in half a decade, my dragon wanted, no, needed, more.

"Being a parent is tough stuff," Alec agreed, ducking Lucien's playful swats. "I learned that fast. Still learning. Couldn't imagine going it alone like you did. But you know what that tells me?"

"What?"

"That you're strong enough, wise enough, and totally badass enough to win him back. If you run back to his place now, you can catch him before the council meeting...I'm sure no one will notice if he's a bit late." Alec gave me that knowing wink again.

"Hey, I will!" Lucien clamored, but with a good-natured grin.

I glanced out the window at the sun. It was barely midday, and Lyria would be on her playdate for another few hours.

I had an idea.

"Go on, go get him." Alec shooed me from the room. "And remember, the secret to any alpha's heart is food!"

"Thanks," I said to both of them with a chuckle, bowing my head in gratitude.

"It's not totally selfless, you know," Lucien called from behind me. I threw on my cloak and was already halfway to the door. "Tell Marlowe to get that stick out of his ass! I want my friend back too."

I considered that mental image, amused, and rushed off across town.

10

MARLOWE

I f fucking-things-up was an Olympic sport, I'd take home the gold. No question.

Days passed to bleary routine as I threw myself into my duties. I made the rounds, sat in on every boring meeting with the scouts, even helped the schoolmaster Thomas wrangle children. I had motives other than pure altruism, sure. I thought I'd catch another glimpse of Lyria, but she wasn't there.

It kept my hands busy. It kept me moving.

That was what mattered, right?

I hadn't dared return to Nik's place. My dragon had been ready to pounce. The magical energy had reverberated between us, pulled taut like a perfect lute string.

And then I opened my big mouth.

With a dissonant twang, there went the string. There went the connection. Gone.

So deep in my thoughts was I that I barely noticed the knock at the door. It came again before I fully registered.

"Oh, who it it now?" I mumbled and rubbed my forehead. I had mistakenly thought that perhaps I'd get some alone time once we returned to Darkvale. But it seemed like the requests came in even more furiously. There were things to repair, to rebuild, to restore. And somehow that fell to me.

I glanced at the simple clock on the wall, heralding the arrival of midday. That meant there was only an hour till the next meeting, and I'd intended to use that time to relax.

The knock came again.

"What is it?" I growled irritably. "It can wait till the meeting!"

Silence.

Then—"It's me."

I'd know that voice anywhere.

"Nik?" I asked, my voice faint.

"Yeah. Open up."

Why of all times had he chose to visit now? He clearly was upset with me, and yet...

A rumbling of fire coursed through my chest as I heard the words in my mind. A faint echo at first, like a voice reaching through thick mist.

Come on, Mar. I know you're in there.

I froze. I'd closed off any connection I had to my mate and our Link long ago, to keep from hurting further. And yet there it was. He'd reached past those walls, for the briefest of moments. Now there was no doubt in my mind about his sincerity.

I can hear you. Come on.

My mouth hung open as I moved toward the door. I took a deep breath, ran a hand through my hair, and slid the latch.

Nik stood on the other side, hands in his pockets but with a desperate fire in his eyes. One I'd only seen once before, when I'd so foolishly challenged him to a duel.

I'd felt stupid then. But even stupider now.

"C'mere, you idiot." Nikolas stepped over the threshold and threw himself at me, wrapping his arms around my neck in a hug.

I stood motionless, not daring to believe. His heady scent invaded my nose. I groaned and lost myself in the scent, rousing not only my dragon but also my cock.

"I'm sorry," Nik breathed as he captured my lips. "I'm here now."

It didn't take long for my dragon to catch up and I held him closer, pressing his heated skin to mine.

Oh, Goddess. Was he in heat? Was that what this was about?

Nik locked eyes with mine. "Heat would imply I'm looking for just any alpha." He kissed me again, slow and deep. "But I'm not."

"And what are you looking for?" My voice quivered. I wanted to praise whatever had brought about this change of heart, but it was too sudden. Too strange.

"We need to talk," Nik said, pulling at my shirt buttons.

I laughed incredulously. "This doesn't look like talking to me."

"I can multitask." He finished the buttons and pulled my shirt away, leaving my chest on full display for him. My brain was still racing to keep up, still echoing with alarm bells, but the feeling of his hands on my skin muted out those worries.

"I thought you were dead. Hated it. Hated myself. Hated you. And then I had her, and hell, Marlowe, I don't know anything about kids—"

"Looks like you did an okay job. She's beautiful." I rubbed little circles on his back, suddenly desperate for more. Taking my turn, I slid my hands under his shirt and lifted it over his head until we stood there, bare chested and face-to-face.

"I want this to work, Mar." Nik's voice cracked as he stared deep into my eyes. A man could lose himself in those fiery orbs. I certainly had. "Lyria needs a family. Two dads. Love. Learning. Opportunity. And she can't have that if you leave me again."

I winced.

"Promise me, Mar." He nuzzled my neck, moving down to the collarbone and planting a line of kisses there. My head spun, but I was still rational enough to process Nik's words. "Promise me, for her."

I breathed in his scent, roaming my hands down the heated flesh there. Warring emotions battled inside me. I was a commander. A fighter. That was my identity, who I'd always been. I couldn't just give that up. But I couldn't lose Nik again either. I remembered again the reason I fought. I wasn't just some bloodthirsty barbarian. I was a protector. Of myself. My people. My family.

My daughter.

The words spilled out of me. "I love you more than life itself. You should know that. Always have. Always did. I'm...not too good at handling emotional stuff. When we left, when all was lost, I..." I brushed a nervous hand across my hair again. "Goddess, I thought you were gone for good. I tried to get back to you. But it all came down around us and next thing I knew, you were gone, and off we went. I did what I had to do for our clan, but damned if I don't regret that decision every day."

I pulled away to get a good look at his face. His eyes were half-lidded with desire, the other half shining with emotion. The tingling connection ignited between us once more. Our relationship had been a ripped fabric for so many years, but finally we could patch that wound. A single thread of soul-bound magic moved through my heart, my arms, my eyes. It pushed out through my fingertips and crackled wherever we touched like an electric shock. Slowly but surely, this ripped fabric could become whole again.

"I want to be with you." Nikolas squeezed my hands, his eyes all liquid amber. "Not just for her. But for us. We really had something, didn't we?"

I chuckled. "Yeah, we sure did."

"Take two?" Nik mumbled against my lips.

"Take two," I promised, and closed the gap.

———

I GAVE myself over to instinct, trusting my dragon to lead the way. The clock still ticked ominously in the corner, counting down the seconds until my next meeting. Right now, though? It didn't matter. I had my mate, and we were together again.

"How do you feel about a quickie?" I whispered in his ear, grinning.

"Good," Nik breathed. "The sooner the better. But only if there's more to come later."

I rumbled low in my chest. "There will be much more later. That is a promise."

"Now show me what you're made of, alpha." Nik taunted me, holding his arms out wide. "Come and get it."

I charged. Our bodies met in a resounding crash, the air rushing out of us as we came together. I raked my hands everywhere I could reach—his neck, his abs, his back. They traveled down, toward the waistband of his pants.

Yes, there was that magnificent ass.

"Good to see that's one thing that hasn't changed." I gave it a squeeze and produced a high-pitched yelp from my omega in return. That just made me want to do it more.

"Careful," I warned him with a nip at his neck. "You don't wanna release the dragon, do you?"

"Maybe I do," Nik retorted and his hands were at my pants, unfastening.

I could only growl in response.

"There's no bed," Nikolas said breathlessly.

"No," I agreed with a mischievous quirk of my eyebrow. "But there is a hammock."

"Can we—?"

"Only one way to find out."

I took Nik's hand and led him to the hammock, my heart beating a steady tattoo in my chest. After the long years of silence, of cold nights sleeping alone, it was finally happening. I was back. He wanted me. This time I wouldn't let him down.

"Are you sure it will hold?" Nik asked, eyeing the swaying cotton hammock.

"Shh," I pressed a finger over his lips. My breath came in hot pants, and if alphas could have heat I'd be lost right now. He was here, so hot, so ready. My dragon vibrated with pleasure, with recognition, with magic. "Trust me." The words bounced off the walls and back onto us. It was a near repeat of our first mating. Seemed fitting.

Nik opened his mouth to speak, then pressed his lips shut. He leaned backward, settling into the hammock and throwing his hands over his head. He wove his long fingers into the netting holding the cotton to the stand and gripped tight. Nikolas threw his legs over each side of the hammock, spreading them wide to reveal his wet and ready channel. Even from this vantage point and the dim light I could see the glistening slick calling to me. "Come and get me, alpha." He grinned with a raised eyebrow and I was powerless to resist.

Be gentle, I tried to remind myself as I lowered myself onto the sleeping hammock. Up until now it had been purely utilitarian. My years on the road had given me no time or reason to collect furniture, and I'd gotten used to the relaxed slumber that a hammock brought me. But now there was an omega in my bed. A very wet, very needy omega. And if I wasn't careful, I'd bring the whole thing down on top of us.

I hooked a leg over the side and lowered myself onto Nik as the wooden stand squealed. I froze and waited a moment—it held. With another breath I lowered myself all the way down, onto Nik's bare skin as our groins pressed together in a hot, heady dance. My hips thrusted of their own volition, seeking him out. The hammock swung and bounced, adding momentum to my movements.

Nik grasped the ropes above him and bit his lip, staring off into space. "Fuck, I thought you said this was a quickie."

"It is." I grabbed my throbbing cock in my hand and guided it to his channel, relishing the breathy moans as I pressed against the opening. Goddess, he was wet. My mind was nothing but a haze of lust and fire, the dragon within me roaring and begging for control. "You like that?"

"Yes," Nik gasped. "Please."

With a push, I guided myself in. A groan rumbled out of my throat before I could stop myself and I clamped down on Nik's shoulders, my fingers momentarily lengthening into claws. Nik sucked in a breath and I pushed myself deeper to savor that sweet heat.

The hammock squealed and rocked with each motion of my hips, the two of us swaying together in time with each thrust. I pressed myself deeper, all the way to the hilt.

"Goddess," I cursed, leaning forward to plant a few kisses down his collarbone. "I missed this."

"I missed you." Nik whispered.

There was no doubt about that any longer.

I bucked and twisted. My motions became more desperate, more ragged. Breath came in quick gasps as I held onto him for leverage, the squeaking of the hammock stand in the background the only anchor to reality.

After all this time, my dragon had not forgotten the scent of his mate. Nor had I.

The connection between us strengthened and closed, linking our minds and souls in a way that only true mates could. In that moment, the brain fog cleared. The walls I'd so carefully erected crumbled down. And there he was. There he always was. Waiting for me.

I eyed the mating bite I'd placed on Nik's neck so long ago. The scar still showed, a shiny white reminder of the past. What if I could do that a second time? What would happen?

I roared and smashed my hips into Nik's. Sweat and pheromones filled the tent and my omega's sounds of pleasure kept me going. "I'm getting close," Nik wailed, using his feet on the floor to push himself up around me even further. Flames crackled in the back of my throat and the sparks danced on my tongue. Battle, violence, blood—they had nothing on this.

My knot began to swell as I felt my balls tighten. I held my breath, freezing for only a moment. There was no turning back now.

"Take me, Mar." Nik pumped upward furiously. "Take me." His eyes rolled back into his head as his dick jerked and spurted gobs of hot nectar across his chest and mine. The scent rose up and smothered me. I was lost.

The dragon pushed forward and I threw my head back, smoke boiling from my nostrils. With superhuman strength I thrusted madly into him and just as I reached my breaking point, so too did the hammock stand. A resounding crack of splintered wood and the sensation of weightlessness gripped me for only a microsecond before Nik and I tumbled to the ground in a heap.

"Fuck you're heavy!" Nik groaned. He held on for dear life as the roller coaster took us higher, higher, higher, then...

"Goddess, Nik!" The world came undone around us in a million sparkling points of light as I thrashed against him and my knot locked us together, panting, in the wreckage.

11

MARLOWE

The afterglow would have to wait.

A glance at the clock sent my heart into overdrive. I dislodged myself as soon as my knot would let me. "Shit, I'm late!"

"Wha?" Nikolas mumbled sleepily, blinking up at me. He was still sprawled out on the floor with that lazy, sated expression. Couldn't blame him.

"The council meeting," I mumbled as I wiped myself down with an errant towel and threw on my uniform. "We've news from the Sorcerer." I cinched the belt around my waist and pulled on my boots.

"The hell are you doing with a Sorcerer?" Nik's eyes went wide.

"Long story," I muttered. "Little bastard was spying on us."

Nik sat up at that. "I'm coming with you." He rolled to his feet, only a little wobbly.

I threw the cloak around my shoulders and looked back at him. His hair stuck out in all directions, his face was sweaty, and he smelled like sex.

Just wait until the council members get a load of this, I snickered to myself.

"You sure about that?" Waiting for Nik would only slow me down, but the fading soul magic that had bound us together urged me to give him another chance. We couldn't be a true family if I kept sticking to my old habits. I stood my ground and waited.

He pulled on a pair of pants and ran a hand through his hair. Nik's hand on my shoulder steadied my racing heart. "We're mates. No more secrets."

No more secrets. What would that even feel like? I didn't know, and didn't have time to figure out.

"Come on. And hurry." I grabbed his hand as he threw on a jacket and we stumbled out into the city.

———

YOU MIGHT AS WELL CALL BEING LATE my brand, by now. When I entered the chamber with Nik in tow, the officers looked up at me with carefully schooled expressions.

"I do hope we weren't interrupting anything, Commander." Lucien gave me a knowing grin as we entered. I glared daggers at him. The other men didn't dare say a word.

"Not at all," I said in my practiced commander voice. "My mate has some...ideas on how we might subdue the oncoming threat." I squeezed his hand and gave him a warning glance as his eyes widened.

"Very well, then." Tork folded his hands and sat. He gestured at the two seats at the head of the table. "Let's get started."

Nik followed me silently and sat in the strong wooden chair to my right while I took my place at the head.

"What news of the Sorcerer?" I asked, looking around the chamber. "Where is he?"

A moment of silence. Lucien looked to Andreas, our intelligence officer. "He's on his way back as we speak." Andreas said, furrowing his brow. He placed a hand to his temple as if with a headache.

"You sent him into the field without my knowledge?" Sparks burned on my tongue as I turned my ire on Andreas. "What if he betrays us?"

Andreas did not so much as flinch. "He's not alone. We've sent guards along with him and we'll know if anything goes awry. If his information proves true, we'll keep him. If he's lying, he'll die. Simple as that."

I leaned back in my chair and folded my hands, grumbling low in my chest. I didn't like that they were doing things behind my back. What else had I missed out on?

"Anything else you've been loath to tell me?" I asked, trying to keep the venom from my voice.

"Nothing else, Commander." Andreas lowered his gaze.

A knock at the door cut through the tension in the room as we looked to see the visitor.

"Who goes there?" Lucien called out. "This meeting is for Firefang Council members only."

"We've returned with the Sorcerer. He speaks the truth." The voice came muffled through the thick iron-banded door, but audible enough.

"Let him in," Lucien waved a hand, and the guards at the door drew the latch. Two men in Firefang garb led another man in shackles through the door, and not gently either. One of the men I recognized as Kaine Maxwell. He was joined by his cousin Ward. Despite Kaine's age he was as strong and quick as any of our young alphas.

The captive's hands and feet were bound with glowing chains, the ankle shackles only far enough apart to take stumbling steps. No running away for this one.

The man's face was drawn and gaunt with age, but his eyes burned when they recognized me all the same.

"Elias," I said, standing to tower over him.

The Sorcerer sniffed and screwed up his face in disgust, spitting to the side. I grabbed his chin and forced it toward me, boring into him with my burning gaze.

"We meet again. Tell me, what have you found, mighty Sorcerer?" My lips quirked up at the last words. They were powerful, sure, but subdued by our poisoned shackles? They were no more than mortal men.

"There's a camp nearby. I don't like the look of it." Elias jerked away, trying to wrench himself from my grasp. That only yanked on his shackles further and he yelped as the metal bit into his skin. "That's all you're getting from me, though."

"If I may, Commander," Kaine started, digging through his pockets.

I tore my gaze up away from the Sorcerer. "Go on."

"He led us to an abandoned camp not far from here. Whoever was there left not too long ago—the coals were still a bit warm, in fact. The air was thick with magic. His kind of magic." Kaine gripped his captive's shoulder tighter. Elias grimaced.

"And?" I continued. "You mean to say there's more of them? What are they after?"

"We found this," Kaine tossed a string of beads onto the table. They clattered across the smooth wood and skidded to a stop.

"Wait a second." Lucien rose. He brushed a hand over the smooth carved beads and a rare shiver racked him. "I've seen these before. Quite recently, in fact."

The rest of the officers, myself included, turned to face him.

"I remember seeing them when I went with Alec to Steamshire, there was a woman selling them there, she had dozens of them..." His voice trailed off. Lucien's throat worked as he swallowed hard.

"You think the humans are onto us?" Kaine asked. "After your...ahem...exodus? Surely they have not taken such an affront lightly."

Lucien rubbed his chin and sunk back into his chair, still fingering the beads. "I will take them to my mate Alec and see what he has to say. He is much more familiar with the human tribes than I. But if it's true and the humans have found a way to harness magic, we're in a lump of trouble indeed."

"You have anything to say about this?" I rounded on Elias again, the new knowledge pulsing through my blood.

"I've told you everything I know. I found that stupid camp. What more do you want?"

"You'll keep tracking them." I commanded. "You'll go with Kaine here and you'll keep us informed. We can't fight a war on two fronts. Our biggest weapon right now is knowledge."

"And in return?" Elias asked, looking around at the splendor of the council hall. It was one of the few places that had not been destroyed in the battle for Darkvale, and for that I was glad.

"I've told you before. You will be safe within our walls, so long as you heed our word. That's more than you can say out in the wilds."

The Sorcerer's lip curled as if he was about to say something, then he relaxed. "Very well then. You have my word."

"A Sorcerer's word means nothing." I spat back at him. It was a risky game we were playing here, but rebel Sorcerers joining the human cause could mean devastation for our troops. "Fools talk, heroes walk."

I looked to Kaine and his cousin Ward, nodding at them. "Remove his shackles, but be on your guard. One false move..." I made a slicing motion across my neck and made sure Elias saw it.

"Don't make me regret my decision." I stared deep into his sapphire depths, ensuring the message reached all the way down to his soul.

There was a metal clank as the shackles fell away and the two guards led him out of the council hall.

A collective exhale of breath. We all looked at one another silently. "Goddess," Tork starting, rubbing the back of his neck. "We can never get rid of those bastards, can we?"

I placed my hands flat on the table and glanced at each of my men. They looked to me, waiting for direction. For answers. Even Lucien. I snapped my gaze over to my mate Nikolas, who had sat silently next to me the entire time. His eyes didn't have the far away look of someone who was bored or uninterested, though. I could nearly see the gears churning through his mind.

He was on to something.

"There's something else." Nikolas broke the silence. He fished a pen out of his pocket and started scribbling on the map before anyone had a chance to tell him no. He marked big rough X's at intervals around the fortress walls and then an arrow from one of them leading off toward the east.

"You all are outsiders—sort of, anyway. Darkvale's changed. You all know that. For the last five years, I've been here. They kept me cooped up, but I could still listen. I heard many things over those years. Heard plenty of plans, gossip, chatter. Things I wasn't supposed to hear. Not like I could do much with the info if I was locked up, right? Well, I happen to know that they planned for secret entrances and exits to the fortress. They didn't manage to finish all the tunnels, but there's one—" He tapped the map.

"It's no good," Lucien interrupted. "We blew it up during the siege. All that's there now is dust." His voice was a little harder than usual, betraying some hidden emotion I couldn't name.

"Ah," nodded Nik, "But you only got the one." He crossed out the cave-in and drew another line snaking around the perimeter and to the south. "Started out as a ventilation shaft from what I can tell."

"There are ventilation shafts all over the city," I said, furrowing my brow at Nikolas. "What makes this one any different?"

"If you'd let me finish..." Nik flicked his gaze up to mine and flashed me a teasing grin. I shut my mouth.

"This *was* a ventilation shaft, but I kept hearing this weird grinding noise in the middle of the night. Almost like they were trying to bore it out for some other reason." He struck a bold line downward, leading away from the fortress. "I say we go check it out."

Lucien and I exchanged glances. Tork cracked his knuckles. As the demolitions expert, there was nothing he loved more than blowing shit up.

"Shall we?" Tork gestured to the door, clearly ready to jump into the action.

I held up a hand as I scrutinized the map further. I looked up at Nikolas with a new sense of gratitude. As bad as I felt for leaving him behind all those years, he'd been gathering crucial information from the enemy. If there really was another tunnel open, then perhaps we weren't as safe as we thought.

And perhaps we could use it to do a little counter spying of our own.

"Wait till nightfall," I said, tracing the path of Nik's pen across the map. If it went all the way through... where would it lead? What would be waiting for us on the other side?

Only one way to find out.

"Dismissed," I waved to the officers, still staring at the map. "Tork, meet me here at sundown."

"Will do, Commander." He saluted and walked off.

As the rest of the men gathered their things and filed out of the Council Hall, I felt a pair of eyes on me. Nik's eyes.

Now that we were alone once more, a resurgence of desire crackled over my skin and left me hot, wanting. Warring emotions clashed in my mind like soldiers on a battlefield, and I didn't quite know which would win out.

Love.

Lust.

Surprise.

Admiration.

Grief.

My head buzzed with the weight of it all and left me breathless.

Nik put a hand around my waist to steady me. He nuzzled into my neck and took a long breath. I held him there for a few moments, the only feeling that of our chests rising and falling in unison.

"I've got to go," Nik whispered, resting his forehead against mine. "Lyria's playdate is over soon. Said I'd pick her up."

"Ah." The reality of it all came crashing back in on me like a ten foot wave. No matter what happened, I had something to fight for. Not only my mate, but my daughter. She deserved all the world had to offer.

"What are we gonna tell her?" I asked. "I can't very well move in right away."

"We'll take it slow. For her."

"You'll let me know what happens, right?" Nik looked up at me through his long lashes. "I wish I could go with you."

I cupped a hand around the back of Nik's neck and

pulled him closer, planting a kiss on his hairline. "Take care of our girl. I'll be careful, I promise."

I won't leave you again. I projected to him when the words wouldn't come.

I know, he sent back, and we parted ways.

As I watched him leave, there was a feeling not unlike that of the most action-packed battle. It was heady, intoxicating, tingly. But not blind bloodlust, no.

Family.

I picked Lyria up from school just in time. She stood there with hands on her hips, clearly indignant about me being five minutes later than usual.

I took her small hand and we headed back to the house, but my normally bubbly Lyria stayed silent.

"You doing okay?" I asked her over dinner. She stared into her soup without making eye contact. I fought down the fear in my gut. If anyone hurt my girl…

"Lyria," I said again, and she finally looked up.

"You're seeing that man again." She said the words simply, matter-of-factly. Goddess, she was too perceptive for her own good. "The alpha."

I chewed my lip, trying to figure out how to explain this to her. "Yes," I said finally. "He's not so bad, you know."

"He's not my daddy. You're my daddy." She shoveled more soup into her face and broke my gaze again.

I rubbed the back of my neck. This was gonna be harder than I thought. Things were moving forward with Marlowe, but if Lyria wasn't happy...

"I'll always be your daddy, sweetheart." I reached forward to cover her hand with my own. "I'm not going anywhere, you know that. You're my little princess, and you *always* come first. Nothing's gonna change that."

She looked at me through those wide, shining eyes. "Promise?"

I gave her hand a squeeze. "Promise. Now finish your soup so we can get you cleaned up and ready for bed."

We passed the rest of the meal in silence, but the tension in the air still hung thick and heavy.

One step forward, two steps back.

———

AS THE SUN began to wane and cast the city in its warm, sleepy glow, I heard Marlowe's voice in my mind.

How's she doing?

I gave a wry grin I knew he couldn't see and gathered my thoughts. *She's...okay.* I didn't want to worry him right before his expedition.

I would be lying if I said it had been far from my mind all evening. All the whispered snatches of conversation, all the secrets, all the things I'd gathered while in captivity came back to haunt me. What if I was wrong? What if something happened to him?

I squeezed my eyes shut.

What's wrong? You seem...disquieted.

The fact that he could tell just from the mental static on the Link unnerved me, but at the same time, I felt a little more at ease. The Marlowe that left me behind five years ago had been a harsher man. The years had done their toll on him, to be sure, but as he reached out to me I felt true concern. Even in the light of war and doubt, he found a place for me.

And that, more than anything else, brought me hope.

I'm worried about you, I admitted.

An electric jolt flashed through me, like being shocked. *As I am about you. Take care of our girl. I will be fine.*

I hope so. I thought wearily. *I sure hope so.*

Lyria emerged from the bathroom buck-naked with a pile of soap bubbles atop her head like a hat. She grinned from ear to ear and dripped water onto the floor.

Oh, crap. I was supposed to be giving her a bath, and then I'd gotten distracted by Marlowe's psychic call.

"Lyria," I breathed, wondering how she'd gotten into the soap. I couldn't help but laugh though. She was my little girl. My baby. Even though she could be impossible sometimes, she made up for it with sheer adorableness.

"I took a bath, daddy!" She spun in a circle and bubbles went flying. I'd been so distracted worrying about Marlowe I hadn't noticed her sneak off, hadn't heard the splashes of water coming from the bathroom.

I chuckled and took her hand. "Yes you did! Let's go finish up now."

I ushered her back into the bathroom to assess the damage. Luckily, she hadn't made too big of a mess. There were splotches of water all over the floor and a spilled container of soap but nothing I couldn't clean up.

"You did a good job," I assured her, "But next time wait for daddy."

"What's wrong?" She asked sweetly.

I froze. She somehow saw through even my most valiant attempts to stay cool, calm, and collected.

"I'm fine," I said casually, brushing the soap suds off of her head.

She stayed silent while I washed her face and helped her into her clothes, but she still had a knowing look in her eye. It unnerved me and a curl of nausea roiled in my stomach. I burped loudly, tasting dinner.

Must not have sat well with me.

I had a lot on my mind, after all. I was worried about Marlowe. Worried about the tunnel and what they'd find. Worried that my intelligence wasn't correct and I'd be leading them straight into a trap. Having an over-inquisitive child? Well, that was just another addition to the already long list of stressors weighing on me.

When Lyria spoke up again she startled me from my worries. "Some of the other kids have two daddies. I guess it's not that weird." The words came out of nowhere; I had no idea she'd still been thinking about it.

I brushed hair back from her forehead and gave her a kiss. She yawned, eyes drooping.

"Marlowe likes you," I offered. "You should give him a chance."

She looked at me, confused. "Do you like him?"

Ah, the innocent questions of youth.

I turned the question over in my mind. "Yes," I said at length. "I do." A pause. "But you're always gonna be my number one girl, even if our family grows. Daddy loving someone else doesn't take any away from you. Promise."

Lyria grinned and stuck out her arms for a hug. I held her tight, feeling the warm weight of her skin and the pitter-patter of her heart. For her, I would move the world.

"Are you going to see him again?" She asked with her head on my shoulder.

"What do you say he joins us for dinner again sometime? Just the three of us."

"Okay," she agreed sleepily, and relaxed against me.

"Let's get you to bed," I whispered, and carried her to the bedroom. She curled under the covers without complaint and as she looked up at me with tired eyes, she had one more question.

"What did you mean about him being part of our family?"

I had no idea how to respond to that. She was so sweet, so innocent, laying there with a sleepy grin and the covers wrapped around her.

"We'll see," I said evenly, and kissed her good night.

13

MARLOWE

The last rays of sunlight faded over the horizon and threw the city into darkness. The air cooled, leaving with it a gentle breeze that stirred my hair and made my skin prick with gooseflesh. Shadows lengthened. The time was nigh.

Knowing that Nik was there, connected to my mind should I need him, brought me some small measure of comfort. Before when I thought Nik had died, I'd had no one. But I had a purpose much greater than that now.

"At your word, Commander," Tork said, his hot breath billowing into clouds of mist in the still air.

We'd both brought with us all manner of tools and accoutrements to scout out the mysterious tunnel. I knew deep in my heart that if the information was wrong, we'd been in for a whole heap of trouble. But if he was right...it could give us the tactical advantage we so desperately needed. Who knew where such a tunnel could lead?

Retaking Darkvale wasn't enough. We had to hold it.

And with spies and Sorcerers on the loose, not to mention vestiges of the Paradox still operating on the fringes of the world, we needed all the information we could get.

I peered at the map again, thankful for my night vision. Dragons didn't have much trouble seeing in the dark—the Goddess Glendaria had gifted us with sight when my ancestors still lived underground. Still, we were much less likely to be seen under cover of night. Less likely to be followed.

"This way," I whispered and nudged Tork to follow me. We crept along the perimeter, eyes pinned to the ground. Since Darkvale was covered with a protective dome we had ventilation shafts that brought in air from the outside. They were small, too small for anyone to fit through. But if Nik was right, they could have widened one out large enough for passage.

The usual sign of an air shaft was an old iron grate sunk into the ground, usually with grass or flowers growing around it. Lucien embarked on a beautification project some years ago before the city fell, citing that the Firefangs deserved to live in a place they were proud of. Seeing random metal grates all over the city wasn't exactly conducive to feelings of calm and comfort.

When Darkvale was under Paradox control, however, the landscaping had totally fallen by the wayside. One would think that would make the grates easier to find if all the vegetation had wilted and perished.

Quite the opposite. Thorny, brown weeds crawled across the ground, grasping at anything they could find. It was yet another bygone facet of the Darkvale I'd once known. Teams would move on to prep the land for farming and production soon enough, I was sure, but rebuilding a city took time.

We scrambled through the morass as the weeds grew thicker. I pulled out my blade and chopped through the brush, Tork doing the same.

"You sure we're going the right way?" Tork asked. He yanked away a particularly thorny vine that left a red scratch across his cheek.

I glanced at the paper again. Any minute now, we'd be right on top of it. "Sure."

My foot stepped on something hard and I looked down, kicking aside the mess.

A discarded iron grate lay at my feet, the bars twisted and mangled by some unimaginable force. A sick feeling of fear twisted through me. What had they done?

"Well, there's the grate," I said, kicking it toward Tork. He took one look at it and grimaced the same way I did.

"But where's the tunnel?" He asked, scanning the ground with slow steps. "It's like they just tossed the grate away into the weeds—" His ankle twisted as a patch of dirt gave way. "Found something!" Tork yelled and I whirled around.

After yanking his foot free, we inspected the crack in the land. It wasn't the entrance to the tunnel, no, but someone had dug so close to the surface that the top layer had given way under Tork's weight.

"Shoddy work," Tork said, shaking his head. "Poor craftsmanship all round."

He continued muttering as we dug through the brush, looking for the entrance. I kicked an old wooden plank aside. A rough hewn hole in the earth looked back at us. It wasn't very large, no, but big enough for one person to squeeze through. Dust and dirt crumbled from the entrance as I examined it. The hole went down about five feet and then expanded south, as Nik had suggested.

"Over here," I called to Tork and he came over to inspect the tunnel. He crossed his arms and frowned. "I don't like it. Tunnel like this could give in at any moment. You saw how I knocked out the ceiling just by walking a little too heavily."

"We need to find out where it goes. If it goes anywhere, that is. Perhaps they didn't finish it."

"You're not thinking of going down there." Tork raised an eyebrow.

"Unless you want to?" I shot him a teasing grin. Pulling a length of rope from my bag I tied it around my waist and handed an end to him. "I'm going to go check it out. You wait out here and stand watch. If you feel a yank on the rope, that's your cue to get help. Understand?"

Tork clenched his jaw but nodded. "I still don't like it."

"Didn't ask you to," I said and crouched down next to the tunnel's gaping maw. It would be a tight fit. I had a brief thought about sending a scout to explore the tunnel instead. They were smaller and quicker, meaning they could probably escape a cave-in better than I could. But I'd put enough lives on the line already.

I needed to do this myself. For Nik. For Lyria.

"I'm going in." I said, as much to myself as to him. Then I eased myself off the ledge and into the dark tunnel below.

———

IT DIDN'T TAKE LONG for my eyes to adjust. Without even the moon's light, the tunnel was near pitch dark. I could still make out the rough shapes of the wall and floor, though. Whoever had come through here had done, as Tork pointed out, a "shoddy" job. They focused on speed rather than precision, as if in a last effort of desperation. I crept down the path, unreeling the length of rope as I went. I had about one hundred feet of rope on me. I figured if I ran out before coming to the end of the tunnel, I'd return to the surface and circle back with more men and supplies.

Dirt clung to the walls and floor, leaving an uneven walking surface littered with roots and stones. I sniffed the air and caught a strange metallic scent, unusual for underground. I'd smelled such a scent before, sure, at our forges. But in a hastily dug and hastily concealed tunnel? Never.

The thought spurred me on and I kept walking, keeping a hand to the right side of the wall.

I considered letting out a brief jet of dragonfire to illuminate the passage further, but I didn't want to roast myself in such an enclosed space. I unreeled more rope, felt out my next steps, and moved on.

The smell grew stronger the further I worked my way in to the tunnel. The ceiling and floor rose and fell. It was over seven feet deep in some parts, and only about five in others, making me crouch low as I walked. My curiosity drove me forward in spite of the danger, and I was nearly out of rope when I saw the glint of metal out of the corner of my eye.

The tunnel opened up onto a larger chamber and I straightened, able to stand at full height. My shoulders and back complained from the constant crouch and I stretched. The air was cooler here and thick with the scent of smoke and iron. I focused on the faint silver glint and realized with a gulp what I was looking at.

A workshop.

The magitech engineers used all manner of gadgetry and gizmos combined with their magical energy to create fantastic inventions. And they did their best work in labs like these. Engineers pushed the boundaries of the possible and allowed us to protect ourselves, detect intruders, and devise new and interesting ways to solve problems. While dragons excelled in the magic part of magitech, our talents could only go so far. It was only through cross-species collaboration that the most advanced creations came to life.

But that was a different time, before the war.

I nearly tripped on something as I stepped into the chamber and bent down to look.

A hand.

A metal hand.

The thought chilled me all the way to my core and I looked away. I thought to yank on the rope and alert Tork when I saw something else even more damning.

Eyes. Two pale, shining eyes watching me from the darkness.

"Hey!" I screamed and lunged forward. The rope ran out and I staggered, yanking it out of Tork's hands. The eyes blinked and disappeared, fading into the blackness. Just like that, they were gone.

I spun around and drew my sword, looking for any sign of movement. Sparks rumbled through my chest and onto my tongue, looking for an outlet. Everything was still. Quiet.

Too quiet.

I heard footsteps behind me and a scattering of dust as Tork barreled into the tunnel after me.

"What are you doing?" I hissed. "You were supposed to sound the alarm, not come in after me!"

Tork's eyes were wild with fear and widened further at the sight of the metal skeletons littering the room. It was a dead-end, as far as I could tell, but I couldn't shake the thought of those shining eyes...

"Thought you were hurt," Tork said. "Thought you needed me."

I let out a breath. "Well, you're here now. What do you make of this?" I waved a hand at the workshop.

"Engineers," he nodded. "Good ones."

"I saw a pair of eyes, over there." I pointed to the spot

where I'd seen the eyes. Tork squinted and even stepped over to the dark corner, waving an arm through the air as if trying to catch smoke. "There's nothing here. No secret doorway. We would have seen them."

I shivered again, not able to shake the chill. If anything happened to us, no one would know where to look. No one except Nik, anyway. I reached out to him with a thought, hoping I could at least contact him.

If you don't hear from me in an hour, get help. I'm on the south side of town past the overgrown weeds. There's a twisted iron grate nearby.

A pause.

...shhhkkktt...

Static.

No reply came, even as I waited out the harrowing moments in silence. I just had to hope he'd heard me. I projected an image of where we'd entered the tunnel. Perhaps he'd see that if nothing else. Then I came back to the present, squared my stance, and prepared for the worst.

"Watch out!" Tork cried as I stepped backward onto a pressure plate. It clicked into the ground. Too late. Noxious green gas poured out of a crack in the wall, filling the small cavern. It worked its way up my nose, into my mouth, through my lungs. My eyes watered and I coughed. I tried to release a jet of flame but none came. The air was still and bitter with the taste of magic.

I screwed up my face, trying to will the fire out of me. Nothing. No wings. No shift. No claws.

Goddess-damned Sorcerers!

"I can't shift!" Tork yelled between hacking, wheezing coughs. "Run!"

I stumbled toward the exit as my throat closed up on me. Tork was a few paces ahead of me but by the sound of it, he wasn't faring too well either.

Just keep running, I told myself as I pushed through the pain. Not far now. Get to Nik. Get to Lyria.

A cold, numb feeling sunk into my skin and through my veins like being doused in ice water.

Each step felt like trying to wade through waist-high water. My steps slowed. The world grew dark around me as my knees gave way, and the last thing I remember thinking was *Nik. Please. Don't hurt Nik.*

14

NIKOLAS

Something was wrong. Very, very wrong.

I felt it all the way down to my soul.

Like a badly tuned radio station, I heard Marlowe in my mind. I saw an open field covered with tangled brush. I saw a gaping hole in the ground. Then nothing.

I tried to tell myself that I was overreacting. Surely he was fine.

But the nagging feeling in my gut wouldn't let go. I had to do something.

I looked over at Lyria's sleeping form and frowned. I hated to wake her, but I couldn't sit here and do nothing.

Who would I even tell? My first thought was to go to Clan Alpha Lucien himself, but he had his hands full.

Him and Alec had left only today on a diplomatic mission to seek out other shifter tribes and gather allies.

Adrian was a kind omega with a beautiful young boy named Finley. We'd spoken a few times and he was exceptionally good with children. But I needed somewhere safe for Lyria while I looked for Marlowe.

There was Myrony, who had probably just finished scrubbing the plates for the night and was turning in around this time. She was a real sweetheart, but she worked so hard already.

Then there was the schoolmaster, Thomas. He was an alpha in status but treated everyone as equals, making him a perfect choice for a teacher. Since the influx of human children from Steamshire, he'd taken them under his wing. During the day him and a few other volunteers would watch over and teach the human kids alongside the shifter children. Despite the cries of panic from more traditionalist factions such as the Iron Paradox or the Elders of Steamshire, the combination had been successful for both human and shifter. Children were born without prejudice, after all.

I sighed, rummaging through my mental list of contacts. Who could I tell? Who could help? And more importantly, who would let me go after him?

During the Paradox days, omegas taking any position of initiative or power was highly frowned upon. Even though they were gone, I'd been around them for so long I'd started to internalize some of their harmful ideas. But I had to be better than that. For Marlowe, for my clan, and for my daughter.

I gently shook Lyria awake and held her at my hip, listening to her groggy questions as I grabbed a few things from the closet.

"Where are we going, daddy?" She mumbled against my neck, and my heart nearly broke right there.

"I'm sorry, sweetheart, but we've gotta go on a little trip, okay?"

"Daddy?" She asked again, yawning.

I gulped and steeled my resolve. Leaving her would be the hardest thing. But it wasn't forever, and I trusted my clansmen.

"We're going to go see Mr. Cadbury," I soothed her as I ran a hand through her hair. "I heard he has a lot of toys at his house."

Another sleepy yawn. "It's the middle of the night."

"I know, darling. Just trust daddy, okay?"

"Okay," she whispered, but as she burrowed into my shoulder, I knew she was anything but.

———

"I'M SORRY, Thomas. You know I wouldn't be here if

it wasn't an emergency." I looked up into Thomas's tired and confused eyes as we stood at the threshold. He was still wearing pajamas and fluffy bunny slippers.

I lowered my voice and leaned in closer. "Marlowe's missing. I think I know what happened to him."

Tom's face blanched. "Come on in." He opened the door wider and we stepped inside.

True to my word, Tom's place was full of storybooks, blocks, and other toys. Though he didn't have kids of his own, he often ran a daycare for kids in the school program out of his house. I set Lyria down next to the building blocks and Thomas followed me into the kitchen.

"What is this about, Nikolas?" He asked in barely more than a whisper. "Have you any idea what time it is?"

"I do, and that's why I need your help."

Thomas crossed his arms. "By watching your little one while you go off to play the hero?"

I clenched my jaw. "Look, I know what I'm doing. I know where he is, I know where to find him. It has to be me." When he continued to look at me like that I added, "I'll be careful. I promise."

"Lyria needs her father," he warned. "Don't go doing anything stupid. Take someone with you, at least."

"Fine, I just...I need to go. My mate's in danger and I can't sit here and do nothing."

His eyes lit up as if remembering some far-off memory. "I'll watch her. You go get your mate." He clapped me on the back. "But don't say I never did you any favors."

"You're a lifesaver, man. I'll make it up to you, promise."

Tom shooed me away and I gave Lyria a last hug and kiss before we separated and I headed for the door.

"I'll be back soon," I promised Tom. "No more than a few hours, tops. If I'm not back by sunup, well..."

"I'll get in touch with Lucien."

"Thanks."

I turned my gaze inward, looking through the bits and pieces I'd picked up over our Link. It was still early days, still weak from the years of neglect, but I could see enough. The words were mostly garbled, but I could make a few of them out. South...weeds...gate...

He'd gone for the tunnel.

I took off at a run, trying to reach out to him in my mind. No response. That made me run faster, and I nearly ran right into one of the Firefangs in my path. The man dropped a toolbox with a clank and wobbled on his feet, looking at me wide-eyed.

"Whoa, where are you going so fast?" It was Ansel

making his nightly rounds to maintain the magitech wards over the city. He wore glasses and had perpetually mussed hair. If you got him started talking about engineering, he'd talk your ear off, but was normally pretty silent.

"Can't talk now, Ansel. Gotta run." I took a few steps then skidded to a halt with an idea. "Actually, follow me. Need your help."

"Wha?" He started but I grabbed his sleeve and yanked him along.

"Tell you on the way!" I yelled as we set off to the south.

———

"WAIT, so you mean to say there's been a secret tunnel here all this time and no one thought to tell me?" Ansel breathed heavily as he tried to keep up. I couldn't tell if the deflated tone of his voice was from fatigue or if he was actually hurt.

"Recent discovery," I clipped. The weeds were growing thicker now, and we fought through the brambles in the footsteps of the men who had come before us. "Marlowe didn't come out here alone," I mused as I eyed the sets of footprints. "Tork, that's who it was."

Ansel gave a little squeak as he quickened his pace to

keep up. I could have sworn I saw the hint of a blush creep up his cheeks, but it was too dark to really tell.

"You work with him, don't you?" I remembered now that Tork worked in the engineering department too.

"Something like that," he muttered and looked away. He pointed to the discarded metal grate. "There!"

I sucked in a breath as we approached the entrance. It wasn't far from the grate, and whatever had happened to that poor piece of iron, it wasn't pretty.

The entrance was visible enough—there were skid marks where the men had slid into the tunnel but not a clear way back out. I called down into the depths at the top of my voice.

"Marlowe! Tork! You in there?"

My voice echoed off the walls. Nothing.

"You smell something?" I said suddenly, wrinkling my nose.

It took only a second for Ansel to go into full-on panic mode. "Shit, it's emerald gas!" He covered his face with his hand and fished out a mask, throwing it to me. "Quick!"

I'd never seen the normally calm Ansel look so afraid. I wasted no time strapping it to my face and breathed a clean breath in through the filter. "What's going on?" I asked in a muffled voice as Ansel fitted his own mask.

"The tunnel's poisoned! We gotta get them out of there!"

Before he could finish his sentence I leapt into the tunnel and skidded to a stop on the rough dirt-packed floor. Ansel wasn't far behind me, his eyes still wide with alarm.

"Come on," I urged him, and we ran.

I continued to call out their names, the only sounds that of my voice reflected back to me off the uneven walls. I thought back to the grinding, scraping sounds I'd heard in the middle of the night so many times. This must have been what they were working on. But why? And why so hastily?

"Marlowe!" I yelled again through my mask.

"Tork!" Ansel called.

It wasn't long until we found them.

I rushed forward, my heart in my throat. They lay collapsed on the floor, unmoving. I bent down to check for a pulse. Good, they were still alive.

"Got any more of those masks?" I asked Ansel as I struggled to roll Marlowe over.

"I'm fresh out," Ansel wrung his hands and glanced down the tunnel. "It's coming from in there. We've got to plug the source before it reaches the surface!"

I froze with fear. Oh, *shit.* If the gas was that powerful, and that deadly, could it knock out an entire city?

"I'll get them out. Can you plug the leak?"

Ansel nodded, digging through his tool bag. "I'm on it."

We locked glances for a brief moment. No matter what people said about omegas, they could be damn resourceful in times of need.

Especially when it came to their mates.

I crouched down and hooked my arms under Marlowe's armpits, groaning as I lifted him into a sitting position. He must weigh twice what I did!

"You start getting sick, you get out. Get help. You hear?" Ansel warned with a last glance at Tork.

"Same," I nodded. "Now go!"

He took off at a run, and I was left alone with two unconscious alphas.

15

NIKOLAS

"Wake up," I projected at Marlowe through our Link. "Wake up, wake up, wake up—damn you're heavy!"

Are you trying *to dislocate my shoulder?*

I let out a breath as I heard his response in my mind. Marlowe's eyes fluttered open, widening as he saw me there. His face no longer had the ruddy gleam it usually did. Even his eyes, once shining with the light of the fire within him, were no more than dull embers.

This was bad.

"What are you..." he started but cut short in a fit of coughs.

"Saving your ass," I responded and offered him my hand. "Come on!"

I braced myself against the wall and pulled, Marlowe stumbling upright at last. Sweat already started to bead up on my forehead, and we weren't out of the woods yet. Marlowe leaned against the wall, heaving and shaking as he ejected the contents of his stomach. The smell mixed with the cloying emerald gas nearly made me gag, even through the protective mask.

Marlowe wiped his mouth with the side of his hand and looked to his fallen comrade.

"Help me," I commanded, pulling at Tork's jacket to turn him over.

Marlowe could barely stand, though, let alone lift another person. I had to do this myself.

There was a crack and the sound of a muffled explosion from down the tunnel and I bit my lip, hoping it was Ansel stopping the gas leak and not getting blown up himself.

No time to think about that, though.

"Stay close to the wall and run." I squeezed Marlowe's hand as our eyes connected. A fraction of the fire returned and he set his jaw, nodding.

"Go, I'm right behind you!" I yelled and pushed him away. Marlowe staggered down the tunnel away from me and away from the gas.

Now there was just the matter of Tork.

I'll never be able to lift him, my mind wailed as I dug in my heels and struggled to get him upright. I called his name over and over, but he wouldn't wake. He was still breathing, slowly, raggedly, but breathing. For now.

I didn't know how much longer he had.

As I narrowed my eyes and the world fell away, I felt a rush of strength surge through my muscles. I had to do this. No other choice.

You saved me, the faint voice echoed through my mind. *Save him too. Take my strength, get him out of there.*

A dozen firecrackers went off inside my body all at once. I let out a roar and heaved, Tork's body coming off the ground. My eyes widened as I froze for only a moment, stunned at myself.

Go! I heard Marlowe's voice again, and I looped one of Tork's arms around my shoulder, dragging him toward the exit.

Footsteps pattered behind me and Ansel emerged. His face was drawn, dirty, and sweaty, but he was alive. Without a word he took Tork's other arm and lightened my load. With Tork's weight distributed between us, we moved faster this time, our own breaths coming in shallow gasps from the exertion.

Tork still wasn't awake, and despite my newfound strength the dead weight was anything but easy to carry. I set my sights on the goal and kept moving. It was all we could do.

Neither of us said anything. Couldn't. Too focused in the moment, the only thing that mattered was the tiny point of light at the end of the tunnel.

Freedom.

Safety.

And not dying in this poisonous cave.

A hand shot out as we neared the ragged hole that marked the exit. Then a rope. Voices echoed down into the cave.

We pushed on the last few yards even as the world began to darken around me. My head swum, my vision blurred, and the strangest fluttering sensation seized my stomach.

I grabbed on to the rope and held on for dear life. The volunteers had arrived.

I felt cool grass under my feet and saw the prone form of Tork and Ansel lying, exhausted, on the ground. The volunteers shoveled dirt into the hole and covered it with the grate, then at last we could breathe once more.

I looked to Marlowe, who leaned against a tree and was being tended by two healers. They lifted Tork onto a makeshift gurney to do the same.

Safe.

The price of the harrowing rescue caught up with me at last. My muscles ached. My stomach roiled. I couldn't see. My dragon took hold and smothered out the light as I collapsed, soundless, onto the ground.

16

MARLOWE

T he fact that I could barely breathe was secondary.

My mate had saved my life, and now he'd collapsed in front of me.

I pulled myself away from the healers, their squawking cries no more than background noise.

"Nik," I breathed, brushing a lock of hair from his face. "I need a healer!"

"Damn right you do, now stay still!" Meryl grabbed my arm and reattached the air-filtering mask. "We've got to remove the toxins in your lungs, hun."

My dragon roared from deep within and I nearly swiped the mask away again. "You've got to help him!" I pointed at Nik, still laying unconscious.

"We will, but you've got to let us do our job." Kyva, the

other healer nearby, sidestepped me to crouch down next to Nik. She hovered a hand over his face, taking a few long, deep breaths. A gentle golden light emanated from her palm and washed over him. Kyva's eyes flicked back and forth as if she was reading something, but I could see no inscription. Then her eyes widened in surprise.

She turned to look at me with a raised eyebrow and then gestured to Meryl. "Get both of them inside, now."

She slapped me on the back as she moved on to evaluate Ansel, but I couldn't get that expression of surprise off her face. What was she hiding?

"Come along now," Meryl prodded me toward a nearby shelter. "Let's get you somewhere more private."

My blood ran cold at her words. Private? What could have been so bad? I looked over to Nik again, still unmoving. A lump forced itself into my throat and I tasted bile. What if...I shuddered from head to foot. What if he wasn't going to make it?

My dragon didn't like that idea one bit and it reared inside of me, smoke pouring from my nostrils as I ran to Nik's side again. A dull, throbbing pain shot up my leg with each step and I was sure to feel even more sore once the adrenaline wore off, but Nik needed me.

I wouldn't leave him to suffer alone again.

I'm here, Nik, I projected to him over our Link. No response came. I squeezed his hand, still hanging limp by his side. I'll take care of you.

Another healer came by carting a gurney for Nik and looked me up and down. "You the omega's mate?" He asked.

"Yes," I said and tightened my grip on Nik's hand.

"I'm Nolan. Come with me."

Him and an assistant lifted Nikolas carefully onto the gurney and pushed him into a small shelter where two more healers waited.

"What's going on?" The healers converged on him, speaking in hushed tones and working quickly with practiced motions of the hand.

Nolan approached, appraising me over the wire rims of his glasses. He spoke slowly, weighing the importance of each word.

"His dragon, as a means of protection, has gone into hibernation. Not unlike the Dragonheart Curse, shifters in times of crisis can go into a coma-like state as their beast fights to restore balance. It's not harmful... usually...but we'll need to keep an eye on him, just in case."

"Nik," my voice came out as a croak. I stepped toward him and lay a hand on his forehead. His eyes were closed, staring at nothing. Breaths came in and out slowly, his chest rising and falling. This was all my fault.

If only I'd escaped faster...

If only I'd brought more backup.

If only I hadn't failed him once again.

"But he'll be all right?" I asked, almost fearing the answer. "You can fix him?"

Nolan rubbed his chin and conferred with the two healers working over Nik's prone body.

He paused, taking a breath, then continued. "Chances are good, and our healers are top-notch, you know that. But there is a...complication." Nolan rubbed the back of his neck, eyes darting around the room.

"Well what is it?" I burst out, not able to take the silence.

"He's pregnant."

All the world screeched to a halt as I heard those two simple words. I blinked at Nolan a few times, registering his words.

Pregnant...oh, *Goddess*.

"Makes sense why his dragon retracted. It's gotta protect the little one, after all."

"Wh-what do I do?" I was used to being in charge. Being

the tough guy, the warrior. Nothing fazed me. Until this omega came along. Now he'd brought down all my walls, and I would do anything just to see him wake again.

"He has a daughter, yes? She'll need to be informed."

My throat stuck together like that time I ate too much honey. Oh no. *Lyria*. How could I break this kind of news to the girl? Even if I was her daddy too, we'd hardly gotten to know each other.

"Wh-what do I do?" I was used to being in charge. Being the tough guy, the warrior. Nothing fazed me. Until this omega came along. Now he'd brought down all my walls, and I would do anything just to see him wake again.

I ran a hand through my hair and let out a sigh. Guess we were going to be spending a lot more quality time together.

"You don't happen to know where she is, do you?" Darkvale wasn't *that* big, but I still didn't have any idea where to start.

"I don't, but ask around. I'm sure someone's seen her."

I took a last longing glance at Nik and leaned down to plant a kiss on his forehead. *I'm so sorry*, I mindspoke to him, even though I knew I'd get nothing in return. *I'll come back for you soon.*

"Let the healers work. Go find the girl," Nolan

suggested, and I stepped out of the shelter into the rising sun.

————

THE FIRST RAYS of dawn spread out across the city, reflected in prisms of light through the protective dome that kept Darkvale safe. The giant orb of fire was only a sliver on the horizon. Already the land was awash in gold and red as the light banished the darkness for yet another day.

At any other time, it would have been beautiful.

As it stood, it reminded me of only one thing: time was running out.

Thoughts sped through my mind quicker than I could run. The filtration mask had done quick work, but I still felt a little hoarse.

The bitter tang of metal stuck to my tongue, a constant companion as I rushed across town. Where could she be?

The early risers of the Firefangs were only just now starting their day, and they looked at me with tired eyes and confused expressions when I asked (albeit a bit frantically) if they'd seen Lyria.

No one had.

After the fifth rejection, I stopped a moment to reconsider my strategy. If she truly was my daughter, then we'd have a Link connection too, right? It would be weak, for sure, but she was my flesh and blood. If I could just seek that out...

There.

A faint, vibrating energy called to me out of the east. It was almost imperceptible, and it probably would have been had I not been specifically looking for it. I couldn't hear much or see anything at all, but I had a feeling. And that was enough of a start.

I turned and followed the source, letting her light lead me like a compass. Follow your instincts, my old master used to say. They will show you the path.

When I ended up in front of Thomas's quarters, I kicked myself for not thinking of it sooner. Some lovingly called him the 'clan daddy' for how much he cared for the little ones. Him and the other volunteers at the makeshift school spent all their time and energy preparing both shifters and humans alike for a better life.

It only made sense that Thomas would be the one to take her in.

I raised my hand to knock but the door opened before I had a chance.

"Thomas," I breathed. He stood there with an arched

eyebrow and a poorly concealed mask of worry. "How did you—"

"You sneak about as well as a goat with tin shoes. Get in here."

He shooed me inside and shut the door.

I saw Lyria out of the corner of my eye, hands grabbing at a bowl of cereal on the table.

Thomas pulled me into the kitchen, looking me up and down. "What's this about, Marlowe? Where's Nikolas?"

I ran a hand through my hair. There was no easy way to say this, was there? "He saved my life. There was an emerald gas leak and I passed out. Tork too. But he and Ansel came and dragged us out. Saved us."

"Goddess," Thomas breathed, leaning back against the wall. "Emerald gas is nasty stuff. Where were you?"

"We found a secret tunnel on the edge of town. It's all cleared out by now, but someone was using it as a workshop right under our noses. The gas was there as a trap, and I accidentally triggered it."

"And Nik?" Thomas asked, his face growing increasingly fearful. "Did he—?"

I licked my lips, trying to find the right words. "He dragged us out of the tunnel and then collapsed. The healers say his dragon..." I stopped, my throat closing up. "...has gone into hibernation. They don't know when he's gonna wake up." I shoved my hands in my pockets and stared at the ground.

Even saying the words lanced a pain through my heart so sharp I winced. When I ran five years ago, I closed myself off to avoid the pain and fear. Now I was feeling it full force, and I felt ready to drown with the intensity of it.

Thomas let out a slow, shaky breath. "Glendaria save us."

"That's not all," I grimaced, wringing my hands. "He's pregnant, Tom."

Thomas's eyebrows reached for his hairline. He shook his head and scrubbed a hand over his face. He took off his glasses, rubbing them on his shirt, then blinked at me through them again.

"How far along?"

"Don't know. They told me to come get Lyria, take her to him. Came as soon as I could."

The schoolmaster walked to the closet and pulled out a spherical decanter and two glasses, pouring us a few fingers each of a dark, smoky spirit.

"Here, drink." He pushed the glass at me. "You look like you need it."

"Thanks," I said wearily as I downed the stuff in one go.

It burned through me from head to toe, but unlike my dragon fire it dulled the pain, terror, and hurt. Everything became just a little easier to bear.

"There is a silver lining in all of this, you know." Thomas sipped at his drink slowly, savoring the smoky aroma where I just wanted it to start working as quick as possible.

I scoffed and my dragon riled inside me. How could he say such a thing? "What's that?"

Thomas tilted his head toward the living room. "Now's your chance to be the alpha father she never had."

A crash sounded from the other room and he stood at once to find Lyria now wearing her food. She'd knocked over the bowl and soggy lumps of cereal peppered not only her face but also the table and floor.

Lyria froze, eyes wide as her lip trembled with fear. She looked at the mess and her breathing quickened. When she caught my eye, she began to wail.

I sat the glass down with a clunk on the table. Alphas didn't back down. That had always been my motto, but the fight I faced now was scarier than anything I'd seen on the battlefield. I needed to be there not only for my mate, but for my daughter and my unborn child.

I leapt into action and joined Thomas in the living room where he started cleaning and I tried to soothe Lyria. I brushed a hand through her hair and squatted so that I was eye level with her. She had the beautiful amber orbs of her father, no less brilliant in their light. She'd grow up to be a fine dragon.

"Hey, it's all right, iskra. No harm done." The word for 'spark' came to my mind in our language, and I used it to get her attention. It fit her. All energy and life and potential. My little spark.

"Where's daddy?" Lyria sniffed, pulling away from Tom's attempts to wipe her face.

I swallowed the lump in my throat and held her gaze, reaching for that pinpoint of energy I'd sensed earlier. *It's going to be okay*, I projected.

I knew it, she sent back, astonished. *You* are *my daddy!*

I heard her small voice through the Link. I froze, not expecting to hear anything in return. She knew I was her dad. She felt it, same as I did. The feeling bolstered me for what I had to say next.

"That's right, iskra." I said the words aloud. "I'm your alpha daddy. You can call me Papa, though. Your Daddy is sleeping right now. He's hurt and needs to heal. But I'm here, and you'll never be alone. We need to go see him so he can feel our love. It will be sad to see him hurt and sleeping, but he needs us. Can you be a brave dragon for Papa?"

She stared at me, her food all but forgotten. That tiny pink lip quivered as she tried to be strong. It broke my heart in all the worst ways—there was nothing I wouldn't do to bring a smile to my little girl's face again.

"Come here, iskra." I held out my arms. "I think we both need a hug."

Lyria held my gaze for a long moment, the stubbornness in her eyes conflicting with her need for reassurance. Finally she flung herself at me, throwing those small arms around my neck and burying her face in my shirt. She was so small in my arms, so delicate. A rush of warmth and emotion flooded through me all the way down to my soul as I held her. There it was. A true bond forged between us for the first time.

"There's one more thing," I said, brushing my hand through her hair. "You're gonna be a big sister soon. Do you know what that means?"

"We're getting a dog?"

I laughed. "No, not a dog. Daddy's pregnant. He's going to have a baby, and you'll have a new brother or sister."

"Whoa..." Lyria gasped and clung to me tighter. "When?"

"A few months from now."

I had no idea how I was gonna handle this whole fatherhood thing, especially with another baby on the way. I didn't even have Nik to help me out. But I knew as I held my daughter in my arms that I would do whatever it took to make this child feel safe and loved.

"Let's get your things," I stroked a hand down her back as her breathing slowed. "Then we can go see Daddy. Say goodbye to Mr. Cadbury, okay?"

When she broke away, an odd void filled her place. I knew how Nik made me feel, sure, but a child's love was different. So pure. I watched her go and snapped myself out of it long enough to pick up her things.

"Come back and see me sometime," Thomas smiled at her. "And don't forget to take these cookies with you!" He handed her a box of sweets. "I can't eat them all by myself, now can I?"

Lyria grinned and took the box, holding it close to her chest. "Thank you Mr. Cadbury." She shot me a mischievous glance.

"Any time, Lyria. Any time."

He waved and I gave Tom a weary look.

I wasn't sure if she picked up something from my conversation with Tom or if she was just shocked into silence but Lyria didn't say another word as we left the schoolmaster's house.

Now the hard part began.

17

NIKOLAS

I had a feeling I wasn't in Darkvale anymore.

I floated on endless clouds of cotton, adrift in a sea with no beginning and no end. Thoughts and sensations came and went, passing me by like ships in the night.

It was like the most surreal dream I'd ever had, but I was strangely lucid. I stretched out my fingers and toes, looking down at my body. Two arms, two legs. A haze of sleepy green light fluttered past my eyelids then left as soon as it came. I tried to turn my head but I stood rooted to the spot.

Where was I?

My mouth opened, but made no sound. It was like floating, no, falling, through a vacuum. Completely airless, directionless, lifeless.

Was this the Great Beyond the shamans so often spoke of? Was I dead?

I furrowed my brow trying to bring up the most recent memory I could. Last thing I remembered was pulling Marlowe out of that poisonous pit he got himself stuck in.

I was tired, sure, but I'd been lucky enough to have a filtration mask from Ansel to block out the negative effects of the gas. Marlowe, on the other hand, wasn't looking so well.

I remembered looking around for him, reaching out to grab his hand, then the world fell away.

The ground crumbled, reality evaporated. And here I was, suspended in time and space with no notion how I got here, or how I might leave.

Flames flickered around me, lapping at my skin, my clothes, my hair. The heat was warm, though not searing. I should have burnt up a thousand times by now. I turned inward, asking my dragon for answers.

No response.

Instead I felt a tiny, almost imperceptible kick, right around my abdomen. It was the strangest feeling, like something was *moving* inside of me. And not just my MIA dragon, either.

I reached out for my dragon again and felt only air. The

void crushed in around me, sucking out all the light. The flames died down, and I was alone.

18

MARLOWE

The closer we got to the healers, the more strongly I could feel Lyria's pain. It mirrored my own. Neither of us knew what was going to happen, but we were going to face it together.

"Want a ride?" I asked, holding out my arms.

She tilted her head in question.

"On my shoulders." I pointed. "You'll be able to see better from there."

Lyria wrapped her arms around me and I lifted her up and over my head, straddling her legs around my neck. She wobbled and grabbed onto my face.

"Wow, you're strong!" She screeched, taking in the view from above. "I can see everything!"

I chuckled. "We're all strong in our own ways. Even you."

"Even me?" She gasped, flexing one of her small arms.

"You're going to be quite the dragon when you grow up, you know that?" I adjusted her on my shoulders till we were both comfortable.

"That's what Daddy says, too."

"That's cause it's true, iskra." The feeling of her tiny hands on me set off a spiral of happiness. I knew well the pride that came from winning a battle, but this was a different sort of victory. A personal one. The pride and connection I felt with this little one stirred deep into my chest and my dragon adored her.

Ours, it roared in delight.

"How's that?" I asked, craning my neck upward. "Ready to go see Daddy?"

"Ready," she said, and pointed west like a captain commanding her troops. I grinned and took off toward the healers, my heart still beating in double time.

Please let them be safe.

———

"IS DADDY GOING TO BE OKAY?" She asked out of nowhere as we drew closer. I nearly stumbled on a rock. Lyria had caught me off guard with her question. My heart thrummed in my chest and roared in my ears, the fears I'd worked so hard to control roaring back. Was he?

I chewed my lip for a few seconds in thought. "I don't know, iskra. But that's why he needs us."

"Can we help?" Lyria asked.

"We can," I agreed. "Daddy might be sleeping, but we need to be there for him. Can you do that?"

"Yes, Papa."

"Good."

We approached the makeshift hospital at long last and I helped her off my shoulders. She looked up at me with windswept hair and a wavering smile. Her eyebrows crept upward.

"Daddy's in there?" She pointed to the burgundy canvas, worn and dusty from the winds. The color took me back to my wartime days. That red always signified a field medic—the cloth was dyed to mask the deep crimson of blood.

The entry way flapped open from an errant breeze and I could see nurses and healers moving about inside. I didn't, however, catch a glance of my mate in those few seconds.

"Yes, he's in there," I said, taking her hand. "Ready?"

She stalled, clinging to my sleeve. I heard the fear in

our Link before she voiced it. "I'm scared. What are they doing to him? When is he coming home?"

"They're making sure he gets better, and they're making sure the baby is okay. They're very smart, so we should trust them. They've patched me up more than a few times, too. And I'm all right."

We pushed through the doorway and the nurse directed us to Nik's cot. She pulled aside some curtains to give us a little privacy and then left us with him.

Lyria toddled over to his bedside. "Daddy?" She said softly.

Lyria looked back at me and then fixed her gaze on Nik again. Her mouth hung open, lip trembling as she stared at his unmoving form.

"I love you, Daddy." She lay her head on his rising and falling chest.

Emotion tugged at my chest and I squinted my eyes, suddenly burning with unbidden tears. I sniffed and shook my head.

I rested a hand over Nik's own, his skin still flushed and warm in his comatose state. I tried to project to him again, but it was like shouting into a void. He was in his own little world now, cut off from our own. The healers kept him stable, but his mind and soul were elsewhere.

The thought that maybe, wherever he was right now he could hear me gave me a small measure of comfort. As far as I knew, only one thing could wake a sleeping dragon.

Time. How much was anyone's guess.

I eyed my pregnant mate's belly, only starting to swell under the blankets. Dragon pregnancies were notoriously short—only three months. We liked to say that dragon babes were just so eager to meet the world, they couldn't wait the full nine that human babes did. What if Nikolas wasn't awake by the time the baby came?

I love you, I projected over and over again. *My best friend. My forever mate. I love you. I love you. I'm sorry. I'm ready to be the mate, and the father, this family needs.*

A tear crept free of my eyelid and dripped down onto Nik's face, leaving a wet trail.

On instinct I leaned down and kissed him, the lips unmoving against my own. But I could still breathe his scent, feel the connection of our dragons there. Buried deep within him, sleeping, but alive.

"I love you," I whispered aloud, breaking the kiss.

"He's due for his medicine," A nurse said, holding a vial of blue liquid. "And then he needs to rest."

I tore myself away from him reluctantly, every fiber of my being still crying out to be next to him. But the healers had to do their job, and I had to take care of Lyria.

"Ready to go home?" I asked Lyria, and she gave his hand a last squeeze.

"Do you think he heard us?" Lyria wondered.

"I'm sure he did." I assured her. Mates were two halves of a soul, bound together inseparably by the mating of their dragons. Surely a little barrier like consciousness wouldn't stop us, right?

19

MARLOWE

W e were walking down the road back toward Nik's place when I heard it.

A small bell jingled and the shouts of a traveler rung out as an overloaded wagon trundled down the road. I craned my neck to get a better vantage point, but I couldn't see anything, just a mass of dust kicked up on the road. By someone, or something.

"What's that sound?" Lyria asked.

Children of humans and shifters alike flew past us, their parents chasing in their wake.

"The Flower Festival's starting!" A girl with messy red curls screeched as she swooped past me.

Goddess, it was here already?

I suppressed a chuckle. The first time Nik ever asked

me out, it was to the Flower Festival. A Darkvale tradition, it was the one time a year when merchants came from all over the realm, flowers and delicacies of every kind could be found, and the Firefangs celebrated food and family.

We've come full circle, I thought to myself with a grin.

Lyria still gazed up at me with excited eyes. Exhaustion reached all the way to my bones and the early wave of merchants always drew the most customers. I had no desire to push past the throngs of people and buy things I didn't need, but I couldn't say no to the look on her face.

A festival was a big event for a child. It often made their day, week, hell, their whole year. I remember how much I looked forward to them and the giddy gleam of excitement when the first caravans rolled into town.

Besides, it would give me a distraction from worrying about Nik, and it would lift Lyria's spirits at the same time. Win-win.

"Let's go find out," I grinned to Lyria and lifted her onto my shoulders as we joined the exodus of people heading for the gate.

Score one Good Dad point for Marlowe.

The first merchant had indeed made his way down the road and approached Darkvale, his caravan sagging with all manner of plants, flowers, and herbs of just about every shape and color I could think of. Even some I couldn't.

Lyria watched with the rest of the crowd, her eyes large as saucers. The merchant was old, with a few tufts of white hair and a speckled face. He had friendly green eyes and a long tufted beard he wore a few shining baubles in. All the hair from his head had migrated downward, it seemed. He gave us a gap-toothed smile and waved a meaty hand as he pulled his horses to a stop.

A creaking hand-painted sign swung back and forth from the side of his wagon. Abernathy's Apothecary, it read.

And I supposed this must be Abernathy.

"There's so many!" Lyria gasped as she took in the bundles of flowers spilling over the sides of the caravan. Indeed, this was quite the harvest. My last Flower Festival was my first date with Nik, to be fair, but I hadn't remembered how resplendent it all was.

For those of us who had little else, a festival of food, family, and exotic delights could brighten the darkest mood.

"Can we get something, Papa?" Lyria asked excitedly.

I eyed the rows of colorful flowers, thinking again of

Nik. Before becoming mates, we'd been childhood friends. Those were simpler days, spent lounging in the sun or playing hide and seek with the other kids. Nik had always had an eye for color, and it pained my heart that he wasn't here to see this.

That doesn't mean he has to completely miss out, I reasoned. *The room the healers kept him in was so awfully dull. Why can't we brighten it up?*

"How about we get some flowers for daddy?" I proposed.

"Good idea," Lyria agreed. "And we can make flower crowns too!"

I blinked. Flower...crowns? I'd never heard of such a thing. "What's that?" I asked.

"I saw some of the girls making them at daycare. They're so pretty...you weave flowers together and wear them. I wanted one, but they ran out." Her lip stuck out in an adorable pout.

"A crown for my princess it is, then." Lyria bounced with excitement and I couldn't help it, I got a little giddy myself. Even in the midst of crisis, her spirit was infectious.

And I could get used to that.

"Let's see what they have." I wove through the crowd to get a better look, Lyria taking in all the blooms from above.

"Why hello there." Abernathy waved, looking at us over his ancient spectacles. "It's good to see this fortress alive again."

"You can say that again," I agreed, and my dragon roared with triumph. "The Firefang clan and their human allies have returned home to Darkvale, and we intend to stay."

Abernathy's bushy mustache bristled as he shook his head in wonder. "I must say, humans and shifters living together...I've traveled far across this world and never seen such a thing. How do you manage?"

"The world is changing," I said proudly. "We change along with it. Our Clan Alpha mated a human, for instance."

"My word."

"Through working together, we build something greater than ourselves." I recited the Firefang creed to him. "We share this land with all our brothers and sisters, not only those of our flesh and blood."

The merchant gave us a surprised but warm smile. "It warms my heart to see. And what's good for you is good for me, as well. Good for my wallet, too." He gave us a wink. "See anything you like? Perhaps a trinket for the darling girl?"

He produced a smooth ivory shell seemingly from nowhere, gleaming in the light and carved into a perfect heart shape. "For the little princess." He offered it up to Lyria and she clutched at it with wide, awestruck eyes.

"Thank you," I bowed my head to Abernathy before continuing. We were here on a mission, after all. "I've got something of a special request."

"Do tell," Abernathy's eyes twinkled with curiosity.

"My mate is very sick, hibernating in fact, and I thought we might bring him some flowers."

"Say no more!" The merchant cried as he rushed through a curtain into his stores. "I've just the thing!"

I let Lyria down from my shoulders as we exchanged confused glances. She hugged the ivory carving to her chest, still admiring the smooth milky surface that shone in the light.

What Abernathy returned with was even more stunning.

A brightly colored bouquet emerged from the wagon, resplendent in reds and golds, the petals each perfectly shaped as if by a master artist. It looked too precious to be real.

"This is the rulo flower," he said in a reverent tone. "Came from all the way across the sea, very exotic, very rare even in those parts. Early explorers used to mistake it for gold, if you can believe it." He stroked the metallic petals. "Imagine their surprise when they found it was simply a flower!"

"It's pretty," Lyria breathed, just as enraptured as I was.

"Pretty, yes, but that's not all. The real magic lies within." He peeled back one of the delicate petals to reveal a cache of pollen at the center, glittering like tiny diamonds.

"The pollen that the rulo flower produces is said to bring vitality, abundance, and good fortune." He took a whiff of the bouquet and gave us a satisfied smile. "In fact, they say this was the Goddess's favorite flower when she walked these realms so long ago. That she's said to bless anyone in their presence. And if that's not enough," he wiggled his eyebrows, "It's also known as The Lover's Bloom. I'll let you figure that one out yourself." He gave me a wink.

Heat rose to my cheeks and I hoped Lyria didn't notice. I knew merchants were always out to make a sale, but what could I say? They were perfect.

"How much?" I asked, internally cringing at what I knew would be an exorbitant price.

Abernathy stepped back, holding the bouquet to his chest as if protecting it. His gaze bored into mine, those green eyes flashing. He studied me from head to toe, as if looking for something beyond just my body. As if he were looking *inside*. I shivered, suddenly uneasy.

Then the merchant spoke again.

"This is one of my most exotic finds. You must understand I cannot let it go easily." He looked lovingly down at the bouquet then back to me, his gaze no less intense. "But I have seen your heart is true."

"What are you talking about?"

He continued in that same eerie tone, yet I couldn't deny it: everything he said was true. "You've been through many trials, yes. But many are still to come, Peter Marlowe." He considered me for another long pause as the beating of my startled heart counted the seconds. "I've traveled a long way. Longer than you know. But I believe the Goddess has led me here for a reason, and I heed her cosmic signs. We were meant to meet this day. Of that I am sure. Take these flowers as my gift to you, and send my best wishes to your mate."

I blinked, muscles relaxing only a little. "I couldn't," I said warily. "Let me pay you—"

"I wouldn't hear of it," Abernathy insisted, pressing the bundle of flowers into my reluctant hands. "Though..." He continued, rubbing his beard. "If you wish to buy something else I wouldn't say no..." He regarded us both with a wink and a friendly grin, and my dragon uncoiled little by little.

He was just a kooky old man.

I snapped my gaping jaw shut and turned to Lyria.

"While we're here, how about we get some seeds for the garden? You'll have to help me pick out the best ones, though."

"Thank you," I mouthed to Abernathy and Lyria led me away.

————

A BIT of haggling and an exchange of gold coins later, we had seeds for tomatoes, corn, potatoes, rosemary, and sage.

Oh, and a rare bouquet of impossibly pretty flowers.

"Ready to go home?" I asked Lyria, who was sucking on a maple candy she'd conned me into buying for her. I hefted my bags in one hand, teetering a bit as I balanced everything just right. Then I took Lyria's small hand in my own and we pushed our way out of the growing crowds.

If there were this many people gathered for such an early arrival, I couldn't imagine what the festival would be like in full swing.

As we walked back home hand in hand, an unfamiliar feeling shone down on me like the sun. For the first time ever, I didn't feel that urge to run away or drown myself in battle. I liked this feeling, this calm, confident assurance that I felt when I was around her. When I was around Nik. The warmness of gratitude bubbled through me and filled me up, my dragon coiling and uncoiling as he took all of it in.

No more running. This time I had something worth staying for.

Family.

20

MARLOWE

If someone had told me a year ago that the rough and tough commander Peter Marlowe would be kneeling at a too-small table making flower crowns with a little girl, I would have laughed in their face.

But now? There was nowhere I'd rather be.

I'd changed a lot since then, I mused as my fat fingers struggled with the stiff vines. We all had.

"No, no, no! It's like this, see?"

Lyria grabbed the mangled flower stems from my hand and twisted one over the other, linking them together so that the blooms formed a crescent shape.

"That's what I was doing," I complained.

"You were doing it wrong."

"How's this?" I offered. It was still a bit wilty, but hey, I tried.

Lyria regarded my attempt and shrugged. "Better."

No one ever told me there was a "right" way to make a flower crown. But apparently, according to Lyria, there very much was. I let her direct me. Those small hands twisted the stems together and handled the petals with such delicate ease I was jealous. For a four year old, she was quite good with her hands, I'd give her that.

I felt a little bad for ruining several of the precious flowers in my misguided attempts to make a crown. But luckily there were more than enough. After a a few false starts and more than a few "no, do it *this* way"s from Lyria, three flower crowns of red and gold sat on the table in front of us.

They weren't perfect, no, but that didn't matter. They were ours.

One for Lyria. One for Nik. One for me.

"We should make one for the baby, too!" Lyria cried suddenly, her eyes wide. "I forgot!"

I chuckled. "The baby isn't even born yet."

"The baby's in Daddy's belly, right? We can just put the crown there!" Before I could say anything else, she grabbed a few more stems and set to work.

Four crowns. Four members of our growing family.

"Papa?" She asked casually as she worked. "How did the baby get in there?"

Good thing I wasn't drinking anything at the moment, cause I nearly choked at those unexpected words. I schooled my features into the best poker face I could. "Magic," I said with a straight face.

"Oh," she said, but gave me that "I don't believe you" face. Thankfully, she didn't press further.

"Ready?" I looked to Lyria, who'd settled her own crown into position. It was a little too big and fell down toward her brows, but even I couldn't deny it looked adorable. The vibrant petals, the delicious scent, and the allegedly magical qualities made it even better.

"You've got to wear yours, too." She handed it to me, her little arms reaching upward but not far enough. I gave a good-natured sigh and ducked my head, and my daughter placed the crown of flowers atop my head.

I was sure I looked ridiculous, but for once I didn't care. I was bonding with my little girl, and we had some flowers to deliver.

———

I IGNORED the whispers as we made our way across town. We weren't the only ones who'd dressed up. The flower merchant had made his rounds to just about everyone, it seemed, and the air was heavy with floral perfume.

When we approached the healing station the nurse that usually stood watch by the door wasn't there, so we let ourselves in. Nik lay alone on his cot, still drowsing. A blanket covered his midsection, but even so I could see the beginning swell of new life.

We must have looked quite the sight, standing over him with our flower crowns and Lyria carrying two more in her hands. When all was said and done, we were left with one perfect rulo rose. I placed it in a glass by his bedside.

There. A little color.

We spent a few moments in silence, just watching the steady rise and fall of Nik's chest. *Please bring him back to me*, I prayed under my breath, beseeching Glendaria to hear me. *Let us be a family once more.*

I sniffed back a few tears and gestured at Nik's stomach. "You wanna do the honors for the baby crown?"

She placed the tiny red and gold crown on the crest of Nik's stomach. I couldn't help but smile as I thought of what the future would bring. If—no, when—Nik woke up, there would be a new baby on the way. New life, and new beginnings. Not only for this child, but for all of us.

There was still the mystery of the workshop to figure out, sorcerer spies on the loose, and a constant quest to rebuild Darkvale to its former glory, but I remembered one thing Lucien used to say to us all every night we were in exile:

We are Firefangs. And Firefangs mean family.

I had let my mate down once before, but those days were over. I was here now, and I would fight until my dying breath if that's what it took to ensure my family was safe, happy, and loved.

"Last one," Lyria said, her voice wobbly with emotion as she handed me the crown we'd made for Nik. "You do it."

I looked down at the petals in my hand, woven together with the flexible leaves and stems to make a headband of sorts. My mate. My friend. My lover.

He was beautiful now and always. But combining the breathtaking colors of the flower crown as they accentuated the glow of his skin, his hair, his freckles?

It was almost too much to bear.

I leaned forward, holding the crown reverently as if it were a sacred artifact. If this worked, it might as well may be. *Please, Glendaria. Bless us with your holy light.* I mumbled a few more words in the Dragon Tongue of my people before settling the crown to rest over Nik's mussed-up hair.

My dragon roared within me, protective and fierce and very, very alpha. I wanted to wrap my arms and my wings around him and never let go. I wanted to fight off whatever demons he was fighting there inside his mind. I wanted to stand in the way of anything and everything that might hurt him, just because he was mine.

But I couldn't do any of those things. Winds prodded at my back, desperate for release. My vision flickered and changed back and forth across my dragon sight. Fire built in my chest, smoke filled my nostrils. I needed to shift, needed to protect him, needed to tear limb from limb whatever had hurt him this way.

I felt my daughter at my side, watching with wide, teary eyes. For Lyria, then. And for the babe.

I let out a long, shaky breath. My hands trembled as I gripped the sides of the bed. And then I wept.

"I'm sorry," I whispered as I kissed Nik's forehead.

"I love you," I mumbled as I kissed his nose.

"Now and forever, my mate, my everything." I kissed one cheek, then the other.

"Come back to me," I sobbed, and planted a kiss on those unmoving lips.

When our lips touched, there was more than a spark between us. It was like a bolt of lightning. The tapestry of souls that mates formed together became whole once more. Perhaps Nik had heard us. Perhaps the Goddess had. Who could say?

Nik shuddered, dragging in a hoarse, shaky breath.

Then he sneezed right in my face.

I staggered backward as my heart leapt into my throat. I didn't even have a chance to wipe my face before he sneezed again. And again.

Nik's eyes fluttered open as his body spasmed.

"What's on my head?" He moaned and then sneezed again. "Gnah—I'm allergic—achoo!"

I was still staring at him, mouth hanging open in shock.

And then I laughed. A little chuckle at first, it soon became a roaring, raucous sound. I snatched the crown off his head and tossed it over my shoulder. He was awake, and that was all that mattered.

Lyria leapt on top of him in her joy, wrapping her thin arms around his neck. She'd forgotten to remove her flower crown, though, and Nik started sneezing all over again.

"Seriously," he groaned between sneezes. "Get that stuff away from me!"

I couldn't stop laughing. Tears formed at the corners of my eyes, but they weren't tears of grief this time. Relief, love, amusement, embarrassment, and the irony of the situation flowed through my veins in equal measure.

These supposedly magical flowers had woken him up all right—just not in the way we'd expected.

I plucked the crowns off Nik's belly and Lyria's head, discarding them to the side along with the single rose I'd placed on his bedside table. It was just too funny. My chest shook with laughter and joy as I watched Nik try to get his bearings. He was alive. He was awake. And we were all here to greet him.

"Why was there one on my belly?" He mumbled, eyes still squinting against the light. "This was all part of your plot, wasn't it? Wake me with allergies?"

"No," I laughed, brushing a tendril of hair off his forehead. "It was Lyria's idea, actually. She wanted to make you something pretty. And the one on your stomach was for...well, you didn't know? You're pregnant."

Nik's hand shot to his stomach and he felt the small lump there. His face went from confusion to shock to fear to joy in a matter of seconds. "Goddess...the baby... is it all right?"

"I'm sure it is. Your dragon took good care of them, I'm sure."

Nik slumped back into the pillows, closing his eyes again.

"Nurse Meryl! He's awake!"

The omega woman stopped what she was doing and

rushed to Nik's bedside, feeling his temple then taking his vitals.

"The baby..." Nik mumbled, still sniffling in the wake of the flowers. "Is the baby okay?"

She ran a hand over his stomach, letting it hover there for a moment. A few seconds later, she smiled. "The baby is healthy."

Nik let out a sigh of relief. "Thank Glendaria."

Thank Glendaria indeed, I repeated in my mind.

"I can't say how, but you've done it." The healer said as she finished her analysis. "He seems to be stable, but we still need to monitor him for a day. I know you're impatient, but he'll be free to go tomorrow."

"I missed you, Daddy," Lyria sniffed, laying her head on Nik's chest. It rose and fell more easily now, and Nik ran a hand through her hair.

"I missed you too, sweetheart." He held her close for several long moments, and Lyria, who'd been so stubbornly strong all this time, finally broke down in gasping sobs.

I leaned over to envelop both of them in my arms. We were one, and nothing would tear us apart again. Not if I had anything to say about it.

As I drew away, not one of us had dry eyes. I sniffed, looking at the ceiling.

Nik turned over on his side with great effort and leveled his gaze at me, suddenly serious. "What happened, Marlowe? I was there with you, and then everything went black, and…"

"You saved my life," I shrugged. "Tork's too. No big deal."

Nik snorted. "Yeah, only you would say saving lives is no big deal." He chewed his lip, considering his next words. "You came back for me."

His eyes were so innocent, shining with that perfect amber glow that melted me from the inside out.

"I will always come back for you, Nik. Now and forever. I know I wronged you in the past. But let's make this a new life, a new day. Just the three—soon, four—of us. Will you give me a chance to be the mate and the father this family needs?" I went to one knee and kissed Nik's hand.

He caught me in those amber eyes again and this time I couldn't look away. Didn't want to. My mate, my omega, the missing piece of my soul. He was alive, and he was mine.

"Yes, Marlowe." Nik said at last. "I will." He stretched his arms toward me. "Now come here!"

Our lips intertwined in one of the most passionate kisses of my life. Into it I poured my grief, my love, my hope. All the pain of the past and the fear of the future melted away. In that moment, we were one.

"Ewww, kissing!" Lyria teased, and I pulled away from my mate, admiring that sleepy expression of joy written all over his face.

We laughed together. Couldn't help it. We were all here. We were family. And we were safe.

21

NIKOLAS

I woke in the middle of the night to the sound of footsteps. I looked around, squinting my eyes against the darkness. The healing ward was eerily silent at night, since most of the daytime healers were gone to be with their families. There were a few on night shift, but much fewer and farther between.

Ever since Nik and Lyria awakened me from that eternal dream world, my strength had returned little by little. I was still weak, sure, but the healers said I was progressing nicely and could go home on the morrow if all things continued well.

So when I heard the sound of sneaky footsteps entering the darkened ward, my ears pricked up.

I tried to sit, but my muscles didn't obey. Not to mention they had me wrapped up in about a million blankets to keep the drafts away. I peeled one to the side, then another.

The hairs on the back of my neck stood up. Someone was behind me. Watching me. I dreaded to turn around and see who it was, until...

It's me, dummy.

I swallowed the lump forming in my throat and whirled around. Marlowe crouched at the edge of my bed, his eyes flitting back and forth as if afraid he'd be spotted.

What are you doing? I hissed at him over our Link.

I had to see you.

I'm fine, I'll be home tomorrow.

Couldn't wait that long. How are you doing? He trailed a hand down my face and I shivered at his touch, my wakening dragon purring with delight. Heat flooded through me where before there was only ice, lighting up the atrophied muscles. Energy and power flooded through our bodies as one and I stared wide-eyed at him, relishing every second.

I need *you, Mar...* I growled in my mind, pulling him closer. *I thought I was gone, thought you were gone.*

We'll have to be careful, Marlowe raised an eyebrow. *No wrestle fucking, no crying out, and no breaking things this time.*

No promises, I smirked, and pulled him into bed with me. The stiff tiredness fell away in the presence of my mate as his skin, his eyes, his breath lit me up with desire once more. My dragon called out to his, finally together, finally safe. He placed a hand possessively over my stomach, feeling the subtle curve there then dipping lower. I gasped.

No secret babies this time, either, he growled, leaning down to kiss a trail of hot fire down my lips, my neck, my chest, across the swell of my stomach down to my rapidly hardening cock. *This one's all mine.*

I propped myself up to sitting with a few pillows, stuffing the blankets behind me for extra support. Marlowe tilted his head in question as he watched me move, his hands never leaving my flesh. They roamed up and down, wherever they could reach, leaving a shivery electric frisson in their place.

I locked eyes with him. My mate. My alpha. My best friend.

Suck me, I commanded, grabbing a handful of his hair and pulling his face toward me. *Now. Before the healers come back.*

Marlowe's eyes lit up with a possessive fire and he growled just low enough for only the two of us to hear. I fisted my hand in his hair, pulling him onto my cock. His wet, ready lips enveloped my shaft and I threw my head back, sighing breathily.

Uh-uh-uh, Marlowe chastised me in his mind. *Gotta be silent, or no pleasure for you.*

I ground my teeth and curled my toes, taking in a shaky breath through my nose. I could do this.

I call this the thank Goddess you're alive fuck, Marlowe chuckled, and dipped his head lower, suckling the rest of my shaft in one long stroke. His tongue lapped at the underside and head, his cheeks hollow to create a suction as he moved up and down. I guided him with my hand, pulling him closer then pushing him away, using the bed and my hands in his hair for leverage. My hips rocked forward, thrusting into his mouth.

Fuck, I missed this, Marlowe growled.

Missed you more, I shot back.

Challenge accepted, pretty boy. He redoubled his efforts, sucking me off with a passion I'd never seen before. My dragon was burning up, wings tickling at my back and nails lengthening into claws. I bit down on my lip. If I didn't control myself, I'd shift right here.

And that would *definitely* attract attention.

We rocked there together, me fucking his face and Marlowe moving his hands to caress my balls. I felt something tighten within me as I pumped harder, hitting the back of his throat with every thrust.

I was close. Really fucking close.

Don't ever leave me again. I pumped into him mercilessly, Marlowe's gaze never leaving my own. We were locked together in time and space, completely oblivious to anything else but our own pleasures.

Never, he promised, and I couldn't hold it anymore. Everything shattered around me, and I careened over the edge.

I came with a muffled groan that sounded like I was in pain more than pleasure. Breaths came hot and heavy through my nose, my chest heaving as I pumped my load into my mate's mouth, hungry and waiting. And that would have been that, had we not heard the damning sound of a clipboard clattering to the floor.

Marlowe startled at the sound and lost hold of my cock, whirling to see the intruder. I'd already passed the point of no return, though, and cum spurted from my dick in long jets. It splattered into Marlowe's hair, the floor, and the poor nurse's shoes as I watched in horror.

I froze, all the blood rushing straight to my neck and face. Shit. I imagined the harsh sort of reprimand I was in for.

The nurse stood there, fumbling with the buttons on her coat. She stared intently at the ground, unable to meet our gaze. Even in the dim light I could tell she was more than a few shades of red. Absolutely mortified was more like it.

Hell, I was too.

"I was just coming by, to, ahem, check your vitals, Mr. Lastir. But it appears you're doing quite well at the moment." She gave me the most awkward smile I'd ever seen and a nervous, shaky laugh. "Carry on." She winked and turned the corner as fast as possible, leaving us alone again.

As soon as she was out of sight, Marlowe burst into peals of laughter. His chest shook as he lay his head in my lap, wiping a stray tear from his eye.

I reached out a hand to stroke his hair and it came away covered in cum. I grimaced and wiped it on the sheets, which made my mate laugh even harder.

"Come on," he breathed. "That was fucking funny. Did you see that cumshot? That's like world record material, man."

"You're so full of it." I rolled my eyes, but he had a point.

"I think *you're* the one who's full of it." Marlowe waggled his eyebrows. "Or at least...you were."

We held each other and laughed until our sides ached. Whatever. Mates would be mates. It would be a good story, right?

22

NIKOLAS

"You're free to go, Mr. Lastir. May the Goddess be with you." Meryl patted me on the back and gave me a sly wink. Color rushed to my cheeks all over again.

They'd never let me forget that.

I wobbled to my feet and emerged from the healing ward for the first time in what felt like forever. The waning sun cast the world in golden light as I squinted toward the horizon.

Marlowe would have come to meet me but he'd been tied up taking care of Lyria. I couldn't blame him; I was glad he was taking good care of my girl.

But it didn't make it hurt any less.

I gathered my things and set off on foot. Luckily home wasn't far. I reveled in the soft grass and solid ground beneath my feet, drawing in the scent of flowers on the breeze.

What my mate and daughter didn't know was that when I was stuck in that dream-world, when my dragon had pulled away and had taken me along with it, I heard them. I heard every word they said when they thought I was out cold.

Their words and feelings came through like water through a sieve, wrapping around me and arming my soul against the night. I tried to respond, to call out to them, but my voice wouldn't come. I railed against the darkness, shrieking, clawing, sobbing. The pull of the tide was too strong. It pulled me under and locked me away.

Until they put all those blasted flowers in my face, that is.

I heard their words. I felt their love. I experienced their grief.

That's when I knew that what I had with Marlowe was real.

Despite his sometimes cold exterior, Marlowe had a soft gooey center filled with love and longing. I'd always known that, in some way, but there was no better way to tell the character of a man than what he says when he thinks you're not listening.

Not to mention I had teasing ammunition for pretty much forever, now.

I let that thought lift my spirits as I neared the house.

Here's to day one of the rest of your life, I told myself, and opened the door.

———

"SURPRISE!"

I stopped dead in my tracks. My house was full of my friends and family, leaping up to greet me with smiles on their faces.

I couldn't believe it.

Adrian and Finley were there. Alec, Lucien, Samson, and Corin waved brightly. Thomas and Tork and Myrony and Ansel all made a showing, drinking and laughing and celebrating as they welcomed me home.

I stepped over the threshold and Lyria ran into my arms, throwing herself against me. "Daddy!" She shrieked and wrapped her arms around my neck. I lifted her and hugged her as tight as I could. My little girl was safe.

Marlowe looked on with a grin, arms crossed as he watched each person in the crowd offer their well wishes.

All these people came out here, for me.

I sniffed, my eyes welling with tears as I took in the smiling crowd. After being held hostage for so long... after feeling abandoned, forgotten, unloved...we were all here now. We were all together.

Welcome home, sweetheart, Marlowe spoke in my mind.

Lyria wriggled in my grasp and I let her down as she led me through the throng of people to the kitchen. What I saw there destroyed the last of my resolve to keep from crying.

A tall chocolate cake sat on the table, decorated with intricate icing flowers. Each one was a different color, forming a rainbow around the perimeter. A small paper flag on a toothpick stood in the middle of the cake and below it in curling script was a message:

Welcome home, Nikolas. We love you.

I covered my mouth with my hand and admired the cake closer, sniffing again against the tide of emotion. It was more than delicious-looking, it was a work of art.

Marlowe came to my side, looping an arm around my waist. "What do you think?" He asked.

"Where'd you get so much chocolate?" I said in awe. Chocolate with a prized treat, accessible only in small quantities and at infrequent intervals. And here was a whole cake of it. "It must have cost you a fortune!"

Marlowe's eyes glinted as he pulled me to face him. "I

have my ways. And I'll do anything for my mate." He pulled me to him and his lips captured mine, not violent and demanding as they had been the night before, but sensual, passionate, loving. "I love you," Marlowe said against my lips. "Welcome home."

"Glad to be back," I gasped when I found my breath again. I pulled away to look at the gathering group of people through the doorway. Even more of my old shifter buddies muscled through the door, their eyes lighting up as they saw me for the first time in years.

"To the man that saved my life." Marlowe pushed a drink into my hand. He grabbed something bubbly and raised his glass in my direction. "To my best friend, my omega, my mate."

"Cheers!" The house rumbled with the celebration of human and shifter alike.

I took a long sip with the rest of my friends and family, smiling at the delightfully fizzy nectar.

"Speech!" Tork clapped, jostling his mug in the process. "Speech!"

I scoffed, my face growing red again as everyone's eyes watched me. Gosh, I didn't know I was gonna have to make a speech! I took a deep breath and addressed the crowd.

"My friends, my family. My clan. Thank you all for being here. It warms my heart more than I can say that you've chosen to celebrate here with me today. When my dragon retracted, I saw what some might call The Great Beyond. I could reach out and touch it. I thought I was dead. But the Goddess decided my time on this world is not done just yet. When I was there I heard voices cutting through the darkness. I heard my daughter. I heard my mate. The last few years have been difficult. Many things have changed. When Darkvale fell I lost everything. I didn't believe in second chances. But I've never been so proud to be wrong in all my days, and I'm truly blessed to have this man as my mate. To Marlowe, everyone!"

"To Marlowe!" The clan roared in agreement. I had my mate and my girl by my side, my friends all around me, and a little one on the way.

It was the best day of my life.

23

MARLOWE

Two weeks later

"You may enter," I said without looking up. Weeks after Nik had returned from the healing ward, I was still buried in diplomatic bullshit.

The door opened and Elias stepped through, joined by one of my guards. I looked up when I saw the flow of his robes across the floor.

I didn't want to admit it, but Elias had become quite the asset. Despite his cantankerous personality he was smart as hell, and knew how to get information we couldn't by ourselves. I'd tasked him with analyzing the findings from the underground workshop we'd discovered, and I could only assume he was here now to share his results.

"Elias," I said, bowing my head slightly. "Sit down."

The Sorcerer swept his robes behind him and sat, the guard still standing vigil by his side.

"You may leave us, Kaine. I wish to speak to Elias alone."

Kaine hesitated. "Yes, Commander," He said at last, leaving with a short bow.

"Now," I leaned forward at my desk, considering him over my steepled fingers. "What news have you brought me?"

Elias fished a scroll out of one of the voluminous pockets of his robes. I gestured for him to bring it forward.

He removed the metal ring holding it in place and spread out the crumpled paper on the table. Scratches of ink and calculations littered the page, along with some foreign language I'd never seen before. What I did recognize, however, was the eerie replication of the discarded metal limbs I'd seen in the workshop. Only, they weren't disembodied anymore. Elias had added on a torso, arms, and even a head. What I saw could only be described as a "metal man."

"What is this about?" I said softly, my breath catching in my throat. The thought of that metal coming to life... I shivered. I may be a dragon, but to animate lifeless metal? I couldn't imagine the amount of power that would take.

"I've inspected each of the artifacts recovered from this workshop of yours. It's quite incredible, I've never seen readings like these before."

"But what does it mean?" I pressed him. "We need to know what we're up against. We need to keep Darkvale safe."

Elias pursed his lips. "I don't know." His shoulders slumped over the parchment. "I've been trying to figure out how it's even possible, but..."

"Try harder." I commanded, leaning back in my chair. "The fate of our people is at stake."

"Yes, Commander," he bowed his head. "I will do my best, but I need more resources."

I gazed at him. Of course he did.

"I'll contact the magitech engineers and send one along with you. Will that be enough?"

"It's a start, but this is complicated stuff." Elias wrung his hands. "I think I'm on to something big, but I need more time."

I drew in a deep breath.

"Time you will have, Sorcerer, but if I get even the faintest hint of foul play..."

"You have my word. That still stands from before."

I considered his proposition. True, he hadn't led us astray yet. In fact, quite the opposite. Maybe all Sorcerers weren't so bad, after all.

"Am I free to go?" He asked at length. "I need to get back to my studies."

"Leave." I waved him away.

Without a word he gathered up his papers, refastening them carefully, then exited through the double doors.

I let out a breath and ran a hand through my hair when he was gone.

What in Glendaria's name were they working on? And *who* was 'they', for that matter? The Paradox? The humans? Or someone else entirely?

If they were even close to building a mechanized warrior like in Elias's drawings, we were in a lot more danger than I thought.

Especially if that kind of technology fell into the wrong hands.

I was making a note to report this news to Lucien when I heard Nik's voice in my mind.

Dinner's almost ready. You about done over there?

Yeah, I mindspoke back to him. *I'll be right there.*

My stomach growled as I stood up from my desk. I'd

been so caught up with meetings and paperwork all day I had barely eaten anything. Even from here I could smell the delicious scent of the night's clan dinner.

After a full belly of food and the company of my mate and daughter, things would look brighter. They had to.

24

MARLOWE

"Ugh, I feel like a balloon." Nik fell backwards into the bed with a thump. He was quite pregnant now, the swell of his stomach forming a graceful arch from his torso down to his legs. It didn't look easy to carry that much extra weight around. I couldn't have done it, that was for sure.

"Why don't you rest?" I suggested and kissed his forehead. "I've already told the Council I'm not coming in until after the baby's born. Should be any day now." I grinned and caressed Nik's stomach, still marveling at the smooth, round shape and how well it fit in my hands. I leaned down to kiss him there and I got a kick to the face from the little one. It wasn't very hard, but I could definitely feel it.

"Ouch," I joked, rubbing my cheek. "Your baby is feisty."

"You have no idea," Nik rolled his eyes. "Keeping me up at all hours of the night, running to the bathroom every hour on the hour...and don't even get me started on the swollen ankles."

I rubbed his back in small circles, focusing on the tense muscles there. "It will all be over soon."

"Yeah, and then the hard part begins—actually being parents."

"It's difficult, sure," I admitted. "But we're in this together. And I'm sure the baby will be just as strong and beautiful as you are." I kissed his shoulder and held him close to me.

Nikolas let out a sigh and turned away. I thought I could detect the hint of a blush there.

"What?" I asked softly.

Nik mumbled something too low for me to hear. He was a bright beet red now, which made me even more curious.

"What's the matter?" I asked again.

"I miss feeling you inside me," he mumbled and hid his face in the pillows.

I stared at him, mouth open. Between work and time with Lyria, neither of us had had much time or energy to be intimate. And with the fatigue and swelling from

Nik's pregnancy, I falsely assumed he wouldn't want to.

How wrong I was.

"You'd want me to...like this?" I caressed his stomach and kissed my way down his back, leaving gooseflesh there.

Nik rolled over and caught my gaze. "Why not?" His eyes glittered with need, and my dragon couldn't resist.

Still, I tried to keep a handle on my feelings. Protecting my mate and my baby was most important, even if I did want to pound him into the mattress.

"I'm not gonna...I dunno, hurt the baby?" My heart had already started going double-time, and blood rushed to my cock as I thought of fucking my pregnant mate.

"We'll just have to be gentle. Here, lay behind me. We can spoon."

"What about Lyria?" I cocked my head toward the hallway. She was sound asleep in the next room, and if she was going to stay that way, we'd need to be quiet.

"She sleeps like a rock. You've seen her. Come on." Nik stroked my neck and I closed my eyes, tilting my head back.

"Okay," I said shakily, but my dragon was already raring to go.

Nik didn't know what he was talking about when he said he felt gross and ugly. Nothing could be further from the truth. He positively glowed with pregnancy, and he was carrying my child. Nothing could be hotter than that.

I positioned myself behind him, one arm behind my head while the other wrapped around his torso. I put a hand protectively on his belly and kissed his shoulder again. "This okay?"

"Yeah."

I rubbed my rapidly hardening cock against his back and Nik responded in kind, moving back and forth with me in a steady, slow motion.

"That feels good," Nik sighed. "Want more."

I used my free hand to snake down to the curve of his ass. Goddess, he was so wet already. My fingers came away coated in his slick juices and I brought them to my nose.

The scent of him drove my dragon wild. I nearly vibrated with need but held myself back. "Tell me if I'm being too rough."

"I will. I'm not made of glass, you know."

Wasn't that the truth. "Far from it," I agreed as I aligned my cock with his opening. "You are the strongest, kindest, bravest omega I've ever met. And I'm honored to have you as my mate." I pressed into him gently as I said each word, inch by delicious inch until I was buried to the hilt.

Nik made a soft choking moan, rocking against me. A sigh of pleasure, of relief, almost.

His warm, tight walls gripped my cock and shot sparks of pleasure up and down my spine. I wrapped my arm around him again and pulled him even closer, desperate for connection.

With a slow, tortured rocking of my hips, I drew out of him, listening to Nik's shuddered gasps. His body twitched with each passionate thrust, shivering and shaking in my arms.

"Goddess, you're so fucking hot." I growled next to his ear. "You're gonna make me come just from the sounds you make."

Nik blushed again and gave me an embarrassed grin. "I can't help it," he mumbled with hooded eyes. "You feel so good."

"So do you," I replied, capturing his lips in a kiss as I drove into him again.

This time as we joined together, it was more than a feral clash of bodies. It was more than a reckless pursuit of pleasure. We gave and took, rocking into one another with a slow, passionate rhythm that drove each breath, each sigh, each beat of our hearts. It was a glowing ember of sensuality instead of a fiery explosion.

And everyone knows that embers burn hottest.

It was a slow ascent that took over each of our bodies and souls, keeping us locked in the moment and completely at one with one another. It consumed me from head to toe as I pressed into him again and again, picking up the pace and possessively stroking Nik's pregnant belly.

My mate. My lover. My baby.

My breathing became labored and my thrusts quickened as I clung to Nik for dear life. My balls tightened, edged to the point of insanity. And then I broke down, shuddering and coming deep inside his channel as we shook and spasmed in each other's arms. My knot swelled within him and held us there, locked together in our passion, as Nik turned his head and eyed me with a sleepy, sated gaze.

"I love you, Marlowe."

"I love you too, Nik."

We lay there, joined as alpha and omega, until our breathing slowed and sleep came for us both.

———

I WOKE the next morning to a panicked yelp coming from the bathroom.

All vestiges of sleep left me in an instant. My eyes shot open, my dragon ready to pounce.

"What's wrong?" I called, my voice still hoarse from sleep.

Nik's muffled voice came from the other side of the door. "My water broke! And I'm cramping like crazy!"

Oh, Goddess. I sat bolt upright in bed, my head spinning. The baby was coming. The baby was finally coming!

"Stay calm!" I called through the door, as much to myself as to him. "Can you come out here?"

"I think so," he groaned and the door opened. Nik emerged in a robe. His face was a pale white and he clamped a hand over his stomach, wincing.

I felt fear greater than any battle. My mate was hurting, and I had to do something!

I spread a blanket out over the bed and eased him down onto it. "Stay right here, I'll get the doctor."

"As if I could get very far," Nik grimaced. "I blame you for this! You're the one that had to go and shake things up in there last night." His eyes were alight with mischief and it took me a few seconds to figure out what he was talking about.

"Ohhh..." I groaned. Excitement and fear washed through me in equal measure.

This was it.

I was thrilled to be there for my mate and see the new

addition to our family, but what if I messed it up? What if I wasn't a good father after all? I'd had some practice with Lyria, but this was a *baby*.

My protective instincts won over and spurred me into action. I nearly tripped over the bundle of clothes on the floor when I heard Lyria from the other room.

"What's going on?" She emerged from her room in a nightgown, still rubbing the sleep from her eyes.

I knelt down to her at eye level. "You're gonna be a big sister, soon. The baby is coming, and Daddy needs you to watch over him while I go get the doctor. Can you do that for Papa?"

"Is he gonna be okay?" She warbled, those innocent eyes worried.

"He will be okay. I promise." I drew her into a hug. "I'll be right back. Don't go anywhere until I return."

I heard Lyria rush into Nik's room, shouting at top of her lungs. "BABY! ARE YOU IN THERE?"

I choked out a laugh, then got to my feet and ran.

———

NOT TEN MINUTES later I returned with Doctor Parley and his assistant Anna in tow. One look at Nik's pained face and he turned to me.

"Usually we do deliveries in the medical ward, but the

baby's coming now. Little bugger is persistent. There's no time."

"What does that mean?" I croaked, my heart hammering against my chest.

"We'll have to make do," he said, and snapped on a pair of gloves.

I hovered around the room, watching with wide eyes as Dr. Parley and Anna rushed about, propping Nik up on a pile of pillows and pulling a blanket over his lower half. I held Lyria as she buried her face in my shirt.

Nik yelped again and clenched at his stomach. It took all my willpower not to run to him and grab his hand.

The doctor twisted his lips and gave a weary shake of his head. "We're gonna need to do a C-section."

"What?" I screamed, and this time I actually did lunge forward. "You can't!"

"Mr. Marlowe," the doctor scolded, pushing me away. "If you can't keep your wits about you, you'll have to leave. Your mate is in good hands but only if you leave me and my assistant to do our work. What will it be?"

My dragon heated up, ready to let him taste my fire, then Nik reached out and grabbed my hand. He gave me a tired smile. "Hey. Don't worry about me."

"I always worry about you," I admitted.

"Take Lyria and wait outside. I'll be okay. I promise."

I took a long last look into his eyes and squeezed his hand. "You better be."

Lyria looked at me and then at Nik with wide, worried eyes. "I'll be all right, sweetheart." Nik soothed her. "Go with Papa. Your baby brother is coming."

"Brother?" I raised an eyebrow. "How do you know?"

"I don't," Nik shrugged, then groaned again as another contraction hit him. "Just a hunch. The way this one's been kicking? Definitely an alpha, and probably a boy too."

"Clear the room," the doctor commanded. "We need to get started."

I love you, I sent to Nikolas over our Link.

I love you too.

I took Lyria's hand and left the room, but it felt like I left a piece of my soul behind.

———

I PACED BACK AND FORTH, back and forth. Lyria sat in a chair and watched as I chewed my lip, fidgeted, clenched and unclenched my fists. Sweat beaded up on my forehead and I could barely think straight. Every fiber in my being screamed at me to barge back in there and protect my mate, but I could not. The doctors knew what they were doing, and Dr. Parley was right. I'd only get in the way.

Lyria dangled her legs off the chair and sat silently, but I could hear all her worries in my mind. Trying to soothe myself and her at the same time was a hell of a job.

She started talking, perhaps to distract herself from her fear, but it helped me calm down as well.

"I didn't like you at first," She admitted. "But you take good care of Daddy."

I scoffed at her candor. At least she'd come around. "I do my best."

"Are you gonna stay with us, Papa?" She clung to my sleeve. The idea that she'd even had to worry about that broke my heart, so I wrapped my arms around her and pulled her into a hug.

"I'm not going anywhere. Papa is here to stay. I'm sorry I was gone before, but I'm gonna be the best Papa ever from now on. Give me a chance?"

Lyria nodded and buried her head in my chest again. *I love you, iskra. I'll never leave you again.*

A cry came from the next room and startled us both. I leapt up, ready to attack. But that cry wasn't a cry of pain. No.

It was a high-pitched, gasping cry of new life.

My heart nearly stopped right then and there.

A spark of life jolted through our Link, branching off from my mate's connection into a new one all its own. Another branch in our growing family tree.

A moment later Anna returned, wiping her hands on a towel. "You can come in now," she beamed at Lyria. "Come see your new baby sister."

"Sister?" Lyria cried, and ran into the room.

I followed her and the sight took my breath away.

Nik lay in bed, flushed and exhausted, but happier than I'd ever seen him. He held a screeching baby in his arms and a smile on his face. I stood in awe of how small she was.

Lyria covered her ears. "How is something that small so loud!?"

Boy, was she in for a surprise.

I chuckled and led her to the bed where the baby quieted for a blessed second. It was almost as if she felt our presence. Her wide amber eyes latched onto mine and I felt the reverberation of our dragon souls mingling.

"Hey there," I cooed. "I'm your Papa, and this is your big sister."

"Hey, baby." Lyria still stood back a bit, ready to cover her ears again at the next screech.

How are you doing? I asked Nik in mindspeak.

Tired, he responded. *But look at her.*

I couldn't take my eyes away from our new child. She was the most beautiful thing I'd ever seen.

A storm still gathered over Darkvale, but that didn't matter at the moment. As long as we had each other, we could weather any obstacle. We had friends, family, and allies on our side.

"She's everything I could ever wish for, and more." Nik mused without taking his eyes off our girl. "I've got my mate, two beautiful girls, and an entire clan at our backs."

"What should we call her?" I asked Nik, gently brushing back the tiny tuft of hair on the baby's head. She whimpered again and wobbled her arms and legs, clinging close to her Daddy's warmth.

"I have an idea," Lyria piped up, and we both looked at her.

"What's that?" I figured she would come up with some silly, out of place answer, and I was already concocting a careful reply when she spoke.

"How about Hope?"

Hope. I repeated the word and looked at Nik. His eyes shone with what could have been tears.

Hope was what got me from the trenches of warfare

back into my mate's arms. Hope was what won back our homeland from the intruders. And hope was what would carry us into the future, come what may.

"It's perfect." I said, and Nik agreed.

"Hope it is," Nik said, snuggling her close to him. He kissed our daughter's forehead, and closed his eyes to rest.

We were together.

We were family.

We were Firefangs.

And nothing would stand in our way.

THE DRAGON'S FORBIDDEN OMEGA

DARKVALE BOOK 3

1

TORK

"You'd sooner find me with a bag over my head," I told Lucien with a scowl. "I'm not going to the ball, and I'm definitely not dressing up or wearing a mask."

Lucien's shoulders slumped. "Not even if I lend you one? It's been a long time since we had reason to celebrate, Tork. Join us. You don't have to dance or anything, but there's going to be a lot of food there, at the very least..."

There was no winning with this guy. He had a point, though. The last days, months, hell, years had been spent in isolation, battle, and a constant state of moving, running, protecting. Not to mention my buddy Marlowe just reunited with his long time love Nik and they had a darling baby girl. The smell of love was in the air, I guessed. Not too long ago Lucien himself had brought home a human mate, of all things.

There was so much to be grateful for.

When I looked at it that way, the Flower Festival was the most normal thing to happen to us in years. The Firefang tradition celebrated family, beauty, and each other. It had been a wonderful festival, and the week wound to a close with an extravagant ball complete with musicians, food from across the world, and jaw-dropping performances.

I huffed out a breath through my nose.

"Fine, I'll go." I held out my hand. "But I'm gonna need that mask."

My lips quirked up in a grin, and Lucien's did the same. "I knew I'd get you to see reason." He shook my hand briskly, then his eyes glinted again.

That meant there was a "but..." coming.

"Now there's the matter of your date."

I rolled my eyes. "Don't push your luck. We gonna go get that mask or stand around talking?"

Lucien led the way off toward his home but kept talking. "We're not on the battlefield anymore, Tork. I bet there's more than one omega out there that would love to have you."

"It's not like that," I shrugged. "I've got everything I need already. Date...mate...it's all the same. All a distraction, if you ask me."

Lucien chuckled. "Whatever you say."

I grumbled and quickened my steps to keep up with him. "Let's just get this over with."

We arrived at the door to Lucien's home and he swiveled to face me before opening the door.

"A tip from your Clan Alpha? Keep your eyes open. Never know what you might find."

———

THE BUBBLY CHAMPAGNE burst across my tongue and tingled as it went down. I sat down the glass flute and gazed out at the couples gliding across the floor in merriment.

Alphas and omegas of all shapes and sizes had come out to the ball tonight, humans and shifters alike. I scratched my chin underneath the full-face mask Lucien had lent me. At least no one would recognize me like this.

The clash of floral scents hung heavy in the air, making me a little lightheaded, if I was being honest. Perhaps that was just the drink, though. Lucien twirled around on the dance floor with his mate in his arms, both of them wearing expressions of unfettered joy. They clung to one another so closely, as if they were one person instead of two.

Must be nice.

I couldn't help thinking about what Lucien had said on the way to pick up my costume. Sure, I was busy with work and loved what I did, but that didn't change the fact that I was a dragon shifter, and an alpha at that. My beast, much as I didn't like to admit it, had needs too.

Needs that I'd been willfully ignoring more often than not. I told myself I didn't need anyone, that it would be too complicated, too messy. I'd seen plenty of relationships go sour, including my parents'. I wasn't in a hurry to replicate that any time soon.

But the way people like Lucien and Alec looked at one another was different. Any bystander could clearly see they adored one another, trusted one another, leaned on one another when the other couldn't be strong. Maybe it wouldn't be so bad to have someone like that.

Keep your eyes open, Lucien had warned me. I straightened my back, squared my shoulders, and ran a hand through my hair to slick the wavy strands back across my forehead.

A dangerous scheme began to brew in my head as my dragon twisted its way through my chest, aching for release. I hadn't lain with anyone in a long, long time. Longer than even I could remember.

Don't you want something like that? My dragon urged me on. I glanced at the couples again.

Yes. Yes I did.

What if I could learn to let go, just for a night? What kind of man could keep up with not only my fast-paced lifestyle but the dangerous nature of my profession?

Not many, that was for sure.

I raked my gaze over the crowd. There were plenty of single omegas in dashing costumes, but none of them caught my eye. Lace and flowers and dyes assaulted my eyeballs at every turn, and they were lovely, yes, but who could say what kind of man lie beneath?

Fuck it, I shrugged. *One night is hardly forever.*

My stomach growled in protest after the multiple rounds of champagne and no food. "Fine," I muttered to myself and pushed through the crowd to the snack bar.

A delicious array of fruits, cheeses, crackers, and other delicacies decorated the long serving table, all arranged in artful patterns while the ball-goers filled plates and chatted among themselves.

I had my eye on a chocolate-covered strawberry when my hand brushed a silk glove reaching for the same morsel. I jerked my wrist away, looking up in surprise.

A thin, shorter man stood before me, decked out in an elaborate costume of black, cream, and gold. He cut quite the dashing figure; even under the intricate swirls of the mask he wore I could see glowing embers of eyes.

A spark shot up my arm as we touched. Even through

the silk glove, his presence was electrifying. I could tell right away that he was an omega, but his floral perfume covered any other scent coming off him.

"Excuse me," the man said softly and drew his hand back, shoving it behind his back.

The strawberry, chocolate covered or not, was all but forgotten. My gaze rested on the flamboyant omega, so different from the shifters I was used to seeing. Perhaps it was something in the man's voice. Something in the way he held himself or the way he slightly tilted his head when considering me. Whatever it was, I couldn't shake the feeling I knew him from somewhere.

I shook my head. Maybe I'd had a few too many glasses of that champagne. I fought back the urge to say "do I know you?" and instead offered a greeting. "Good evening."

"Is it?" The man asked quizzically, now leaning over me to fill his plate. A smell wafted off of him I'd never noticed before. It was omega, all right, but different than the other shifters I'd been in contact with in the village. There was only the faintest hint of it, but as I considered the omega smell grew stronger, and stronger still.

My mind reeled and I yanked my gaze away as he straightened with his plate.

He cocked an eyebrow in my direction.

"It's the Flower Festival," I said, suddenly flustered. "The ball. Most people wait all year for such an occasion." And surely this one's costume was long in the making. The sequins caught my eye in the light, feathers blossomed from his shoulders, and he presented himself with all the elegance of a jeweled peacock.

The omega shrugged. "I'm not most people."

That was for certain.

I gave an amused chuckle as that current of desire flickered through my veins again. "Nor am I, Sparkles." I grinned at the nickname, stroking my chin. Where did I know him from? Surely somewhere, right? I would have noticed such an omega before.

Now he'd roused me both body and mind. I wanted, no, needed to know more about him. But not here.

Sparkles tilted his head away from the snack bar to a quieter corner of the ballroom, shrouded by heavy velvet drapes and whispering couples. He pointed at his ear and gestured for me to come close.

I held my breath as I leaned in. The scent of him poured off his skin and invaded my senses, lighting up my dragon from deep within.

He'd do. He'd do nicely, the dragon crooned.

"It's a bit loud around here, yes? I'd like to hear the man I'm talking to."

I nodded and Sparkles led the way. He slipped through gaps in the crowd so easily, twisting and turning as he danced to the rhythm of the music. I...well, let's just say I wasn't nearly so graceful. After a few awkward jostles and mumbled apologies, I made it to the other side of the room. Only, Sparkles was nowhere to be found.

"Over here!" His glittery head poked out from behind a large flowerpot and waved at me. He patted a plush cushion in an alcove where tiny globes of dragonfire floated on garlands and gave off a flickery, cozy light. Totally romantic...if I was into that kind of thing.

I grabbed another glass of champagne from a passing server and joined him, my long legs sticking off to the side of the planter. *Not so private now*, I chuckled to myself.

Sparkles continued to eye me. Was he struggling with the same hidden mystery I was? Was he feeling the same inklings of desire?

I took another sip to steel myself and leaned back against the cushions. My ears rang. I hadn't realized just how loud the ball was with all the people and music and talking. But now that I was away from it all, my senses were still catching up.

Delicate hands picked up a strawberry and popped it into his mouth. I couldn't help but watch the way those luscious lips closed around the fruit. Couldn't help but wonder what they might feel like around my...

"I'm not much for crowds," Sparkles said sheepishly, interrupting my wayward thoughts.

"I never would have guessed," I teased. He carried himself like a peacock, but perhaps it was all an act? A character he put on like a costume for this occasion alone?

A hint of chocolate smeared on the corner of his mouth. A vision flashed through my mind of grabbing him right then and there, of licking that sweet filling off and so much more. This was so unlike me. I shook my head and put a hand to my temple.

Other alphas got all worked up over sex and mating.

Not me.

I swallowed hard, straightening and taking a deep breath. Wrong choice. I got a lungful of that intoxicating scent and my cock grew even harder as I watched him enjoy the strawberries one at a time. He closed his eyes as he bit into each one, a low sigh escaping from his lips.

"You really like strawberries," I chuckled, grasping for what to say next.

"They're my favorite," Sparkles agreed. "And the chocolate...mmm! I haven't had chocolate in years. Such a delicacy! This has been the best Flower Festival ever, wouldn't you say?"

His eyes locked with mine and I couldn't tear myself

away. I was trapped there, held in this omega's burning gaze as he set the plate aside. The familiar rumbling of fire rose in my chest, sparked on my tongue. But this time it was more than a passing annoyance. It was a strong, all-encompassing heat that soaked through me and wiped out all other thoughts.

Take him, my dragon screeched. *Take him now!*

I couldn't taste the champagne on my lips. Couldn't smell the fresh scent of the flowers. There was only him. I drew closer to him as if pulled by some external force, my lips slightly parted as I honed in on that perfect mouth...

"Oh, shit!" Sparkles yelped in what sounded like pain and shrunk away from me. I blinked, my mind screeching to a halt with the whiplash. The omega scrambled to his feet and put a hand to his forehead, wringing his hands. "Shit, shit, shit!"

"What?" I rasped, my voice husky. Lust still simmered there, hot and ready, but there was something else, too. My protective alpha instincts kicked into full gear. What was wrong? Had I hurt him?

"I'm...oh, Goddess, I'm so sorry, I have to..."

Sparkles scrambled off through the crowd without another word, disappearing easily among the throng.

"Wait!" I called after him, lumbering to my feet and scanning the crowd. He might have been small, but I could see over many of the bobbing heads. Not to mention that costume made him pretty easy to find.

There he was.

I pushed through dancers and servers, accidentally trampling a few toes on the way. I knocked over a wobbly vase and it shattered on the ground in an explosion of glass. It only barely registered in my mind as I fled toward him, every alpha instinct roaring to the surface. My heart leapt into double time as my eyes locked on to his small form, crouched and panting near the end of a long hallway. His eyes widened in fear when he saw me.

Not so sparkly anymore.

That's when I realized what was happening. Why his smell had come on so strong. An unexpected heat, right in the middle of the whole town.

Goddess, no wonder he was panicked.

I held up my hands in a gesture of peace, taking a few cautious steps in his directions.

"Hey, it's okay. I'm here to help."

As much as my dragon wanted to take this omega right here right now, I pushed through it to a higher plane of reason. He needed help. He needed to get to safety before some less scrupulous alpha got to him first.

The scent and energy in the air was electric. It crackled

with power and arousal and possibility. And I couldn't have any of it.

Sparkles shrank back further, his small body quivering.

"I'm not going to hurt you," I said slowly, and our eyes locked.

There. Hidden within those masked depths was the shining amber core I was looking for. It called to me like a magnet to my soul.

Mate...? The word bounced around in my soul but I pushed it away. It couldn't be. Not here. Not now.

I took a breath and extended my hand. "Let me help you."

"You know what this is, don't you?" The omega whispered, voice shaking. His forehead shone with sweat and the very visible evidence of his arousal pressed through his pleated pants.

"Yes," I growled.

Focus, Tork, focus.

I grit my teeth and reached out to him, knowing what I'd feel when our skin touched. But I couldn't leave him here. That wouldn't be honorable at all.

"Should I be scared?" He breathed.

"No," I assured him, and he took my hand.

His skin on mine lit up every pore, every nerve, every

cell. My vision narrowed to focus on him, only him. "I won't hurt you," I assured him and gave the hand a squeeze. "There are other alphas I would not be so sure about, but you're in good hands. You're safe with me. Let's get you out of here."

I looked to my left and right down the hallway. No one was coming, which was good. No one to see our particular predicament. I ducked around a corner and found a spare room. "Come on," I beckoned. Sparkles followed.

The omega sank down onto a plush couch as I slid the door closed. It wasn't exactly the lap of luxury, but we could hide out here until the crowds died down, then make our escape. Sparkles let out a sigh and put a hand to his head, swaying a bit before righting himself.

"Do you need water? A blanket? Anything I can get you?" The words tumbled out on top of one another. Speaking too fast again. I wanted, no, needed to help him, and seeing the look on his face made me even more concerned. My pulse raced in my veins and my dragon begged for release as I realized just how close we were.

We were alone. Alpha and omega. And he was in heat.

Goddess help me.

I wanted him more than I'd ever wanted anything. More than the new chemicals for my lab. More than a new adventure. This little omega *was* the adventure, and this was an adrenaline rush greater than the most action-packed heist. Red flags flew up in all directions in the back of my mind, but the intoxicating smell of an omega in heat wiped them all away.

I promised to look after him, and I had to do that. No matter how much my cock ached.

"I'll just be outside, I'll watch the door and send for someone to help..." I needed air. Yes, that was it.

My hand was on the doorknob when the omega responded.

"No," he rasped. "Stay."

I turned slowly to face him, blood roaring in my ears and sparks crackling on my tongue. Did he know what he was doing to me?

"Are you sure about that?" I rumbled, my self restraint holding on by only a thread. "In your condition..."

He leapt to his feet and grabbed my hands, pressing me into the door. His scent smothered me. I was lost. The omega's lips whispered over my chest, my neck. He looked up, locking eyes with mine.

"I said...stay."

Even through our masks I could see the flaming desire there, like molten metal ready to be forged. My body strained against him as he pressed me against the wall, and even though I could easily push him away, I didn't want to.

May I be damned, but I didn't want to.

"You wanted to help me. So help me," he whispered. His hand was soft in mine, only a few calluses on the fingers and palm. I didn't care. He led my hand to his bulging crotch and left it there. My eyes widened and I sucked in a breath. Omegas were known to be forward while in heat, but this was something else.

"I can't," I groaned through gritted teeth. I'd never lost control like this before. Never. I prided myself on it. But here I was, every inhibition and shred of decency gone. It should have been humiliating.

But I'd never been so turned on in my life.

"Please," the omega moaned. He fumbled with the layers of costume and soon the bottoms came free, exposing his hard and leaking cock.

The moment I saw it, there was no turning back. My dragon roared to the surface, blocking all out reason, all honor. This omega was mine.

"You sure about this?" I rumbled, running a hand down the omega's cheek to his shoulders as I held him to me. Goddess, he was so warm. And he smelled incredible. Like my favorite food and my favorite hobbies all rolled into one.

This was my mate. Had to be. And to think I'd met him at the Flower Festival ball I'd been so reluctant to attend.

I smirked at the thought, remembering how Marlowe and Nik had first found one another at the Festival all those years ago.

Guess love was in the air.

"I want this," the omega mumbled. "Want you."

That was enough for me.

My alpha senses took over as I loomed over the small omega. He was small, yes, but with a fire that roused me even further. What was it about this man that stood out among all the others? Whatever it was, I was going to find out.

Right after I buried my cock all the way to the hilt in his sweet, hot channel. Right after I made him mine.

"Is here okay?" I asked, arranging a pile of pillows and laying him down gently. It took all my resolve to keep from throwing him down and taking what was mine, but I was better than my instincts. Omegas deserved to be loved and treasured, not fucked and discarded like pieces of meat.

I was going to treasure this one with all I had.

"Take off your mask," he breathed, eyes shining. "Want to see you."

I froze at that. Peeling away the layers of mask and costume might break the spell between us. I recognized it as an irrational fear, but couldn't bat it away for long before it resurfaced.

"We have our whole lives to look upon one another," I replied, toying with the feathers that splayed out around his head like a crown. "Tonight, let's preserve the magic."

My omega was silent for a moment, still holding my

gaze, our dragons reaching out to one another in a primal dance neither of us could resist. Now or never.

"Fair enough," he responded, and kissed me.

It took a moment to get over the initial shock. Not only was this omega the hottest shifter I'd ever seen, but he was willing to take the initiative, too. My dragon growled in response and I pressed myself closer, spearing my tongue into his mouth as he opened to me with a moan. We clasped at one another, giving and taking that delicious chemistry that flowed between us.

This wasn't just the champagne. This wasn't just a fling.

This was fate, and both our dragons knew it.

It didn't matter that I didn't even know his name. It didn't matter that I couldn't shake the strange feeling of familiarity. All that mattered was getting inside him, joining us the way we were meant to be joined, as alpha and omega.

I wasted no time in fumbling with the buttons on the tunic Lucien had lent me. My fingers rushed over the brass fast and clumsy. I feared I'd rip away a button or tear right through the fabric for a harrowing moment, and then the fasteners came free. My mate sucked in a breath at the sight of my bare chest, toned and muscled from long days of working in the shop. Demolitions and magitech was no easy business, and I had to be on my toes, both physically and mentally, to do the work I did.

One false move could mean death, after all.

Sparkles followed suit, divesting himself of the glittery garment and tossing it aside. It crumpled to the floor, forgotten, and I grabbed him with such ferocity he squeaked in surprise. The feeling of skin on skin burned me up from the inside out. Already I could feel the pull of his dragon to mine. Already I could feel the ancient mating rite beginning as our souls reached out and intertwined.

"Fuck," the omega breathed, and I leaned down to plant kisses across his smooth, toned chest, his sides, down to his abdomen. He sucked in a breath and I continued my trail of pleasure, nipping at his hips, his thighs, and finally centering in on his hard and weeping cock.

"You're beautiful," I rumbled, admiring his proud length.

"What are you gonna do about it?" He quirked an eyebrow.

Goddess, I could get used to this.

I slipped a hand out from around his back to snake down toward his crotch, watching the contortions of my mate's face as I went. Even behind the mask, I could see the gasps and moans of pleasure perfectly. And I hadn't even touched his cock yet. I shuddered to think of what came next.

When I reached his opening, my fingers came away soaking wet. I brought them up to my face and sniffed, the pheromones surrounding me and blocking out everything else. With a throaty groan, I slipped a slick finger into my mouth. Flavors exploded on my tongue, musk and herbs and the overwhelming feeling that this was *right*.

My mate looked up at me with wide eyes. He wiggled his hips toward me, mewling with desire as his cock twitched. I wasted no time getting rid of my pants and my cock sprung free, hot and heavy against my already overheated skin. I propped myself on one arm and leaned over him, gathering our cocks together in one hand.

The omega hissed. "Goddess..." he swore.

"More where that came from." Sparks of need zigzagged all over my body as I pressed our cocks together. The friction built and my balls tightened. I would come right here if I wasn't careful. The omega's velvety length slid easily against mine, making my dragon all kinds of crazy.

"Please," the omega panted. "Now." He lifted his hips and angled himself toward me. My heart nearly stopped—I'd never seen anything so hot in my life.

My human mind went blank, but that didn't matter. The dragon took full control and I guided my cock where it needed to go. My vision sharpened. Prisms of light danced before my eyes. This was it.

Gently at first, I hissed as his hot, tight channel enveloped my cock. I pressed into him inch by torturous inch and my heart sped into double time. As soon as I seated myself all the way to the hilt inside him, I let out a long, shuddery breath. This was what I was made for, what I'd been waiting for all these years. The old ideas about not needing a mate or not understanding the appeal faded into the background. This was better than flying.

My partner's arms wrapped around me and pulled me closer until I covered him with every inch of my skin. Only our faces remained concealed, but it added to the eroticism of the moment, if anything. I felt wild and free, burying myself in a mystery omega I never knew I needed. This was what people wrote songs about, I realized. This was what people went to war over.

The omega rocked beneath me, his breaths quickening as he dragged his small hands down my back. I growled deep in my chest and thrust into him again. My head still spun with the overwhelming sensations of his tight heat around me and the connection of our dragons, our souls. I let it spin. Wouldn't give this up for anything.

My dragon rose dangerously close to the surface and I tasted fire, felt my fingers morph into claws as I pounded into my mate's wanting flesh. I fought to keep from shifting on the spot. Shifting indoors would bring down a whole pile of rubble on top of us.

Decidedly not sexy.

The omega beneath me seemed to be struggling as much as I was as his eyes and reptilian pupils flickered between human and dragon form. He was getting close, I realized as he squeezed me with his legs. This was the point of no return.

Mine! My dragon soared within me, and I pushed into him one, two, three more times. Then the world shattered around us. I let out a roar as my knot swelled, locking us together as mates. I'd never felt so full, so wanted in all my years. And with the spirits looking down on us from above, I shuddered and filled the omega with my seed, panting, as we held on to each other for dear life.

Mine. My mate. My destiny.

———

IT WASN'T SUPPOSED to end like this.

"You've got to take care of Ansel. Please," the weak words of a dying man rung in my ears. I held his limp body in my arms as fire and screams echoed around us. My best friend. My partner in crime.

"Don't say that." I growled. "You're going to be okay." I pressed a makeshift bandage into the wound at his side.

It soaked through almost instantly. He was losing too much blood, and his eyes already had that glassy, far away stare.

He was going to die.

Veltar gripped at my shirt with surprising strength for a dying man. "Please, take care of my son. He will come of age soon, and he needs a mentor. I can think of no one better." He coughed and his body shook. Blood bubbled on his lips.

My entire body felt cold. Battle raged around me, but it was faint in my ears. My own aches and wounds meant nothing. In this moment, there was only us. As a warrior and a Firefang, I knew that death was part of life. But I never thought it would be like this. Without Veltar, who was I? What was I? I was an alpha, and a weapons scientist. I had no idea how to take care of a child.

My throat dried as I watched my Veltar's life force fade before my eyes. There was nothing I could do.

"Please..." Veltar panted. "Promise me, Tork."

"I promise," I swore, and Veltar passed into the Great Beyond.

———

THAT DREAM AGAIN.

My heart ached and a lump of emotion still wobbled in

my throat, even nearly a decade after the fact. I groaned and opened my eyes to the shimmery rays of sunlight.

My body ached all over, and I had a raging headache. I was naked, which wasn't unusual, but the room was unfamiliar. What had happened last night?

Memories filtered back in slowly as the dream lost its hold on me. I sat up so fast I nearly fainted, my head protesting as I put a hand to my temple. The Flower Festival. The ball. The omega...

Oh, no. I didn't...

I snaked a hand down to my crotch. My cock was still sensitive from the night before, and my muscles screamed as if from the hardest workout. I could just about hear the grinding of gears in my brain as it rushed to process the new information.

Last night was the Flower Festival ball. Last night I ran across an inexplicably endearing omega. Last night I mated him.

So where was he?

The room was empty, save for a few pillows and a lingering floral smell. Guess I'd spooked the guy.

I scrubbed a hand across my face. What the hell had gotten into me? As one of Lucien's right hand men and head of weapons and demolition for the Firefangs, I needed to be calm and in control at all times.

And what happened last night? That was about as far from control as you could get.

As I quickly threw on my clothes and schooled my hair into some semblance of order, I pushed away the nagging anxiety that bubbled up in my gut.

My omega was out there. And I didn't even know his name.

ANSEL

W hat a night.

As soon as I woke up and found myself in a strange alpha's arms, I bolted. Didn't know what else to do.

Goddess-damned heat.

There I was, just trying to have a little fun at the Flower Festival ball. I'd made an outfit just for the occasion. It was one of the only times per year I got to have a little fun and dress up. Couldn't exactly go into work covered in feathers. *What a fire hazard that would be*, I chuckled to myself as I swung my legs over the side of the bed.

And then I'd went and done it. I slept with an alpha last night when my heat overtook me. Not only did we have sex, if my hazy memory was correct, he'd knotted in me too. That probably meant we were mated now, and probably meant I was gonna be carrying a little dragon inside me soon.

Conflicting thoughts and desires fought their way through my mind. Did I regret it? Not exactly, but the guilt was still there.

What would Tork say?

Ever since returning from a four year stint at Magitech Academy, I saw things in a new way. Returning to Darkvale after studying abroad had not only sharpened my skills as an engineer, but also my perceptions. I saw things, and people, in a new light. My mentor Tork, in particular.

He was handsome, no one could deny that. But he was also my father's best friend, and totally off limits.

I swallowed and buttoned up my flame-resistant tunic, stopping to glance in the mirror and make sure it was on straight. Couldn't tell you how many times I'd missed a button and came into work with a lopsided shirt.

After my parents passed away in battle when I was only thirteen, Tork took me in. I knew him from my childhood as my father's best friend, but in the year before I went off to the academy, he took care of me best he could and taught me what he knew.

I'd always had an inclination for engineering, sure, but getting to work alongside Tork? It was like a dream come true. He was incredibly brilliant, if a little brash, and I respected that about him. His rigorous training paid off once I got into Magitech Academy, and then I was off to learn amongst the greatest engineers in the country.

Now that I was back, I couldn't shake the feeling that there was something...I don't know, more for me out there. Getting back into my old routine of working in the lab and joining up with the local magitech guild was all fine and good, but my dragon, my omega, needed more.

I squeezed my eyes shut and drew in a long breath through my nose.

It wasn't like I was ever going to mate with Tork anyway. He was not only my mentor, but had served as a kind of father figure to me after my parents died. Talk about forbidden.

Brushing away the pangs of guilt, I threw on my jacket, slipped on my boots, and made my way out the door. Whatever had happened, I could deal with it later. For now, I had work to do.

———

"YOWCH!" I hopped on one foot, holding my

throbbing toe after dropping a wrench on it for the second time that day. One of the other engineers eyed me warily, flipping up his welding mask to watch my theatrics.

"You doing all right there?" He asked, raising an eyebrow. "Forget your steel toe boots today?"

"It's nothing," I muttered. "Just clumsy today, is all." I put my throbbing foot back on the ground and tried to shoot him a smile.

"You're normally not like this," He pressed on, putting down his tools to approach me. "Why don't you take an early lunch break, clear your head?"

I swallowed and turned my head, staring at the ground. Now I was fucking things up at work too.

"We've got a lot of work to do and need everyone in top form. If there's anything I can do..."

"There's not," I cut him off, and grabbed my lunch sack. "I'll be fine."

I breezed out the door, my skin cooling rapidly in the breeze. I always worked up a sweat in the workshop. Who wouldn't? The place was covered with forges and fire. But out here, everything was quiet. I could finally hear myself think.

Putting a few paces between me and the workshop, I wandered over to a small clearing with a bench and a few trees. I thought better of it when I realized how popular as a lunch spot it would be. I didn't want to run into anyone right about now. Definitely not Tork.

I turned on my heel and headed off in the opposite direction, trying to ignore the unknown feeling of guilt that rose within me.

Why did I care so much about letting Tork down? He was my mentor, not my mate. There was nothing between us. I respected him in a totally business way, but that was it. That was all it would ever be.

I sunk down onto a fallen tree branch behind a building with a sigh. No one to bother me here.

The air hung silent save for the distant mechanical whirring and clanging of the workshop. Birds fluttered through the trees and the air carried the last fading scents of the Flower Festival. As enjoyable as it all was, reality started to filter back into day to day life here in Darkvale. Although things on the war front were calmer than they had been, there was still the matter of the mysterious "metal men" uncovered by our resident Sorcerer, Elias. I shivered at the thought as I took a bite of my sandwich. Lucien had recruited just about all of us engineers to research the possibility of this kind of contraption and to see if we could replicate something similar. We needed to know what we were up against, and if a raging automaton struck Darkvale now, we'd be woefully unprepared.

The sound of a snapping twig yanked me out of my

thoughts and I looked up to find the man I least wanted to see right now.

Tork.

My cheeks flushed as I stared at him with a bit of bread hanging from my mouth. He stood there, hands on his hips. He panted as if he'd run all the way here. "There you are."

I put down the sandwich as a thread of fear twisted through me. Something was wrong. I didn't know what, but I could feel it, all the way down in my gut.

"What's the matter?"

"It's Lucien. He's got news of the metal men. Needs to meet with us immediately. All hands."

I nearly choked on my sandwich and swallowed hard. "He never calls unplanned all hands meetings."

"He does now. Come on." Tork outstretched his hand to help me up and I grabbed it without thinking.

A spike of electricity shot through me as we touched and I gasped before I could stop myself. I looked to Tork to see if he was feeling the same, but if he was, he didn't show it. Didn't expect him to—years of working together taught me he didn't exactly wear his heart on his sleeve.

Get your head in the game, I scolded myself, and yanked my hand away. I wiped it on my pants and slung my bag over my shoulder. "Let's go," I said, and we rushed off toward the workshop.

This was no time for worrying about mates and babies. I had a job to do. Grateful for the distraction, I pushed my legs harder, focusing on the wind in my hair and the cool breeze on my face. My clan needed us, and I wasn't about to let them down.

The mystery of my midnight mate would just have to wait.

———

"COME IN, COME IN," Lucien ushered us through the door as he shut the heavy iron behind us with a eerily final thunk. "Thank you for coming on such short notice. I apologize for interrupting your lunch break," he lowered his eyes to me, "but I have urgent news from the field. And I need your help."

I hastily took my seat next to Tork and watched as Lucien walked over to the head of the crowd that had formed. My heart still raced and my blood felt like it was on fire. I told myself it was just the adrenaline of having a good run back to the shop and wondering what Lucien had to tell us, but with Tork sitting there so close to me, I couldn't be sure.

All of those worries seemed insignificant, though, as I listened to Clan Alpha Lucien's announcement.

"It is with a heavy heart that I bring you news from the field. We've received reports of these...metal men being sighted only a day's ride from here."

Murmurs of surprise and shock filled the crowd and my veins turned to ice as I considered the ramifications. All we had found were remnants...they found one operational?!

Lucien held up his hand for silence and I held my breath, waiting for the next bombshell to drop. "Yes, it does appear that our enemies have an early prototype afield, and in a skirmish we've lost not one, but two of our prized scouts." He placed a hand over his heart and looked upon us with sad eyes. "They are with the Goddess now, watching over us from the Great Beyond. But we shall not let this slight go unanswered. We must root out this prototype before it ever reaches our walls. The future of Darkvale, and of the Firefangs, depends on it. I've chosen several warriors and scouts to intercept and neutralize the threat, but I need engineers, as well. The road ahead will be dangerous, and I will not force you to fight. But think of this: your families, your children, your mates, all depend on what happens in the next few weeks. Will you join us?"

The room filled with muttering for a moment, each of us waiting for someone to speak up first.

"I will," I heard myself say. I stood, the wooden chair squealing behind me as I pressed my hands down on the table. "I will go with you." I needed a distraction. I needed time to think. And the chance to get up close and personal with such an elaborate specimen was just the icing on the cake.

"I'm coming too," Tork chimed in beside me almost instantly. He stood and gave me a glance I couldn't decipher. I tensed. So much for that idea.

Lucien nodded at us both and marked our names on a list. "We need one more."

"And I," Rex agreed with a dip of his head.

"It's decided," Lucien regarded us with a flick of his pen. "Glendaria smiles upon you. All others, you may leave. Tork, Ansel, and Rex, you'll need to attend the briefing. At dawn, we depart."

My stomach roiled at the thought as men and women pressed their way past us out of the workshop. The walls seemed to close in on me, and the air was suddenly too thick, too full with the pungent odors of oil and metal. I swallowed and tasted bile.

Spending who knew how long in close quarters with Tork was just about the last thing I wanted to do right now. He'd smell the alpha on me if he hadn't already, and if I was pregnant...

What would he think of me then?

Goddess help me, I prayed I wasn't making the wrong choice. I could barely stomach the idea of keeping this secret from him, especially when he'd find out soon enough. I had to clear the air before we left. It would be just too awkward otherwise.

I turned, hoping to find him still standing there next to me. "Tork, I wanted to—" The words were no sooner out of my mouth than the alpha slipped away through the doors, leaving the thoughts trapped on my tongue.

Dawn came much too early for my liking. I yawned and stretched, rolling over in bed and burying my face in the pillows for just a few more seconds.

I'd been in a lot of messy situations, but I'd never felt so dirty. Not even an hour-long shower with Myrony's best scrubbing gel could get rid of the thoughts that plagued my every waking moment.

Dishonor.

Shame.

Impropriety.

I was guilty of all three of those and so much more.

When I agreed to take Veltar's son under my wing, he became the number one priority in my life. Work and loyalty to the clan came a close second. With both of those duties taking up my time, there was no room for a mating.

And yet that was precisely what I'd done at the Flower Festival ball.

It was no wonder the omega hadn't sought me out after that scandalous night. Omegas went into heat at intervals, that much was known, but they usually kept to their homes when it occurred. Being caught out in public was a predicament indeed. I'd only wanted to protect him, care for him, keep him away from alphas that may do him harm.

And I became the very alpha I wanted to save him from.

He'd begged me for it in the heat of the moment, but didn't all omegas? I rubbed a hand over my face and threw myself out of bed as my front door rattled on the hinges.

"Coming!" I growled, gathering up my bag and slinging my sword over my shoulder. The door shook again, this time louder.

"The clan's gonna leave without you if you don't get your ass out here!"

"Goddess, give me a moment," I grumbled. I stashed a few of my best reagents in a hip pouch and strapped my water flask to my side.

When I opened the door I found Arthur standing there, looking rather displeased.

"Bout time you showed up," he huffed. "Now come on, the rest of the group's already started moving!"

I picked up my steps and followed Arthur until we came to the giant gate at heading out of the city walls. Marlowe and Kari were there, along with Rex, another scout I couldn't name, and Ansel. I winced at the sight. I was gonna have to tell him sooner or later, but personal drama had no place during a military mission. We'd already lost two of our best scouts to the infernal contraption and if I didn't keep my wits about me, we'd lose even more.

"There you are," Marlowe nudged me as I joined their ranks heading out of the city. "Thought you weren't gonna make it."

"Slept in," I grumbled.

"As always," Kari said under her breath. I shot her a glare and she shut up.

"All right, Firefangs. Our mission is clear. Track down the prototype. Find out who's controlling it. Neutralize the threat. Engineers, you're to salvage everything you can and bring it back for dismantlement. Warriors: you'll hold the line while the engineers do their work. Scouts: you'll clear the way and update our trackers. Is everyone ready?"

"Sir," we said in unison, and I felt the familiar splash of adrenaline.

This was going to be an adventure.

———

THE JOURNEY STARTED out well enough—all of us were in high spirits and we joked and chatted before getting too far beyond the walls. There would come a time for silence, and soon. Our good humor wore off quickly when the skies parted and unleashed a heavy rain on our heads. It slowed our progress and made the road like quicksand to walk through. We weren't talking and laughing anymore, no. More like the grumbles and grunts of exertion, and the slurping sound our boots made in the mud.

I avoided catching Ansel's eye. Didn't want to have to break the uncomfortable news to him while we were out in the field. Didn't want to break the news to him at all, really. But I'd have to sooner or later.

I had to admit I snuck a few glances in as he stumbled in the mud. The strangest pull came from deep in my gut, urging me forward to help him up. I didn't think much of it; I'd spent most of the last decade looking after him and mentoring him in the magitechnical arts, after all.

But that's not all, my dragon urged me on with a flicker of what almost felt like arousal. I shook my head and hoped the thoughts would leave. They didn't, only rolling about like the ball bearings we used in the workshop.

Ever since Ansel returned from Magitech Academy with a degree in hand, he'd turned into a different person.

Well, not different exactly. That wasn't the right word. Perhaps I was just now noticing what had been there all along. The years at the Academy had toned not only his mind but also his body, and I couldn't help noticing how much stronger he looked. When I looked at him, I didn't see the scared young teen I'd taken in anymore. I saw a man.

I saw an omega.

And that scared the shit out of me.

Not that it mattered now, though. I'd gone and lain with another omega in the heat of the moment, and now he was probably out there alone, and pregnant, and...

"Hold up," Arthur hissed, holding out a hand for us to stop. That snapped me out of my thoughts and back into the moment, my ears pricked up for any sound, my eyes scanning the horizon. I sniffed the air and didn't pick up anything unfamiliar.

As the team grew silent and listened, I heard what Arthur was talking about. Low voices murmured on the breeze, carrying over the rising hills to us in a garbled mix of sound. I strained my ears and wished I was in my shift. Dragon senses were a lot more perceptive, but shifting out in the open like this would definitely get us noticed.

I couldn't decipher many of the mumblings, but I did manage to pick up a few words, and they set my blood afire.

Attack.

Darkvale.

And then there was the name Elias...

We stared at one another, eyes wide. Elias was our resident Sorcerer, and a spy for the Firefangs. He'd sworn his loyalty. Did they know he was working for us? Or was there some deeper intent at play? I shivered at the thought.

Had the Sorcerer double-crossed us?

I listened harder but the voices carried away, gone like the ashes of a fire. The land was silent once more, and Arthur motioned for us to get off the road. We crept away from the open plains toward the cliffs while the scouts watched our back and the warriors held their weapons at the ready. None of us dared to breathe.

Arthur and Anya forged ahead once we'd cleared the area behind us and leapt down a series of ledges.

We followed on foot, still glancing behind us as we scrambled down the rock.

"What's going on?" Ansel hissed at me as we gathered on the small stone shelf. There wasn't a lot of room and we were all pressed together, which made my awareness of Ansel that much stronger. It was also the first time he'd spoken to me since the ball.

"Dunno," I mumbled back. "There's a troop nearby, heard 'em. We can hide out here till they pass."

The voices grew louder again and footsteps crackled down the dusty path. I held my breath and pressed myself against the wall, hoping they wouldn't notice us.

Just then, a rock tumbled from the precipice and splashed into the water below.

I let out a shaky breath and closed my eyes. Now we'd done it. No one moved.

The footsteps above us stopped and a voice rang out clear as crystal this time.

"I heard something."

Shit.

I shot my gaze to Marlowe, looking for direction. He gave an almost imperceptible shake of his head, commanding us to stay put.

"It came from over here," a second man's voice said. So

there were at least two of them, four if I had to guess from the sound of their footsteps.

I heard them coming closer. We couldn't just stand here and get caught!

I shot a panicked glance at Marlowe and he tilted his head off the cliff and toward the splashing of the sea below. "Now," he mouthed, and we jumped.

We sailed through the air in free fall. Goddess, I'd missed that feeling. Wind whipped at my skin and the water rushed toward us below. I heard shouts from above but they all but faded into the background as I gave myself over to my shift. My muscles bulged and changed, my teeth lengthened into fangs, my mouth became a snout. Wings burst from my shoulder blades. I let out a roar and the sound of dragons filled the air.

Messing with a clan of dragon shifters? Bad idea.

I flapped my wings to gain altitude and saw the men that had almost uncovered our hiding place. They wore heat-resistant armor and glowing green gauntlets. They knew we were coming.

I wanted to blow them up right then and there, but then I heard a familiar screech. I whipped around. It was Ansel. He flailed and roared in a combination of pain and fear.

My heart leapt into my throat. *No! Not Ansel!*

I swiveled to find the source of the attack and locked

eyes with a red-headed woman shrouded in a deep green robe. They had a fucking Sorcerer!

She swung her arms in a terrible arc and I knew I'd be next. Her energies surrounded Ansel and he quailed, limbs flailing frantically. He began to lose altitude.

I rushed forward, folding my wings to my sides to gain more speed. I didn't have time to think about it. All I knew was I had to save him.

Screams and roars of panic echoed in my ears. Steel clashed as both human and shifter collided. Marlowe lost his shift and fought hand to hand on the ground. The scouts kept their distance and blew flames from above.

I took it all in at a moment and filed it away. My protégé, my Ansel, was falling.

The wind roared in my ears as I fled toward him, ignoring the spike of pain that lanced through my side. Had to get to him. Had to save him.

Ansel lost his shift in in mid-air, his frail body falling limp to the craggy beach below.

Time trickled by in slow motion. I focused on the sight of him, on my wings to carry me forward at just the right moment. At the last second before his body collided with the ground, I swooped beneath him and he landed on my back with a thud.

"I've got you!" I roared, skimming the surface of the

waves. His weak arms clasped the pockets behind my wings and held on for dear life.

Tork...

This time I heard Ansel's voice not out loud but in my mind. I nearly fell out of the sky with the shock of it.

Ansel?

Everyone knew that fated mates had a mental connection, a Link on which they could speak telepathically. But we weren't mates. Far from it. There were reports of Links being formed between soldiers or other incredibly intimate relationships, but it was rare.

I heard Ansel again, and this time it was no hallucination.

Let's get those sons of bitches! He looped his legs around my torso and tightened his grip. A shiver of pride, purpose, and pleasure flowed through my every vein. I'd never felt anything like it before. It was like breathing fire, only times a thousand. My every cell vibrated with light and life and power.

I didn't have time to think or question. Only to act.

Go! He cried, I roared in triumph.

We sailed through the air like the riders of old, the force of our bodies and souls combined like a multiplier. I appraised the field at a glance—Marlowe grappled with what looked to be their leader while the scouts circled above and burned a ring of fire into the earth, preventing any escape.

Kari rejoined the fray, facing off against the sorcerer while Rex scavenged through their wagon of supplies.

First matter of business, the Sorcerer. With her neutralized we could use our powers again.

You gonna be okay if I shift back? I spoke to Ansel, still reveling in the knowledge that he could hear me.

Yeah, I'm good. Put me down.

I won't leave you, I promised, and we alighted on the cliff face. I took advantage of the Sorcerer's momentary distraction to shift back to human and run toward her full speed. I caught her in a tackle and she crumpled to the ground, eyes wild and teeth bared. She dug her knife-like nails into my arms, leaving a trail of fresh blood. I grunted in pain.

Rex tossed Kari a metal spike that he'd found in their stores and she leveled it at the Sorcerer's throat.

The mage narrowed her eyes at me, spittle forming on her lips. "You wouldn't kill me. Neither of you."

"Try me," Kari hissed, pressing the sharp point against her exposed skin.

"You're coming with us," I told her. "Or you can die. Your choice."

She snarled at me but there wasn't much she could do with the two of us restraining her.

I heard a shout and a thud from behind us and I nodded to Kari. "Hold her!"

I gave the Sorcerer a last withering look and released my grip, spinning around. I saw with horror that Marlowe lay on the ground unmoving and his attacker lunged at me with wide, angry eyes. He swung his blade toward what would have been my back if I hadn't moved at that exact moment. I feinted to the side and grabbed a vial from my hip, throwing the contents in his face. He screamed and I wrinkled my nose at the smell of burning flesh. His sword clattered to the ground and I lunged to pick it up, still on my guard.

Ansel ran to Marlowe's side as the scouts circled closer. I held my wounded ribs and rounded on Rex, digging through the wagons and totally unguarded.

Look out for Marlowe, I'll cover Rex.

Deal.

I coughed as the fumes from the reagent burned my nose. I spent a long time gathering that. Didn't expect to use it to burn a man's face off, but hey, improvise.

"Find anything?" I asked Rex breathlessly as he looked up.

"There's a whole load of stuff here, looking like some

parts for their automatons too. We need to get somewhere safe and study it."

"Can do. Is the wagon intact?"

"Looks like it."

"Good, let's get out of here."

I looked to the sky and signaled to the scouts. They circled lower now, back into the range of the Sorcerer's abilities. Though Kari held her hostage, she could still do a lot of damage if things got out of hand.

Arthur settled to the ground first, shifting back to human form as he ran to Marlowe's side. Anya joined me and Rex, a breathless look of terror in her eyes.

"There's more," she breathed. "A lot more. There's an unoccupied cave not far south but we gotta be careful."

My gut clenched and I motioned to Rex. "Pack up everything you can and follow me."

Ansel and Arthur helped Marlowe to his feet, unsteady but very much still alive. I let out a breath of relief. Thank the Goddess.

"Come on!" I waved to my team. "We've got to get settled before nightfall."

Anya led the way with me and Rex close behind. Ansel and Arthur took up the rear as they helped Marlowe along and Kari dragged the Sorcerer with her, still angling a knife at her throat if she dared try anything.

I kept my eyes peeled for any signs of movement as we moved toward the cave. Nothing save for the screech of sea birds and the smell of salt on the air.

I glanced back at Ansel more than once. Just to make sure he was all right, I told myself, but there was something else there too.

What had happened to us back there? Why could I suddenly hear him in my mind? And what was that power I felt flowing through my every cell when we touched?

"Stay on your guard," Anya reminded me, and I kept close to her with my sword drawn, just in case.

As the dry plains gave way to hills and then the rise of mountains, the air cooled and the birds disappeared. It happened as sudden as walking through a veil. This was no place for life. No place for anyone. We crested a hill and the land stretched out around us as stony spires reached toward the sky. The ground hardened and cracked from sun or from some other force I couldn't tell. A crow perched on a petrified tree branch, staring straight at us with his glassy eyes.

Caw!

I hated crows.

"You sure this is the right way?" I quickened my steps to catch up with Anya. She lengthened her spyglass and peered through it for a moment, her lips pursed. She collapsed it and turned to me, pointing.

"There, see that?"

I tried to follow her finger but all I could see was the rough outline of the oncoming mountains. The terrain all flowed together and made it hard to pick out any individual pieces.

She grabbed my shoulder and pulled me toward her, so I could see where she'd been standing. "Straight ahead." Anya handed me the spyglass to take a look. Before she relinquished her grip she narrowed her eyes and added, "Don't drop it."

I extended the spyglass and closed one eye, trying to make out what she'd seen on the horizon.

And there it was. Barely noticeable even with a spyglass, a darkened area between two rocky crags looked back at me. A smattering of white stone surrounded the entrance but I could not see any further within. It was well out of the way, through, and obscure enough we wouldn't be stumbled upon for the night. "How long?" I asked.

"Flying, we'd be there in no time." She shrugged. "But with our cargo," she nodded toward the hostage Sorcerer, "I wouldn't risk it."

I let out a breath. "How long on foot?"

"If we hurry? Till nightfall."

"Noted."

I hung back to relay the message to the warriors. Some of the color had returned to Marlowe's face but he still walked with a limp. If we were caught that off guard by a surprise attack, the chances for finding and neutralizing the automaton didn't look good.

"How are we doing back here?" I asked, noting that Ansel's shoulders sagged under the weight of helping Marlowe along. "Why don't you let me take over for a bit? Go help Anya."

Ansel's face twisted. "I can handle myself."

"I know you can, I just..." I wrung my hands. "Fine. Whatever."

"I could use a break," Arthur said, stretching his arms. "I need to go check in with Anya anyway." He gave me a queer look and extricated himself. He hurried off before I could ask what he meant by it.

My heart skipped a few beats in my chest. Something weird was going on between Ansel and I, and having to be in forced proximity while we headed for the cave? Not exactly what I'd had in mind.

"Sure," I said tonelessly, and I stepped in to loop Marlowe's shoulder over my own.

"I'm fine," Marlowe complained. "Stop treating me like an omega."

Ansel bristled at that. "You're hurt. Alpha or omega, doesn't matter. you need medical attention."

"It's nothing," he brushed off. "Really. I'm just slowing you down."

"No Firefang left behind," I reminded him, and we carried on in tense silence.

T alk about awkward.

Here I was, trying to ignore the feelings I got around my mentor, and now we were stuck together helping our commander Marlowe along. I focused on the task at hand and tried not to meet his gaze.

But I couldn't get him out of my mind.

What had happened back there was incredible. Beyond anything I'd ever felt or heard of. I didn't know how to explain it, but it looked like we were gonna have to have a talk sooner rather than later.

My stomach roiled at the thought and a wave of nausea passed. I heaved a little, doubling over as Marlowe stumbled. Tork appeared at my side instantly.

"You okay?" He asked, placing a hand on my shoulder. There was that spark again, the electricity that crackled between us like a live wire every time we touched.

"Fine," I muttered and wiped my mouth. "Got a little shaken up back there is all. Don't worry about it."

Tork narrowed his eyes in that "I don't believe you" look, but didn't press. Thank the Goddess for that. We resumed our positions and carried on across the wilds.

What he didn't know couldn't hurt him, I told myself as I cradled my upset belly with one hand. But the alpha I saw that night, the way I'd given myself to him...

Something like that couldn't stay a secret for long, especially if I was—I gulped—pregnant.

We arrived at the cave under the last vestiges of sunlight. Thankfully the trip had been mostly uneventful after the ambush on the road, but that didn't mean we could let our guards down.

No, all of us were tired, sore, and totally on edge.

We still had our hostage Sorcerer, after all. And although Marlowe gained color with each step, I still worried for him.

I worried for everyone. Part of being an omega, I guess.

After the scouts cleared the cave for us to enter, I set about building wards for the door to make sure no one would stumble upon us in the night. With a little bit of magic-infused metal and a sweeping sensor no bigger than a fingertip, I could track movements in a wide radius around the doorway. They were a simpler version of the same wards I used to protect Darkvale, only on a more impromptu scale.

I knew they'd brought me along for that reason. Even if I hadn't volunteered, they likely would have drafted me all the same. I was the only one that knew all the inner workings of the wards and how to build the magitech shields to keep out prying eyes. And for us on this kind of mission, staying out of sight was crucial.

I didn't mind the work. No, I relished the chance to throw myself into something other than my jumbled thoughts and the tug of my dragon toward someone I knew I couldn't have.

When I got home, I realized as I wiped my brow, I'd have to seek out my real mate. He'd want to start a family, no doubt. Heat or not, I couldn't deny the feeling of connection I'd experienced that night in the alpha's arms.

Heats were nothing new for an omega like me. I should have known better. But even before it came on, my dragon awakened at the sight of the alpha at the snack table. Even behind the mask and costume, it knew. This one was mine.

I shook my head and tightened the last bolt, fastening the new wards to each side of the cave entrance. With a mechanical buzzing sound, they activated and a barely visible sheen of light laced between them like a force field. I waved my hand through the entrance and they turned red, letting out an awful klaxon of sound. I flinched at the noise, even though I knew it was coming.

"Keep it down, won't you?" Rex muttered. He crouched over a circular indentation in the ground where he'd piled firewood. "Do you want to alert every living thing in a mile radius?"

"You'd rather we wait till something comes to eat us for dinner to see if it works or not?" I shot back. While he was a talented engineer, Rex played a little too fast and loose for my liking.

Rex grumbled into the fire and sparks flew from his mouth, catching the dry wood at once. It didn't take long for the pile of kindling to become a merry crackling fire, spreading some much needed warmth to my tired bones.

Long shadows flickered on the walls as we settled in for the night.

Anya distributed dinner in the form of dried jerky and rice cakes that tasted like dirt. I choked it down all the same with a splash of water from my skin—didn't realize how ravenous I was.

When was the last time I'd eaten, anyway?

The Sorcerer sat in chains near the fire, watching us with a sullen expression as she chewed on one of the cakes Kari had offered her. She was calmer now, her shoulders slumped in resignation as she stared into the flames. Kari fitted her with a set of sublimation shackles to quell her powers, then set to the task of interrogating her.

Dinner gurgled in my stomach and I worried that I might not keep it down. More unsettling still was the thought that perhaps this was more than just a stomachache.

I prepped my bedroll for the night and little by little movement died down. Everyone was tired, and dawn would come early. When it did, we had to be ready to go.

I fell asleep to the crackle of the fire and the rustle of the wind through the trees.

———

WHEN I OPENED my eyes again, the fire had all but burnt itself out. It glowed in a lump of burning embers, throwing warm slants of light across the cave walls. As I opened my eyes a little further, I could see someone sitting in front of the fire, warming their hands. I couldn't tell quite who it was, the fire cast them in a dark silhouette, but I knew the answer anyway.

"Hey," I mumbled without moving from my bedroll. The man turned to look at me. Just as I'd expected, Tork's warm amber eyes looked back at me.

"You're awake," he said.

"Couldn't sleep."

Tork shrugged. "Me neither. One of us needs to keep watch, anyway."

I bristled at that. "The wards should do just fine. You know that."

"All the same." Tork stretched and avoided my gaze. He stared off into the distance, across the burning coals and up toward the small ventilation shaft through the ceiling. "I've got a lot on my mind," he admitted.

"Mind if I join you?" I whispered, moving quietly to not disturb the rest of the party.

"Sure," he said and patted a spot on the ground next to him.

I pulled the hide blanket away from my body and crawled over to the fire on hands and knees. Tork watched me each step of the way, his gaze hot on mine.

The tired embers glowed and sparks crackled from the coals up toward the sky and through the shaft to the sky beyond. Crickets chirped their persistent song outside, and the echoing hoot of an owl came at intervals.

"You ever been in the field like this?" Tork asked, giving me a sidelong glance. "They train you in that at your Academy?"

I blinked. Not once had Tork asked about my time at the Academy. I knew he was proud of me, sure. I knew he was glad to see me back home with degree in hand. But we never really talked about what went on there. And if I did tell him the truth, I doubted he'd ever believe it.

I shivered at the memories, even right next to the fire. "Not really," I replied, trying to sound casual. "More theory than practice. I learned a lot, sure, but—" I rubbed my arms and the gooseflesh there—"It's different in the real world, you know?"

"Don't I know it." Tork leaned back and propped himself on his elbows, his eyes still appraising me. For what, I didn't know.

We sat there in silence for what seemed like ages. The air stretched out in front of us, heavy with tension, with secrets, with that undeniable energy that linked us both. Finally, I couldn't take it anymore. I had to say something.

"We need to talk."

Tork raised an eyebrow. "About what?"

I swallowed. First things first. "About what happened

back there. About the ambush. I was unprepared. I fell, I lost my shift, I..." I shook my head. "You caught me."

"What about it?" Tork asked slowly. "You're part of the clan. No Firefang left behind. I had to help."

I scoffed. "And that's all it was? Just doing your duty?" I wrung my hands. "Come on, Tork. That's not what I mean. I heard you, man. I *felt* you, for Glendaria's sake. What was all that about?"

Tork frowned and looked away now. Even in the dim light of the coals, his face flushed a shade I'd never seen before. Was he embarrassed?

"I don't know anything about that," Tork said finally. "Doesn't make any sense to me either. It's a mate thing, and we're not..."

The words spilled out now, flooding my tongue as the dam of pent up emotion broke. All the shame and guilt and fear washed over me like the sea, cold and just as drowning. "Speaking of mates," I continued in a low, strangled voice. "I need to tell you something."

Tork's throat bobbed as he listened. His hands were fists at his side, and I could practically feel the anxiety pouring off of him.

"I need to tell you something too," Tork sighed, rubbing the back of his neck.

I froze, my throat suddenly dry. Tork was a professional. He didn't get to be the head of demolitions and weapons science by fucking random strangers at balls.

When my dad died, Tork took me in and taught me everything he knew. And part of that was how to be a proper omega in society. How to serve the clan and do my duty. He taught me the importance of loyalty, respect, and honor.

I'd sullied all three.

I closed my eyes and thought again of my dad. Always there for me. Always strong. Powerful. Alpha. He sacrificed so much for me to have a good life. "I never thanked you properly," I said with a shaking voice. "For what you did for me. When my...When dad died." I choked out the last words.

"He was a good man," Tork said, his eyes far away. I wasn't the only one who'd lost someone. Veltar was his best friend, and the entire reason he'd become my godfather.

"He was," I agreed, remembering his smile, his scent, his strength when he'd pick me up and carry me around on his back. It was the closest thing to flying I'd experienced before I'd been able to shift myself.

I blinked at the tears welling up in my eyes. I gave a choking chuckle. "Sorry," I murmured and wiped my face.

"No," Tork started, and reached out a hand toward me.

Then he stopped in midair, as if thinking better of it. His hand fell, and so did my spirits. "No sorries necessary."

He paused for a moment, then added, "You're a good man too, Ansel."

When I looked up those glowing orbs were boring into mine, full of emotion and purpose.

I wanted to look away, but couldn't. It was like some otherworldly force held me in, drawing us together like iron filings to a magnet.

"I don't know about that," I whispered, my cheeks hot with guilt.

"Oh yeah?" This time Tork didn't resist. He reached forward and planted a hand on my chin. "Why's that?"

He tilted it up toward his own and my lips parted slightly. I was suddenly too aware of Tork's touch, the tingle in my lips, the shiver of pleasure that crawled all the way down my spine.

There was no way this could be happening. No way my body would respond this way. I'd worked with Tork for ages and he'd never affected me this way. Until...

The pieces clicked together and I scooted backwards, gasping for breath.

"It was you," I rasped, my voice cracking.

"It was I, what?" Tork crossed his arms. "English, please."

"That night, at the festival, it was you..."

Tork's eyes widened and his mouth hung open. He blinked as if seeing for the first time. "No..." He started. "No..."

"Does this look at all familiar to you?" I pulled out a single silver feather and dangled it next to my ear.

"It can't be..." Tork whispered, turning away. "It's not right. It's not honorable. Just think of what Veltar would have said!"

"Why can't it be right?" I pressed. The vibration in my soul resonated ever stronger now with the knowledge that this was my mate. Not some random stranger from a party. Tork. "Tell me you don't feel this between us." I laced his fingers with mine and he sucked in a breath, still avoiding my gaze.

"You're Veltar's son," he moaned. "I could never..."

"Don't you believe in fate?" I asked him, gesturing to the stars above.

"Never did," Tork responded in a gruff tone.

"Ever since I was a kid, I heard that Glendaria has someone for us all out there. Our destiny. Our fated mate. Sometimes it just takes a while to find them, even if they've been in front of your face the whole time."

Tork frowned and chewed his lip. "I don't know what to think anymore."

"You felt our powers combine!" I beseeched him now, my voice raising by a hair. "You felt the mating pull, same as I. You heard our Link. We're mates, Tork. I'm sure of it."

The fire crackled on, spewing sparks and smoke toward the ceiling. Neither of us spoke for a long time—we sat there as the information sunk in. Tork didn't yank his hand away from mine. We sat there, fingers linked, and stared at the flickering coals in silence.

"I..." Tork opened his mouth at last, then a loud snore cut him off.

We both turned at the noise and saw Marlowe rolling about in bed, snoring and mumbling to himself.

"Go away, why don't you...I'm busy." He snorted and threw a hand over his face. "Making...flower crowns...gotta...be pretty." He snored again then rolled over on his stomach and back to sleep.

We glanced at one another and couldn't hold back our giggles anymore. My body shook with repressed laughter. Marlowe was never gonna live that down. For that moment, we weren't on a deadly mission to save Darkvale and all we held dear. We were just friends, enjoying one another's company, the heat of the fire, and the antics of our clan members.

Tomorrow's struggles couldn't touch us. The war loomed far off like a misremembered dream. Tension and anxiety melted away from my bones and we sat there, leaning on one another.

My mentor. My friend. My mate.

Maybe this would work out after all.

I opened my eyes to a new dawn, and a new revelation along with it.

I couldn't believe it. Didn't want to believe it. It hovered in my mind like mist, and I feared if I grasped at it too tightly, it might fly away for good.

Ansel...my mate?

When I looked over at the sleeping omega beside me, I knew it was the truth. Doubt and tension faded away to leave only a warm, grateful feeling in its place.

Mine to behold. Mine to protect.

I couldn't deny what I'd felt between us, sure, but I couldn't shake the guilt that seized me like a vise.

Was I confused? Definitely. Was I aroused at the same time? Hell yeah.

When we touched, my dragon responded in a way I'd never felt before. When we fought together, our powers combined. By standing together, we became greater than ourselves.

But whatever this was, exploring it would have to wait. We had an important mission to do, and this trick of ours just might be the thing to turn the tides.

———

THE SUN PEEKED through the shimmery veil of the entrance, casting the rest of the clan in a warm glow. My clansmen stirred one by one, righting themselves for the day.

Only, one was missing.

"The Sorcerer!" Kari cried out. "She's gone!"

"What?" Marlowe snapped, rubbing the sleep from his eyes. "How?"

"Dunno," Kari wrung her hands.

"Check your packs, everyone. Make sure she didn't steal anything."

That got the clan moving, and I raced to check my stores with my heart in my throat. Ansel made better wards than anyone I knew, and they would have gone off if the Sorcerer tried to escape. Must have found another way out. I grimaced and pawed through my supplies, letting out a breath. Everything in its place.

"We're good," Rex announced.

"All clear for us," Arthur echoed, nodding at Anya.

"Then what happened?" Marlowe asked, folding his arms. "She may be a Sorcerer but she didn't just vanish in a puff of smoke. Ansel, check the wards."

"On it, Commander." Ansel was already up and moving, peering at each of the mechanical sensors he'd attached to the doorway. He leaned in close, staring at them through a magnifying crystal, then shrunk back. "They're intact, sir. Nothing's come this way."

"There must be another exit," I suggested.

"Shall we track her?" Arthur asked.

Marlowe let out a string of curses and finally a long ragged breath. "Let her go. We've got bigger matters to deal with."

The clan grew silent at Marlowe's edict. All of us, me included, were thinking about what might happen if the Sorcerer got back to her buddies and told them where we were.

"We pack up. We get out of here. We find the infernal contraption we came for, and we do our duty." Marlowe's voice echoed off the walls and sent a chill down my spine.

"Very well," Arthur said with a nod. "You heard him, get moving!"

―――――

PACKING our things didn't take long—we'd traveled light to begin with, and pretty much crashed as soon as we reached the cave last night.

The trouble came when Kari distributed the morning rations.

Everyone else was on their way out, but Ansel hung back. He dragged himself across the cave like it cost him incredible effort, his eyes far away. Despite the professional front he'd put on this morning, I could see now that his skin held a sickly pallor and he struggled to nibble on the square of ration provided. His forehead shone with a delicate sheen of sweat, even though it was far from warm out. When he doubled over and started heaving, I rushed to his side at once.

I held his hair back as he gagged and shook, watching with horror as he ejected the past day's meals. It was then that I caught the scent that had been flickering in and out for days. It was then that I finally put the pieces together and realized.

Ansel wasn't just my mate. He was pregnant.

My chest squeezed and my heart raced as I held him. My dragon protested noisily in my chest. Alpha instincts took over and I brushed a hand through his hair, helping him wipe his mouth and right himself. "You okay?" I asked softly.

"Yeah, I'm fine, I'm just..."

"Pregnant," I finished, looking him dead in the eye. "Why didn't you say something?"

"Didn't know," Ansel whispered, staring at the ground. "Not for sure, anyway."

"It's for sure, all right. My dragon won't shut up about it."

That got a little laugh out of him, and I couldn't help smiling as well. "We've got to get you back to Darkvale." I took hold of both his hands. "It's not safe out here."

Ansel twisted out of my grasp, frowning. "What, cause I'm an omega?"

"No, cause you're pregnant. If something happened to you..."

"I knew the risks, Tork. I chose to come along."

"Yeah, but that was before..." I put my hands on my hips. He was being so difficult!

"And who's going to man the wards if I'm gone?" Ansel shot back, slinging his bag over his shoulder and turning for the exit where the rest of the clan waited.

I groaned and rolled my eyes. "Look, you're an adult, and you can make your own decisions, but think about the baby, Ansel. Our baby."

That seemed to get through to him and his face softened, his muscles slackened. He sagged and looked a little green again until I put a steadying hand on his shoulder.

Trust me? I asked over our newly-formed Link, knowing that he'd hear me in his mind.

Ansel leaned forward and rested his head on my chest as I held him close.

I made a promise to Veltar to keep him safe. And that's just what I would do.

"Guys, come on! I found something!" Arthur's voice drew me out of my trance and Ansel broke away from me at once, jogging to catch up.

I shook my head and followed after him.

He never had been too good with authority. Should have known.

———

WE CRESTED a hill to look down on a sandy plain below. Between the rocks and weeds there was a strange circle burned into the earth, a sort of sooty black halo. The ground inside the ring bore no such burn marks. It was fine and crumbly, freshly turned.

"Someone's been here," Anya said, bending down to brush at the dirt. "Whoever was here was trying to cover something up. And they didn't do a very good job of it."

We brushed at the perimeter and the hastily dumped dirt fell away, exposing the scorched earth beneath.

What was even more interesting was the trap door concealed there.

"What do you think?" Marlowe asked me.

I sniffed the air and caught the scent of iron and oil and soot.

"That's them, all right. Same kind of residue we found on the automaton."

"I say we go in," Kari suggested, drawing her weapon and kicking the last debris away from the hinges. "Bet they're hiding."

I remembered the last time I'd gone to explore an unknown tunnel and shivered. I would have died down there if it weren't for Nik and Ansel finding us. "You all have masks? You know what happened last time."

Kari strapped a filter to her face and tossed a few out to the other members of the team.

"Someone's gonna need to stand watch. If we don't come back..."

I nodded. No rushing in to save the day this time. Last time I tried that, I nearly got both Marlowe and I killed. "Ansel and I will stay."

Ansel opened his mouth like he was about to retort but I shot him a glare and he quieted down.

"Very well," said Marlowe as he strapped a mask over his face. "You see anything out of the ordinary, anything at all, you call us out and we'll be right there."

"Same goes for you," I nodded to him and clapped him on the back. "Glendaria go with you."

"And with you," he echoed, and heaved open the dusty trap door.

"You know what to do," Marlowe reminded me, then each of them disappeared down the hole and out of sight.

Then it was just the two of us.

Volunteering Ansel to stand watch with me had a twofold purpose. I didn't want him to get into any more danger than needed, but I also needed a moment of privacy to speak with him about this whole mating thing.

But no sooner had the trapdoor thudded closed than we

heard a metallic grinding sound behind us. I whirled and what I saw approaching took my breath away.

Nearly twenty feet tall, a cobbled together monstrosity of wires and metal stood there, gazing down on us with shining white eyes. I saw spots and took a few steps back, spinning around to wrench at the trapdoor.

"It's a trap!" I yelled through the wood. "Get out here! Get out here now!"

I pulled at the door with all my might, but it wouldn't budge.

Trapped.

I sucked in a breath and rushed to put myself between the monster and Ansel. He would have to go through me first.

It creaked its way toward us, smelling like smoke and sulphur. Ansel grabbed my hand and linked our fingers until I felt the sparks of connection rage through me once more.

"Let's do this," he said, and I squeezed his hand in return.

I dug into my bag for one of the portable mines I'd brought along. Just in case, of course. They packed a mighty punch when activated, but I had to get close enough to the thing to place one. And if I messed up, it might blow on me instead.

"Stay with me," I commanded Ansel, who already wove a tenuous thread of silk between his fingers, lashing it together and whispering an inscription into the rope. It shone with a pale blue light for a moment, then faded away.

"Here," he offered an end of the reinforced strand to me, and when I didn't immediately respond, he said, "Tie it to the mine, we can use it like a lasso."

"Genius," I said excitedly and tied the end through an opening in the mine's mechanical underbelly. I had to hope the string wouldn't trigger the switch in the meantime.

"We need some kind of adhesive," I muttered, digging through my stores as the automaton grew closer.

Sleeping draught...explosive merryroot...no, no, no.

Then my fingers closed around a small glass vial I forgot I even had. There!

I pulled out the vial and tossed the cork aside. A thick brown substance rested within, congealed with age.

"Terra sap," Ansel breathed, "Brilliant."

I shook the vial vigorously over the mine's backside, but the liquid stayed put. "Come on," I grumbled, shaking it harder.

"Was Terra sap the one that thins like honey when you

warm it up, or the one that explodes?" Ansel looked to me with wide eyes.

"We're about to find out," I said after placing it on the ground, and let out a jet of flame.

The substance bubbled and boiled almost instantly, but the mixture remained stable, thank the Goddess, I grabbed it, burning my fingers in the process, and dumped the sticky sap in a puddle onto the backside.

"There we go," I grinned and gave Ansel a high five. "Self adhesive lasso mine. Easy."

"Let's see if it works first—duck!"

I threw myself to the ground just in time. A sharpened metal bolt whizzed over my head so close I could feel the air rush through my hair. Any closer and I would have gotten a face full of metal. I rolled to the side and regained my feet. Adrenaline coursed through my veins and pushed away all second thoughts, all fear, all pain. I swung the contraption over my head in a circle once, twice, three times. It gained speed and the mechanics within grated, then whirred into action.

"Armed and ready," I muttered to myself, then narrowed my vision to the huge metal man in front of me. I had one chance to get this right.

The automaton reeled back and pummeled the ground with both fists, sending a shockwave out in a huge radius. The ground shuddered beneath my feet and I miscalculated my target, letting the rope free a moment too soon. I could only watch with wide eyes as it sailed through the air.

With a splat it came to rest on the beast's knee, and thank the Goddess, it held! A far cry from the headshot I'd been aiming for, but good enough.

"Move!" I barked at Ansel, covering him.

The monster tilted its head and looked, confused at the whirring, beeping contraption attached to its leg. The noise grew louder, the beeping faster. I squeezed my eyes shut.

Boom.

I shielded Ansel with my body as the explosion shook the ground and roared in my ears. Heat seared my back and metal crashed to the ground, then all was silent. When I turned around to look, my heart dropped even further.

The blast had torn off the thing's leg, but it was still moving! Those shining white eyes locked onto us with even more malice than before, and it reached out with its clawed hands, scraping through the dirt toward us.

Ansel stumbled back a few steps with a wail.

What now? I raced through my mind trying to come up with a solution. I only had that one mine left, and to detonate anything else this close to the entrance would cave in the tunnel. The rest of the team would be trapped.

We needed to lure it away.

"Hey pea brain!" Ansel taunted. He set off at a run in the opposite direction, waving his arms madly. The automaton took notice and dragged its head away from me to zero in on Ansel's fleeing form.

No!

"Ansel you idiot!" I bellowed, but my voice was lost in the metallic screech as the automaton let out another razor-sharp bolt, whizzing right toward Ansel's skull.

Watch out!

He swerved to the left at the last second and the arrow buried itself, quivering, in the dirt.

He was moving too fast for explosives and it was too big for my puny sword. I had to protect my mate, at any cost.

Dragon power flowed through me as I began to shift and leave my human body behind. Wings sprouted from my shoulder blades, my teeth lengthened into lethal daggers, my legs and arms grew stronger, deadlier, faster. I let out a roar that shook the ground beneath us and lumbered toward him, the both of us comparable in size now.

Dragon versus giant robot.

Never thought I'd see the day.

I had one massive advantage over the crippled automaton, however.

I wasn't missing a leg.

I barreled into the contraption full on, the shock reverberating through my scales. We crashed to the ground together and the air was a haze of metal and spikes and screeching. I let out a column of flame right at the things face. The metal withstood the heat, and I kept flaming, using all my energy and spark. I was going to roast this son of a bitch no matter what it took. He was threatening my omega!

The metal glowed a bright red and seared through my armored flesh as I ran out of steam. A compartment near the head sprung and steam billowed out.

Inside the giant robot was...a man.

His face was bright red with sweat and exertion. Blood dripped from his forehead and he regarded me with a delirious grin. Then I saw it.

Holding the collar of the man's shirt together was a metal buckle with an insignia I only faintly recognized. When I did, though, it took my breath away.

A cog with a lance through it. The emblem of Steamshire.

"What are you doing here?" I demanded, looming

over the wreckage and pinning him to the ground. "What business does Steamshire have with the Firefangs?"

The man gave me a grim smile showing a few missing teeth. His eyes flashed. He knew something I didn't. "You're too late," he coughed. "You have no idea what's coming, do you? Filthy animals."

"Say that again!" I bellowed and prepared to strike.

"Wait!" Ansel cried, rushing toward us. I held my tongue.

"What?" I spat. "This man, this *human*, seeks to undo us all!"

"Let him speak. He's no use to us dead."

My dragon grumbled deep in my chest but I relented. Still kept a wary eye trained on his weapons, though.

"No longer will your kind threaten us with your powers," the Steamshire man rasped. "Turns out we have powers of our own."

He pressed a button on the inside of his suit. I didn't have time to react. The automaton, human and all, exploded in a storm of fire and debris, throwing us backward with the blast. My ears rung, deafened. I knocked my head on the ground. The world spun.

But all I could think about, all I could see, was Ansel's still body spread out on the ground beside me.

I crawled over to where he lay on his stomach and flipped him over. Good, he was still breathing.

"Ansel!" I called both out loud and through our Link. "Ansel, talk to me!"

I shook him by the shoulders but he didn't move. My pleas remained unanswered.

"Ansel, baby, no!" Tears sprung to my face now as I leaned over him.

There was a wooden knock from beside me and I turned to see the trapdoor shuddering. The blows came again. I held my breath. Either it was the rest of my clan coming back to the surface, or it was whatever fell beasts had befallen them within.

I heaved Ansel into my arms and stood on shaky legs. The pounding came again and the wood splintered with a crash. A hand shot out, then another.

It was them.

I let out a breath. Marlowe surfaced first, dragging himself back onto the earth. He leaned down and offered a hand up to the rest of the men and women, each of them clambering out of the tunnel dirty, bloody, and totally spent.

When Marlowe saw the scattered debris, he froze. Then he looked to me, still holding Ansel in my arms.

"Goddess, don't tell me..." He said weakly.

"They snuck up on us." I grimaced. "Doesn't look like you fared much better."

Marlowe ignored my question. He nodded to Ansel warily. "Is he...?"

"No," I said a little more forcefully than I intended. The reptilian rasp of my dragon forced its way into my voice as I thought of my mate, my Ansel, passing from this world into the next. "He's knocked out, is all."

"You ran into one of...them?" Marlowe eyed the wreckage.

"We did, and it wasn't pretty. Permission to return to Darkvale, sir. We need to warn the others."

He brushed off his clothes and looked around at the team, then at me and Ansel. "You're taking him back too, I wager?"

"I am," I said protectively, holding him closer. "He's not only hurt, Commander. He's pregnant."

Marlowe's eyebrows raised so high on his forehead I thought they'd fly off. "My word."

"I'm taking him home," I said. It was more of a statement, not a question. If I got in trouble, if they labeled me AWOL, I didn't care. It didn't matter. My mate was in trouble.

"Does his mate know?" Marlowe asked softly, still staring at us in awe.

"He does now," I confirmed with a wink, and pushed off the ground with my strong back legs into the air. Ansel clung to my back and as I gained altitude, I watched the gaping faces below.

Let them talk. The dragon and the alpha in me had other plans.

7

ANSEL

W ind rushed through my hair and tickled my nose. I was afloat on clouds of cotton, resting peacefully while the world flowed around me.

Achoo!

I sneezed and jolted awake so violently I nearly fell off Tork's back.

I gripped onto the pockets behind Tork's wings for dear life and squeezed him with my thighs, ignoring the aching pain that sprouted up all over my body. I blinked my eyes once, twice, three times.

Then I made the mistake of looking down.

My stomach rebelled once more and I heaved, bile burning the back of my throat.

You're awake, I heard Tork's voice in my mind. It soothed me, just knowing he was there.

Where are we, I sent back. *What are you...*

I'm taking you home.

I swallowed past the lump in my throat and renewed my grip. My mate's wings flapped easily, gracefully, riding each current of wind and floating through the clouds with ease. The world was nothing but a speck of tiny trees and houses below. Little black dots like ants were the sign of people.

Images of metal and fire and ash flickered through my mind again. I was there. I was next to him. We finally found one of the mysterious automatons. And Steamshire was behind it.

Then he self destructed, I flew through the air, and then...

I was here.

I shook my head and blinked against the tears in my eyes.

The mission, I breathed. *Tork, the mission! What happened to everyone else?*

Some things are more important than the mission, Tork assured me. *I made a promise, and I intend to keep it.*

But, I started.

Tork was never one to run from a fight. Never. And to think he'd do that for me?

We've got to get back to Darkvale and warn them. If we can get there in time and tell Lucien to call in reinforcements, we might have a chance.

He had a point. Just one of those things was difficult enough to take down. If we were up against a whole army of them? I heaved again, only dry hacking sobs this time.

Hang on, Tork urged me. *We're getting you home as soon as possible. We're gonna see Doctor Parley when we get back. And then we've got work to do.*

I grumbled, but couldn't do much to resist. I was too weak to shift, and exhaustion draped over me like a blanket, warm and inviting. Sleep beckoned me once more and I settled into the warm, smooth scales on Tork's back.

"Do you smell chicken?" I mumbled, sniffing the air. "Cause I do."

Tork's body shook with laughter. "What are you talking about? You get knocked on the head too?"

"No," I insisted. The smell was there, all right. I could nearly taste it on my tongue, it was so strong. "Chicken," I continued. My mouth watered at the thought. "Hot, greasy, delicious....do you think we can get some fried chicken back in Darkvale? I'm so hungry."

Tork didn't stop chuckling for a good while. I lay sleepily on his back, glad to have amused him. "You always were a handful," he muttered. "And yes, when we get back, you can have all the chicken you want."

"Good," I mumbled, half asleep now. "You sure everyone will be all right? Now that we've left?"

It would be a lie to say I didn't feel a little guilty. But we had an important mission, perhaps more important than our work in the field. If shit was gonna hit the fan, Darkvale needed to know sooner rather than later. And that's where we came in.

"Here, I'll show you," Tork offered. "Open your mind, see what I see..."

I felt the same rush of power and energy as he reached out across our Link. Then the world faded away and a new landscape built itself up around me.

———

IT WAS the cave we'd spent the night in. I could see myself, still sleeping. Marlowe approached Tork as they readied themselves for the day and gestured for him to come closer, speaking in a low tone only he could hear.

"I don't know much about people. I definitely don't

know much about relationships. But I saw the way you leaned on each other last night."

I snorted and my face flushed as I thought about our secret night together. Marlowe had been sleeping...or so we had thought.

Believe me, I was mortified too, Tork said in my mind. The scene continued to play out, and I looked on in wonder.

"It's not so unusual, you know." Marlowe put a hand on Tork's shoulder. "Glendaria has plans for all of us, even ones we don't understand sometimes." He stared at the ground for a moment, chewing his lip, then spoke again. "For what it's worth, I think Veltar would be proud that such a strong, capable alpha was fated to his son."

I couldn't see Tork's face well, but the corners of his mouth twitched up in a silent smile.

"Better than some prick that would abuse him, right?" Marlowe shrugged. "I know you'll do right by him. You'd do right by anyone. You're a good man, Tork."

Tork nodded his head. "My thanks."

"If what we've seen and heard is true, Darkvale is gonna need a lot more men."

"Don't I know it." Tork sighed. A moment passed between them, then Tork bowed his head and pressed his hands together. "Thank you, Commander. I won't let you down."

"Glendaria go with you, Tork."

"And with you, brother."

The walls faded away, the voices no more than mumbles in the background now. Tork and Marlowe dissipated like mist, and then they were gone.

———

WHEN I COULD SEE AGAIN, the great towering walls came into view. The shimmering dome of Darkvale glowed and sparkled in the sunlight, and I'd never been so glad to see it.

"Come on, Ansel. We're home."

8

ANSEL

"Looks like you've got a baby dragon on the way. Two, if I'm not mistaken."

"Two?" I said hoarsely. "Twins?"

"Looks like it," Dr. Parley nodded and stuffed some paperwork into a folder. "Don't worry about a thing, though. I've delivered babies for quite a few omegas now, no problems."

I gulped, still digesting the news. *Twins.*

I wasn't so sure I could handle one baby, but two? Good thing I was already sitting down.

Tork placed a hand on my shoulder to steady me and I leaned forward into his warmth.

"How are you doing?" He asked, rubbing small circles on my back.

"Okay," I mumbled. "Still hungry."

"Let's go home and get you that chicken." Tork held out a hand and I grabbed it, sliding off the observation table.

"Don't hesitate to let us know if there's any problems." Dr. Parley said as he handed Tork the folder. "And Ansel?"

"Yeah?" I turned to see his mischievous grin.

"Take it easy on him. Alphas go a little crazy during pregnancy too."

"Hey!" Tork retorted, but I just laughed and let him lead me out of the clinic.

With that out of the way, now we had to go see Lucien and tell him about the oncoming threat. My stomach roiled again at that.

"You sure you don't want to go home?" Tork asked, rubbing my back. "I can deal with Lucien myself. You need your rest."

"I'll be fine," I insisted. "I want to be there. I'm not gonna turn into some helpless omega just cause I'm pregnant, you know." I brushed his hand away.

"I wouldn't dream of it." Tork kissed my hand and we headed toward Lucien's office.

———

WE OPENED the door to Lucien's office to a bit of familial chaos. Lucien hunched over his desk, trying to read a book, while Alec fought with little Corin to eat his food. The baby definitely had some dragon in him, I noted with a smile. He was a feisty one, knocking away Alec's hand at each turn.

Lucien looked up as we entered and tilted his head in confusion.

"You're back so soon. Is something wrong?"

"Yes...and no." Tork started. He cast an eye over the screaming child and gestured toward the door. "We should go somewhere private."

Lucien's throat worked and he gave us a terse nod. "Very well." He stood up from behind his desk and followed us to the door. "Around the corner to the left, there's a unused storage room I like to go and think sometimes."

When I entered the "storage room", I had the strangest sense of deja vu. It looked just like the room Tork and I had mated in, back at the Flower Festival. I shot him a glance and I saw the same secret gleam in his eye. I cleared my throat, hoping the blush hadn't reached too far up my cheeks, when Lucien came in behind us and shut the door.

"This will do," he said, brushing dust off the old armchairs and the futon. "Sit, sit. Tell me what's going on."

I took a deep breath and sunk into the cushions. Tork joined me and put a protective hand around my shoulder.

"Don't tell me you two have finally mated..." he grinned.

Finally? Was it that obvious?

"Yes," Tork said simply, to save me the embarrassment. "But that's not what's important right now. We've news from the field, and we need your help."

"I'm all ears." His voice remained even, his demeanor professional, but I could tell underneath there was an undercurrent of despair.

"We found the automaton," I began. I took a breath. "We found a lot more than that, too."

"There are more of them than we thought," Tork added with a furrowed brow. "They're operational, Lucien. Huge. Powerful. And we found out who's behind it all."

Lucien didn't respond, just watched us silently, his chin resting on his hands.

"It's Steamshire!" I blurted. "They're out for revenge." A chill passed through me.

This time the Clan Alpha shrunk back as if shocked by lightning. The color drained from his face. "Goddess preserve us," he muttered. "The humans...I'll need to tell Alec at once."

"There's more," Tork cautioned. "They're on their way here, now. We came back to warn you, to call in reinforcements. If we're going to make it through this, Darkvale needs backup."

Lucien rubbed the back of his neck and regarded us. "Diplomatic relations have been...strained, to say the least. But we've made contact with a tribe of elementals on our last journey, Alec and I. We'll reach out to them now, call them to our aid. Is Marlowe still in the field?"

"He's right behind us," Tork promised. "They'll be back soon."

"Well we must get to work, then," Lucien stood and brushed his hands on his pants. "There's no time to lose."

"You've got that right."

Lucien hurried to the door and ushered us out. "Thank you, Ansel. And you too, Tork. Your information may just save us all."

"It's my pleasure, Clan Alpha." Tork bowed his head. I did the same.

"Oh, and Ansel?" He added as an afterthought. "Congratulations."

He eyed me with a knowing grin, and then he was gone.

I wanted to go after him, to help call in the allies and do anything I could to prepare for the siege, but my body had other ideas. My head pounded and my limbs felt like bricks. I sunk back into the chair as soon as Lucien had left.

Tork didn't say anything, just took my hand. "Let's get you home."

Home, I thought with a smile.

"We'll go back to my place. It's closer. In the meantime, I'll see what I can do about those cravings."

For once, I didn't have the energy to challenge him.

———

I'D VISITED Tork's place many times, but none since returning from the Academy. It looked much as I'd left it, but everything seemed smaller than I'd remembered. I reminded myself that I'd been smaller too, back then. He sat me down on the bed and brought me a huge cream-colored blanket. I had to laugh at the ridiculousness of it all. Even though he was my godfather and mentor, he'd never been so fussy over me before.

I guessed Doctor Parley was right. Pregnancy drove more than just omegas crazy.

I wove my hands through the delicate stitches and wrapped myself from head to toe.

"Where'd you get something like this?"

"My grandmother made it. She was great at stuff like that. Used to always give it to me when I was sick."

I snickered at that. "I'm not sick, Tork. Just pregnant."

"I know. But I want you to have it."

I yawned and curled up in the blanket, my eyes drooping closed. Tork still rushed around at a pace that made me dizzy. Finally, I said something.

"What about you? You doing okay?"

"What?" He asked, looking up. "I'm fine."

"You've been spending all this time worrying over me, but what about you? I know you got hurt back there. I know you've been ignoring it. And they probably need you back at the lab, and..."

"Shhh," Tork cut me off as a knock sounded at the door.

My muscles tensed up involuntarily. "Who's that?"

"Special delivery." Tork made his way to the door and said his thank yous to the courier standing there. Even though I didn't have a clear line of sight to the doorway, I could smell my present before I saw it.

"Chicken!" I shouted.

"Just the way you like it." Tork placed the package down on the kitchen counter and unwrapped it. An entire steaming chicken looked back at me, glistening with grease and breading and herbs.

"Goddess, that smells good," I moaned, twisting in my seat.

"You wanna eat over there or come in here?" Tork asked as he plated the meat.

"I'm basically a blanket burrito right now, so..."

Tork chuckled. "Anything for my omega."

My face burned at that, but the lightness I felt in my heart more than made up for it.

I was his, and he was mine. This was what all the old songs spoke about. What people went to war over, what people died for.

Having a mate, a true mate, was the best feeling of my life. And getting to start a family with him?

Well, that was just the icing on the cake.

He rounded the couch and sat down next to me, handing me a plate and some utensils.

I paid them no mind—I was so hungry! I picked up the chicken leg and bit right into it. The juices exploded in my mouth and dribbled from my fingers and lips. I let out a moan. I could taste each herb, each bread crumb, each bite more than ever before. My taste buds had rocketed up along with my sense of smell, and I was in heaven.

Tork watched me and the discarded utensils with amusement. I didn't care.

"This is really good," I said between bites. "Thank you so much."

Tork beamed and tore into his own plate. "Looks like you needed it."

"Did I ever," I agreed, and we passed the evening with food and comfort.

———

I'D NEVER FELT SO SATED in my life.

Well, maybe except for my mating night.

Speaking of...

I glanced over at Tork, who was just finishing his meal.

"So..." I started, but the words stuck in my throat. This was all so sudden, for the both of us. I knew Tork was doing his best to be a good alpha and a good partner, but his initial apprehension still ate at me. What if he didn't really want to be mates? What if he regretted what we did?

"I know this has all happened so fast. And I know you weren't exactly, um, on board with it at first." My words trailed off as I peeked through my eyelashes at Tork. "I never had a chance to really ask you though. Are you...okay with all this? I don't want to force you into anything."

Tork wiped his mouth and put his plate aside. He took my hands in each of his, and those glowing amber eyes searched deep into mine.

"I made a promise to Veltar, the day he died." Tork's voice was reverent now, echoing all the way down to my soul. "I will admit that mating his son wasn't part of the deal. But the more I think about it, maybe it was. My dragon wants to take care of you, Ansel. Body and soul. I thought I was doing just that before, but then at the Flower Festival..." he stopped, pursing his lips. "I should never have taken advantage of you that night. And for that, I am sorry. But when our souls combine, Ansel, it feels right. It feels like maybe we *were* meant to be mates, after all. And I want that. I want you, and everything you are."

He leaned forward and kissed me, and every doubt faded away.

My dragon responded instantly, pulling me closer like a magnet as I returned the kiss, hot and fierce and demanding. His lips captured mine, his tongue teased me in an impossibly frustrating dance. I grasped the back of his head, pulling him closer as I shot my own tongue out. He growled with satisfaction, and then I was airborne.

Tork's strong arms lifted me off the ground and into his embrace, his kisses landing on my face, my neck, my chin. He carried me down a hallway as I clung tightly. Through a doorway with a cloth banner for a door, and we were in his bedroom.

He let me go right over the bed and I bounced into the plush mattress, the air whooshing out of me. No sooner had I sunk into the mound of pillows than Tork was on me, his shirt thrown to the side in a heap.

This time I was in control. This time I would feel everything. Remember everything.

I ran my hands down the muscled planes of his chest and stomach, arching my back upwards.

He batted my hands away and ground his groin into mine. If my cock hadn't already been hard and begging for release, it was now. It strained against my pants, aching and twitching at each movement of his hips. I reached a hand down to my fly but he batted it away again.

"Let me do it," he rumbled, and made quick work of the zipper. My pants came away and my cock was left throbbing against my underwear. Tork tugged at my shirt and I obliged, throwing it over my head. I wound my arms around his neck and sunk back down into the bed, bringing him with me.

His arms wrapped around my back and kneaded the tight area between my shoulder blades. I groaned in delight and my dragon responded in kind, the wings tickling at that very spot, eager to come out.

"Careful," I breathed, looking up at him with a mischievous eye. "You're gonna make me shift."

"Maybe I want that," he purred, moving his lips down to my collar bone and leaving a series of nips that took my breath away.

"Tork," I sighed, throwing my head back as he moved lower.

"Yes?" He asked, raising an eyebrow.

I grit my teeth and fisted my hands in the sheets. He had to know what he was doing to me! My heart thudded like a war drum, each pulse of blood heading straight for my cock and leaving me in a breathless, lightheaded trance.

When I didn't answer he continued his downward assault, stopping to nip and kiss at my hips and thighs. He orbited around the area of my most essential need, giving everywhere attention but my hard and leaking cock. He knew what he was doing, and he knew how it made me feel. My shuddered moans were proof of that. When he finally closed his lips over the head of my cock, it was like fireworks. Literal fireworks.

Tork's mouth was hot and greedy, sucking at my tender flesh. He bobbed up and down, his strong hands moving to cup my balls. I gasped at that—because it was unexpected, and because it felt so damn good. That in tandem with the way he pleased my cock with his mouth...I nearly came right then and there.

"Stop," I gasped through gritted teeth. Tork looked up at me. "I don't want to come...not yet...please..."

My staff slipped out of his mouth with a pop and he kissed his way back up my torso before whispering in my ear, "No. You're not going to come until you've had all you can take, and more."

I shuddered at the thought, but my cock had other ideas. It twitched again, leaking precum. My dragon fell into a full on frenzy and I couldn't stop myself from grabbing, touching, scratching anywhere and everywhere that I could. Tork took this new development in stride.

He pressed his hips into mine, our heavy cocks brushing past each other in the most delicious kind of friction. The way he rocked back and forth against me sent spark after spark of adrenaline, endorphins, and white-hot desire crackling across every vein, every pore, until I was no longer myself. I was his.

"Need to feel you," I whimpered, arching my back to grind against him again. "Inside me."

Tork rumbled low in his chest and dipped a hand below to test my opening. When he brought it back, his fingers were wet and covered with slick. "Looks like someone's quite excited," he teased and brought the fingers up to my mouth. I sucked them between my lips, licking him clean of my juices. It was so wrong, so embarrassing, so personal...

But so. Fucking. Hot.

"Please," I whispered, my voice breaking. My wild, half-lidded eyes met his, and in that moment our dragons sensed one another, soaring together and beginning their primal dance.

Tork stuck his hands under my buttocks and lifted my hips, putting my legs over his shoulders. I was so vulnerable, so exposed to him like this. But I'd have it no other way.

He slid into me without warning, the hot, hard length stretching and filling me completely. It wasn't long until he was seated all the way to the hilt, so deep inside me it pressed upon a secret place that came alive with the added pressure.

I moaned and rocked toward him again. Why wasn't he moving? Why wasn't he pounding me yet?

"A pounding, you say?" Tork teased me.

My face grew bright red, burning with the realization I'd said that to him in our minds. I had to learn how to split out my regular thoughts versus what I transmitted over our Link. I bit my lip and nodded. "Yes," I got out, but no other words would come.

"Hold on tight, baby." Tork gripped my hips and drew

out of me, plunging back in so deeply and so suddenly that I cried out, my head arcing backward.

"Like that?" He asked, doing it again as if to demonstrate.

"Ah…Goddess…yes!" I could barely breathe, much less get out the words I needed as he dove into my channel again and again, stretching me beyond what I thought was possible and hitting that delicate spot each and every time. The tension drove higher still and my hand found my way to my own cock, pumping it in time with Tork's thrusts.

We rode together on a sea of sensation, each movement sending us higher and higher until…

"Goddess! Tork! Yes!" I spasmed around him as my release came, shattering and hard, echoing through every part of my body and spewing out of my cock in long white ropes. The mere sight of my pleasure took Tork over the edge with me, and he let my legs down to hold me, skin to skin, while he cried out and pumped into me, filling me with his seed.

It didn't matter that he was my father's best friend. It didn't matter that he was nearly twice my age. It didn't matter what people would say.

Let them talk. We were mates, fated by Glendaria herself. And as I came down from the heights of ultimate pleasure, I realized I wouldn't have had it any other way.

9

TORK

Another night, another bout of insomnia. I laid awake in bed next to Ansel, staring at the ceiling. No matter what I tried, my mind just wouldn't shut up.

I sighed and gently pulled myself out of bed, being careful not to disturb Ansel. I needed a drink of water, and I needed to think.

Just as soon as I'd poured myself a glass I heard a knock at the door. A soft, tentative knock, as if they weren't sure whether they should be here or not.

When I went to the door, I saw Lucien standing there, wearing a robe and holding a steaming mug in his hands.

"I figured you'd be up," he said softly. "Come, let's talk."

I glanced back at Ansel, still sleeping peacefully. "Okay, but make it quick." If he woke up and I wasn't there, I would never hear the end of it.

We walked through the alleyway with our drinks in hand, stepping over the loose cobblestones and taking in the silence of the night. Darkvale served as such a hub of activity during the day. But in the dead of night? It was like a graveyard.

"How is Alec doing in light of all this?" I asked after taking another sip of water. "With the Steamshire reveal and all."

"He's scared," Lucien said without missing a beat. "He's angry. We all are."

I stepped over a tree root that had bulged out of the ground and continued. "Do you think he could get through to them? The humans, I mean. They're from his village. Perhaps he could get them to see reason."

Lucien shrugged. "He couldn't before. That's why we got him and most of the kids and omegas out of there. Don't see why this time would be any different."

"Hmm," I groaned. He had a point. "I'm ready to fight with you," I blurted out. It was the only thing I could think to say in the moment, and that's what this was all leading to, wasn't it? Another battle. Another war. Would it ever end?

"I only wish it didn't have to come to that," Lucien said

softly, kicking at a stone. He shook his head and changed the subject. "How's he doing?"

"Who, Ansel?" I took another sip of my water before responding. Even though just about everyone knew we were mates by now, it was still a little awkward to talk about. "He's fine. Tired, is all. The hormones are getting to him."

Lucien nodded knowingly. We came to a clearing lined with stone pillars, a vine covered trellis, and two great stone benches. We sat, listening to the high pitched whine of the wind.

"I remember when Alec was pregnant," he said with a smile. "There was nothing I wouldn't do to make sure he was comfortable and safe. Omegas aren't the only ones that change during pregnancy. I ran from our greatest battle to rescue him, remember?"

I nodded, remembering the day we took back our home. Remembering how Lucien rushed off in an instant and left Marlowe in charge.

"I remember."

"You know, a lot of people gave me weird looks for mating a human. I'm sure you'll get some of the same for your pairing. But I want you to know that you have my support. You two are perfect together."

I smiled and reflected on his words as a lightness filled me. It burned through my heart like honey, like a warm drink on the coldest winter's day. How grateful I was to have someone so special in my life!

"I guess I never let myself think of him that way, before." I shrugged and remembered the first time I'd seen him after he returned from the Academy. I'd noticed him. My dragon noticed him, too. But I hadn't thought anything of it, until that fateful night... "After the ball, I couldn't stop thinking about him. Hell, I didn't even know it *was* him back then. Just that something really big had happened, and I didn't know how to feel."

Lucien let out a hearty laugh at that, placing his hand over his belly. I hissed at him to quiet down, but we were surrounded by only trees. No homes nearby.

"Sounds like someone had a good time after all. Aren't you glad I dragged you along? Mr. 'Grr, I'm not going even if I have to wear a paper bag on my head'!" He kept laughing, and I grumbled.

"Whatever." I rolled my eyes, but could stop the laughter from bubbling up in my throat. It was kinda ridiculous, actually. So we laughed, letting go of all fear about the future, all tension, all stress of constant battle and paranoia. This was nice.

But nice things, shoulda known, never last.

Our reverie shattered as a whining alarm cut through the night. It chilled me right to my bones as the klaxon wailed and I leapt to my feet.

"What's going on?" Lucien cried over the din. He covered his ears and peered up at the sky, where the sound seemed to come from nowhere and everywhere at once. My thoughts instantly went to Ansel. He was alone. I had to get to him.

Stay right there, I warned him on our Link as I took off at a run. *I'm coming to get you!*

Lucien's footsteps pattered not far behind.

"The wards!" I shouted back at him. "Something's wrong, something's set them off—"

Just then a great shattering sound shook the earth. I nearly lost my footing and Lucien just about did, grabbing on to my sleeve as he swayed to the side. Electric arcs like lightning flashed through the sky as the magical dome protecting Darkvale disintegrated. A huge gaping hole yawned open in the force field and grew wider, like a mouth determined to eat everything in its path.

"You know how to fix it?" Lucien barked, staring up at the breach.

"I could try, but—"

"I can." We stopped short as Ansel appeared at the door of my house, fully alert and suited up in his work clothes. He cracked his knuckles. "Sounds like you need a wardsman."

My heart and dragon soared when I saw him like this.

Even though he wasn't feeling well, even though his hormones were going crazy, he was always ready to step up and defend his friends, family, and clan. Just one of many things I admired about him.

I regarded him with a wide, growing grin. "Yes. Yes, we do."

"Cover me," Ansel commanded, slinging his bag of tools over his shoulder. "I'm going in."

As the alarms roared above us and confused villagers began to emerge from their homes, Ansel ran off straight for the source of the danger. And even though part of me was terrified for his safety, another part had never been so proud in my life.

10

ANSEL

I fled through the chaos, my bag bumping against my leg as I set my sights on the control room housing most of the machinery for the wards. Part of my duty in Darkvale was to perform regular maintenance and updates, but since going on the road I hadn't had a chance to check on them again.

Good thing I was here, I thought in a flash as I ran. *What if the dome went down while I was away? Or worse*, I gulped, *if something happened to me?*

I made a mental note then and there to start training an underling of my own, so we'd have back up on the wards once I had the baby. My heart thudded faster at the thought.

That's right. I was having a baby. Two babies, actually. And I would protect them with everything I had.

I skidded to a stop in front of the control room and wrenched open the door, the warm, dry air of exhaust hitting me full in the face. I sputtered and dived in, squinting through the dim light to get to the control panel.

The ground shook again with the force of another blast. I fell against the wall with a yelp, the doorknob poking into my ribs. It stopped nearly as soon as it started, though, and I threw myself back into action. The control panel was locked for security reasons, but in the moment it was proving to be quite the inconvenience. I dug into every pocket for the key and turned up empty. Where was it? I finally found it at the bottom of my bag and yanked it out, my shaking hands only barely managing to get it into the keyhole before the ground shifted beneath me once more.

I threw open the panel and the scene that looked back at me couldn't have been much worse. The wards were fried, like some kind of electrical surge had come through and burned the lot of them out. We had override switches in place for just such a contingency— things sometimes went haywire during storms—but they weren't so easy to activate. You had to really get into the mechanics of it and align the resonance of the existing wards to the override. Not an easy task at the best of times, and when the world was crumbling around you? Even less so.

"Who designed this crap?" I grumbled to myself as I pulled out my screwdriver and slipped magnifying goggles over my face.

Oh right. Me.

Thanks a lot, asshole.

I poked around the bits of frayed wire, trying to feel through the metal to the resonance of magic within. That was the core of all magitech, after all. Imbuing a machine with one's essence allowed the engineer to create all sorts of improvements or abilities. But only if the correct resonance frequency was applied. Anything else, and the magic would backfire, causing a very messy, and very dangerous, result.

Sweat beaded up on my forehead as I let out a slow, shaky breath to still my hands. There were six switches marked in red that would turn on the backup wards, but to do that, I had to imbue them first.

Here goes nothing.

I reached out beyond the metal, deep down into my soul and the well of energy there. I listened for the calm, steady hum of the machine, almost like a beating heart. Each machine had a differing frequency that, when matched, upgraded the whole system. I tried to match what I heard, slowly letting go of a little bit of magic at a time, but it wasn't right.

The metal grew hot beneath my hands and I jerked my wrist back as a white shiny burn shone on my finger. I hissed and sucked it into my mouth, narrowing my eyes. *Come on, Ansel. Come on, they're counting on you.*

As if in response I felt an almost imperceptible pressure against my stomach, sorta like a gas bubble but stronger. I placed a hand over my swelling navel, wiping the sweat from my brow.

"Daddy's here," I soothed them, and prayed that I wouldn't let my babies down. One false move in here and I'd be blown to kingdom come, along with anyone unfortunate enough to be standing nearby.

A ripping sound echoed through the air and a panicked glimpse toward the small slatted window told me the rift was widening.

Dammit!

No matter what I tried, how deep I reached or how much I focused, I couldn't seem to get it right. I needed more. And I knew just where I might get that.

Tork, I called out on our Link. *Get your ass over here.*

What? The response came almost instantly. *What's wrong?*

Now!

My heart thudded in my chest as I groped out for the right resonance. Every time I started to grasp the elusive pattern, it slipped through my fingers like sand. I grit my teeth and tried again and again, watching in horror.

This didn't make any sense. I knew all the wards here in Darkvale. Built most of them myself, and yet this one continued to elude me. Any other time, it would have been routine, but not today. Stress? Hormones? Everything else that had been on my mind recently? No way to tell. I remembered the amp in power I'd felt when working with Tork. I remembered how every muscle lit up with strength and purpose, and I felt like I could move the world. To reinstate the wards after such a massive blowout, we were gonna need power. And a lot of it.

A scraping sound caught my attention and I whirled around, my hand on my weapon.

It's me, you bonehead, Tork's voice came from the other side of the door. *Open up.*

I let out a breath and let him in. Before I knew it he was on me, his arms wrapped around my waist and his face nuzzled in my neck. Already the humming, tingling flow of energy flowed from him to me, and back again like a live circuit.

Perfect.

"What's the crisis?" He asked, drawing back to look me in the eye.

"I need your help." I said, pointing to the control panel.

"With the wards?" Tork cocked an eyebrow. "Can't say it's my specialty, but..."

"No," I insisted and held him back. He watched me silently, waiting for my next move. "Listen to me and do exactly as I say. Take my hand."

Tork covered my hand with his own large and well-weathered one. He gave it a quick squeeze, sending blood to all the wrong places when I needed it to think.

"Feel that?" I asked breathlessly. My cock twitched in my pants. My dragon pouted in my chest.

One track mind, that one.

"Yeah," Tork rumbled, his breath hot against my ear.

"Now focus," I commanded as I moved back toward the control panel and began the ritual once more. "I'm gonna need all the juice we can get."

The world faded away as I tapped into the energy source coming across our Link, using it to refine the pattern in my mind, chipping away the rough edges until it matched that I saw in the machine exactly.

I gave his hand a squeeze and called upon my powers once more, pushing that energy into the metal. It flowed around each of the six wards like water, covering every crack and crevice. Then they started to heat up again, but the indicator lights still hadn't come on.

Something was still wrong.

"Come on, come on, come on," I muttered to myself as I screwed up my eyes, squinted through the metal to what I knew intuitively lie beneath. The energy that poured out of us reached around the core, but couldn't quite touch it. Like a badly copied key, the resonance was still not quite right.

The twins shifted in my belly once more and this time I felt a third surge of energy, small but definitely there. It flowed up into me from my center, reaching down my arms toward the tips of my fingers and out into the world.

Tork shivered and didn't let go. "Looks like they're getting into it too."

"Yeah," I breathed, and this time I knew it would work. It had to.

I reached out like before, but the energy came easier now. It wasn't like trying to jam a key into a rusty lock, but a gentler, smoother motion. It flowed in and around each of the wards in turn and I held my breath as the bright white indicator lights clicked on, one by one.

Six backup wards operational.

"Flip the switches," Tork said without taking his hand from mine.

Click. Click. Click. Click. Click. Click.

The mechanical whirring started again. The wards glowed white then green as they came online, and the wires crisscrossed themselves out of the control box down underground where they would, hopefully, restart the shield protocol.

The ground stabilized. The tearing sound stopped. I dared to throw open the door and peek out at the aftermath.

Healing over like a bad scar, tendrils of white light pressed up over the wound and across it, healing the part that had faltered. The air shimmered as the sun rose on the horizon, then with a flash of light the dome became whole once more.

"Woo!" I yelled, pumping my fist at the sky. Tork stood beside me and hollered his own triumph. He lifted our hands, still entwined, to the sky.

"We did it," I said, my shoulders slumping as the adrenaline began to wear off. "We're safe."

"You did it," Tork reminded me, and kissed my forehead. "My little engineer."

I blushed. I pressed my face into his chest and breathed in his scent. So good. "Thank you," I muttered without moving. It came out as no more than a mumble through the fabric of his shirt.

Tork grasped both sides of my face and tilted my head up to look at him. I grinned and gazed deep into those amber eyes, eyes that I could spend a lifetime admiring.

"I love you," Tork said, and then he kissed me.

11

ANSEL

After the shield crisis, things calmed down considerably around Darkvale. Well, calm for us. It had been almost two whole weeks without any life-threatening disasters!

I counted that as a win in my book.

The rest of the team had arrived from the field, bringing a wagon full of artifacts with them. Tork, of course, wanted to start delving into them immediately and holed up in the lab at just about all hours. I would have been helping him too, but I had other matters to attend to.

After the debacle with the shields, I realized we were going to need a more robust system if it ever came time for a real full-scale assault. The metal man we'd encountered still plagued my nightmares, and I'd be damned if they were getting through our shields.

I spent my days strengthening the wards and redesigning the override system. Of course, the work was a lot of stop and go. The twins were growing rapidly now, and I was constantly waylaid by bathroom breaks or sore joints. Dragon pregnancies were notoriously short, everyone knew that, but it was still early days. The fact that there was not one, but two babies inside me made everything feel twice as intense.

In just a few months time, I'd be a father. Tork and I both. The thought sent a chill down my spine. I had no idea how to be a father. No one ever taught me this stuff. How the hell was I going to take care of two babies at once?

Sure, I'd always thought about being a father. All omegas did, I figured. It was part of our DNA. But all that talk about mates and babies and knotting and heats was just that—talk. It sat peacefully in the back of my mind as something that happened to other people. Not to me.

Now that I was pregnant, it was like a whole new world of possibilities opened up for me. Things I hadn't considered before.

Perhaps having a baby was like the biggest science experiment of them all. I huffed in amusement at that realization, cupping my stomach with my free hand. I crafted all manner of magical and mechanical things in the lab. Things no one had ever thought of before.

Things people thought were impossible. But this? This would be my greatest achievement: creating new life.

I drew in a slow steady breath through my nose and then let it out through my mouth, counting the seconds that passed. *In....out.* It was one of the first techniques Tork taught me when he became my mentor. Right after my dad died, my emotions, my mind, they were all a wreck. He helped me then, to put me back together before we started working. And those simple techniques? That kindness he'd shown me back then?

I still used them today.

I let out one more long, slow breath and stretched my shoulders, taking off my work apron for the day and discarding my gloves on the lab table.

Another day's work done.

Tork let me know on our Link he'd be working late, so I headed to dinner alone. As soon as I sat down Nikolas found me.

"Mind if we sit?" He asked. He bounced baby Hope on his hip and his five-year-old daughter Lyria stood beside him, balancing a plate of food.

"Go ahead, Tork's skipping dinner again." I rolled my eyes. "He gets way into stuff sometimes, and all those artifacts the team brought back are no exception. I figure I'll take him a plate later."

"Good man." Nikolas got everyone settled and then turned to me, looking me up and down.

"How are you doing with everything? Marlowe told me how brave you were out there."

I looked away, my cheeks suddenly burning. "It's nothing."

"So you and Tork, huh?" He continued. "Can't say I'm surprised. I saw the way you looked when we dragged him out of that tunnel."

I snorted. "That obvious?"

"Totally."

"You don't think its, I dunno, weird?"

Nikolas clapped me on the back. "Look man. I fell for my best friend. Lucien fell for a human. We're all a little weird around here."

"How's Hope doing? Keeping you busy?"

Nik hoisted her. "Unbelievably. Her and Lyria both."

"I'm five years old now!" Lyria grinned at me, holding out five tiny fingers.

"Her birthday was just last week," Nik said while spooning some baby food to little Hope. Gotta say, the ability of parents to multi task was impressive. "She's starting school soon. Thomas won't know what hit him."

I watched the little family eat together, Lyria chewing on a roll while Nik fed Hope what looked like creamed peas. They looked just like him and Marlowe, perfect little renditions of the both of them. They made for adorable children, and even fiercer dragons, I was sure. My heart filled with gratitude and wonder as I watched them interact. What must that be like, having children? Having a family to love and care for?

One day soon, I'd have that too.

Our own little family.

"Hey," Nik said and shook me out of my thoughts. "You need anyone to talk to about...I dunno, anything, you come to me, okay? I got your back."

I had a mate. I had friends. I had a clan that supported and surrounded me. And soon, two tiny baby dragons.

"Thanks man." I nodded. "I appreciate it."

"What are friends for?" Nik wiped a smear of peas from Hope's cheek and looked back at me. His voice dropped and he leaned closer as if he was about to share a secret. "Oh, and tell Tork not to freak out too much. Alphas, man. they get so wrapped up when we're pregnant, don't they? Can't help themselves."

That got a full on laugh out of me. My shoulders shook. "You got that right." My mind drifted to the way he always double checked to make sure I had everything I needed before going to bed at night. The way he'd bend over backwards to get whatever I was craving, no matter how weird it was. "He's been great."

"That means he's a keeper. Where is he tonight, anyway?"

"Couldn't make it," I said after a spoonful of hot stew that burned my throat as it went down. Myrony had really outdone herself this time. Carrots, celery, and potatoes floated in a beef broth rich with salt and spices. "He's been working day and night on the prototypes Rex brought back from the field. He keeps saying he's close to a breakthrough, but..." I shrugged.

"Typical Tork."

"He's passionate," I said after another spoonful of soup. *In more ways than one.*

Hope made a wet coughing sound and green goop spewed out of her mouth, dribbling down the sides of her face and dripping onto Nik's clothes. He grimaced and held her at arms length, but his expression was still every bit the loving father. I offered him a towel to clean up with, but he brushed it away.

"Looks like that's my cue," he said, untangling himself from the long communal bench. "Bedtime comes early, anyway." He balanced Hope on his hip and waved to me with his free hand. "It was great to see you again."

"Take care!" I waved at him as they headed off back toward their home.

The pregnancy hormones were definitely having their way with me now. Did I just find a puking baby cute?

Tork would never let me hear the end of that.

Tork.

The thought sliced across my mind like a knife. No, a hot knife, being struck by lightning. My dragon cried out in pain and spikes of terror raced across my flesh. My hand shot to my temple.

Something was wrong. Something was happening to Tork!

My vision faded in and out, leaving me seeing double for a few seconds as I shook my head and blinked my eyes. What was going on? Where was he? I tried to call out to Tork on our Link but got no answer. Only cold, empty static.

Ice water dumped into my belly and my skin broke out in gooseflesh as my dragon cried out once more.

Find him! Find him now!

I nearly knocked over the table as I ran toward the lab, terrified of what I might find. *Tork, answer me! Tork, it's Ansel. Are you okay?* I called out to him again and again in my mind, hoping that perhaps he was just too far or was too entranced in his work to notice. But no, there was no answer. And that worried me even more.

I fumbled with my keycard and threw open the door to the laboratory, only to find it cold, dark, and empty.

Tork was gone.

The sun sank low over the horizon and cast a warm red glare over everything. The hot fumes of the workshop broke out in sweat over my skin, not to mention the way the mask over my face recirculated the same stale air again and again.

But I couldn't stop yet. I had to figure this out.

Ever since Rex had brought back a wagon full of mysterious artifacts from our scouting journey, I was obsessed. There was mostly scrap metal and other assorted traveling supplies, but some very interesting pieces as well that I'd never seen before. A little voice in the back of my head kept telling me that if I kept working, kept pushing, I could find that hidden key to turn the tides in our favor.

As of yet, I hadn't found it.

I wiped my brow and moved on to the next item, an

ornately carved mirror framed with ivory and perfectly reflective, even after the dusty journey. It was far too nice a piece of work to be carrying in a travel wagon. Looked like it would be on display at the Flower Festival or in a merchant's cart, not some roving band on the road.

I flipped it over and examined the backside. Smooth, cream colored ivory encircled the glass and shone in the light. I rubbed the pads of my fingers over the surface and closed my eyes.

There.

I couldn't quite tell what it was, but there was some form of engraving on the back. I could feel it, but no matter how I tilted the mirror I couldn't get it to come to light. Finally I moved to the wood-powered forge and grabbed one of the blocks there. I shoved it into the furnace and charred only the end, then rushed back to my work.

Using the firewood like a giant pencil I scraped it over the pristine ivory, throwing crumbs of wood and black dust everywhere. It ran over the fine engraving and the charcoal dust stuck into the grooves. Now each letter stood out plain as day. I wiped away the dust with a smear of my hand and there it was: the inscription.

It didn't look like any language I'd seen before, though I wasn't a linguistic expert like some of the other engineers. I mostly just blew shit up. Something about this mirror gave off an eerie presence though. Like it was some precious, mystical artifact I should never have picked up in the first place.

I mouthed the words scratched in to the back of the ivory.

~ *Andelra intimi laosin acree* ~

Beneath it was a scratched insignia of six points in a hexagon shape connected through by lines. I furrowed my brow as I studied the strange markings. What did it mean?

That's when the mirror started vibrating in my hands.

I nearly dropped it in my surprise, but that would have broken the glass. Then whatever knowledge this thing had would be lost. Thoughts flashed briefly in my mind of putting this off till later, of recruiting someone that knew more about this kind of stuff than I did. but I was in too deep now. I had to keep going.

I flipped over the mirror, the ivory and glass still buzzing beneath my fingertips. Only this time, when I peered into the smooth glass surface, I didn't see my face staring back at me. It was like looking through a portal. Or a window, maybe. Green hills rolled across the landscape and clouds drifted lazily by in the skies above. It looked sorta familiar, like I'd been there before. Nearby, if I had to guess.

Then they crested the hill and my heart froze in my chest.

Not one mech. Not two.

Five of them. Five fully operational, totally badass automatons, controlled by the humans of Steamshire and rumbling across the way. That's when I realized where they were. That was not half a day from here. That was part of the ground we'd covered not too long ago.

They were coming. They were coming for Darkvale. And they were close.

I couldn't tear my eyes away as I watched all five of them creaking and rumbling and tearing up the ground in their wake. This was bad. No, this was more than bad.

This was a disaster.

Lucien had reached out for aid for but as far as I knew, they weren't coming. At least not in time to save us, anyway. Guess we were gonna have to go this alone.

We'd protect our home, or go down trying.

My dragon did a panicked dance in my chest, begging to come out and roast anyone or anything that stood in our way. I had more than just myself to live for now. I had a mate. And not only that, my mate was pregnant, with twins of all things.

They wouldn't get to my family. I'd die before I let that happen.

The emotion surged through me and blocked out all reason. I had to protect him. No matter what.

I looked across the lab table to the work area where I'd been building a new type of explosive mine. Using what I had learned about the automatons, I had specifically engineered a new prototype to take them down before they ever neared our walls.

Five mines lay on the table.

Five automatons approached our walls.

I chewed my lip. They weren't quite ready yet, was the problem. There were still a few bugs I needed to work out, like the one where the trigger mechanism occasionally didn't stay locked. I could arm the mine, walk away, and it would switch off on its own without warning. A lot of good that did.

But it was this or nothing.

The mirror clattered to the desk as I made up my mind. I took a deep breath, stuffed the mines in my bag, and flew out the door. As soon as I breached the castle gates, I gave myself over to the shift.

Dragon time.

———

I FLEW FASTER than I'd ever flown in my life, the bag at my side dangling precariously as I flapped my wings faster, harder. Wind wailed in my ears and my eyes watered. But the heart of a warrior beat within me, the heart of an alpha, a mate, a father. *Protect your clan. Protect your family*, it told me. My dragon was on a mission, and it would not be deterred.

I landed on the grass right over the hill that shielded Darkvale on one side. I couldn't see them yet, but the echoes I heard in the distance told me they wouldn't be far. My fingers fumbled on the switches as I placed each of the five mines and used the mounting spike I'd developed to bury them into the earth. They weren't going anywhere. And once the automatons ran over them, neither would they.

My brain reminded me that this was crazy. That I was breaking just about every clan law and I should have gone to Lucien first, to warn him. And I would have, really, had things been different.

There was no time.

By the time I'd alerted all the proper authorities and gathered a team to help head them off, they'd be upon us, and we'd be toast. But if I could set up this first line of defense, if I could blast my way through their defenses before they even got close to the walls...

Maybe we'd have a chance.

Glendaria preserve us, I muttered in an incantation, crossing my hands over my heart.

I armed each of the mines one by one, holding my breath as a little red light flashed on the side then faded away. Now as long as they didn't malfunction and trigger early, or turn themselves off like my early prototypes had...

When I flipped the switch on the last mine, it came off in my hand and the mine blinked an angry red, flashing its warnings at me. I sucked in a breath. Two choices spread out before me:

I could stay here and manually configure the last mine.

Or I could run and hope it didn't blow before I got out of range.

Both of them, I realized grimly, likely ended in a fiery death. Mine, to be exact.

I'm sorry, I thought through my Link, praying that Ansel would be able to hear me. *I'm sorry and I love you.*

Then I held tight to the mine, suppressing the trigger, and roared out my defiance into the night.

If I was gonna go out, I'd go out with a boom.

13

ANSEL

I heard Tork's plea at the same time the alarms started going off.

I'm sorry and I love you.

What kind of crazy scheme was he up to this time?

My heart cried out in protest and I nearly shifted right there in the middle of the lab in my haste to get to him.

Sirens wailed and I heard Lucien's voice, amplified one hundred times as he announced that the final battle was at hand. He called us to arms, not only the alphas, but omegas, women, everyone who could fight. Especially without reinforcements, we needed every fighting hand we could get.

I rushed through the chaos and into the throng of shifters pushing their way through the gates. Marlowe led the vanguard, his eyes fierce and furious as he beckoned to his strongest fighters. They shifted as soon as they were clear of the gates and sailed high into the sky, encircling the fortress with a moat of flame.

I escaped the ring of fire just in time, grateful for my small stature.

That's when I saw him.

Our eyes met and time stopped for a split second as I realized his predicament.

Ansel, no! He screamed in my mind, but I was already running toward him.

If you touch me, you'll trigger it! We'll both blow!

No we won't!

I wouldn't let that happen. Not to my mate, not to my babies, not to anyone. This time, I could be a savior.

A wall of metal crested the hill and turned my blood to ice. So that's what all the alarms were about. So that meant they were coming. They were here. I eyed the line of explosives and realized that Tork had snuck out to do this on his own, before any of us even knew they were coming.

He wanted to protect me.

But now it was time to protect him.

I grit my teeth and threw myself into the shift, my wings sprouting from my back just in time. I swooped forward and never took my eyes off Tork, who looked on with fear, surprise, and what I thought could have been admiration.

Energy and adrenaline pumped through me and my heart hammered like a drum even in my dragon form as the wind rushed against my scales. I hovered low, reaching out my strong back legs and stretching the claws there. If I could just grab him in time, we could get out of here and away from the blast.

And if I messed up, I'd both impale my mate and get blown up at the same time.

No pressure.

I sucked in a breath and locked my sights on my mate.

Too late, he realized what I was doing and put his hands up to shield his face. My legs reached down and caught him around the middle, careful of my talons. Tork yelped as he flew into the air with me and as we sailed away from the scene, the malfunctioning mine exploded in our wake. Fire and heat burned at my back but I couldn't stop. I pushed my wings harder, up and away.

Let me down! Goddess please, let me down! Tork screeched from below me, still wriggling in my grasp.

Oh, thank Glendaria. He was alive.

I flew in a wide circle over the plains, past the encroaching automatons and over the wall of flame protecting Darkvale. I landed as gently as I could and Tork tumbled out of my grasp, rolling a few times before coming to a stop, dusty and scraped up, on the ground. He stared at me, open mouthed, brushing his torn clothes off with skinned hands while he fought to catch his breath. I watched every move.

Fucking hell, Ansel. Tork grumbled on our Link. *Warn a guy next time!*

You were about to die, I shot back. *I'm supposed to let you sacrifice yourself like that?*

*Just...*he shuddered. *Never do that again.*

Stubborn, I teased. *I saved your ass.*

Reckless, he muttered.

My dragon huffed. He was one to talk.

I changed back to human form, my limbs already exhausted from my frenzied rescue. Tork ran forward and threw his arms around me, squeezing me so tightly I couldn't breathe.

"I get it, I get it," I squeaked and pushed him away.

"If something happened to you..." he said out loud this time. "You scared me, Ansel."

"Ready for a little more of that teamwork magic?" I asked him as I took his hand. The power of our ancestors flowed through us and strengthened my will, my resolve, and my courage. All past hurts and fears fled away in the presence of my mate and the growing life within me.

"Let's do this," Tork agreed and kissed me on the cheek. "Dragon style."

In that moment no one else mattered. Our dragons united, our bodies and minds totally in sync. We shifted in unison, and took to the skies.

———

WE SAILED over the front lines, watching as man and dragon converged on the battlefield.

Marlowe and his team circled above with fire and fury, but what surprised me most of all were the forces on the ground.

None other than Alec Cipher led a team of omegas into the fray, shouting war cries to the heavens and pumping his fist to the sky. They followed him. They believed in him.

And his band of freedom fighters weren't just shifters, either. There were humans there, too. Former Steamshire refugees. With Steamshire insurgents clattering over the hill in their massive metal men, it would be a sight to behold.

I had always known that humans and shifters didn't like one another very much. But to stoop to this level…it chilled me to the core. And here they were, in their own little civil war, right at our doorstep. Because this was more than just a fight over land or property. This was a fight of ideals, and the victor would pave the way for the future of their species. Humans and shifters had learned to work together in Darkvale because of Alec and Lucien's firm belief that we could live as one.

But if Steamshire were to win today? I shuddered to think.

"For Darkvale!" I roared and let out a jet of flame. We would never go back. Never.

The automatons continued to roll forward, the weapons built into their hulking hands quivering at the ready.

When they hit the mines, we blast 'em, Tork said in my mind. *I'll take the west flank. You take the other*.

Deal.

We split off and came up on them from either side, drawing their attention away from the oncoming army. One raised its arm and shot a bolt toward me. I swerved to the side just in time. Tork barrel rolled through the air and picked up speed, dodging in and out of their attacks.

Three... Tork breathed.

Two, I joined in.

One.

"Boom," I mouthed.

The mines exploded on impact and created a wall of debris as metal and dirt flew everywhere. I didn't waste any time unleashing my fire, spraying death down upon the wreckage. I couldn't see through the smoke and ash, I couldn't hear over the deafening sounds of the explosion, but I continued breathing fire with all my heart, and Tork's too.

This went past any limit I'd set for myself before. I was putting my all into this and then some more. As the fire dried up and sparks coughed up and I heaved for breath, I prayed to the Goddess above it was enough. That when the dust cleared and the smoke settled, those awful things would be dead.

No such luck.

Through the fire and explosions of the mines, four out of the five automatons still stood. Still advanced. My stomach heaved, another wave of nausea seizing me like a snake. This time it wasn't morning sickness. This time it was the crippling, crushing realization that despite our best efforts, we'd failed.

Fall back! Tork called to me, and I didn't waste any time.

We sailed over the crowd of humans and shifters pouring from the gate, and I shifted back into human form to join them.

"We've weakened them," I called out to Alec as soon as I touched down. "But they're still coming. You're gonna need to give it everything you've got."

"You hear that?" Alec projected to the crowd around him. "Today is the day we fight! Not only for our home, not only for our safety, but for our freedom! It does not matter, brothers and sisters, what land you hail from, what species or race you are, what powers you have or don't have. What matters is our drive, our dedication, our love for one another and for our family. I know many of you are refugees, just as I once was. It saddens my heart to see the Elders have done this. But each and every one of you means more to me than a thousand Elders and their schemes. Today we fight! Today we win! Will you join me, Darkvale?"

The crowd roared, brandishing whatever weapons they had on hand.

Dragons shifted and roars crackled through the air like lightning. It was now or never, and I'd never been so proud of my clan.

Just then, the mechs slashed through the flames, stepping through as if they were nothing. My throat closed up in horror. The mines hadn't worked. Fire hadn't worked. How were we gonna take these bastards down?

One of the automatons spoke for the first time,

amplifying his own voice as him and his cronies moved ever closer.

"Alec Cipher…it's no wonder I should find you here. Still dwelling with the animals, I see. And got a whole army of traitors with you too. How…quaint."

Alec bared his teeth and I wanted to blast the metal man right then and there.

"You've gone too far." Alec stood his ground and gestured to the fighters around him. "We don't subscribe to your ways of fear and hate anymore."

A moment of defiant, taunting laughter. "You brought an army of *omegas* against us? That's the best you can do?" The man laughed again, momentarily off his guard.

"Get them," Alec commanded.

A whole horde of men, women, and shifters surged forward like the tide, spilling over the ground and screaming their defiance as they faced off against their former masters. Dragons shifted and took to the air, flapping their wings in a swirling air current around the automatons.

The automatons stood ready, firing charges into the crowd. In unison they brought their feet up and then down in a mighty stomp, sending a shockwave through the earth. People stumbled and fell to their knees as the charges triggered and let out spurts of corrosive poison all over the onlookers. The mass of people soon devolved into chaos, humans shrieking and flailing as flesh sloughed away on impact of the ghastly green stuff from the charges.

It didn't stop everyone though. I ran forward with Adrian and Nik at my side, the three of us sharing a glance. Tork flew on scaly wings above us with Marlowe, leading the charge and pummeling into the mech firing the charges. They collided with a bone-jarring crash and and ear-splitting screech of metal and monster.

I set my sights on the rightmost mech and bared my teeth. This ended now.

Nik and Adrian flanked me and we converged on the monster, weapons at the ready. I gripped the gun I'd grabbed from the lab and took a deep breath. I hoped it would do what it said on the tin. Electromagnetic Pulse Detonation Device—Single Use, it read in silver engraving on the long polished barrel. My hands shook. I'd never fired a gun before, but here, in the presence of my kinfolk and all I held dear, there was no other option. I looked down the iron sights, lined up the pulsing heart of light at the mech's center, let out a breath, and pulled the trigger.

It hit the mech dead center like a load of invisible bricks. The metal man stumbled backwards and the throbbing ball of energy at its core flickered, faltered, and went out. The animated metal slumped and squealed, crashing to the dirt in a pile of dust.

"Woot!" Nik shouted, pumping his fist in the air. But as I kept my eyes on the now-unmoving automaton, I felt a chill of terror down to my very soul. This was wrong, this was very, very wrong. I stumbled back just in time.

The trapdoor holding the driver sprung open and a hooded man leapt out, eyes shining with supreme hatred and fury.

The driver wasn't a human at all.

It was a Sorcerer, and he didn't look happy.

W e were in deep shit.

I knew Steamshire had Sorcerers on their side, sure, but to have them piloting these monsters?

My blood ran cold as I felt the clash of our energies in mid air. My throat dried up, my dragon quailed as I tumbled to the ground in human form. No shifting here.

I bared my teeth and clenched my fists.

"Sorcerer," I spat.

"Shifter," she responded, and when she let down her hood I saw with horror it was the same woman who'd escaped us.

Why had we ever let her escape? I bet the slippery

bitch told them all about us, too. That's why they withstood the mine blasts. That's why they kept coming through the wall of fire.

The echo of steel sounded behind me as my clansmen drew their swords. Sorcerer or not, they could still bleed. And they would pay for what they'd done here today.

"Grenya, is that you?" Heavy footsteps pushed through the crowd and I glanced over my shoulder long enough to see Elias striding toward the front lines.

Turns out we had a Sorcerer too.

"Elias..." The woman growled, narrowing her eyes. Her pale, glistening eyes tore straight through the crowd and chaos, straight to him. "How interesting to find you here. Thought you'd died."

"Far from it," Elias said. "Let's just say I turned over a new leaf."

"Traitor!" Grenya yelled so loud I took a few steps backward. "You've betrayed us all, Elias. Allying with these beasts? What were you thinking?"

"That we deserve more than a life of running from one job to the next."

"If your father could see you now..." Grenya's face twisted in disgust. "I should just get rid of you myself."

"Then come at me," Elias taunted. "But I'm not going anywhere."

I dodged out of the way just in time as their spells collided in midair.

A Sorcerer on Sorcerer battle? Not something you want to be caught in the middle of.

"Tork, come on!" Ansel's voice snapped me out of it. I joined him at his side and only then noticed the spent pistol in his hands. My pistol. It was nothing more than a hobby project I picked up on spare nights and weekends, yet Ansel had picked it up at just the right time to save us all.

"It worked!" I grinned, letting out a relieved laugh. "Awesome!"

"Celebrate later, we've got company!" He yanked me to the side just in time to miss a bolt flying through the air and burying itself, quivering, in the soft wet ground.

With a lump in my throat, I whirled around.

Those bastards!

While we'd been preoccupied the last remaining mech had snuck their way up to the gates, fighting now in close quarters with the omega army.

And we were losing.

Fear squeezed my heart like a vise. All those omegas, fighting for their home and their freedom, some even younger than Ansel. The alpha instinct in me riled up and my dragon strained to break free, but the sorcerer was still too close, still doing her dirty work.

No matter. We had other means of fighting.

Ansel must have heard what I was saying, because he grabbed my hand and gave me a encouraging nod. I focused all my attention on the incoming mechs and charged forward, picking up a long spear from a fallen warrior as I went. I yelled and leapt into the air, aiming right for the gap between the monster's head and body.

The blade slipped into the gap in the metal and sent a shock of vibration from my hands all the way down my body. I cried out, hanging on to the spear for dear life as it lodged itself deeper into the machinery. There was a grinding, scraping sound and the mech wailed in a great rusty scream, flinching away so fast I nearly flew through the air with the force of it. I growled and held firm, driving it ever deeper, into the pulsing core and through the other side.

But when it flailed again and headed straight for my friend Adrian, I lost my grip and tumbled to the dirt.

No, Adrian...

No!

I skidded across the ground and held my breath, waiting for the screams.

"Don't mess with Darkvale!" A voice bellowed, and

Adrian appeared on the other side, landing a roundhouse kick right at the weak part where the spear protruded. I let go at the last second and the spear snapped as the force split the mech in two, the pieces crashing to the ground in a smoking heap.

"The driver!" I cried to Adrian as I picked myself up. "Get the driver!"

By this time the driver's compartment had opened and a small, gangly man scrambled out, eyes frantic with fear. He held up his hands in surrender, but it was too late for that. Adrian and Alec grabbed him around the middle, holding him still while Ansel and I advanced.

I prepared to unleash a bout of flame but the sparks dried on my tongue and wouldn't come. Goddess-damned Sorcerer! I dared not look back, I dared not focus on anything but the present moment. The human screamed and tried to wriggle away, but was no match for his captors.

He didn't look so scary now, out of his giant metal contraption. He looked terrified.

Alec broke the silence before I had the chance to. "Why are you doing this, Hans?" His voice took on a pleading quality. He knew the man, I realized with a shock.

Hans sputtered and gulped, looking wildly at the battle raging around him. "I didn't have a choice, man. They made me..." He stopped, panting and coughing. "They made me a deal and I..."

"Denounce them and their ways," Alec commanded. "And you may yet live."

The man panted, eyes flickering between him and us. Fire still boiled in my gut, and I knew were I in Alec's shoes I would not have such mercy. These people had betrayed him, attacked him, killed members of their own tribe! There was no greater crime.

"Alec, you can't be serious—" I started, my own rage bubbling over. Ansel put a calming hand on my shoulder and I snapped my mouth shut.

"Lucien will deal with him," Alec sneered and passed him off to two burly-looking guards who dragged the screaming man away. Then he turned his gaze to me.

"You don't know what its like," he said softly, his voice wavering. "I lived with them for so long, and some of them were my friends, and..." He ran a hand over his face. "It's just hard to believe they're all bad, you know?"

I nodded and Ansel squeezed my hand.

A resounding boom echoed from behind us and my hands shot up to cover my ears, still pounding from the blast. I whirled around and found Elias standing over the rebel Sorcerer, his hand clenched in midair. Grenya gasped and clawed at her throat, her mouth opening and closing silently.

"You will not harm me and my friends anymore." He said it simply, as a statement of fact. Then he closed his outstretched hands into a fist, and the woman's eyes bulged and tongue sagged as her face turned a bright, beet red. She scrabbled at her neck until her arms went limp, sagging loosely by her side as her body gave up the fight. She was dead.

Elias stood over him for a long moment, considering the face of his enemy, a Sorcerer just like him. I knew how hard that must have been for him. When I first met Elias, he was a snarky little brat that wouldn't listen to anyone, least of all any Firefang. But he'd been such a resource to us as time went on. We'd developed a working relationship that perhaps was not close like friendship, but a solid trust and sharing of skills and ideals.

And this, here today? Elias had faced off against his own kind to protect us. He'd chosen a side at last. And he'd chosen us.

Elias turned, caught my eye, and bowed his head. "Kill them," I saw him mouth over the roar of battle.

Didn't have to tell me twice.

The roar of dragonfire filled the night as my people regained their powers. Men and women shifted all around me, taking to the sky and surrounding the remaining mech. Now that we knew their weakness, it was only a matter of time. The circling dragons built a towering prism of fire surrounding the mech and the ground armies stood on the other side, waiting to strike. I saw them dive-bombing from above, their claws outstretched, their wings folded to their side to pick up speed.

At the last second they leveled out, three dragons grabbing the mech in their claws and lifting it into the air. I heard screams now, human screams.

I watched with horror as they flew up, up, up, then split off in opposite directions while still holding the mech firmly in their claws. A great screech rent the air as debris tumbled to the ground. They had torn the mech limb from limb, and the driver along with it.

I tried not to think about the wet squish the body made as it hit the ground. I didn't think about the smell of soot or iron or smoke. In that moment, there was silence. Pure, blessed silence. The mechs were destroyed. Their masters incapacitated.

It was over.

Ansel leaned into me and let out a breath. He squeezed his eyes shut, breath coming in quick gasps. I held him there in the middle of the battlefield, brushing a hand through his hair as the chaos died down around us.

After all the fear and blood and death, we'd done it. We'd won.

Over Steamshire and humans and Sorcerers, we'd come out on top.

I heard shouts and cheers of triumph behind us, but they faded into the background as I held my mate close. There was only one thing my dragon wanted to do right now, and we'd need a little more privacy for that.

A fter the Battle of the Mechs, as we'd come to call it, things actually calmed down around Darkvale for once. We repaired, we recuperated, we recovered. Us Firefangs were nothing if not resilient.

Weeks passed as we fell into a sort of routine once more. We'd salvaged what we could from the wreckage of the automatons and brought it into the lab for testing and research. No one had been more excited about that than Tork, but we'd all had a hand in deciphering their technology.

After long nights of trial and error, combined with Elias' help, we'd managed to dissect the molten core that powered each automaton. It was such a marvelous source of energy, capable of more than just terror and destruction. In fact, I had an idea in my mind that we could make our own mechs in the future. Not for war, no. But for assistance. Several of our fighters had been injured, some even crippled in the attack. Add to that our elderly population and you had a contingent of people that could use a little help now and then.

All that had to be put on hold as I grew more and more pregnant, however.

The cravings were driving both me and Tork nuts, even though he didn't want to admit it. He was a good sport about it, though. He brought me pickles, ice cream, even a few rare berries. Whatever I asked for, he made it his mission to find. And that was only one of the reasons I loved him so much. As the days droned on though, I had to take leave from the lab because the little ones were not big fans of me standing around all day. My ankles swelled, my back ached.

I was ready for this to be over.

My stomach had ballooned out like I'd swallowed a watermelon whole, and even though Doctor Parley assured me everything was progressing smoothly, most days I felt like a beached whale.

It was only a week and a half before my due date when we received a formal message from Steamshire. Lucien gathered us all together in the great hall to read it aloud.

Steamshire had surrendered, at long last.

After years on the endless cycle of war and recovery, it

felt weird to go about my daily schedule without waiting for the other shoe to drop. After I got used to it, it felt kinda...nice.

Clan Alpha Lucien announced a feast of epic proportions that weekend to celebrate our victory and to rekindle our spirits.

I was so there, of course. Only problem was all my fancy costumes wouldn't fit my over my belly. Believe me, I tried.

Tork, on the other hand? He was gonna take a little more convincing.

———

"COME ON," I knocked on the bathroom door. "Come out already, you can't look that bad!"

I heard a muffled grunt from within and he finally emerged.

My mouth hung open as I took in this new Tork. Not only had he actually brushed his hair for once, he was wearing a suit. It hugged him in all the right places, accentuating his broad chest and the long lines of his legs.

"Like what you see?" He quirked a grin, turning around to give me a 360 view.

Damn, those pants were *made* for his ass.

"Oh, um," I rubbed the back of my neck and cleared my throat. "You look great. More than great, actually."

"Oh yeah?" He murmured, towering over me.

"Makes me wanna tear those clothes off right here." I grinned and dropped my voice. Even though no one else was around, it felt like our little secret.

"This is a brand new suit," Tork said in mock affront. "At least let me get through the dinner first."

I laughed. "You don't even want to go. We could stay here, you know...skip out..." I tried to give him a coy glance.

His eyes flashed with desire as he leaned in close, his hot breath whispering on my ear. "No, we're going. But after? After is fair game."

"Deal," I breathed. My dragon was already starting to get excited and a rush of heat down to my groin short-circuited what I wanted to say next. Waiting through the feast would be torture.

"The most delicious kind," Tork nipped at the side of my neck. Had I said that aloud? "But come on, let's get going."

He helped me to my feet—the babies made it hard nowadays—and we headed out the door to the ballroom. The very place where we'd ran into each other that fateful night.

THE FESTIVITIES WERE in full swing when we arrived. It wasn't as extravagant as the Flower Festival —but then, what was—but there was a colorful array of foods, live music, and every one of my friends was in attendance.

It was like a big family reunion. All of us, at last, were together. Were safe.

"You scout out a seat," Tork offered. "I'll grab us some food. What are the little ones craving today?"

I chewed my lip, thinking. "Pretzels? Or anything salty, really. And chocolate, if they have it."

Tork's face twisted into a grin. "Your wish is my command." He gave an exaggerated bow and headed off. I had to laugh.

"You've got him wrapped around your finger," I heard a voice from behind me as I watched him leave.

It was Adrian, one of the local omegas and a friend to Alec and Nik. I hadn't had a chance to get to know him very well since I was off at the Academy, but I'd heard great things.

I laughed again and shrugged. "Yeah, guess I do. He's just trying to help, is all."

"He's a good alpha. Takes care of his own." For a second his face sagged with something like sadness, or a long-forgotten memory. Then it was gone, as quickly as it had surfaced.

"He is," I agreed. "He's a keeper, for sure."

Adrian held a small boy by the hand. He looked very much like Adrian, with a hint of more angular features as well. Blond hair lay messily over his forehead and he gaped at me with wide amber eyes.

"This is Finley," he said. "Say hi, Finley!"

The child buried his head in his daddy's pant leg instead. Adrian shrugged. "He's feeling shy tonight. Heard you have a little one of your own coming soon." He grinned and eyed my midsection. It wasn't exactly easy to hide anymore. My due date was still a week away, but I didn't know if I could wait that long. Pregnancy was awesome in a lot of ways, but I was ready to move on. I was ready to meet my little darlings and welcome them to the world.

"He's adorable," I cooed at Finley. I instinctively placed a hand over my stomach, thinking about my little ones on the way. "And yeah, you're right. Two, actually."

Adrian's eyes widened. "Twins? No way, man."

"Twins," I confirmed.

"Wow..." Adrian seemed at a loss for words. "They're incredibly rare, you know? I can't wait to meet them."

"Neither can I," I said, and my heart surged with pride.

"I don't envy all the work, though." Adrian said. "This little guy keeps me on my toes, but two? Sounds like a party."

I laughed. "I'm sure it will be." I wasn't as nervous about the birth as I probably should be. It was scary, sure. And having two babies to take care of instead of one was gonna be a lot of work. But I had faith that Tork and I could pull it off. When I was with him, anything seemed possible. Even raising twins.

Tork returned to the table with a plate full of food and set it before me. A big pile of pretzels, cured meat, and even a small wedge of chocolate. I stared at the plate and back at Tork. "Have I ever told you how much I love you?"

"Regularly." He sat down next to me and pecked my cheek. "But I never get tired of hearing it."

The moment was broken by the high pitched sound of silverware on glass. We all looked up to see Clan Alpha Lucien standing at the front of the room. He was joined by his mate Alec and their baby Corin. Nikolas and Marlowe were there too with Lyria and Hope by their side.

The gang's all here, I thought with a smile.

"Greetings, Firefangs," Lucien said in a loud projecting voice. It reached across the room without amplification. He didn't need it. Everyone was still and listening. "Greetings to our friends and allies from Steamshire and abroad. We dine together tonight beyond the bounds of clans or races or labels. We dine together tonight as family. We've been through a lot in the past years. No one will deny that. But it is our commitment to our duty, and to each other, that has brought us here today. I say we toast to our friends, toast to our fallen comrades, and toast to all the bounty that is to come." He raised his glass high and the rest of us followed suit.

Alec spoke next. "The night I left Steamshire, I didn't know where I was gonna go, or what I was gonna do. I just knew I was destined for something greater than their ritual sacrifice. That night, I met Lucien. He took me in, showed me what a real family could be like. And what do you know? I fell in love. Dragons, shifters, sorcerers, humans, it doesn't matter. Alpha or omega, it doesn't matter. What we've built here is a model for the rest of the world, and I toast today to all the days to come, and all the new allies we'll meet along the way."

"Cheers," the crowd rumbled.

Nik now took the platform, raising his glass to the sky. "When I saw Darkvale burning around me, when I lost my mate that terrible night, I thought that's all life was. When I had my daughter and her alpha daddy wasn't there to see her beautiful smile, I kept moving. Even though I was treated no better than a hostage, I held that hope in my heart, night after night. *Firefangs mean family*. That's what Lucien told us. And when the Paradox finally fell, I knew my waiting had paid off. I not only re-united with my long lost mate, my best friend, my lover, but we had another perfect child together to add to our family. So my toast is to Hope—both the baby," he kissed his daughter's cheek—"and the concept that's brought us through so many trials to this day. To Hope!"

"To hope!" Voices echoed through the halls.

Marlowe was last, and he looked upon the crowd of friends and family, spreading his arms wide as if in a hug. "I'm not sure what I can say that hasn't already been said," he started. "I've fought with many of you throughout the years. I've worked with more. I've seen men and women, alphas and omegas, rise above their circumstances to greatness when called upon. And I have never been so proud to be surrounded with so many strong, caring, and generous people. So my toast is to strength—both the inner and outer strength that each and every one of you has inside. To strength!" He ended on a yell, jutting his glass into the air so quickly his drink splashed out.

"To strength!" The crowd echoed, and the air vibrated with the roars of dragons.

All the excitement must have gotten the little ones worked up too, because at that instant I felt a squeezing sensation in my lower abdomen. Like a cramp, but stronger. I shot a hand to my stomach and winced.

"What's the matter?" Tork was immediately at my side. "Is it the baby?"

The cheers and celebration of the crowd faded away as my stomach cramped again. "Yeah, I think its the baby."

"Now?" His eyes widened like saucers. "You sure?"

"Yes, now!" I snapped with a little more venom than I'd intended. A rush of wetness seeped through my pants and I winced again.

My water's broke, I thought hazily. *It's coming. The babies are actually coming.*

"Stay right here," Tork grabbed my shoulders and looked into my eyes. "It's gonna be okay. I'll get the doctor. He's gotta be here somewhere."

"You stay with your mate," Adrian interrupted us. He must have noticed my predicament. "I'll get Dr. Parley."

"If you can find him in this mess," I moaned, looking around at the crowds of people. It would be like finding a needle in a haystack.

"I'll find him," Adrian promised and gave my hand a squeeze. "Just stay calm. I'll be right back."

With that he rushed off, pushing through the crowds of people.

Tork brushed hair away from my face and held me close. "How do you feel?"

I shifted in my seat, still cradling my stomach. "Hurts. Feels like the twins are ready to say hello. Guess they wanted to be part of the party, too."

Tork huffed. "Glad you can have some good humor about this. But what timing, huh?"

"Yeah," I chuckled. "We knew it was coming, just..."

"It's still a week away," Tork pointed out. "Your due date."

"The twins don't seem to care about due dates." I shot him a grin but it was cut off by another contraction.

"Breathe," he whispered in my ear as he rubbed my back. "Remember what I taught you. Breathe."

He was right. I let everything else fall away. The sounds of the other people around us, the music, the clink of plates and glasses. I held Tork's gaze and squeezed his hands. He kept me grounded, kept me from flying away.

"You're going to be all right," he promised. "The doctor's on his way."

And indeed he was. Adrian had located him in record time and when the doctor saw me sitting on the bench and panting for breath, he leapt into action.

"You his mate?" He eyed Tork.

"I am," Tork said. "How can I help?"

"We've got to get him out of here, back to the medical ward. The sooner the better. I've sent word to Anna to set things up and I need to go change, but you bring him right there, you hear me?"

"I will," Tork promised. "I will."

"Good. See you soon." He rushed off as soon as he'd come, and another contraction hit me like waves on the shore. I moaned and looked up at Tork through blurry eyes.

"You heard the good doctor," Tork said. "Let's get you out of here." He hooked his arms under my shoulders and knees and lifted me into the air, carrying me easily toward the door.

I knew people were staring. I knew everyone would be talking about this for weeks. But that didn't matter right now.

Tork pushed through the crowd like a steamroller, and I was once again grateful for his large stature. "Pregnant mate coming through, make way!"

People scattered in all directions and at some point I must have blacked out, because when I opened them again, we were in the medical ward.

W e were having a baby.

No.

We were having two babies.

I couldn't believe it.

After watching Ansel grow into a man, after teaching him, mentoring him, and finally mating him, here it was. The ultimate moment. Ansel's grip just about crushed my fingers, but I let him squeeze. It was all I could do for him right now.

Doctor Parley and his nurse Anna had prepared a room for us in short order. Ansel lay on a cot with a blanket over his lower half while the doctor checked his vitals.

"Good thing you found when you did," he said, snapping on a pair of gloves. "These little dragons are ready to meet their daddies."

Ansel gave a weak smile and I squeezed his hand again. *Remember to breathe,* I told him on our Link.

Of course I know how to breathe, you asshole. I've got babies coming out of me, that's the problem!

The sudden outburst caught me off guard and I stifled a laugh. Ansel's eyes were like daggers boring into my flesh.

So he was a little feisty while in labor. Got it.

"I'm gonna need you to push," the doctor said to Ansel. "In three...two...one..."

"Push!"

Ansel moaned in pain, his whole body tense. He squeezed my hand so tightly I lost feeling and he kept squeezing, kept yelling, kept flinging curses at me over our Link.

It will be over soon, I tried to assure him telepathically, but he wasn't having any of it.

"Almost there, I can see the head!" The doctor announced. "Push!"

Beads of sweat broke out over Ansel's forehead as he tensed and released, groaning and screaming and gritting his teeth. Whoever said omegas were weak clearly hadn't seen one giving birth. It was nothing short of miraculous.

A gasping cry of new life rent through the air and in

that instant my world stopped. Nurse Anna swiftly took the baby away to clean them up, but we weren't done yet.

"One more good push for me," the doctor prodded. "I know you're tired. The little one's on the way. Now push!"

One last gasping, crying, shaking moment later, another cry joined their sibling's.

I looked to Ansel to see how he was doing. His eyes were half-lidded, his face red and covered with sweat. But in those eyes, laced with exhaustion and pain, I saw something else. Triumph. Joy. Hope.

"We did it," he muttered, finally loosening his hold on my hand. I stretched the sore fingers. "We really did it."

He closed his eyes for a moment, resting against the pillows as his breaths returned to normal.

The nurse returned with not one but two little babies in her arms, each wrapped in a swaddling newborn blanket. "Congratulations. Your little dragons are healthy and beautiful. One girl, one boy."

I let out a breath as I watched her place them into Ansel's waiting arms. I'd never seen anything so perfect in my life. Chills ran down my spine and my dragon woke up, taking notice of the two new souls flickering to life on our Link. One girl, one boy. Ten fingers, ten toes. We'd done it.

Ansel stared at them like they were the greatest treasure on Earth. And in this moment, they were. His mouth opened and closed as he tried to find his words. Those beautiful amber eyes brimmed with tears.

"One boy, one girl," I caught Ansel's eye when he finally tore his gaze away from the twins. "What shall we call them?"

"Hmm..." Ansel thought. "You pick one, I'll pick the other?"

I shrugged. "Works for me."

"Just nothing crazy like Shadowbane or Mistwalker."

I raised an eyebrow at him. "Would I do that?"

"Knowing you? You would." He chuckled to himself.

I rolled my eyes. "Fiiine."

"Now, serious names. What do you think?"

I looked at the little girl now resting sleepily in her fathers arms. She had almost a full head of hair, unusual for a newborn. She took after her father, then. "Juno." The word came out of my mouth before I'd even realized I'd said it. The impulse came from deep within, like I somehow knew what this child would be called.

"Juno," Ansel repeated, brushing a lock of hair from the little girl's face. "I love it."

"And for the boy?" I asked.

He was a little larger, with my nose and Ansel's eyes. While his sister had calmed down and was resting on Ansel's chest, he was still screeching bloody murder. He was going to be a handful and a half, I knew.

"Ray," Ansel said and looked at me. "What do you think of Ray?"

Ray and Juno. Our twins.

"I love it," I said, and this time my voice broke with emotion. "And I love you, *nyota*," I said, slipping into the old tongue.

"Nyota?" Ansel muttered sleepily.

"My star. My shining star." I spoke reverently, to both my mate and my children. "No matter where I am, or what happens to us, you'll always be my guiding light. I'll always find my way back to you."

I love you too, Ansel said to me, only this time in my mind. I felt it latch on and take hold, deep in my soul.

I'd gone on a lot of adventures in my life. But this, right here? My mate, my two smiling babies, my family?

This was the greatest adventure of all time.

SNEAK PEEK OF BOOK 4!

Many readers have contacted me asking about Adrian's story. He's always there to help out the other omegas, is a friend to all, but where's his happy ending? How's his little boy Finley doing? And what happened to his mate?

Finally, your questions will be answered. Read on for an exclusive sneak peek of Darkvale Book 4! You won't find this anywhere else.

Thank you for reading and supporting my work, it means a lot to me <3

ADRIAN

ONE YEAR LATER

"**D**addy!"

The sounds of children echoed through the halls even before I opened the door. Finley wobbled back and forth on the balls of his feet, looking up at me nervously. It had been so long since we'd had a chance to do anything...normal.

Nik opened the door and smiled at both Adrian and Finley. His little one Lyria had just started school and was one year younger than Finley. She peeked out from behind her dad, holding a steamed bun in her small hands.

I gave them both my warmest smile, but Finley remained hesitant. Poor kid. He'd had trouble talking to other kids ever since...well...

I sniffed and tried to will the thoughts away. Just accept it. He's not coming back.

And what about our son? What about him?

My shoulders slumped and I plastered the grin on my face. None of that now. Finley needed to have a fun, relaxing day just as much as I did. So I led him inside and Nik shut the door behind us.

Why did it have to sound so final?

"Finley, you remember Lyria, right?" I gestured at the girl. She held out a bun in Finley's direction and stuffed her other hand in her mouth. "She's in school with you."

Finley took the bun after a moment of consideration. He sniffed it, as if he wasn't sure what to expect. "Thank you," he mumbled, and took a bite.

His eyes lit up when he reached the bits of meat inside. "Good," Finley announced, then turned back to me. He held out the bun.

"Oh no, that's yours." I waved him off. "Lyria gave it to you. Say thank you."

"Thank you," Finley muttered around a mouthful of bread.

Nik smiled at them both, then led us into the den. Mountains of fluffy cushions covered the floor and stretched wall-to-wall. The chairs and furniture I remembered were no longer there.

I raised an eyebrow at Nik, who chuckled. "Lyria's

taken up tumbling. She's been bouncing off the walls, climbing on everything. I didn't want her to get hurt, so I 'padded' the floor."

"Daddy, watch!" Lyria said, drawing our attention to the center of the room. Lyria raised her arms then lurched forward, springing off the cushions and tumbling into a full cartwheel before landing back on her feet. "Tada!"

I clapped when she stuck the landing, and Nik did the same.

"Hey, you're really getting good at that!" Nik said. He lifted her in his arms and spun her around.

Just like Darius used to do.

Even a year later, thinking about him felt like a punch to the stomach. Not only had I lost my shift, but my son was still having trouble, too. He was just getting to the age where he'd be mature enough to control his shift, but so far, he'd shown no signs of doing so.

Ask the multiple burn marks on the furniture back home.

Finley froze, watching them. He was remembering the same thing I was, then.

It's all right... I tried to tell him over our Link, but he didn't want to hear it. Little bugger kept shutting me out. If he was like this at six years old, I could barely wait till Finley was a teen. I'd have my hands full, for sure.

Marlowe, Nik's alpha, stepped out of then kitchen. Despite wearing and apron, his clothes were covered in flour. He raised a hand in greeting.

"Get in a fight with a bag of flour again?" I teased him. Marlowe was the commander of Darkvale's military forces, but during peace time he'd taken up baking at Lyria's request. The man that waved at me now was the same Marlowe I knew and loved, only with a softer edge. Mating had been good for him.

"You try making Batya Buns. It's not as easy as it looks!" Marlowe's lip jutted out in a pout, but his eyes were still full of good humor. "It's good to see you, man." He came forward and before I could stop him he clapped me on the back, sending a cloud of flour flying everywhere.

I waved the air and sneezed, sending even more into the air. Lyria giggled, and even Finley broke a smile when he saw me.

"How's Hope?" I asked. She'd had her first birthday recently, and was just as adorable as ever.

"Sleeping, thank the goddess."

"I hear that," I agreed. First Lucien, then Marlowe, then Tork had mated and had children. While they were just about the cutest things ever, babies were a lot of work! Especially at that age.

"I thought you could use a little down time." Marlowe flicked his gaze toward Finley, then to Nik. "There's a band of traveling performers, just came by this morning. Was planning to take Hope and Lyria. Finley can come too if you like."

Honestly? That sounded wonderful.

"You sure you'll be all right?" Nik asked, throwing his arms around Marlowe's neck.

Marlowe gave a low, hearty laugh and kissed his mate. "I took care of Lyria when your Dragon slept, remember? I can take three kids to a play."

I looked to Finley now. He loved seeing performers, but I was wary he wouldn't want to be separated from me.

"What do you think, Finn? Wanna go see the play with Uncle Marlowe? I hear they brought puppets..."

Finley's eyes widened. "Puppets?" he repeated.

"It's true," Marlowe nodded. "And we can go as soon as I grab a change of clothes and get Hope into her stroller. What do you say, Finn?"

I held my breath. I half expected Finn to say nothing, or shrink back into his shell. Apparently Lyria's welcoming gesture had worn off on him though. "I'd like that," Finley said, nodding.

"Excellent," Marlowe beamed. "Now you wait right here, I'm going to go get Hope and then we can leave. You might want to grab another bun to go, yeah?"

Lyria was on her feet at the mention of food and dashed into the kitchen, Finley not far behind.

Marlowe watched them go, his whole demeanor still alight with the love of his children.

"Lyria seems to be doing well," I remarked to Nik when Marlowe left the room.

Nik rolled his eyes. "Where she gets all that energy I have no idea. It's not from me, that's for sure."

"And Hope's well, too?"

"Keeping us busy." Nik shrugged. Then his face turned serious. "There's something I've been meaning to talk to you about, but with both our kids, haven't found a good time...wanna go for a walk?"

I eyed Finley. "You gonna be okay, Finn?"

He nodded. "Yeah."

I still didn't feel great about leaving him, but we both needed the time to relax. It was good that Finley was getting out and socializing for once, and I'd been meaning to talk to Nik too.

"All right, go on then." I ruffled his hair and grabbed my coat. Marlowe emerged from the other room with Hope in a stroller. She was still sleeping soundly, somehow.

"How'd you get her into the carriage without waking her up?" I asked. Hope lay in the carriage, mouth slightly open, a pink beanie on her head and a fuzzy blanket wrapped around her small body.

Marlowe smiled. "What can I say, Hope loves her sleep. She'd sleep through a thunderstorm if we let her."

"Lucky," I laughed. "Finley kept me up all hours of the night when he was little."

"Come on, now," Marlowe gestured for Lyria and Finley to follow him. "The performance awaits!"

With one last look at me, Finley followed Marlowe out the door.

Nik grabbed his coat and met me outside. The air was starting to cool, with a whispery breeze coming through the stone walls and howling through the cracks. I used to be scared of that sound as a kid, but now it was almost soothing, in a way. It reminded me of home. Of safety. Inside these walls, nothing could get us.

Or so I'd thought.

He walked up beside me, leading the way through one of the rarely-used tunnels beneath the castle. The stony floor was uneven and since I could no longer use my dragon-sight, Nik held out an orb of his own flame in front of us.

"He's taking it hard, isn't he?" Nik broke me out of my reverie.

"Yeah." I stared at the floor. "We always thought...I dunno."

Nik turned and put a hand on my shoulder. "We lost a lot of good men in the war. I would like to say it was worth it in the end, but we both know thats not true." He sighed, his shoulders slumping. "Darius was a good man. A good fighter. He would want you to stay strong. For Finley."

And that's what hurt most of all.

"Finley used to be such a happy kid." I kicked at a pebble on the walkway. "And then Darius never came home, and..."

"I know, man. It's been hard for all of us."

We made our way out of the castle and along a sloping path leading to the shore. The air was chill and biting, but the first snows hadn't begun to fall yet. The cold was actually bracing, I thought. Gave me something to focus on other than my grief.

Just then, we heard a long, pitiful yowl. I spun and looked at Nik with alarm, my muscles tensing up. It could have been the howl of the wind, but what if it wasn't?

"What was that?" I asked. My heart thrummed in my chest and when I looked back I noticed how far away from the fortress we'd strayed. If something happened to us now, no one would hear us scream...

Nik froze and pricked up his ears, listening again. He had better senses than me on a good day, especially ever since the Curse had befallen me.

The howl came again, and it sounded even closer this time. It wasn't the roaring battle cry I'd heard all too often, though. It was...sad, somehow. In need.

Hurt.

"Let's go," I nudged Nik and started toward the sound before I knew what I was doing.

"Are you kidding me?" Nik panted as he jogged to keep up. "You're going toward the sound? We don't know what's out there!"

I didn't speak. All I knew was that I had to find the source of the sound, had to help whoever it was. They sounded so helpless, so in pain...

"Adrian!" Nik called again, but I barely heard him. We came to a rocky cliff near the shore where scraggly brush and little pebbles littered the ground before turning into sand. The cliff was steep, dropping down to the crashing waves of the sea below.

That's when I saw him.

Broken and bleeding, his fur caught in the thorny brambles of the shoreline, lay a wolf.

A wolf!

Nik sucked in a breath. He looked at me, eyes wide, as if he couldn't believe what he was seeing.

"Is that...?" He started, gesturing at the shoreline.

"A wolf," I confirmed.

"But there haven't been any wolves around these parts since..."

"Never mind that, he's hurt!" I scanned the rocky cliff for a path down, and saw a spot where the grass and rocks were flattened, as if someone had come this way before. "I'm going down there," I said without waiting for Nik's approval. "Cover me."

"Wait, you can't be serious!" Nik yelled, stumbling after me. "Adrian, come on! Let's go back, let the others know at least!"

But his cries were wasted. I was already half way down the slope. My feet skidded and scrambled on the loose rocks and dirt, muddying my pants and scraping my palms raw. In the moment, though, it didn't matter. It was as if an almost supernatural force drew me down the cliff toward the wolf, as if all my questions would be answered if I could just reach him.

Nik was right. I'd never even seen a wolf before. Only heard about them in stories. They weren't native to this part of the world, and were wiped out by poachers so many years ago. Maybe the rarity of it pressed me forward. But maybe it was something else entirely. My body reacted instinctively and soon I was down there at the shoreline, next to the broken wolf.

I heard Nik's faint calls from above, but paid them no mind. The wolf lay on the rocky beach, his chest rising and falling slowly. Good, he was still alive. The eyes were closed, though, and the mouth hung open as the tongue lolled out. I crept closer. He smelled like the sea. Like the sea and...pine trees. Yes, pine. The smell nearly bowled me over. If he'd gotten caught in the waves, it would have washed off any scent he'd been carrying.

But my nose didn't lie. There was a very strong pine and sap smell over the salty undertones. Now that I was closer I could see a bloody scratch across his gray, matted fur. It was a jagged line, like he'd been attacked by a beast.

I bit my lip and glanced up at the cliff again. Nik was gone. Probably gone to get help. But that meant I was all alone with the wolf now. What if he woke up? What if he was mad, tried to attack me?

I couldn't shift. I couldn't overpower him. My flame died out the night Darius passed, and it had never returned.

Then something happened I didn't expect. The wolf turned its head, let out a long, high-pitched whine, and shifted. There on the sands with the cold wind blowing off the ocean and the waves lapping at the shore, the injured wolf transformed into a human.

I took a few steps back in shock. My voice deserted me. Only a lump in my throat remained. A shifter...

Not only was he a wolf, but he was a shifter!

And he needed my help.

The man opened his eyes slowly, warily. They were crusted with sand and salt from the sea, but when they locked on to me, I could see nothing else.

A brilliant, blazing blue, so light it could have been silver bored into me. I felt like I was the naked one, standing there in the gaze of this man. He was strong, I could tell that much. His skin was tanned and his toned muscles told me he was likely an alpha. Or a very athletic omega.

That scent hit me again, and my head spun.

The man opened his mouth and his body heaved as he coughed up sea water. It splattered onto the ground and splashed onto my shoes. I lurched forward to help him.

"Who are..." His voice was hoarse, like he'd just crunched a load of nails for breakfast.

"Don't talk," I whispered, kneeling next to him. "You're hurt."

The wolf scoffed. Even in his pain he rolled his eyes t

me. "That much is obvious. Now are you going to stand there gawking or you gonna help me up?"

Of course. I put an arm around the man's shoulders. His skin was warm despite the chill of the air and the fact that he'd just come from the sea. Almost like our dragon babes before they'd had a chance to shift. Were wolves the same?

"Let's get you out of here." I helped the man to his feet, but it wasn't easy. He was larger than me, way larger. I wished again that I was able to shift. I could simply fly him away, no problem. But that would be a problem for a different day, a different time. Right now, I had to focus on getting this man...this wolf...the help he needed.

"Can you stand? My friend's nearby, he can help us get back up, but..."

Before I could warn him, a roar crested the cliff and green scaly wings flew forward, blocking out the sun.

Nik circled the air a few times, the air buffeting his huge wingspan. The man in my arms gasped and his muscles tensed. "Is that..." he whispered.

"It's okay," I promised him. "We're here to help."

"A dragon..." the wolf murmured again, and then he went limp in my arms.

Nik landed with a thud, rocks and sand spewing out

around him. His amber eyes blinked at me, as if to say, "what?"

"Way to make an entrance, asshole." I huffed at my friend. "You just scared the poor man half to death! Come lower, help me get him on your back."

Nik took a few steps backward. I clenched my jaw. "Come on, he's injured! And he's a shifter, Nik! When have we ever met any other kind of shifters? This is a new discovery, for all of us. We gotta take him back to Lucien, please..."

Nik let out a burst of steam through his nostrils and then relented. He lowered his head and torso to the ground, low enough to where I could reach. I basically dragged the wolf's dead weight the few feet toward Nik. His scaly back was still too high for me to lift the wolf's body, and I didn't want to reopen his wounds.

"Come on," I muttered under my breath, grunting as I heaved his weight upward. I grumbled and cursed, wishing I'd taken Marlowe up on his offer of weight training. Guess I was more out of shape than I thought.

By some miracle of the Goddess or a burst of superhuman strength, I managed to get the alpha wolf situated on Nik's back.

"Good thing we didn't stray too far, huh?" I said more to myself than to Nik.

The more I looked at the broken, hurting alpha on

Nik's back, the more that supernatural sense of belonging rose within me. I couldn't leave him like that. What if he fell off? What if he needed me?

I knew in my mind that it sounded ridiculous. But finding a shifter that we didn't even know existed was pretty ridiculous, too.

"I'm coming with you," I said before Nik had a chance to protest. Clambering up the side of his scales wasn't easy, but it was a lot easier for me than for an out-cold wolf shifter. I leaned into the alpha, wrapping an arm around him protectively.

I mean, I needed to grab the scaly "pockets" on Nik's back to hold on to, right?

Don't judge me.

Nik just grumbled again, a jet of steam issuing from his snout, then he pushed off with his strong back legs, and we were flying.

Thank you for reading! Keep an eye out for Adrian's story :)

Turn the page to find out how you can be the first to know about upcoming books —>

When the kids are away, the mates will play…

Sign up here for your FREE copy of ONE KNOTTY NIGHT, a special story that's too hot for Amazon!
https://dl.bookfunnel.com/c1d8qcu6h8

Join my Facebook group Connor's Coven for live streams, giveaways, and sneak peeks. It's the most fun you can have without being arrested ;)

https://www.facebook.com/groups/connorscoven/

Printed in Great Britain
by Amazon

59861285R00388